P9-DFO-457

Praise for

SEMIOSIS

"This is up there with Ursula K. Le Guin: science fiction at its most fascinating and most humane." —*Thrillist*

"A fascinating world." —*The Verge*

"A solid debut." —*SFRevu*

"A magnetic meditation on biochemistry and humanity." —*Locus*

"This first-contact tale is extraordinary." —*Library Journal* (starred review)

"Sharp, evocative . . . *Semiosis* unfolds the old science fiction idea of first contact in ways that are both traditional and subversive." —*The Christian Science Monitor*

"A clever, fascinating, fun, and unique debut." —*Kirkus Reviews*

"Burke's world-building is exceptional, and her ability to combine the intricacies of colonization with the science of botany and theories of mutualism and predation is astounding." —*Booklist*

"Impressive debut novel . . . lush . . . beautiful." —*Publishers Weekly* (starred review)

"A fresh and fun perspective on planetary exploration." —*The BiblioSanctum* (4 out of 5 stars)

"Filled with questions about the nature of intelligence and how we value it, and humanity's place within the universe, *Semiosis* is a provocative novel." —*Fantasy Literature*

"*Semiosis* combines the world-building of *Avatar* with the alien wonder of *Arrival* and the sheer humanity of Atwood. An essential work for our time." —Stephen Baxter, award-winning author of *The Time Ships*

"Intelligent, riveting, and ultimately uplifting, *Semiosis* asks big questions and gives satisfying answers."
—Emma Newman, author of *Planetfall*

"This is top-class SF, intelligent and engaging, and I loved every moment of it." —Adrian Tchaikovsky, winner of the Arthur C. Clarke Award for *Children of Time*

"In *Semiosis*, Sue Burke blends science with adventure and fascinating characters, as a human colony desperately seeks to join the ecosystem of an alien world." —David Brin, author of *Earth* and *Existence*

"A first-contact novel like none you've ever read . . . The kind of story for which science fiction was invented." —James Patrick Kelly, winner of the Hugo, Nebula, and Locus Awards

"Sue Burke has created one of the most fascinating alien personae science fiction has seen in this decade."
—David Andrew Nichols, early America historian and author of *Engines of Diplomacy*

"A gripping story of colonization and biological wonders."
—Gregory Frost, author of the Shadowbridge novels

"A fantastic SF debut . . . *Semiosis* will remain relevant for years to come." —Professor Daniel Chamovitz, award-winning author of *What a Plant Knows* and director of the Manna Center for Plant Biosciences at Tel Aviv University

SEMIOSIS

SUE BURKE

A TOM DOHERTY ASSOCIATES BOOK  NEW YORK

This is a work of fiction. All of the characters, organizations, and events portrayed in this novel are either products of the author's imagination or are used fictitiously.

SEMIOSIS

Copyright © 2018 by Sue Burke

All rights reserved.

A Tor Book
Published by Tom Doherty Associates
175 Fifth Avenue
New York, NY 10010

www.tor-forge.com

Tor® is a registered trademark of Macmillan Publishing Group, LLC.

The Library of Congress has cataloged the hardcover edition as follows:

Names: Burke, Sue, 1955– author.
Title: Semiosis / Sue Burke.
Description: First edition. | New York : Tor Books, February 2018. | "A Tom Doherty Associates Book."
Identifiers: LCCN 2017049645 | ISBN 978-0-7653-9135-3 (hardcover) | ISBN 978-0-7653-9137-7 (ebook)
Subjects: LCSH: Science fiction.
Classification: LCC PS3602.U7556 S46 2018 | DDC 813/.6—dc23
LC record available at https://lccn.loc.gov/2017049645

ISBN 978-0-7653-9136-0 (trade paperback)

Our books may be purchased in bulk for promotional, educational, or business use. Please contact your local bookseller or the Macmillan Corporate and Premium Sales Department at 1-800-221-7945, extension 5442, or by email at MacmillanSpecialMarkets@macmillan.com.

First Edition: February 2018
First Trade Paperback Edition: March 2019

Printed in the United States of America

0 9 8 7 6 5 4 3

I owe thanks to Gregory Frost, whose writing exercise about a special kind of wall led to this novel. Thanks also to my sister-in-law, Kathleen Daley Burke, who lent her childhood imaginary animal, the fippokat. And thanks to the many people who helped with critiques and suggestions. A version of chapter one previously appeared in the magazine *LC-39*.

SEMIOSIS

OCTAVO
YEAR 1–GENERATION 1

Grateful for this opportunity to create a new society in full harmony with nature, we enter into this covenant, promising one another our mutual trust and support. We will face hardship, danger, and potential failure, but we can aspire to the use of practical wisdom to seek joy, love, beauty, community, and life.

—from the Constitution of the Commonwealth of Pax,
written on Earth in 2065

The war had begun long before we arrived because war was their way of life. It took its first victims among us before we understood what was happening, on an evening that seemed quiet. But even then, we knew we could easily be in danger.

My wife, Paula, shook her head as she left the radio hut in the plaza of our little village. "There's too much interference again. I'll try one more time, but if they don't answer, we'll start a search."

An hour ago, three women had gone to pick fruit. They did not come back, they were not answering their radio, and the Sun had sunk almost to the top of the hills.

Around us, tiny lizards in the trees had begun their evening hoots and chimes. Nine-legged crabs silently hunted the lizards. The breeze smelled bittersweet, perhaps from something in bloom. I should have known what, but I did not.

Uri and I were fixing an irrigation pump, but I knew his mind was on one of the women, Ninia. He had just begun living with her, and he was squinting up the path through the fields where she had gone. And then he was jerked back to the present when the wind tangled his long blond beard around the pump handle. He knelt to free it. I pulled a jackknife from my belt, stroking my own short beard. He saluted with one finger. He was a Russian Slav, and a proper Slav never cuts his beard.

Paula went back to her work at a rough-hewn table nearby, trying to make sense of weather data. A wide straw hat held her red hair in place and protected her skin from the Sun. She took a deep breath and stretched her stiff back. We all struggled with the stronger gravity. Finally she entered the radio hut again.

Everyone stopped what they were doing and listened. The hut's walls were panels scavenged from a landing pod and the roof was tree bark, so the sound carried.

"Hello? . . . Ninia? Zee? Carrie?"

Static.

"Hello? . . . This is Paula. Do you hear me?"

Static.

"Ninia, Zee, Carrie? Are you there? Hello?" After a moment, she came out to the plaza. "Maybe the batteries died again. Let's look for them."

She kept her voice reassuring as she asked Ramona to bring a medical kit and Merl to carry a radio and microphone to listen for emergency whistles. We would also need people to carry three stretchers and someone to bring a weapon: standard operating procedure. Uri picked up his rifle.

We set off westward up the steady slope of a meadow toward a white line of vines and trees a kilometer away, hiking as fast as we could. Low clouds dotted the sky, some already tinted pink. The stronger gravity meant that the atmosphere thinned fast above us, so the clouds were always low. We passed the long field that we had planted with a native grass resembling Earth's wild wheat, whose green shoots stood almost ankle-high. The air smelled of moist soil, and spiny caterpillar-like creatures the size of fingers inched across the surface, swallowing big mouthfuls of dirt and excreting dark castings that seemed to be good manure. The caterpillars might have been larvae of some sort. We had no way to find out except by waiting.

But the presence of the wheat worried me. The wheat was a lot like Earth grass, and if there was grass, then there were grazers, maybe animals like gazelle, moose, or elephant. And if there were grazers, then something hunted them. So far we had seen only small browsers and predators like little land crabs with trilateral symmetry, but we had found bits of big crab shells—and of big stone-shelled land corals with stinging tentacles. None of us went barefoot anywhere.

Uri and Merl took the lead, pointing at tussocks of dry grass or bright coral bushes where something could hide and leap out. Lizards fled at our approach, moving lightning fast. In heavier gravity, things fell faster and animals moved faster. We humans were slow and ignorant, still aliens. I saw a burrow and aimed a flashlight into it. Something inside barked, and we all jumped.

"Just a bird," Merl said. Flightless bird-shaped animals with spiny feathers scurried around day and night, and while some were big, they did not seem dangerous. We kept going.

Merl fiddled with the radio receiver as we walked, pausing when Paula blew a whistle. In the thicker air, the sound would carry far, but it was answered only by musical calls from red-eyed bats swooping overhead.

We were panting and sweating when we reached the west edge of the meadow, where a vine-filled thicket formed a wall a kilometer wide and several kilometers long. Slim gray-barked trees that resembled aspens grew two stories high, their leaves wilted from a lack of water: a dry season or a drought, Paula was not sure. Around them looped tangles of snow-white vines jointed like bamboo that bore dangling thorns and grew so densely that we could barely see inside. Another snow vine thicket rose on the east side of the meadow just behind our village. Finding crops had kept me too busy to investigate the thickets carefully, but I had learned that the vines parasitized the trees.

These vines had also kept away hunger. Shortly after we landed, orange fruit like translucent persimmons had ripened quickly on the east vines and had recently appeared on the west vines. The fruit had tested safe, contained plenty of vitamin C, and tasted like cantaloupe.

The women had been to these vines. To the left, we could see ripe fruit close by, but to the right, the vines had been picked clean. We turned right, north. Ahead lay a river that pierced both the west and east thickets and our meadow. We had a long way to search, but the sunset was throwing a golden light over everything, reminding us with every glance how late it was. We could not pause to catch our breath.

Uri turned his energy outward as we hurried on. He prowled up to a tall blue-leafed shrub as if an ambush awaited on the other side. He paused dramatically, then dashed around it, recounting out loud the events of a war game he had played in the Russian Army.

"We see lasers ahead and we know where to aim!" Abruptly he fell silent.

I began to run even before we heard him howl.

The three women lay on the other side of the shrub, baskets of snow fruit set down beside them. Uri yelled Ninia's name as if he could shout her awake. He fell to his knees and fumbled at her throat for a pulse, and his voice choked. I lifted Zee's wrist. It was cold and limp. Carrie stared sleepily ahead, and a pair of tiny lizards climbed on her eyeball. I gagged and turned away.

But we had expected something far worse. I had tried to prepare myself for dismembered bodies, perhaps half-eaten or disfigured by giant coral stings, evidence of attack and predation in the battle for survival. The women seemed to have fallen asleep.

They had had peaceful deaths. This was wrong.

We looked around, frightened and silent. Something had killed without an obvious method or motive.

"Let's bring them home," Paula said, her voice low and steady. We began to assemble the stretchers.

We grieved that night in the plaza of our little village, a fire burning in the clay-and-stone hearth that Zee had built. Some of us talked quietly, sitting on benches in a corner under a canopy of solar panels. Of the fifty who had left Earth, now only thirty-one remained. Uri, tall and lean like a scarecrow, stood staring out at the fields, where glow-worms and fireflies flickered like stars beneath vivid auroras. Those bright bugs needed to be seen for a reason that only they knew.

Hedike, a concert musician on Earth, played a serenade on a flute, but the song could not hide the buzzes, rattles, and barks of the night, more eerie than anything on Earth because we could not connect creatures to most of the noises. Something far away roared a song of three low, rising notes, and it was answered by a far-off roar in the opposite direction. Stars without constellations and legends shone overhead. A small star in the east was Sol.

Paula walked among us, gazing into every face to see who needed help and who could offer it. Bryan was talking to Jill when his bass voice rang out, "Something killed them!" Paula went to him and talked gently until he became calm.

But it was what we were all thinking. I went to the little lab. Ramona and Grun worked silently on the autopsies while chromatographs and computers hummed. The dead women lay under sheets in a corner. I looked away and pulled a flask from a shelf in the cooler. It contained sap that I had found fermenting in some taproots. It had tested no more toxic than cheap Earth wine and tasted sour and buttery.

The sap did not go far, but I had enough for those who grieved the most. Uri raised a gray clay cup in a toast. "For Carrie, Zee, and Ninia, who will never see the future of the Commonwealth of Pax." He drained his cup like a shot of vodka and hurled it at the hearth. It shattered. Zee had made that cup. We did not have another potter.

I kissed Paula good night and rubbed her shoulders for a minute. She would stay awake until everyone had been comforted, and then, as our meteorologist, would prepare a forecast before sleeping herself. I was tired and had to get up before dawn, less than five hours away in Pax's short days and nights. As the colony's botanist I needed light to do my work.

———

Paula had come to bed and was asleep when I awoke to my alarm clock. I quickly switched it off, hoping not to wake her, but she rolled over to hold me close.

"I was dreaming about children," she said.

We'd talked a lot about children. They'd grow up in this gravity, so they'd be shorter, adapted to their environment, and belong to Pax. Just Pax. Her Ireland and my Mexico wouldn't mean anything to them. I held her tighter.

"Pax will be home." I lay still, knowing that she tended to wake up suddenly and would fall asleep again just as suddenly. In the dark I could see little of the improvised hut that was now our home.

We had not expected paradise. We had expected hardship, danger, and potential failure. We hoped to create a new society in full harmony with nature, but nineteen people had died of accidents and illnesses since we arrived, including three who had died the day before for no apparent reason.

When her breathing became even, I slipped out of bed. Cold air slapped my bare skin. I dressed quietly and stepped outside. Our plaza was the size of a small soccer field, and on two sides we had assembled homes from wood, pieces of landing pods, stone, clay, parachutes, and tree bark. On the third side sat the lab, made from a landing pod designed specifically for that reuse.

The fourth side of the plaza remained open, facing the fields, where a lone aspen tree grew with a snow vine spiraling around it. Loose branches of vine hung down like weeping willow boughs. Zee had thought it looked like a living sculpture, named it Snowman, and watered it. In the predawn twilight, it looked like a phantom standing sentinel at the edge of our village. Overhead, the extraordinarily bright star was Lux, a brown dwarf that orbited the Sun, and Pax occupied its Lagrange point. Lux was bright enough to be visible even in the day.

I walked past the embers in Zee's hearth. In a pen nearby, a couple of furry green house-cat-sized herbivores hopped like springbok gazelle to look at me through the bars. Merl was a livestock specialist, and they were his experiment in domestication. Wendy had named them fippokats after an imaginary childhood animal that had pink noses and curly tails like them, although to me they looked more like rabbits than cats. Someday we would develop complete taxonomies of our new home's life-forms. The most important, we'd agreed, would be named after Stevland Barr, in honor of the first death among us. I intended to nominate the wheat.

Grun left the lab, walked to Snowman, grabbed a fruit, and turned back to the lab. He must have worked all night, not a surprise. He had the nickname "Grim" for being conscientious. I hurried to join him.

"Breakfast?" I asked.

Grun's blue eyes seemed bloodshot even in the faint light. "The fruit the women ate yesterday were poisonous. The ones from Snowman aren't. I think. They didn't use to be. I'm going to check."

"I'll help."

In the lab, Ramona slouched in front of a computer screen, her delicate brown face drooping. A fippokat lay limp on a table. On its side was a long incision, red blood bright as neon against green fur. I quickly looked away. I could stand sap but not blood. I felt relieved to see that the dead women had been taken away.

"We fed a west fruit to Fluffy to observe the symptoms," Grun said. "He just fell asleep. Paralysis. He didn't suffer. That was good, at least."

"What was the poison?"

"We're looking," Ramona said.

"You tested the skin, too?" I said. "Not just the juice. You have to look at pulp, skin, everything."

"We just blended the whole fruit," Grun said. "Even the tiny seeds."

"I can prepare the one from Snowman. Take a rest."

Instead Grun examined the dead fippokat. I kept my eyes on the fruit, and by the time I had the sample ready, Ramona had news.

"Here's a new alkaloid. The fruit you tested two weeks ago hadn't got it, Octavo. I've got lists of both." Her voice, with its thick London accent, began to recover some of its typical energy. "There's some little differences, but this is a big one."

We all knew that alkaloids were often pharmacological, if not toxic. I gave her the sample and went out to the east thicket to pick more fruit, lit by dawn twilight and surrounded by the morning's chirps and buzzes. I thought about the ways that fruit can vary.

"Snowman hasn't got the alkaloid," she said when I got back. She switched to another screen. "Take a look at the structure. It's like strychnine a little, don't you think?"

"We should check sugar levels and organelles, too." I reached for a microscope.

Within an hour, as the Sun rose and lit the room, working as fast as we could, we had learned what had happened. I realized it was all my fault, and I had to stop working for fear I would drop a piece of equipment and break it. Paula arrived as I tried to explain.

"Fruit does not simply get ripe," I said. "It can get ripe and then change again as the season changes. It might become better suited for a certain species of animals that can disperse the seeds more effectively, and it becomes poisonous for other animals. Or maybe the west vine and east vine are different species. Maybe the soil is different."

"Maybe," Grun said. "We've still got a lot to learn."

Ramona nodded. They were exhausted and did not understand.

"I was wrong when I said it was safe, and that is what killed them," I insisted. "Maybe a change in nitrogen metabolism created excess alkaloids. Or perhaps it was a response to pests or pathogens. Or photoinhibition. Maybe it is unusually dry. The trees it parasitizes could have changed in some way."

Paula took my hand. "Come outside and let's talk."

In the warm sunlight, she looked at me gently. "It's always a shock, but we knew things would go wrong."

"I killed them."

"We all ate the west fruit before, and it was fine. It isn't your fault."

"We planted the fields on my recommendation. They could go wrong, too. A lot more people could get killed."

"We'll just avoid the west fruit until we figure it out."

"But what will we eat?"

"We'll find something. I know you're doing your best." She took me by both hands and kissed me.

My job, besides searching for edible plants, was to describe and classify Pax's vegetation.

At first glance, it looked Earthlike: trees, vines, grasses, and bushes. But the bushes that had leaves like bluish butterfly wings were a sort of land coral, a three-part symbiont involving photosynthesizing algae and tiny animals with stony skeletons that held locked-in-place winged lizards. Other kinds of land corals captured and ate small animals, and at some point bush coral had discovered that keeping prisoners had advantages over hunting.

A second glance at the sky, although it was blue, also proved that we were not on Earth. Green ribbons knobbed with bubbles of hydrogen floated in the air and got tangled in treetops, or perhaps they anchored themselves there. Other floating plants resembled cactus-spined balloons.

Some trees had bark of cellulose acetate plastic that peeled off in sheets with razor-sharp edges. Maybe someday we could process it into rayon cloth or lacquer. One by one, I was finding fruits, seeds, roots, stems, and flowers that might prove useful or edible, which was the pressing issue. Moreover, as the colony's botanist, I had to devise a taxonomy. Every scrap of information would help as we looked for a niche in this ecology for ourselves.

A little before we left Earth, we rehearsed our arrival. Supposedly we did not know where we were, but within minutes after the trucks had left us on a dirt road in a forest, we had guessed.

I noted majestic white pines with long bluish-green needles, coniferous tamaracks, and quaking aspens, their flat leaves rattling in the hot breeze. "This is northern United States, east of the Mississippi," I said. "If we were in Canada, the trees would still be healthier."

Merl listened to birds squawk and sing. "Sure enough. Grackles and

Carolina chickadees." He shrugged his wide shoulders. "That doesn't mean we're in the Carolinas. They've been moving around a lot on account of the heat."

Paula looked at the clouds. "Thunderheads. Let's think about shelter."

Eventually, we got more precise, identifying it as Wisconsin even before we ran into a pair of Menominee women gathering vines to make baskets. The tribal council supported our project and was allowing us to spend two months trying to survive in their reservation's forest, and the women were sorry to spoil our isolation. But before they left, they suggested coating our skin with wood ash and grease to repel the clouds of mosquitoes, advice we badly needed.

Other than that, survival held no major challenges because we already knew a lot about the environment. Deer were edible, for example. Instead, the rehearsal deepened our commitment as we witnessed the disaster of the forest despite the Menominees' careful stewardship. Global warming was turning the forest into a prairie. All around us the trees were dying of heat and thirst and disease, bringing down the ecology with them. But the flora and fauna weren't simply moving north. The disaster was at once too fast and too slow. In southwest Wisconsin, Aldo Leopold's treasured Sand Counties were becoming sand dunes, and their prairie species were going extinct. The forests in northeast Wisconsin hadn't yet become prairies to welcome them, so when the forests finally became grasslands, there would be no surviving prairie species to welcome.

I got to know Uri in the Menominees' forest. His English was even worse then. For both of us, English was a second language, but the colony was strictly monolingual. We would avoid the disputes over language that were poisoning so much of Earth.

"Of course I volunteer for army," he said. "I work for food. Like now, but not so nice food." We were knee-deep in a swamp collecting cattail pollen, which could be used like flour to make pancakes. Actually, every eighteen-year-old in Russia had to serve. He had been a marksman.

He pulled a cattail head horizontal and batted it while I held a clay bowl underneath to catch the falling yellow pollen.

"Rifle is not antique. Is fallback, what we use if high tech would be jammed. And very entertaining. My unit gave shows like circus, even with horses, and was when I decided to join this project after my duty is finish. I saw too much of Mother Russia during travel and give shows. They are raping her. I not can endure stay and see it."

That was true everywhere on Earth, environmental devastation that we wished we could fix, but the best we could do was try again elsewhere.

"I wonder if there will still be humans on Earth when we get to Pax," Vera said one evening after dinner as we worked on the many tasks that survival required. It had been harder than we thought but also more rewarding.

"The people on this planet don't deserve to survive," Bryan said as he made fishhooks out of wire.

"The thing is, we can learn," Merl said. "We'll just have to do better. And how hard will that be?"

We were all in our twenties, selected for our skills and personalities. Merl, a sandy-haired Texan, had scored low on anxiety and high on agreeableness. I was responsible and self-disciplined. We were all glad to have something to hope for.

We awakened, cold and dizzy, with our muscles, hearts, and digestive systems atrophied from the 158-year hibernation on a tiny spaceship. The computer had brought us into orbit, sent a message to Earth, then administered intravenous drugs.

Two hours later I was in the cramped cabin trying to sip an electrolyte drink when Vera, our astronomer, came flying in from the control module, her tightly curled hair trailing like a black cloud.

"We're at the wrong star!"

I felt a wave of nausea and despair.

Paula was spoon-feeding Bryan, who was too weak to eat, and she seemed calm, but her hand trembled. "The computer could pick another one if it was better," she said.

"It did!" Vera said. "It is. Lots of oxygen and water. And lots of life. It's alive and waiting for us. We're home!"

We were at star HIP 30815f instead of HIP 30756, at a planet with a well-evolved ecology and, I noted, abundant chlorophyll. The carbon dioxide level was slightly higher than Earth's but not dangerous. Seen from Earth, both stars were pinpricks in the Gemini constellation near Castor's left shin. As planned, we named the planet Pax, since we had come to live in peace.

Stevland Barr never awoke, dead years before from a failure in his hibernation system. Krishna Narashima developed pneumonia and died on board. Hedike's kidneys had failed, although he was recovering with regrown medulla cells.

Waking up was just the start. Two of the six landing pods crashed. One crash broke Terrell's collarbone and crushed Rosemarie Waukau's chest, killing her. The other, a disaster, killed all twelve people on board and destroyed irreplaceable equipment, including the food synthesizer, too heavy and bulky for backup units.

The gravity, one-fifth stronger than Earth's, caused misjudgments. When I left our landing module, I became dizzy and fell, twisting my ankle but nothing worse, although our bones had lost calcium and grown brittle during hibernation. Breasts and scrotums weighed more and ached, and our hearts labored.

We suffered rashes from Pax-style poison ivies, welts from bug-lizard bites, and diarrhea until we artificially stimulated new digestive enzymes and our intestinal flora adapted. A Pax fungus caused hyaline membrane disease, collapsed lungs. It had killed Luigi Dini, the other botanist, before Ramona found a fungicide. Wendy mangled her foot fixing a tractor, the wound got infected, and the medics had to amputate up to the tarsus bone. Always sturdy, she renamed herself "Half-Foot" Wendy.

Then Carrie, Ninia, and Zee died from poison fruit. We still had enough people to populate a planet, since we had a cache of frozen ova and sperm to fall back on. We did not need genetic material as much as we needed hands to work.

———

Now, a month after we had arrived, I had to figure out what the snow vines were doing. I paced along the east thicket behind the homes of our village. Between the aspens, thorny vines wider than my thumb looped like barbed wire made of bone. I searched for a way in: a tree-fall clearing or an animal path. I told myself I was not afraid of a vine, not me, not a botanist. I walked past one of our outhouses and startled a fippokat. It raced into the thicket. I found its narrow path, dropped to my knees, and, with a shove, shouldered my way in. It was like a cage inside.

Knobby white vine roots and gray tree roots covered the ground, hard as stones beneath my hands and knees. Vines arched across the tunnel and grazed my head. The air in the thicket hung motionless and smelled of exhausted soil. I crawled slowly, bowed to avoid a thorn, and shifted my weight onto a knee already throbbing against a nodule on a root. The thorn slipped across my hair—and stabbed into my scalp. It yanked backward, pulling me up onto aching knees. I groped for the thorn and found it, and its razor edge slit my fingers. The thorn in my scalp jerked again. I fumbled until I could grab it by its sides and tried to back it out. Barbs tore my scalp, and my fingers slipped, wet with blood. Finally, I gritted my teeth and pulled.

I whirled back to see what had bit so deep: a fishhook-sized white thorn, now smeared red. It hung from a tendril that curled like a spring. A sharp little thorn, that was all, just like thorns on Earth, attached to the same kind of tendril that had hoisted bean plants in my mother's garden. These were natural tools for a climbing vine. Their movements were normal on Earth and Pax. Nothing personal, and nothing to be frightened of. Plants don't attack botanists. I tugged on the tendril to test its strength. It could have supported my machete.

Around me stretched vines and parasitized trees but nothing else, silent and empty, with no moss, no ferns, no grass, no competing plants of any type. The vines had eliminated them.

I wasn't sure I could do this job anymore. On Earth, my botany degree had won me work on an industrialized farm to monitor engineered corn. For four years I had watched the near-infrared satellite images of the fields for dark patches that might signal the root blister blight that had caused corn crops to wilt from the top down and had started a war when I was a boy. Sometimes the war had been all I could see, my family running, trying to hide from the spy planes, drones disguised as birds or insects that would call in bigger, armed robot airplanes. If they didn't kill us, we might die of hunger anyway. We were just farmers, no one's enemy, but if we lived, we might join the enemy's forces, so we had to die.

Now I had a planet to explore and people to keep alive, and I was afraid again. Maybe the other planet, the one we had aimed for, would have been better. Here, I was kneeling inside a thicket of a plant wholly unlike docile domesticated corn.

But I was our colony's sole botanist. I had a big job, and I had to do it properly regardless of my fear.

I saw movement out of the corner of my eye. I spotted some moss, a patch of green in the bole of a root. It moved again. It was a fippokat. I looked at more boles. They made perfect fippokat homes. Fippokat feces littered the ground, black raisins melting into the sandy soil. Perhaps this was symbiosis—two life-forms helping each other—with the snow vines providing housing and the fippokats providing fertilizer, like bromeliads and ants on Earth. That didn't explain why the west vines had suddenly made fruit that could kill a fippokat.

I needed samples. With a pocketknife and plastic sample bags that I had been carefully cleaning and reusing since we had arrived, I took bits of vine, aspen, fruit, soil, fippokat feces, dead leaves, and bark, then very carefully I crawled out to uncramped sunshine.

I took samples from Snowman and from the west thicket—which stabbed me just as the east vine had. I tested the samples, and the results explained some things, but not the most important thing. The east thicket and Snowman were genetically the same individual. Snowman must have been a daughter plant from a shoot or underground stem. The west plant was the same species but a different individual. I could not explain why it had become poisonous. I could not predict whether the east fruit would remain safe. I had accomplished nothing.

———

That afternoon, we buried Ninia, Carrie, and Zee where we had buried the others, just south of the village in a little patch of ground next to the east thicket, where a mat of flowering turf covered the soil like a garden. Weeping, we rolled up the fragrant yellow blooms like sod, dug three holes, and lowered in the bodies. Everyone dropped in a handful of soil before we filled the graves and replanted the turf. Hedike led a song. Jill poured water onto the graves and recited a poem about rivers and oceans in a quaking voice. We each recalled our best memory of the women.

Zee had carved the other markers with names and the number of days since landing. This time Merl set plain stones at each grave.

"No names or dates," he said, brushing soil from his hands.

"We need a Pax calendar," Vera said. "And a Pax clock." She pointed to Lux in the western sky. "That sets three hours before the Sun, and it rises three hours before the Sun. That's one way to measure time."

She pointed at another starlike light, an asteroid-sized moon called Chandra.

"That orbit's almost the same as Pax's rotation. It's no good for telling time, except for seasons. But Galileo," she said, pointing to a light in the northeast, "is perfect. It goes backwards, west to east, so anyone can spot it. It orbits two and a half times a day."

Paula squinted at the sky. "Thank you. This—"

"Now we have it," Vera said. "We have our own way. Our own clock, our own sky, our own time. It's what we came here for."

With that reminder of our hopes, we returned to our daily tasks for survival. A Pax day and night lasted about twenty Earth hours, and a Pax year about 490 Earth days. A year seemed like such a long time.

A week passed, busy for both the zoologists and me. A flock of tiny moth-winged lizards arrived, flying as gracefully as a school of fish, and we watched with wonder until suddenly, as a group, they swooped down

and began to bite us. Ashes and grease worked again, then suddenly
the moths disappeared.

Hunting teams found half-eaten birds and fippokats and thought
they saw giant birds running away, but what bothered them more
were the pink slugs twenty centimeters long they found eating old
carcasses. The slugs would attack anything and dissolved living flesh
on contact. Grun dissected one.

"Nothing but slime. No differentiated tissue. If you chop it into
twenty bits, you have twenty slugs."

Merl discovered the source of the three-note roaring songs. "I believe I've found us the big-time cousin of our friends the fippokats." He
had arrived just before the evening meal and sat at a table talking calmly
enough, but sweat soaked his shirt as he petted a fippokat on his lap as
if to assure himself that it was docile. Everyone knew he was not an
anxious man, so we listened closely.

"If I had to use one word, I'd say kangaroo, but that's not quite it
either. Giant kangaroo to use two words, a good sight taller than me, and
judging from the nests they had, they can knock over trees. I believe
they're vegetarians like our friend here, root-eaters very possibly, and I'd
like to believe that the claws are for digging, but they're the size of
machetes. I saw a pack of around ten of them, but I didn't get too close.
And I wouldn't recommend getting close."

Most colonists tended to focus their attention on animals. Merl got
many more questions about his day's finds than I did, which I tried
not to let bother me, but I knew that plants with their poisons and
chemicals were as dangerous as animals, and because there were so
many more plants than animals, they were more important.

"The plants here aren't like anything on Earth," I tried to explain one
night. "They have cells I can't explain. On Earth, all seeds have one or
two embryonic leaves, but here they have three or five or eight."

"And RNA," Grun said, "not DNA. Nothing has DNA except us."

"But it looks the same," Vera said.

"No," Half-Foot Wendy said, "I mean, floating cactuses? Blue ones?
But they have thorns like Earth."

"Yes," I said, "thorns. They need to protect themselves like Earth cacti, so they grow thorns. Plants that need to get water from soil develop roots."

"Not like Earth," Uri said. "No earthworms. We have sponges instead."

"But they do the same thing," Vera said.

"We don't really know what they do," I said.

"But we know what plants do," she said. "They grow. They're useful or they're not. And that's all we need to know."

I knew we needed to know much more, and I wished Luigi Dini had survived so I would have someone to work with and to talk to.

We had already realized from the disaster on Mars that transplanting Earth ecology wouldn't work. Crops would not grow without specific symbiotic fungi on their roots to extract nutrients, and the exact fungi would not grow without the proper soil composition, which did not exist without certain saprophytic bacteria that had proven resistant to transplantation, each life-form demanding its own billion-year-old niche. But Mars fossils and organic chemicals in interstellar comets showed that the building blocks of life were not unique to Earth. Proteins, amino acids, and carbohydrates existed everywhere. The theory of panspermia was true to a degree.

I had found a grass resembling wheat on our first day on Pax, and with a little plant tissue, a dash of hormone from buds, and some chitin, we soon had artificial seeds to plant. But would it grow? Theory was one thing and farming was another.

Then a few days before the women had died from poisoned fruit, Ramona and Carrie had seen the first shoots, and whooped and squealed until we all came to look. They were twirling around the edges of the field, hair and skirts flying, and grabbed more of us by the hands until everyone in the colony, all thirty-four of us, danced with low, slow steps at the first evidence that we might survive.

The east fruit remained plentiful—alarmingly, it became more nutritious, another mystery I should have been able to explain but could not. The west fruit rotted on the vines. Uri toiled in the fields as if he could work out his grief through his hands and his tears through irrigation water from a spring between our fields and the west vines. We had planted a second crop, a yamlike tuber, and I prayed it would remain safe to eat.

"Someday we will have to clear that west thicket for more fields," Uri told Paula after breakfast one morning. We both heard stress tightening his voice.

"I don't think we'll need to clear the thicket anytime soon," Paula said in a deliberately offhand way. We were watching the fippokats play tug-of-war with a length of bark twine in their pen. "We don't want to do anything unnecessary until we understand the effect on the ecology. We're the aliens here."

"But this is necessary. The vine is a danger to us."

"Are you still angry over Ninia's death?" she asked, leaning back and gazing at his face.

Uri looked away. "I want peace. We all want peace."

I kept quiet, but even if he was right, which I doubted, we could hardly eliminate such a huge thicket if we tried.

Paula leaned over the fippokat pen and dangled a stem from a leaf of Pax lettuce. The lettuce was my latest find. The leaves contained folic acid and riboflavin, among other nutrients, but the stems were too tough to eat. We had eaten a slim breakfast of lettuce, nuts, snow vine fruit, and a bit of roasted fippokat.

A fippokat hopped closer to beg for the stem. Paula shook it and the animal turned a somersault in midair. Merl had found them remarkably easy to train. She dropped the stem at its feet. "Octavo," she said, "can you make seeds for more lettuce?"

"Of course."

"Uri," she said, "can you find a field for it? Have we got enough water?"

"I will fill your plate with peaceful lettuce," he said with a toothy

smile. Paula offered a sweeter smile in return, but I knew she sometimes had little patience with his antics.

Uri turned to me. "First, come look at the weeds in the wheat. One
in particular has needles like nettle, so even if it is good for something,
I do not want you to tell me. The thorns stick to the robot weeders and
then stick to me when I clean them, and I do not have enough skin for
this procedure."

Uri pointed out a nettle growing near us. I pulled on gloves to examine the plant. Its leaves were covered with thorns like glass tubes.

"Well, thorns like this might actually have a use," I said. I looked
up. He wasn't paying attention.

"That field!" he said, pointing toward the top of the hill. "The wheat
is flat."

He dashed up the path. I followed. From one edge almost to the
other, the wheat lay flat, every little shoot, and it had stood more than
halfway to my knees the day before. My wheat. Flat.

Uri reached the field before I did. He knelt to look, then pawed
through the dirt. "Root rot!"

I sprinted. Root rot kills. I dropped beside Uri and brushed apart
the wheat to look. Dark rot crept up the stems. I pawed through the
moist soil. The roots had decayed into brown slime.

"This is our bread," Uri howled. "Why?"

I closed my eyes and recited a textbook answer to avoid howling
like him. "Disease, too much water, a nutrient shortage. A lot of things
can cause it." I stood up to look for a pattern, moving too fast and
getting dizzy, but as soon as my vision cleared, I saw one. "My first
guess is disease traveling via water. You can see the rot spreading
downhill."

"Can I stop it? If I stop the water?"

I could only shrug.

He radioed Wendy at the irrigation pumps. I dug out some plants
with my hands and ran to the lab, remembering the Corn War, the wilting fields of my family's farm. But that was blight. This was root rot. The
blight was an engineered disease. This was natural. Both as deadly.

By the time I had results, Uri and Half-Foot Wendy had directed robots to dig a trench straight through the middle of the field to stop the downhill seep of irrigation water. Poison in the soil had killed the plants. It ate through their cell walls, making the cells burst like balloons. Ramona and I searched for something to neutralize the poison or to keep rootlets from absorbing it.

Jill came back from a tour of the fields, her dark eyes shadowed with worry. She had taken a sensor with a probe calibrated to test for the poison to see if it was spreading. It was in only one field, but if we irrigated or if it rained, it would spread.

We worked until long past sunset. We debated whether tilling and watering the field unbalanced something in the soil. We worried that we might have brought a disease from Earth despite our decontamination efforts.

For once I went to bed after Paula. I lay not quite touching her, close enough to feel the warmth of her body as she breathed steadily. The bittersweet scent of the air and hoots of the lizards did not quite feel like home, but Earth had long ago stopped feeling like home, too.

I first met Paula when I went to see a play by her father, Dr. Gregory Shanley, about how misplaced priorities had caused the asthma disaster in 2023, a work many people called apostate for its criticism of Greens as well as governments. I went because it was a fund-raiser for Next Earth, as it was called then, a privately funded project to send a colony to a distant planet. She was staffing a table in the theater lobby, and of course I knew who the small young woman was. Her father had been preparing her since childhood to lead it, which some people criticized as much as the project itself.

On video, she had always seemed serious, maybe even a little quiet, but when I approached the table, she was laughing and talking with other people, and when she saw me, she put out her hand. "I'm glad you could come tonight. I'm Paula Shanley."

"Octavo Pastor."

She gestured at the others. "We were saying—I was saying—that we *could* fail, I know, and we could die, but that's how much it's worth doing."

"Tell that to Goltz's family," someone said. Erno Goltz was a would-be volunteer whose family had obtained preventive detention so he couldn't leave Earth. In fact, Gregory and Paula were not welcome in several countries.

"It's hard for some people to understand," she said. "We're the future of humanity, and we have a duty."

"Can I volunteer?" I said. She looked me in the eyes to see if I was serious. Then she nodded and reached for some papers. I thought perhaps I could help with a scientific committee, but the more I learned about the project, the more I was willing to give everything.

At first I was attracted to Paula's concern for others, then to her iron determination and the way she sacrificed and struggled for the project.

"What human beings and other sentient species bring to the universe," she said, "is the ability to make choices, to step beyond the struggle to survive and be the eyes and ears and minds and hearts of the universe. Survival is just the first step."

I loved her, but I did not dare express my feelings. She approached me. I did not know what she saw in me because I was so unlike her, and I always felt a little awed by her, but I had never been happier. I hoped that happiness would become our legacy on another world.

Our new civilization would be based on the best of Earth. We would respect the dignity of all life, practice justice and compassion, and seek joy and beauty. We brought educational programs in our computers for our children that left out Earthly irrationalities like money, religion, and war. Some thought we would contaminate an exoecology, but we meant to fit in, to add to it, and most of all to ensure that humanity's fate would not depend on a single imperiled planet.

Not all those who had volunteered could go. They had to support the Pax Constitution, which we had written, debated, and rewritten before we left. They needed good genes, strong bodies without artificial parts, healthy minds, and useful skills, including arts, so Hedike and Stevland Barr, musical prodigies, joined us. Eventually, fifty volunteers left Earth, some in tears, some with smiles.

We landed at a lakeshore near a river, delirious with joy to see trees and hear birdlike whistles. The other five landing pods would arrive—or try to—the next day. As part of the exploration team, I waded up-river, past the wide eerie thicket we would later call the east snow vine, past what I thought were slow green fish camouflaged as plants but soon realized were free-swimming plants. Already dazzled by this new world, we arrived at a vast meadow that seemed ideal. The thickets on the east and west would protect us. The forests on the north and south stood ready for exploration. We had found our home.

The hot, dry weather stole more from us. Leaves that would mark edible roots withered and fell from dormant plants. Seeds on wild grains loosened and blew away. Barking flightless birds gathered nuts before we could find them, and giant birds started to menace the hunters, but Uri frightened them off, at least for a while, with well-aimed rifle shots. Red hydrogen-filled seedpods floated in the wind, ready to ignite with the smallest spark, and the dry forest would burn fast. I had failed to predict the fruit, I could not save the wheat, and I was not finding food, but no one blamed me. Except myself. We all knew we would face unexpected dangers and failures, but no one, not even Paula, knew how much I wanted to advance our survival.

My stomach was empty as I left the village at dawn. I carried a geo-positioning receiver tuned to a satellite overhead, all that was left of the spaceship that had brought us here.

I paused at the little cemetery, surprised to see that the yellow blooms above the three women's graves had become balls of dried petals, dead without going to seed. I knelt to examine the plants and dug into the soil. The sod fell to pieces in my hands. Perhaps we had been less careful replacing it than we had thought.

My fingers, brushing through the sod, felt something firm, springy with life. A white shoot, like bamboo and wide as my thumb, rose from the soil. I found another, another, and more. Snow vines sprouted from the three women's graves. The vines had sent out roots to feed on dead humans instead of aspen trees, to tap flesh for food and blood for water. One vine had killed them and the other was feeding on them, as if this were an Earth war where corpses were left to be scavenged by crows and wild dogs. I whipped out my machete and hacked apart the color-less shoots without thinking, kicked open the soil to find every last one, and chopped them all to bits.

Finished, panting in the thick atmosphere, I gazed at the east thicket rising unperturbed and realized I was a fool. This was no Earth war, just Darwinian struggle. The cycle of life always reuses the dead, and I had succeeded only in despoiling the graves. I gazed at clods of soil, dead flowers, and white vines bleeding sap. I smoothed the ground as neatly as I could over the graves, and left.

The Sun had risen above the treetops. I explored the forest until the muscles and joints in my legs ached, but I found precious little for our colony.

I had so much to learn. We knew that Pax was a billion years older than Earth. On Earth, plants had separated from animals less than a billion years ago. Probably Pax plants had had more time to evolve.

The greenery around me held secrets I would never learn.

We ate a small dinner in near silence that night. Uri said that some of the yams had been poisoned, apparently from seepage from the wheat fields, despite the drought.

Later, in bed, Paula awoke suddenly.

"It might rain," she said.

"Soon?"

"It might rain a lot. The planet has seasonal storm patterns. It makes hurricanes, but they're big and low and move slow compared to Earth."

"Can we prepare for them?"

"Not much, not much at all."

After a long while, we both fell back asleep. I dreamed of my child-hood and hunger. I awoke at dawn expecting gunfire—and remem-bered that I was far away from warfare and safe from soldiers, if not hunger.

Before I went on my daily search for food, Uri and I inspected the fields as the early morning Sun cast long shadows. We checked the trench and the wheat below it. Less than one-third of the crop had been saved, and it was wilting for lack of water. We kept walking. I stared down at the dusty poisoned soil beneath our feet. "Maybe if we water lightly—"

Uri grabbed my arm so suddenly I tripped. "Look."

At the west end of the fields, at the top of the hill, like white spears, snow vine shoots rose ten centimeters high. Sandy soil still clung to the sprouts. The field had been bare the night before, I had seen it myself. With one look, I understood the poison.

"It's the vines," I said. Uri stared wide-eyed at the shoots. "The snow vines poisoned the field. It's allelopathy. The plant gets rivals out of the way to clear space for itself. If we test them, we'll find them full of poison."

They were. The snow vines had sent down roots more than a meter deep, found our irrigated field, exuded a poison, and taken the land for its own use. They were in the yam fields, too.

"Plants try to expand. It's a natural thing," I explained in the lab to Uri and Paula. But I felt troubled. The snow vines had sent their roots more than a half kilometer to attack the field, passing other fine fertile ground.

"I say destroy it," Uri said with clenched teeth. "It killed Ninia. It will kill all our crops."

Paula looked at him sternly. I stated an obvious fact.

"It will not be easy to destroy. The thicket covers hectares, with who knows what defenses."

"We stopped Napoleon, we stopped Hitler, we can stop a killer houseplant. We will not fall to siege." Then Uri caught Paula's look and smiled, as if he had told a joke.

"We're not at war," Paula said slowly, smiling back. "It's only vines and trees."

Uri saluted. "I am a lumberjack of a soldier."

Paula's smile faded a bit.

If we were ever going to grow anything, we would need to control the vines, but we needed something in harmony with the environment. An idea occurred to me that I should have had much earlier.

"Nature balances," I said. "Something has to be the natural biological control for the snow vines. We can find it and let the environment take care of itself. Uri, let's go."

Paula gave me a look of thanks.

Our two thickets, east and west, were set apart by the wide meadow we lived in, and bounded by forest at either end. With machetes, guided by the geopositioning system, Uri and I crashed through the forest to the north, sweating under gloves and heavy shirts to protect us from thorns and bug-lizards and spiny flightless birds and coral tentacles. Every slash brought a different scent of sap to the air.

Uri swung hard at a poison ivy fern. "We must find something as good as a missile," he said.

"We will need something even more powerful, but not a weapon. Something natural."

He paused. "You think we will find such a thing?"

"Have faith in nature. Whatever balances the snow vine has to be at least as powerful as it is."

The first snow vine thicket that we located stood in the forest like an island two meters across, a cloud of white vines around a crest of aspen. They arched over our heads like tentacles reaching into the woods. One had wrapped around a palm tree, pulling it over, and another tentacle had clamped over the growth bud at the top. The palm was dying.

"Here is a job for a lumberjack soldier," I said.

With a flourish, he saluted the thicket. "We will meet in battle."

The satellite scan of the forest had located another thicket, big and split in the middle like a lizard eye. In miniature, it resembled the thickets bordering our meadow.

At one end, a gap in the thicket opened like a doorway into the little meadow inside it. Above the doorway, vines arched toward each other and grappled. Thorns cut into other vines, and sap dripped onto the ground. One branch held a tattered piece of another vine clamped in a spiral grip.

Uri stared at it. "The plant grows very strange."

I understood it at a glance. "Two plants, east and west."

"Two soldiers," he corrected, and laughed, entertained by his own idea. I could not manage to laugh.

Inside we found tufts of grass falling over and rotten like the wheat in our fields. With my boot, I cleared away slimy remains to reveal a rotting aspen sapling that had belonged to one side or another. "This might be the real target of the root rot."

He studied it, looked around at the thickets on either side of us, and slowly smiled. "Life again makes sense. We are in a battlefield, a fight between two houseplants."

He was right up to a point. Plants always struggled against each other on Earth. They often fought to the death.

"A fight, yes," I said, "but for survival. They're not mere soldiers. And think how big our meadow is, how big the struggle to survive." I looked around for any hint of a counterbalancing force to snow vines and did not see one.

A stink drew us to a lump of green turf, actually a bloated fippokat corpse. Ripe fruit hung on the vines on one side of the meadow. "I bet those are poisonous," I said.

"Why kill a little kat? You said they fertilize the ground in the thickets."

"Dead bodies might yield more fertilizer. Or you could cut off your opponent's manure supply."

"Plants are not that smart."

"They adapt," I said. "They evolve." At the university, we had joked about the ways plants abused insects to make them carry pollen or seeds, but insects were small. On Pax, the snow vines were enormous. Next to them, humans and fippokats were insects, objects to abuse. I pushed at the dead fippokat with the toe of my boot. It was anchored to the ground somehow. I prodded the corpse with my machete, holding my breath against the smell. A thick root emerged from its belly and buried itself in the soil beneath it. Something poked up under the fur.

I sliced the poor thing open. Inside, a snow vine seed had germinated. I thought of the three women's graves. The west vine had employed them just like this fippokat to carry away its seeds and used the dead bodies as fertilizer. I hacked off the shoot springing out of the fippokat. I had learned everything I needed to know. I knew what we were.

I looked for Uri. Holding his machete like a sword, he had approached one of the thickets walls and was walking slowly down its length. He kicked at the leaf litter and rotting grass on the ground. Leaves and twigs flew, and maybe bones. Beneath the litter, vine roots lay like slithering snakes, reaching out and winding around each other. "Madness," he shouted. "Madness. We are being killed by fighting houseplants."

In the flying leaves I saw our house in Veracruz explode in the Corn War, thatch blasting through the air. My family fled through dying fields to the swampy forest, spy planes buzzing all around us. My mother tried to shield my eyes and told me to be brave, but I saw human bones in the woods, their stinking flesh falling away, and I screamed. Then my mother fell, blood bubbling from her chest and mouth. We had to leave her with the rest of the dead, and I had to be brave.

Uri had been in an army, but I had been in a war. Soldiers win victories, but civilians merely survive, if they are lucky and clever. That can be enough, but the civilians may hate both sides, and I did. I had left Earth to escape them all, every side in every war.

"We can go," I said. "We can go."

The people who caused the Corn War—both sides of that war—were greedy and cruel. But the vines were just vines.

He pointed the machete at me. "The east vine is already our ally, correct? It will serve us."

"Only if we are great big fippokats and do what it wants."

Uri hopped like a kat. "The fippokats will win, then."

"Only if our vine wins."

At my insistence, we dug up the graves of Carrie, Ninia, and Zee. We found a mass of roots at war tangled through their flesh. The seeds from the west vine had sprouted, stems and roots bursting through their abdomens. But roots from the east thicket had countered, strangling the seedlings. The east vine had won. I confessed to attacking the west vine's seedlings.

Uri put an arm around my shoulder. "You helped kill Ninia's killer—and Carrie's and Zee's. You did us a service."

More than that, I had made a decision about the sanctity of a grave, something beyond the struggle to survive. I had brought a mind and a heart to Pax.

At the conclusion of a meager dinner in the village plaza—snow vine fruit but no yams, no bread, and not much of the dehydrated myco-protein we had brought from Earth—we held a Commonwealth meeting about the snow vines. I described how individual vines battled each other, poisoning other plants and using animals to provide fertilizer, to spread seeds, and perhaps more. "We could probably transplant the east vine to guard our fields, but—"

Half-Foot Wendy interrupted me. "Perfect." Other people nodded.

"But we need to be its fippokats," I said. "We will work *for* it, not the other way around. It will help us only because it is helping itself. We give it food and water—our latrines and irrigation and cemetery—and we help it advance, just as if we were a colony of fippokats."

"That's fine," Wendy said, grinning. "We wanted to fit into the ecology. We won't be aliens anymore, and after only a couple of months. Oh, this is better than I thought."

But immediate success would be unlikely. We had to be overlooking something.

"Merl," Paula said, "tell us about fippokats. What are they like, and what do we need to do?"

He stood up and stroked his beard for a moment. "They're herbivores, for starters. Camouflaged, and not at the top of the food chain. And I've discovered lately that they can slide as well as hop."

He continued talking. I wondered what we had not noticed. Ecologies adjust, but two months was fast, especially for plants. Intelligence made humans extremely adaptable as a species. We could probably learn within days to fully imitate fippokats, if we had to make many changes. We already fulfilled many of their behaviors from the snow vines' point of view.

Merl was saying: "I believe I've seen them teaching each other things. They learn mighty fast."

The snow vines had learned fast, too. They had realized that we were like fippokats and used us like them, giving us healthy or poisonous fruit. But the west vine had attacked our fields. It had noticed how we differed from fippokats, that we were farmers, and it had developed a plan that required conspicuous effort on its part. Creative, original ideas and perseverance were signs of intelligence—real intelligence, insightful. It had weighed possible courses of action, then chosen one.

Snow vines could think and plan ahead, and the west vine had made a very aggressive decision. It had decided to kill us every way it could and had invented tactics to do it. We were civilians in a warlord's territory. We were in a genuine battleground.

We were in terrible danger.

I interrupted Merl. "Do fippokats grow crops?"

He looked at me like I was crazy, then shrugged. "Why, no, they don't. Not that I've seen. Not even burying seeds like squirrels, though they might, come fall."

"The snow vine attacked our crops. It knows we are not fippokats. It is like the Corn War back on Earth. Controlling the food supply is one way to win a war."

"Aw, come on," Bryan said. "It attacked the field because it was a good place for it to grow."

"It had to go too far, more than a half kilometer, and it passed better places to grow, like the spring. It analyzed us and made a decision, a complex decision. Then the other snow vine decided to become our ally. They are smart enough to do that. They can think."

"You never said this before," Vera said.

"I only realized it now."

"Plants can't think!"

Paula rapped on the table. "Let's remember to be supportive and listen, not debate. We're here to solve a problem, not to win."

I gave her a look of gratitude, but she was looking at someone else with warning. I took a deep breath. "They have cells I cannot identify. On Earth, plants can count. They can see, they can move, they can produce insecticides when the wrong insect comes in contact with them."

"It could be an instinctual response," Merl said. "Any animal decides what to do about its territory."

"Plants struggle against each other for survival. They fight," I said. "This is a war, an organized fight."

"Aw, come on," Bryan said, then caught Paula's eye. "I mean, this is a lot to accept at once."

"I know," I said, working hard to be patient. "I want us to be sure we understand that we are picking sides in a war that is bigger than we are, and we are making one side a more determined enemy."

"Enemy. A plant enemy," he muttered. Everyone sat quietly for a minute. A couple of crabs started buzzing near Snowman.

"Humans go to war because they're depraved." Vera glanced at Paula, then continued more gently. "This is an ecosystem, so it all works together as a whole." She was an astronomer, so of course she saw the universe as stars and planets with neat and predictable orbits, everything worked out by math: the rest of nature would be the same.

"The plants are fierce," Uri said. "Octavo is right about that. We must try to survive equally hard."

Grun nodded. "He's found out how to fit into nature, harsh as it is here. It's a risky plan and it's good of him to make sure we know the risks, but it's a reasonable plan, and I like it."

I looked around. We all wore the same sturdy clothes, spoke the same language, and shared the same hopes. We had debated this back on Earth and reached an agreement. We would live in harmony with nature, and nature was always in harmony, like the gears of an old-fashioned clock. I knew that the vines had killed us deliberately, with malice and forethought, but that was too hard for anyone else to believe.

"If plants are so smart," Bryan said, "where are their cities?"

"Now, it's an old planet, but it's new to us," Merl replied. "We've not been here but a couple of months, and there's a lot to learn. We might be standing smack in the middle of a city and not be able to see it. Still, we can't take too long before we decide what to do because we don't have that much time. The fippokats have managed to live with the vines, and they're mighty smart for animals. We can do it, too."

"This is the first place where I've felt genuinely at home," Wendy said. "We found what we wanted. We left Earth behind, didn't we? Pax will be at peace as long as we're at peace."

"That's right," Vera repeated. "We left behind the failed paradigms like war."

Perhaps I was using the wrong paradigm. "You are right, it is an evolutionary struggle, and we need to fit in. But I do not know what the snow vine, either snow vine, is going to do next. We will have to keep on doing whatever they want. They might outthink us, or use us and discard us. The east vine might not even fight for us."

"Plants don't control animals," Merl said. "Influence, maybe, so it's right to keep a weather eye, but they can't outthink us."

I thought about agriculture back on Earth. Food meant money and power, and on Earth it was easy to spot the enemy. It had its hand in your pocket or its gun pointed at your chest.

Paula said, "I think we all recognize that our decision might have unforeseen consequences. It will be *all* our decision, though, knowing that nothing's guaranteed."

"If it doesn't work," Ramona echoed, "it's not your fault, Octavo. I think we ought to try being a friend of the east vine for a while."

"It's that or move the whole colony," Vera said, "and we'd starve for certain, and there may be snow vines all over Pax anyway. Let's be practical."

They had no idea what they were agreeing to, but if they wanted to think they were living in harmony with nature, maybe they could sleep more peacefully. War was a human thing, but not just a human thing, and we had not added anything new to this planet. We were at war and only I knew what that meant. But one person knowing what to do might be enough.

Uri still argued for destroying the west thicket, but he was voted down, twenty-four to seven. I voted no because I feared that without the west thicket as an enemy, the east thicket might not need us.

I did what I could. I transplanted snow vines and aspen trees from the east thicket to the western edge of our fields as a shield. They thrived and attacked. We replanted our crops, and they grew unmolested.

Every day, I walked with a machete on the far side of our shield of vines and hacked off any west vines reaching toward it. Sometimes I found combating vines wrapped around each other in struggle, pushing and tearing. With one chop, I rescued our white knight. Underground, I knew, the battle raged even more fiercely.

One afternoon, Uri came with me, shirtless in the heat. A bandanna tied across his forehead caught his sweat. "Who would think farming would be so violent?" He chopped off a vine and hurled it toward a woodpile for burning. He walked on, poking with a stick in the brush for vines hiding like snakes. This was simply weeding a garden to him.

Around us, little lizards hooted under the blue sky and the small bright Sun. Soon we would have our first harvest, and we were planning a feast.

We had said we expected hardship, not paradise, but we really wanted both. We thought we could come in peace and find a happy niche in another ecology. Instead we found a battlefield. The east vine turned us into servile mercenaries, nothing more than big, clever fippokats helping it win another battle. We had wanted to begin the world afresh, far from Earth and all its mistakes. That had not happened, but only I realized it, and I kept my disappointment to myself. Someday I might explain to our children how we had to compromise to survive.

Uri chopped merrily away. We faced more fighting ahead, and I hoped I would be ready.

SYLVIA
YEAR 34–GENERATION 2

Nothing herein shall be deemed to infringe on the individual freedom of belief, right to speech and justice, liberty, and the peaceful pursuit of individual aims in harmony with the welfare and interests of the Commonwealth as a whole.

—from the Constitution of the Commonwealth of Pax

Before the roof blew away, I had to check it, I had to, and it didn't matter who said I shouldn't or if it really wasn't safe to go upstairs. Summer meant hurricanes and I'd dreamed of designing a beautiful building as strong as a hurricane but I didn't get beauty or strength because they wouldn't let me. And this hurricane! It was the first storm of the summer and the meteorologists said it would probably be the worst ever. Rain was plowing against the lodge when Julian and I went up to the third floor. We opened the trapdoor to the attic and I climbed up on his shoulders to look at the roof from the underside.

It rocked like a boat on water. The shingles were ripped off in some places, rain slashed in and filled the attic with the smell of drenched wood, and the wind tugged on the beams and gables and strained every joint. What if I'd woven the studs and rafters as if they were reeds? Then some wood cracked in the corner like an exploding hydrogen cactus.

"Torch!" I shouted at Julian, then motioned since he couldn't hear me over the wind. The flame flickered in the wind as he handed it up and the air smelled of burning resin, then a hard wind swatted the roof and it rocked again.

There was the problem: the improvised tie-down had broken at the northwest corner. I'd designed the roof to be set into the walls with slotted joints and crossties the way the architecture text recommended, but no one had time for the complicated work. No one wanted to give time to a child's dream. They'd used poles and logs not even sawed into real beams. They got what they wanted.

Would the building survive the storm at all? I wanted doubled-up beams, corner braces, and extra ties. Extravagances, they said, and the building turned out weak, cramped, and clumsy.

"Sylvia!" Julian shouted, and added something I couldn't catch. His red hair shone like flame in the torchlight and his eyes suffered for me, for how I felt about the roof, my poor roof.

I began to climb down and there was Vera standing at the head of the stairs. She must have struggled all the way up to check on us, but why? She was the new moderator of Pax so she ought to be concerned about the building but we could have told her all about it. Torchlight lit her face, wrinkled like tree bark, white hair receding like a man's, false teeth bared.

"Julian!" She sounded like an underoiled machine. "Why did you bring Sylvia here?"

"My idea," I yelled so she could hear me over the storm. Julian had followed me, trying to be helpful. But Vera ignored me and motioned for us to follow her.

We trudged down the steps. The wind tore at the building the way a fippolion's claws hunt for roots, and the plaster was cracking as the walls shuddered. Vera descended step by step, leaning on a cane. It would have been disrespectful to get ahead of her, and children must honor the parents! We'd heard that since we were born, and how could we disobey?

She yelled at him all the way down, and when we arrived in the crowded, dark cellar, I put out the torch and tried again.

"I needed to inspect the roof." I kept even a hint of disrespect out of my voice.

"Julian could have gone alone and told you about it." She grunted as she lowered herself onto a bench.

"But he didn't design it. He wouldn't know what to look for."

She waved her cane. "It was too dangerous."

"Don't worry," he murmured. He was still a teenager like me, but his beard had come in red like his hair. He got that from his mother, Paula, and a squarish face from his father, Octavo, and had a smile so wide that it made his eyes crinkle up. He patted me on the arm. She glared at his hand.

Even so, I swear I wanted to like her and I thought maybe she acted angry because she was frightened by the storm. She'd been moderator for only a month, elected after Paula's death, and I hoped that Vera would be as good as her. Paula had been too sick in her last year to be a real moderator and I hoped that Pax would become calm and organized again. I wanted to keep building, to design strong and beautiful homes and barns and bridges. Survival was year to year and survival came first, but beauty was good for the soul. Several Earth texts said that and Earth couldn't have been all bad.

My mother, Half-Foot Wendy, was sitting with Octavo. His white hair and beard looked bright in the dim light of oil lamps. I headed toward them, zigzagging because all twenty-eight residents of the lodge and their possessions crowded the room, all their clothes, beds, tools, medical equipment, and robots. There were three other older lodges, also probably having trouble in a storm so fierce, with cellars full of people, but the cellars were sturdy. Everyone understood the importance of that.

Mama smiled at me as if I'd gone for a stroll to pick friendly fruit, with a wide smile like Julian's, but the corners of her mouth disappeared into her jowls. Her face had once been smooth and full like mine, I'd seen the pictures, but she wasn't made for this gravity. It had pulled her face down, and her breasts, knees, arms, all her flesh drooped. On Earth, according to the parents, I'd be light as a leaf.

"It was a good design," Mama said.

"It was my first real building."

"Not your fault," Octavo said, but he wasn't looking at me.

Mama wanted to go to the gift center and I helped her stand and walk. The top of my head only reached her shoulder because Pax gravity had made us children short and strong and fast like native animals. The parents were crippled after a lifetime of falls and struggling, no matter how many times the medics rebuilt their bones and joints.

"Not bad in here yet," she called from the gift center, which was just big buckets, not a real outhouse, and it didn't stink yet, but we'd be stuck in the cellar for two days with no chance to make a gift to a friendly plant, and they'd get full. She limped out and took my shoulder again.

"Do you know why Vera yells at Julian?" she whispered, and put her arm around my shoulders. "Octavo told me. Julian's sterile."

Sterile? I was so surprised I didn't say anything. Mama shook her head and patted my cheek because she knew I liked Julian.

Sterility was the Pax curse, that's what the parents muttered, and population was the Pax problem. Half the parents were dead now and they'd had only twenty-four surviving children, and half the cache of sperm and ova from Earth had been lost in a refrigeration failure in a storm. We children had produced only thirteen grandchildren so far, none from me, and I was now eighteen Earth years old, fourteen Pax years, and fertile, and a lot of parents thought I had a duty to fulfill. "You have time," Mama always said, but other parents were impatient. I saw how mothers loved their children and I couldn't stand to love anything that much yet because sometimes babies died even before they were born. What if my baby died?

We made the usual hurricane meal that evening, fancy fippokat stew, fragrant with onions and potatoes, but I didn't eat much. I minded Nicoletta's toddler while she fed her father. Later Ramona wanted to play Go and how can you say no to a parent, especially a bossy one like her? So we played and I won, probably because I could see better. Eventually, the roof blew off. The wood tore horribly until there was a thud and shake of released pressure, then rain blasted louder than ever against the attic floor. No one said anything. Without the tug from the roof, the building seemed to creak less. I was sitting on my cot with a piece of paper, designing a temporary roof, when Julian sat down next to me and put his arm around me. I closed my eyes and leaned against him, hoping Vera was watching. I wished I were on Earth.

In my earliest memories I thought Pax was somewhere on Earth because the names of so many things were the same here as in the educational programs. But there were big differences too, so later I thought there was some elaborate Earth-Pax distinction about animals and plants and food. I worried that Earth and all its tall fragile people with their multipart names might be just on the other side of the lake and might cross it, because they'd made Earth a living hell. The parents always said so.

But then I understood that Earth was far away, just a computer library of texts, music, and pictures about complicated histories and places I'd never visit and eventually saw less of as the computers broke down. Besides us, there was no intelligent life on Pax, just the snow vines and some sneaky carnivores. That disappointed the parents and me, too, when I realized that the only new people I'd ever meet were new babies. I wished for aliens.

The architecture texts, when I could access them, showed beautiful and inspiring buildings, completely impossible because we didn't have pre-stressed concrete or structural steel, in fact hardly any iron because the satellite hadn't found any ore deposits. We had only bricks and lumber but I'd tried to learn what was practical and apply it and now my first building was falling apart on top of me because people who hadn't studied architecture were sure they knew better.

Vera stayed anxious during the whole storm, organizing teams to mop up leaks and cook meals. Nights were the worst. It was early lights out because the parents wanted to sleep, but they never slept well, waking at any noise, every clap of thunder, shuffling again and again to the gift center, and snoring louder than the roaring wind, then early lights on when they were done with what passed for sleep. They kept me awake and I began to act like them, inattentive, irritable, and forgetful, chronically sleep-deprived because the days and nights were too

short for the parents, who'd been born on Earth. I wished I were somewhere else.

As soon as the storm calmed, two days after the roof was torn off,
I slipped out of the damp and stinking cellar, finally, with some other
children. I went to the lake with Julian and tall, skinny Aloysha, who
were both hunters, and Daniel, who fished and was almost thirty years
old. We wanted to see how the boats had fared and what had washed up
on shore. It was still raining hard and the clouds were low and dark.
We were wrapped in downy acetate ponchos like cocoons but our feet
were drenched. Puddles and streamlets were everywhere. Everything
we walked past was damaged, buildings and irrigation canals and farm
fields, and the disaster would look even worse when the Sun came out.
Even some of the aspen trees in the snow vine thicket had fallen, although the thicket itself remained sturdy in a way that I envied.

The river through the friendly thicket was flooded. The lake was
flooded too, with only a narrow strip of sand between the water and
the tree line. The other rivers were probably flooded but we couldn't
see them through the rain. The whitecapped waves were dirty brown
from all the soil washed into the water. Rain rattled on the surface of
the water and made it dull as the clouds. The boats had been hauled
up beyond the tree line and lashed tightly.

Daniel, who always worried, checked the boats. "They look good,"
he said, relieved. I checked the wicker fish traps stored under them.
They looked good, too.

Wicker was the reason I'd come to the beach. I made baskets. After
storms, fresh reeds and vines would wash up on the beach, brought to
the lake by the flooding rivers, and there were usually dead natans from
the lake, the swimming plants that dried into silky-soft fibers. I also
hoped that a roof beam might be floating around, because we could
salvage the nails, at least. Julian and Aloysha found an injured fippolion. I didn't look as they pulled out their knives and ended its whim-
pers. It would be a lot of meat, tough and not nearly as good as deer
crab, but we'd have enough to eat.

I saw strange flashes of color in a mat of branches that had washed
on shore. I got closer and saw rainbow-striped pieces of stems and twigs.

But a hungry lizard or worse might be riding in the mat so I teased out some pieces with a stick. Finger-wide rainbows alternated with black bands on the twigs, worn and scratched but still beautiful, and I could weave extraordinary things with it. I took all I could and stuffed it into my bag. I hoped I'd find more down the beach.

On the way I saw something pink in the sand, maybe a chunk of rose quartz, so I checked. A pretty stone could be beautiful, too. Closer, I saw shiny yellow metal with it. Maybe it was a bit from one of the landing pods that had crashed thirty-four years ago. I dug it out of the wet sand and let the rain wash it clean. It was a glass ball, solid and heavy, the size of a baby's fist and faceted, worn on the surface but clear where it was chipped, wrapped in a spiral band of gold.

The gold was battered but I could still see writing engraved in a kind of alphabet I'd never seen in history texts, just lines and triangles. I turned it around and around in my hands and tried to imagine what it was. A machine part? I knew what most machine parts looked like even if I wasn't a technician, and a few lenses sort of looked like this, but lenses were small. A decoration? We didn't have many decorations and nothing like this because gold was too useful to be wasted. A piece of ore? Not even possible. Maybe something natural? Even more impossible. It wasn't like anything I knew.

Finally I began to realize that the only things I knew were either natural or human-made. Maybe I couldn't recognize the ball because it wasn't either. Maybe it had been made by another kind of sentient being. Maybe someone else lived on Pax. Someone who could make things. Someone who could write and handle metal and glass and make something beautiful with it. This ball had sat in the bottom of the lake or washed in from a river or some traveler had left it behind. Someone else lived on Pax. Maybe we could find them.

Julian and Aloysha had tied the dead fippolion to a fallen branch and were hoisting it up, a male big enough to tear apart snow vines, with front claws like machetes. They wobbled with its weight. The rain was falling harder. I ran up and held out the ball. My hand trembled.

"I don't think this is ours," I said, "look, I think this is something alien, I mean Pax, really, we're aliens, it has writing, I found it, really different writing, it's beautiful, isn't it, and it was in the sand over there, and it's not human." I realized I wasn't making sense.

Julian set the branch on his shoulder and put his hands around mine to steady it. He looked at the ball for what seemed like a long time, then he smiled wider than he ever had. Daniel ran over to see what we were excited about and we all started talking at once.

"This is gold, look, and glass."

"We don't make things like this."

"What is it? Let me hold it."

"It's beautiful."

Aloysha howled like a lion.

"Something—someone made this," I said. "We're not alone. Not here, not on Pax, not in the universe."

We stared at it for a moment.

"There's intelligent life here besides us," I said, "somewhere nearby."

"Nearby," Aloysha echoed, squinting. He didn't always catch on fast.

"How old is this?" Julian said.

"The wear should tell us something," Daniel said. He took it and turned it around in his hand slowly. "It can't be that old. I mean, not thousands of years."

"So they're still alive," I said. Daniel handed it back to me, and for a moment I was surprised to feel it was wet because I'd forgotten we were standing in the middle of a rainstorm. I was drenched and rain was pelting on the ball in my hand and all our faces were dripping but I didn't care. We weren't alone on Pax.

"What's it for?" Aloysha asked.

"Maybe," I said, "it's an invitation. We need to find them."

Julian smiled. "Soon."

When we got to the village, he and Aloysha had to take the lion to be dressed out and Daniel went to report to the fishing team while I headed straight for the lodge, where Vera would probably be. The reek from the basement hit me as soon as I opened the door. I knew I shouldn't go into the basement and drip over everything so I had someone ask her to come up.

She huffed up the steps, looking anxious. "Is there a problem? Did we lose the boats?"

"No, they're fine, but—"

"The fields?"

"Well, they're flooded and there's damage, and buildings too, but—"

She shook her head and closed her eyes and sighed. "This is hard, so hard."

"I found this." I held out the ball. Maybe it would cheer her up. She opened her eyes and stared at it blankly. "I think it was made by some other intelligent life," I said. "It was at the lake."

Terrell had come up behind her. He was a parent and metallurgist, so I said, "That's gold around it. We should look for whoever made it."

He was tall and as thin as a parasitized aspen, so when he nudged Vera, she had to look up to see his face as they exchanged a look. They were interested so I pulled out some rainbow twigs.

"I found these, too."

They stiffened with surprise, but Vera said, "We don't have time for that, not now. There's too much to do." She took the ball from my hand. "I'll put it on the agenda for the next meeting."

But the next Commonwealth meeting was in four days. Four days!

Still, people heard about the ball and wanted to see it that night in the dark cellar as we ate dinner.

Ramona said, "It looks like a Christmas ornament," and she began to sing a Christmas song, but Bryan, another parent, complained that Christmas was a nightmare.

"Arguing over the past," said Rosemarie, a child a little older than me, and Bryan overheard and scolded her for disrespecting the parents. I'd read about Christmas and "frivolity" was the word I remembered, and frivolity seemed interesting. And unlikely on Pax.

Survival first. There was a lot to repair and replant but there always was. "Is this really better than Earth?" Nicoletta had whispered once when we were young and no parents were around. Now, she worked as my mother's replacement, scavenging parts from the failed radio system to repair the medical tomography equipment, and if there were parts left over, to keep the weeding machines running. Machines did mindless tasks so we had time to care for sick parents or prepare for the next storm or preserve what food we had for winter.

Nicoletta had borne three babies already and two lived. When we were young, we used to coil her curly black hair into ringlets. These days, she had no time for fussing with her hair. And sometimes she cried for no reason.

Daniel fished but the lake became anaerobic during the bad droughts and all the fish died. My brother tried to enrich the soil in the fields and complained that the snow vines took the nutrients as fast as he could fertilize, but snow vine fruit kept everyone fed when crops failed or were destroyed by storms.

Sometimes, Octavo would stare at nothing and grumble: "Parameters. Fippokats here. Uri, let's go weeding." Uri had died ten years ago. Octavo was sick and would die soon too, and I'd miss him because he was always patient with me.

I was in the plaza weaving a thatch frame for a temporary roof for the lodge when Octavo limped up to ask for a sample of the rainbow bamboo, as he called it.

"Something for the meeting," he said, and coughed with a wheezing bark. "Something that needs an explanation." He knew plants better than anyone and I wondered what there was to explain.

But thunderstorms arrived on the meeting night and no building could hold all residents at once, although we were only sixty-two people. The roof thatched with plastic bark on my lodge held with hardly a leak and some people congratulated me, but not Vera. She was still proving she was moderator and reorganizing our rooms because a lot of them had been damaged in the big hurricane, even though we'd already rearranged ourselves without her help and no one was complaining.

I went to the closet that was my new room, with nothing but a cot and one box that held everything I owned, so angry I almost cried. I should have known then what I realized later, that we wouldn't have voted to investigate the glass makers anyway. The parents would've voted no, the children would've voted the way their parents did, and even the grandchildren would follow their parents' parents. Children didn't think for themselves. We did what we were told because we'd been convinced that we didn't really understand things well enough to make our own decisions. That's what we were told all the time and how could we argue with that? We were supposed to be happy to be just like the parents, and working together in harmony mattered more than thinking as individuals. We were still children even though most of us were twenty or thirty years old.

What would happen when all the parents died?

Octavo came to talk to me the next day while I was working in a corner of the plaza next to Snowman, the big old snow vine. I was making a basket for collecting pond grubs, a wide hoop basket with loosely attached ribs so it would be soft and flexible because the grubs burst so easily. I was thinking about the meeting we should have held. Why wasn't Vera interested in something as big as another intelligent species nearby when something as small as who slept on the sunrise side of a lodge fascinated her?

I could hear her laughing as I worked. She was sitting with some other parents at the far corner of the plaza cleaning trilobites, stinky work, so they were as far from the lodges and the meal area as they could get and I couldn't hear the words, just occasional laughter. She always worked hard and the parents and some children liked her leadership and I still wanted to like her but all I had were questions.

Octavo lowered himself onto a bench, panting. I pulled out some cois twine and anchored the ribs first on one side of the hoop and then on the other. He couldn't tolerate certain fungus spores and his lungs had been regrown three times but they worked less efficiently each time. The same thing had been killing my father, Merl, when a pack of ground eagles got him first. Our hunters tracked down the pack, the last one to bother us, and we put a bouquet of spiny eagle feathers on Papa's grave.

"A Coke would be nice right now," Octavo finally said. Coke was some sort of Earth drink. "You know, snow vine fruit looks a lot like that glass ball, those same surface facets when they're immature."

I glanced up. "Is that important?"

He pulled out the rainbow bamboo twig I'd given him. "Pax is a billion years older than Earth. It has had time for more evolution."

I finished a weaver and reached for another, thought again, and picked a coil of greener cois so I could make a striped basket. "We should find the people who made the ball."

"It might not be that easy, girl. There are two intelligences. The ball is obvious, but the bamboo . . . It belongs to the snow vine family. We set fippolions to graze on the west vine and the east vine rejoiced. Our loyal master . . ."

He paused again to catch his breath and gazed across the plaza. I kept weaving, wondering why he was complaining about the snow vines again.

"This bamboo," he said, "displays a representation of a rainbow, not a refraction like the surface of a bubble. This is made with chromoplasts. Plants can see. They grow toward light and observe its angle to know the season. They recognize colors. This one made colors on its bark to show something. It is a signal . . . that this plant is intelligent. It can interpret the visual spectrum and control its responses."

"So it wants to attract us? Attract intelligent beings, I mean?"

"No. A signal to beware. Like thorns. Who knows what a plant might be thinking? I . . . doubt they have a natural tenderness for animals. We are . . . conveniences."

"But the glass ball is beautiful. It's a fruit, you said, so it must have come from a plant that was friendly or the glass makers wouldn't have made such a nice copy of it. Maybe it came from the rainbow bamboo, since it's like snow vine fruit. We should find it."

Octavo was staring across the plaza. Vera was getting up. He turned to me. "Snow vines are not especially intelligent, less than a wolf. Well, you have never seen wolves or even dogs. . . . But this rainbow bamboo . . . You can predict animals but not plants. They never think like we do. It might not be friendly."

"If the snow vines can decide to give us fruit, then the rainbow bamboo might give us fruit, too. We always need food and a more intelligent plant would know how much we can do for it in exchange for food."

"Exactly, plants always want something." He glanced at Vera, who was walking toward us. "But this cois twine . . . Tell me, have you noticed a difference in fibers in the different colors?"

I frowned. Why was he asking that? But I wanted to be polite so I picked up samples of each color and flexed them. "No. I think the greener is just picked younger."

Vera came up to us and stopped.

Octavo looked at her. "We have been discussing cois. It could have many uses, perhaps like flax. . . . We have been too focused on food sources, I think."

"We always need food," she said.

They were silent for a while and since I wouldn't be interrupting, I said, "I've been thinking about the glass and rainbow bamboo. When can we discuss it at a meeting?"

"Not soon," she said. "We still haven't recovered from the hurricane."

I tried to hide my disappointment, but she was staring at my basket instead of me anyway. The stripe looked good.

"That's the natural variation of the cois fiber," I murmured.

"Efficient," she said, and hobbled away.

"We'll never discuss it!" I said. "Paula wasn't like that." Octavo never scolded when we children complained.

"Paula had . . . training." He looked at the twig. "Not our planet, not our niche."

"Intelligent creatures have no niche." I'd read that somewhere.

Octavo shook his head. He never really liked plants even though he was a botanist, and it was no good arguing with him. He had me help him get up and he went to the lab.

I kept working on the basket and I tried to imagine plants as smart as we were. How would they relate to us? Probably not the way regular plants acted toward bug-lizards or fippokats. And I could make beautiful things with rainbow bamboo. Why wait? I got some twigs from storage, soaked them, and when the grub basket was done, I took a twig, made two loops, and then braided the end through the loops. A colorful bracelet, a whole minute wasted on a decoration. I made seven and set them to dry in the Sun with the basket.

I gave the soaking water to Snowman, put my things away, helped erect a bower to shade some lettuce seedlings, and delivered the basket to Rosemarie and Daniel. I returned to the bracelets, put one on, and gave others to Julian, Aloysha, Mama, Nicoletta, Cynthia, and Enea.

Vera saw them during the evening meal out in the plaza, boxer bird soup and tulip salad. We didn't have much because of the storm, but we sat down happy enough on the benches on either side of the line of tables. It was a comfortable evening, although the parents were bundled up, always cold when we were hot. The bats were swooping and singing, and cactus balloon plants on strings kept them from stealing food. The grandchildren, the pregnant women, and the sick ate well. I got plenty of salad and a bowl of soup with a scrap of meat. Julian got only broth from the birds he'd hunted. The grandchildren were in a giggly mood.

Then Vera frowned at the bracelets. "Those have no place here," she said. "We don't have time to waste."

"Oh, I suppose you'll want me to erase the carving on my walking stick," Mama said. "Everything doesn't have to be useful, does it?"

That provoked more of the endless debate about a flower garden, parents' opinions only, children should listen and learn. Terrell thought we should look for metal, not pretty flowers.

Bryan made a show of standing to speak in spite of his stiff joints, as if we owed him something for chronic bursitis and his drooping skin with scars where skin cancer had been removed. He wanted to require childbearing "in harmony with the welfare and interests of the Commonwealth as a whole," as the Constitution said. Parents liked to quote the Constitution and worried that if we didn't follow it, we'd face disaster, but the Constitution talked about beauty too, and about equality. Parents quoted only what they wanted to.

"I think we've discussed this enough," Vera said. "We should get rid of the bracelets. This is no time for divisiveness."

"Oh, it's only a bracelet," Mama said.

"The problem is with what it represents. This is Pax. A community with peace, mutual trust, and support," Vera said, quoting the Constitution. "The bracelet is a violation of trust. Let's be practical. Symbols are important. The bracelets symbolize a decision we aren't ready to make now. We have too much to do just to recover from the hurricane."

I should have resisted, I should have spoken up, but too many people were looking at me, childless, designer of a failed roof, and a disrespectful citizen, or so they probably thought, and we children were always being suspected of being lazy and greedy. I took off my bracelet. So did the rest. Aloysha and Nicoletta made a face when they did and Julian stamped on his and broke it. Terrell burned them.

That night I was crying in my bed when Julian came to my room and he didn't say a thing, he just hugged me until I stopped crying and we made love for the first time. I'd done that before with other boys so the parents would think I was trying to get pregnant but it was just to satisfy other people, not to make me happy.

Julian wanted to make me happy and I wanted to be happy with him, and afterward I held him and realized I wanted him to be happy forever, too. The parents would have thought the whole thing was a waste of time because he was sterile, but that night was love, real love. It was uselessly beautiful just like the bracelets. And it was the beginning of the revolt.

I looked for the rainbow bamboo in the storage shed the next day and it was gone. There might have been more at the beach but I didn't have time to go to the lake. Julian looked for it when he hunted and finally found a twig, prettier than I remembered.

"It's from Thunder River, at the waterfall," he said. No one had gone upriver beyond the waterfall but the maps based on the meteorologists' satellite pictures showed a long canyon up through some mountains that led to a wide plateau. "And I found this." He smiled and held out some pieces of red, green, and yellow glass. "It might be obsidian or agate, but I don't think so. What do we do?"

I thought hard before I answered. We could continue as usual, working from Luxrise to sunset, planting, weeding, building, harvesting, hunting, gathering, cooking, cleaning, weaving, sewing, caring for animals, monitoring equipment, repairing machines, watching the computers sputter and the robots stop, disassembling dead machines for their parts, helping the parents to and from the clinic, and reengineering the electrical system to run on wind and hand cranks.

We could watch the seasons go by, spring with floods and lizards hatching everywhere, summer with its storms knocking down roofs and trees and fields of grain, autumn with droughts and fires, and winter with frost and fog. Our holidays were harvests, births, funerals, and the solar solstices and equinoxes, and a holiday only meant a bit more to eat. On Earth people went to battles, carnivals, museums, and universities, and on a lucky day I got to go to the lake. On Earth there was protest, revolution, genocide, piracy, and war, and I was punished for weaving bracelets.

"I know what I don't want to do," I said so sadly that he hugged me.

But we kept on doing it. What was our choice? Search for the glass makers on our own? That would be a violation of mutual support.

Besides, Mama was sick with cancer from radiation exposure during the space trip and she got worse until she was bedridden. The same cancer had killed many parents already. I spent as much time as I could with her in her little room in the lodge, wondering if I'd miss her as much as Papa, and one day I asked the question that I'd always wondered about.

"What was Earth really like? Really and honestly?" Books said things, usually bad, but I could tell they didn't say everything.

Mama's bones hurt, her belly hurt, and she was glad for any distraction, that's what she always said. She pursed her gray lips and thought for a while. "Stressful. And complicated. Actually, not that bad for us because we were rich, at least compared to the rest of the world. Other people died of hunger and we could get together enough money to go to the stars."

Rich? She was rich? No one had told me that. "What if you hadn't gone, Mama?"

"We'd have all led easier lives. You too, probably. Oh, they like to tell tales, don't they, about pollution and diseases, the beginning of the end of humanity, but the rich got by. It was only the poor who were killing each other. Or trying not to die of one thing or another. It was so tragic."

"But, then why did you leave? Didn't you have to?"

"No, we didn't, we volunteered, and we wanted to try to do better. People had made horrible mistakes on Earth, fatal mistakes for whole countries, millions and millions of people. Oh, it was shameful how the poor got so little help for problems they never created. You wouldn't understand, but we wanted to try again. To make a fresh start of Earth. To do it right this time, without the unfairness that made some people rich and some people poor. Things you couldn't imagine. I think we made a good new start. And I'm glad we did. Oh, there's hardship, but we expected that. It was like coming home to Eden."

I'd heard of Eden, a mythical paradise, but the book that told all about it wasn't in the libraries. I wouldn't understand anyway according to the parents, but hardship wasn't paradise, I knew that. What would it be like to be so rich you could get any book you wanted and then have time to read it?

"For all its troubles, Earth could get boring." Mama smiled. "Pax was exciting."

I thought about that while I was crying during her funeral. I'd have led an easier life on Earth. We buried her near the friendly snow vines along the western fields, next to Paula, and we buried Mama in rags because we couldn't afford to bury good clothes. Octavo stared slumped and tired at the vines. "Birth to death," he muttered, "they have us."

Octavo didn't like snow vines so he might misjudge the rainbow bamboo and the glass makers. I said that to Julian one morning. He was making poisoned arrows for hunting. We were far away from everyone so that a grandchild couldn't accidentally wander over, and we could say what we thought.

"We need to go up Thunder River and see what's there," I said.

"Up Thunder River," he repeated, watching his work. He wore gloves and goggles as he dipped arrowheads in ergot and set them to dry in a rack in the Sun. "I'm a trained explorer. I can do it."

"Both of us. We both have to look."

He hesitated. Vera would never approve.

"I'll go without you," I said.

After a while he said, "You should never travel alone," in the same voice as if he were saying *Honor the parents*. We started planning while he wrapped the arrows in mullein leaves. Would the glass makers and the bamboo welcome us? Why hadn't the glass makers come to us?

Survival last, curiosity first. Better no life than this life.

So when Vera's weather report said there were no hurricanes in formation, we sneaked off, carrying food, a blanket, a hammock, rope, a lighter, hunting knives, and clothes. All the clothes I owned fit into a single backpack, and people on Earth, rich people like I'd have been, had closets full of clothes.

We left with questions and we came back with answers to questions we hadn't even thought to ask, with thoughts we weren't supposed to think. I almost didn't want to come back but I knew we had to, and so we did, nearly sixty days later, with rainbow-striped hiking staffs, rainbow bracelets, and rainbow diadems. We were skinny, our clothes in rags, our backpacks filled with tokens of another civilization and morsels of bamboo fruit that were dried and shriveled but still delicious. We entered the village, a huddle of mismatched hovels, and the lodge I had designed looked utterly clumsy, still with the improvised bark thatch roof. The fields rose on hills, thirsty, the snow vine thickets hulked like prison walls, and storm clouds churned overhead.

Cynthia saw us and shouted. We were surrounded immediately, smothered with hugs and tears and welcomes, everyone asking questions all at once.

Then Vera hobbled up. "You left us when we needed you," she squeaked.

"We found a city," I said.

"You were incredibly irresponsible. You most of all, Sylvia. We searched for you for days."

"But they're back safe," Ramona said. "That's what matters."

Vera kept scolding. Enea's little boy toddled up, yelling, "Juu!" with arms raised, ready for Julian to pick him up. I picked up Higgins, Nicoletta's boy, and he squirmed with excitement. Octavo was limping toward us, looking at Julian.

Aloysha repeated until we heard, "What city? What city?"

"Another hurricane will arrive tonight," Vera said, "and the buildings aren't ready, and there are animals to be gathered in!"

"A beautiful city," I said, "with sparkling glass roofs and gardens of rainbow bamboo."

Octavo arrived, the wind tossing his long beard. "A city?" He wasn't smiling. He didn't look happy to see his own son.

"Up on Thunder River, Dad."

"That's not important," Vera said.

"The glass makers?" Octavo said.

"They're not there," Julian said. "I don't know what happened to them."

"I brought some fruit," I said. I patted Higgins and hoped Julian would stick to our plan.

"And we brought soil samples," Julian added. "They look rich."

"A hurricane is coming!" Vera said.

Not a big hurricane, though, and finally we were assembled in the cellar. All the people who could had crowded into the lodge with us as thunder rumbled and Vera tried to convince them to start preparing the stew but we respectfully ignored her.

Is it a lie not to tell everything? Julian and I wanted to save certain details for the Commonwealth meeting and there were things I didn't want to tell at all.

"We walked for twenty days," I said.

"It had to be farther than that," Bryan said.

It had seemed farther.

On the day that we left, we circled to one side of Thunder River's waterfall and hurried over the scree and up the ledges on the cliff, then got lost finding our way around a snow vine thicket. The first night, we slept cuddled in a hammock draped with a bug net, and the barks from the digging owls kept me awake for hours because they sounded so human that I was sure they were the voices of people chasing us, and the fireflies whizzed around us until I felt dizzy. When I woke, a slug had crawled into a fold of the net and divided, so slimy little pink things were crawling all around trying to touch us and dissolve a nip of flesh for a meal.

When we got close to the river that morning, we were in foggy, swampy woods, and slithery things moved on the ground, giant slugs, some bright pink and purple, some just clumps of clear slime, and a few disguised like logs or vines, and we had to put spearheads on our walking staffs to protect ourselves but they were sometimes too fast and stung us. Moths swirled around us in patterns like giant thumbprints, each trying for a bite. We were wrapped in raincoats and double pairs of socks and had smeared mud on our faces and still lost bits of flesh.

Beyond the waterfall and its mists and slugs, travel got easier.

"Up above the waterfall," I told the people in the cellar, "the canyon is like the ruins of a giant Greek temple." Everyone had seen a picture of the Acropolis in the history text, the birthplace of democracy. The canyon actually was high and narrow, with the trees arching overhead, more like a cathedral, but only the architecture texts showed churches.

"There are rocks like columns," I said, "and aspens grow free and tall alongside them. No snow vines. There are meadows full of flowers on the riverbanks."

I didn't mention all the rocks to climb over and around, uphill all the way, and some of the flowers were little biting corals with dewdrops of digestive enzymes on tiny teeth. The only food we could easily find were wild onions and palm-sized trilobites netted from the river. Onions and trilobites for breakfast, lunch, and dinner. Once, we were trapped between the riverbank and a cliff by three ground eagles, drumming their air sacs and dancing and snapping their big beaks at us, human-sized and smelly, with spiny feathers that looked so much like bark and dried weeds they'd had no trouble sneaking up on us. We lit a line of fires to hold them off but they were waiting until we ran out of fuel so we caught trilobites and threw them to the eagles until they'd eaten their fill and left.

We left the valley and climbed hand in hand through the misty forest around the final waterfall, up through vines and mosses and clumps of pulsing slime and finally over some rocks and into a forest.

That's when we saw our first rainbow bamboo. A stand of it grew right along the edge of the cliff, taller than some of the trees, with trunks as wide as a human thigh. The bamboo stood straight and proud, not at all like the snaking snow vines. Living rainbows. A few pieces of fruit, pink and translucent and bright in the sunshine, hung face-high.

Julian and I looked at each other. You should never eat something untested.

"It looks exactly like the glass maker ornament, except bigger," I said.

"Snow vines can kill when they decide to."

"But the bamboo hasn't met us yet, so it shouldn't have an opinion." A piece of fruit pulled off easily from the stem. Three seeds were shadowed inside. It smelled like fresh wheat and cinnamon. I took a little bite and the juice was sweet and oily against my tongue. Julian watched.

"If it kills me," I said, "I'll die happy." But that was all I ate for the moment. I stroked the bamboo's smooth and waxy trunk and I imagined it as door frames or roof beams, or split and woven into wall coverings. A small trunk cut into rings would make beautiful bracelets.

We admired it awhile, then walked along the top of the cliff toward the waterfall, hoping to see the aliens behind every rock. We looked down on the canyon, green and long and dropping sharply between the stone cliffs. The view became better as we got close to the waterfall and at the most beautiful spot we found a bench carved into the stone and encrusted with lichen. At first we thought it was natural but there were words carved into the back of the seat, the same script writing that was on the glass ball. The glass makers had been there! We shouted and hugged each other.

We sat on the bench, trying to guess what glass makers could be like. The seat was low and wide. The glass makers were somewhere upstream, so we began hiking. The land became flat and the river got wider and slower. There was a path along it made of flagstones, heaved up by roots. We were going in the right direction, and we walked faster. There were more bits of glass in the river, all the colors of the rainbow. Around the next bend, soon, soon, we'd find them.

That afternoon we spotted a cluster of four buildings with domed glass roofs sparkling in the middle of a grove of bamboo. I ran toward the nearest one. The roofs were rings of colored glass blocks arranged in rainbows, the walls were made of brownish bricks, and the foundations were stone with bands of sparkling gray and white. Julian was right behind me. But as soon as I started running, I saw that the buildings were ruins, the walls cracked and tumbled in, the roofs collapsed.

The glass makers weren't there. They hadn't been there for a long time.

I was crying by the time I entered the closest building. Dirt and dead leaves covered the floor. The walls inside had been faced with glazed tile in a pattern of interlaced red and green lines. I'd seen glazed tiles in computer texts. I tried to wipe away the tears and look carefully. The room was about five meters across. Glass blocks from the roof lay on the floor, half-buried and sparkling.

"Spectacular," Julian whispered.

The building had several low bays, each crowned by a half dome, and one of them was intact. The glass roof was dirty and corals were crusted on the outside.

Someone had stood below this ceiling once, had stared up at the sunlight filtering through it, someone with eyes like mine that enjoyed colors, someone who built buildings like me, someone who thought like me, someone who could do things that I'd dreamed of. Someone had built a bench, low and wide, along the wall. I sat on it and sobbed. Julian sat with me.

The glass makers must have abandoned the buildings before the parents had come to Pax. We'd traveled far to find only ruins, but there had to be more glass makers somewhere. I wiped my face and stood up. I walked over and around fallen brick and stone and glass, trying to see how it had been built. The bricks were slightly offset at about head level, sloping in for a half meter, then changing to glass, and the curve of the domes was parabolic, not circular. One apse seemed to be the entrance to the building and I'd have had to duck a bit if it had been intact. I was taller than the glass makers.

"Come here!" Julian said. I heard rustling. He was already in the next building. He'd kicked some of the dirt and leaves off the floor. It was covered with a mosaic of flowers and plants, including a stand of rainbow bamboo. We cleared away more dirt. The bamboo had flowers and fruit, and what looked like a skinny yellow arm and hand was reaching for a fruit. We cleared more as fast as we could but the rest of the tiles were broken and scattered.

The buildings were surrounded by bamboo and weeds. I picked another piece of fruit and it tasted better than ever. Fippokats peeked out from a burrow between the bamboo roots. The path kept going, straight into a patch of woods. More ruins? Or would the next building be inhabited? We began walking.

Two hours later, just before Luxset, mothbitten, we saw the city on a bluff above the river, a huge city. Sparkling roofs and bamboo rose behind a glazed brick city wall taller than we were. But we knew from the cracked wall and shattered roofs that once we got through the gate, we'd find nothing but fippokats, bats, and lizards. I was already out of tears.

That night, we lashed the hammock between two bamboo trunks and slept beneath a dome that was partially intact. The moths finally left us alone. The wind sighed in the streets, the bamboo stood tall, and its flowers breathed a scent like spices I never wanted to be away from.

But twenty days later we did leave the city.

On the night we arrived back in the village, down in a cellar as a hurricane blew outside, Julian told the people listening, "When we got to the city, it was unbelievable. Nothing on Earth could be as good."

Bryan snorted. He had elbowed in close.

I pulled out a rainbow of glass tiles from my backpack. "The roofs of the buildings are domes of glass bricks. They sparkle like jewels, and the city could hold a thousand people."

"What about the glass makers?" Enea said.

I was watching Vera from the corner of my eye. She sat at the far wall with Terrell.

"They've been gone for a long time," Julian said, "and some of the buildings need repairs, but they left behind a lot of things, useful things."

He took out a heavy steel cup inscribed with the line-and-triangle writing we saw all over the city. We'd found the remains of furniture and bits of fabric in a few houses. Some things were obviously techno-logical, like metal boxes filled with corroded wires or brass housings around lenses, and there was lots of furniture that had rotted over the years, but some of the ceramic dishes in a kitchen building were still stacked up neatly.

Vera and Terrell whispered to each other, and she was twisting a piece of cloth so hard it ripped.

"Most of the buildings are habitable," I said. "We could move in tomorrow with a little cleaning up."

Only a slight exaggeration. Some buildings had fallen down and a central tower had almost completely collapsed because its wooden beams had rotted away. Outside of the city we found round stone-and-brick kilns as tall as me for making glass or working metal.

I added, "There aren't any snow vines." I couldn't tell if Octavo was listening. "Lots of rainbow bamboo. Delicious fruit, more than we could eat. Here are some."

Octavo leaned in to look as I laid out dried samples, little wrinkled purplish lumps, still smelling sweet and cinnamony, thrilling, and I felt desperate to eat one but if I was going to have more I couldn't show how much I wanted one.

Bryan grabbed a piece. "I'll analyze this later." Octavo looked at him, then at the rest of the fruit, but didn't move.

In truth, the bamboo had looked so sickly that it scared me. Eventu-ally Julian discovered a big water pipe that led from the hills to the city but it had broken in several places, so the bamboo was probably thirsty and the only gifts it got were from fippokats. Little corals were grow-ing everywhere.

Julian and I agreed that the walls were probably meant to keep out deer crabs and slugs, although ground eagles could jump over them. I looked and looked but couldn't find anything that showed an attack or a fire, and we couldn't figure what had made the glass makers leave. Everything seemed to say they hadn't left in a hurry. Maybe they'd even meant to come back.

Just outside the walls I found an old grove of bamboo growing around stones with painted ceramic portrait tiles, a cemetery. Digging beneath a stone, I found bones as brown as the soil. They cracked and crumbled as I tried to pull them out but I got several good pieces. I put the soil back and pried the portrait tile from the stone. I'd bring a glass maker back to the village.

We'd learned a lot, including one more thing. The bamboo was very friendly. Fruit appeared right away near the house where we stayed. Then one of the trunks where we'd tied our hammocks grew a shoot. Each of the new leaves had stripes of a different color, a little rainbow built out of leaves instead of bark to show that it had observed us and recognized us as an intelligent species like itself. It had delivered a message, a welcome home, because it wanted us to stay.

But I didn't say that back in the village. Octavo wouldn't want to know that this bamboo was as smart as he'd thought it was.

"This is a glass maker," I said in the dim cellar back in the village as the storm rumbled and splashed outside. I pulled the cemetery tile from my bag.

It showed someone with four spindly legs that supported a body with an overhanging rump. Oddly bent twiggy arms and a clublike head with yellow-brown skin rose from the shoulders. The head had large gray eyes on its sides and a vertical mouth. I'd seen plenty of other pictures and figured out the anatomy. The tile was the best small picture of a glass maker I'd found. There was writing at the feet, five linear marks and three triangles, maybe the person's name.

"It's wearing clothes," I added. A red lace sleeveless tunic fell to just below its body. I'd seen lace in computer texts.

1. Directory
2. ~~Dentist Reschedule~~
3. ~~REP Reschedule~~
4. Aracely
5. Penn Medicine

Chester County Health
Pernal Health
Michele ~~Styner~~ Steiner

610 344-6225
michele Styner

Mon Jun 13

1. ~~Fix Newsletter~~
2. ~~Call/email Library about Internat'l B C on Wed~~
3. Do Exercises
4. ~~Costco~~ - martine Stuff - Front hm Beans
   me -sponges   face
                                  Activa

P 98 line 14-19 go to G.
P 98 lines 20 watchers
P 102 lines 20-30
P 103 lines 1-12

~~Wed Feb 12th~~ SAT Feb 15

1. Call to change Theatre both Mar + May
2. ~~Call Hair Salon to change appt.~~
3. Call Penn Medicine
4. ~~Finish Directory~~   228 precincts
5. ~~Rewrite ZLC notes~~
4. ~~USIA TEAMS~~

Friday Tennis

The portrait went from hand to hand. "Almost a praying mantis," Octavo said. Male or female? We didn't know.

"There's good hunting," Julian said. "The glass makers had farms, and tulips and potatoes are still growing wild." He was sticking to the plan. And Vera did what I'd expected.

"You ran away, and no matter what you discovered, you have to answer for that." She was on her feet, waving droopy-skinned arms, the torn cloth in one hand. "You acted without concern for the welfare and interests of the Commonwealth as a whole. In four days, we'll hold a meeting for judicial proceedings. Now it's time to go to bed."

The grandchildren whined.

"I'll tell you more tomorrow," I murmured to them.

Of course, there was a lot more to be told. Some of what we left out wasn't much at all, like how truly miserable the hike back was. The moths bothered us less but the pulsing slime was worse. It had rained, and the water was higher in the river so the easy-walking sandbars had disappeared. We looked at the flotsam stuck in the tree branches above our heads and worried that a sudden storm might cause a flood. Our shoes had worn out, the packs were heavy with artifacts, and the stinking ground eagles remembered us as a source of trilobites and extorted meals.

The most miserable of all was the end of the bamboo fruit. We stretched it out as best we could but having only a little was as bad as having none at all. I was tired, I had headaches, I was hungry, and Julian felt just as bad.

"The only way to get more is to go back to the city," I said one night in the hammock. "Not now, though. We couldn't survive there alone, not forever. We need to move the village there, everyone. We need to live there."

"The parents can't make this hike."

"Would they even want to come? I don't think so." I was quiet for a while, trying to conceive of life without them. Could they imagine the city, shining in the forest alongside the river? The city was big, really big . . . too big.

They knew about it. They had always known about it. They had been lying all our lives.

I lay silently, too shocked to think, while he stroked me under the blanket. "I wish they could see the city," he said. "Then they'd come."

"They've seen it in the satellite pictures," I finally said. The satellite had surveyed the area carefully for resources. During our hike up the valley, Julian had told me all about a fault line that made the waterfall on Thunder River near the village and about the granite mountains that surrounded the plateau where the glass maker city was. He had a map with enough details to show the major cataracts in the valley and the river snaking through the forest in the plateau. The city's roofs should have flashed out at any observer, but we used the meteorologists' maps and had never seen the survey pictures themselves.

Julian figured it out fast. "They knew. Mom, Vera . . ."

"They saw it every day on the weather scans."

"They knew. They covered it up. Why not tell us? Why?"

"We should ask them. But we should do it in a way to make people want to move to the city."

I convinced him not to confront Vera right away although we wanted to when we got back to the village. We'd discuss her un-community-minded behavior at a Commonwealth meeting. I knew there'd be one and I was right.

Back in the village, the day after the little hurricane, we were answering questions even before we left the cellar. Julian went to hunt and I went to the plaza to make a couple of baskets to sift wheat, and a lot of people seemed to have tasks to do in the plaza.

"Are there fippokats?" asked little Higgins.

"Yes, and they play and slide just like here."

"Is the soil good?" a farmer asked.

"Well, the trees are bigger."

"How was the climate?"

"You'd have to ask Vera, she has the weather data, but it seemed cooler and damper. The fields wouldn't need irrigation. And we know hurricanes break up on the mountains, so we wouldn't have to worry about them anymore."

"Were there ground eagles?"

"Probably, but the town has a wall around it."

"What happened to the glass makers?"

"Maybe an epidemic, or maybe they moved and live somewhere else."

"How much bamboo fruit was there?"

"Plenty."

I learned that while we were gone, the tomography machine had failed for good, Nicoletta's father had died of space travel cancer, and a new kind of lizard had been discovered, tiny and iridescent yellow, that fertilized tulip flowers.

I folded in the spokes to finish the first basket and I measured and cut reeds for the second one. "The rainbow bamboo probably wants what the snow vine does," I said, "gifts and a little help."

"Was it beautiful?"

"You can't imagine."

Ramona limped up to us, leaning on a pair of canes and draped in a shawl. It was odd to see her out of the clinic where she worked and at first I thought she'd come to hear about the city, but she looked too sad. Maybe another parent had died and she'd come to tell someone. But she came over to me.

"Sylvia, I'm so sorry," she said. She leaned against my worktable and took my hand. Hers was cold and twitched with Parkinson's disease. My parents were dead, so what could she be so sorry about?

"Julian is dead. He made a mistake with a poisoned arrow." She went on to explain but I hardly heard her. Julian was dead. Julian.

That couldn't be right.

Ramona hugged me. She was thin and shaking. "I'm sorry. I know you'd gotten close."

I tried to talk and realized I had stopped breathing. I deliberately took a deep breath. "What happened?"

"He died. Julian died when he was hunting."

"How?" Even with one small syllable, my voice shook.

She explained again and I made myself listen. She said it was just a hunting accident in the forest near the lake. He was putting a poisoned arrow on his bowstring and it slipped. But she was lying, I knew it, another lying parent. He'd never have made a mistake like that. He was a fine hunter, as silent as an owl in the woods.

They lied about Earth, they lied about the city, and now they were lying about how Julian died.

He was dead. They killed him.

Everyone told me they were sorry and hugged me and cried. The children's tears were real. And mine.

I'd known him all my life and he wasn't there anymore. I thought about climbing up the valley with him toward that first stand of bamboo on top of the cliff, hand in hand, hoping a glass maker would pop up from behind the next rock. I thought about the long walk home after we'd both learned so much. I slept with him, ate with him, talked with him, expected to be with him my whole life.

Now life was different, never the same again.

We held the funeral that night. Octavo wouldn't talk to anyone and didn't go to the grave. For his own son! He didn't go because he knew it was no accident. But he wouldn't do anything about the people who killed him. Or maybe he couldn't do anything.

I followed Julian's corpse as it was carried to its grave, thinking that I did not, not, not want to die there, did not want to lead a hard, ugly life under the dictates of lying murderous parents and finally be carried in rags through the desolate fields and be left to feed the greedy, stupid snow vine. Vera gave a short bland funeral speech. I didn't say anything. I probably couldn't have. Children were only allowed to praise the dead, anyway.

Late that night, in my room, I ate a dried bamboo fruit, sweet and spicy, and felt worse to know that more waited for me, wanted me to come, gardens decorated with fruit in a city that sparkled in the Sun and that Julian would never see again with me. He was sterile and expendable. He was a warning, the sort of crime they did on Earth, what the parents left Earth to escape, but they were still Earthlings. And I could carry on without Julian. I had to.

I was quiet the next day and the day after that, sometimes pretending he was still with me, sometimes imagining I was back at the city with him or that I was at the city in the future, we'd all gone there to live, and I was looking at the places where we'd been together. The worst was at night, alone, trying to sleep in the same ugly building as the people who'd killed him. I thought about how to get back to the city, about what I had to do, about why they killed Julian to keep me quiet, but I wouldn't be quiet. I'd make them talk.

Bryan told people he'd tested the dried fruit and when they asked him about the results, he sighed. He said he'd explain at the meeting.

That evening, I arrived at the plaza as the benches were being lined up and Cynthia came up to me and asked about the city.

"It's big and colorful," I said.

"Why isn't it on the satellite pictures?" She did a lot of foraging and depended on maps.

"That's a good question."

She frowned and curled a lock of hair around her finger, thinking, as bats wailed overhead.

Vera emerged from one of the lodges with a parent being carried to the meeting in a cot. She called everyone to order and we all sat down. "A long meeting would be difficult for some of us, so let's start. Sylvia's broken the covenant of the Commonwealth, and we must decide how she will be punished."

"What did I do?" I said. She glared at me because I was talking at a meeting in a challenging tone of voice. Aloysha made a fist and winked.

"You ran away," Terrell said.

Octavo said softly, "We ran away from Earth," but no one paid attention.

I didn't have time to waste. "The city is visible from the sky."

"That's not the point of the meeting," Terrell snapped.

"Lying is as bad as running away," I said. "Lying for years is worse than running away once. The satellite can see the city. We were never told."

"Can you prove that?"

"Someone should review the satellite data code," I said. "That's the proof."

Nicoletta stood up. "I will."

I looked at Octavo. He was staring far away, his lips moving silently.

"That's not what this meeting is for," said Vera. "You—"

"What else do you know about the city?" I said.

"There's no city," Terrell said.

"It's that rainbow fruit," Bryan said. "I've analyzed it. An alkaloid. Do you know what alkaloids do to people? Cocaine, nicotine, strychnine. They're addictive. They affect your thinking. Mescaline. People took mescaline and thought they saw God."

And cocaine and nicotine had ruined Earth, he didn't need to say that. Rosemarie and Daniel were sitting together, holding hands. Her other hand covered her mouth, and he was looking all around, nervous.

"Ephedrine is an alkaloid, too," said Blas, the medic, another child speaking up, but he was apologetic, staring at the ground. "It's what keeps some of you breathing."

"The city is there," I said. "The bamboo has fruit."

Vera's wrinkles deepened into valleys. "This is outrageous. You broke the covenant, and now you bring all sorts of false charges. We need to set things right before we continue. But no more talk about this before the next meeting. It's divisive, and we need to put our energies into productive work. And I want everything that Sylvia and Julian brought back analyzed."

"I can do that," Octavo rasped. Bryan looked disappointed. I felt frustrated but I hid it. I'd never convince the parents but I knew that a few children already agreed with me. As we walked back to the lodges, I got some gentle pats of support.

"I will give these things a real analysis," Octavo said when he came to my room, huffing and wheezing. I doubted it because he knew they had killed Julian and he hadn't done anything. I stared at the fruit, dying to nibble it, to feel the dried flesh become alive and sweet and rich in my mouth. "More fruit," he said. "Good."

"I have glass maker bones." I watched to see how he'd react.

"Bones . . . Very good." But he wasn't pleased or surprised.

"You knew about the city."

He wouldn't look at me. "I can analyze these," he said, and shuffled away. Liar. But I didn't think he liked lying. Maybe, just maybe, he wouldn't keep lying.

The methane fermenters in the power units of the weeding robots somehow broke down the next morning, which was cold and rainy, so Nicoletta was too busy fixing them to have time to examine the satellite maps because the crops came first. I was sent to fix the roofs on the gift center and Cynthia met me there.

"We can't even talk about it," she said.

"So don't," I said. "Don't talk about anything."

That evening, seven of us children ate dinner in silence. Some of the grandchildren thought it was a game and joined in. Higgins tried to hush Vera as she talked about the weather and new problems with the medical equipment, which meant more unexpected work for Nicoletta and delays for Octavo's testing, since there wasn't enough equipment to investigate our surroundings and care for Ansel's perforated ulcer, Terrell's this, someone's that, and Bryan's malingering joint trouble. With every sentence, Higgins shook his head, no no no! Other grandchildren joined in. Vera opened her mouth and a half-dozen little heads wagged.

Bryan ran out of patience by the next morning. "You're addicted to the fruit, right? Answer me!" As a reply, I took off my clothes because parents hated nudity for some Earth reason. He hobbled away as fast as he could.

The protest caught on. Higgins and his little friends got naked and tried to undress people.

That afternoon Vera looked me in the eye, deliberately ignoring my body, when she ordered me to make a cage for hydrogen seeds about to ripen, so I was on my way to the shed for esparto grass when Octavo limped up.

"The fruit is fine," he said.

"Bryan lied? And you, will you lie?"

"There has been enough lying, but that is not the important part. It is complicated. We can start with the fruit."

I wanted to start with the lies but he'd get to that eventually or I'd make him.

He walked toward the shed with me. "It has plenty of vitamin E, which might actually help with our fertility problem. We have yet to find a good source of it. And some other oil-soluble vitamins like niacin."

He stumbled a little and I made him lean on my shoulder because liar or not, I still couldn't hate him. He didn't seem to care that I was naked but he kept rambling.

"But vitamins are only natural, just like pyridoxine and their alkaloids. Oh, yes, alkaloids . . . just like the snow vines. We had to rethink the meaning of alkaloids because of that, you know." He looked down at my face. "It is an Earth science assumption. We . . . had always thought they were a leftover from nitrogen metabolism stored in leaves or fruit or flowers to be discarded with them. Useful, of course. . . ."

He was breathing too hard. He needed to rest a moment. I suggested finding a bench but he said he didn't want to keep me from my work and slowly, slowly, we kept walking and he kept rambling and I kept waiting.

"Alkaloids are part of nature, although not as common here. Which seems only logical, since the plants had more time to evolve. Monocotyledons on Earth do not make them often. Apparently . . . they have more efficient metabolisms. Although alkaloids discourage predation. Nicotine is a potent insecticide. The plants here create all manner of toxins. . . ."

He stared at the trees and shrubs as if he'd never seen them before. I reminded myself to be patient, at least for a while.

"The problem with potent toxins being that the learning curve is steeper than the lifetime. The predators never live and learn, which they do with alkaloids. . . . The mere taste is the chief discouragement. If something does not taste discouraging, there usually is not a . . . sufficient concentration to worry about. Addictive in this case, not surprisingly. Alkaloids often are, like caffeine, but harmful is another matter. The plant wants you dependent, not injured. Very wise choice, addiction. . . . You say the fruit is delicious? Bryan is too excitable. And not just about that. . . ." He looked around. "I am too excitable. I taught him, and I suppose I taught him that, my fault, all my fault . . . again, and I paid for it."

"Julian," I said.

He didn't answer, just looked sad.

We'd arrived at the shed and I opened it and pulled out a bundle of grass.

"What?" he said. "Esparto? No, let me see." He grabbed the bundle, squinted at the ends of the stems, and took out a hand lens. He studied it, then threw the grass down as if it would bite him. "Wrong . . . wrong veins. Where did you get this?"

"I picked this a while ago up in the south meadow." But maybe it wasn't the same bundle. It looked a little smaller.

"Ricin. This has ricin." He bent down to rub his fingertips with clay. "Wash your hands, too. This is not esparto, it is *Lycopodium ensatus*. It looks about the same dried, but . . . you would never mistake it when you picked it. Exotoxins . . . it has plenty, a kind called ricin. By the time you wove this all, the skin would fall off your hands." He picked up the bundle with his walking stick. "We must burn this. The grandchildren, you know. They could get hurt."

"How did it get there?" But I already knew. I hadn't gotten the hint with Julian and I needed to get another lesson.

He carried it on the tip of his walking stick and limped toward a hearth near the metallurgy shed. "It does not occur around here. It grows in brackish soils. Bryan . . ."

"Bryan did this?" That made sense.

"He is afraid of the rainbow bamboo. I taught him . . . fear of plants, but the fruit was poisonous . . . the bamboo fruit. After the snow vine, we thought the bamboo would be worse. Understand that. The fruit was poisonous back then. And now . . ."

"You visited the city?" The lies were bigger than I thought.

"Not me, no. Uri, Bryan, and Jill. We were excited. . . . A city. Bryan thought the people had been wiped out by . . . rainbow bamboo. It moved in . . . grabbed their water system. . . . But . . ." He could hardly breathe and looked bad, worse than usual.

"The city was built to copy the bamboo," I said. "Anyone could see that. Look, you need to sit down and rest. I'll take the poison grass. Here, sit on this log."

I helped him sit, grabbed a stick from the ground, took the grass, and carried it to the hearth. I struck a spark and it burned like a torch. They knew about the city, all the parents did, but they were afraid of the bamboo, so afraid that they killed Julian to make sure we wouldn't go back. I walked back to the log, and Octavo tried to stand up.

"Oh, we all knew . . . ," he said, "the only city the satellite found . . ."

"The only city? Here, don't try to stand. I'll sit with you." I wondered if I should get a medic but I needed to hear what he had to say, the truth about the lies, all of them, finally.

"Not everyone believes plants are significantly intelligent, but . . . but we were all afraid of them. The glass makers disappeared for a reason. . . . Snow vines have been domesticated. . . . They are less in-telligent. Bamboo . . . is very intelligent." I wanted to say something but he looked too frightened, and of what? "Do you want a life worth living? It wants to keep you. . . . You will be slaves in a pretty cage."

"A life worth living, that's what I want. You should have told us."

"I think so now. Lies and lies, and Julian died because we need to keep telling them." Frightened or sad, I couldn't tell. "But you will not . . . believe the truth, child. Poisoned by lies. Us and you. Poison fruit."

"I know the truth. The bamboo is smart. It thinks and it wants us to live there. It will help us."

Something about his face looked wrong. "But do not trust it. Plants are not altruistic. . . . Wants you for a purpose." He could barely talk.

"Aren't humans altruistic? Why not plants?"

"Not all humans. That is why we left Earth." His right eyelid drooped. The right side of his mouth had gone slack. I took his right hand and it was limp.

"You need a medic."

"No. Just rest. I need rest. I am sick, Sylvia. I will not live much lon-ger. It is a waste to prolong it."

I got up and ran to the clinic as fast as I could. The medics came with a stretcher and at a glance said he was having a stroke. I followed them to the clinic. Vera arrived but she didn't even look at him before she started yelling at me.

"You attacked Octavo. You've gone too far. Much too far." She waved her cane, but I wasn't scared. She shouldn't be running Pax.

"He had a stroke. I didn't do that. I didn't attack anyone. You knew about the city all along, and I can prove it." I walked out. She didn't deserve respect anymore. Nicoletta could check the satellite scans and whatever she was doing couldn't be as important as proving that Vera lied.

I found Nicoletta over the hills fixing the electronic fence around the fippolions that were clearing unfriendly snow vines for us, and from far away I saw that she'd put on her clothes.

"No," she said, "I can't check the satellite scans." She wouldn't look at me.

"It won't take much," I said. "Repeating code in a photo file. The parents actually visited the place, Bryan and Jill and Uri. We can prove that they knew."

"And then what?"

That was all she'd say. The fippolions looked at us dully. Electronic collars kept them on the other side of the fence but they could kill us with a swipe if they had the chance. I left her alone but at the top of the hill I looked back. It was hard to tell from that distance, but she might have been crying. What had they done to Nicoletta?

I went south on the way home through a field of esparto just about to bloom close to western snow vines. I looked at it closely. When esparto dried, the wavy edges of the leaves would become flat and resemble the poison grass.

Something smacked me hard across the shoulders and I flew face-first into the esparto. Maybe it was an eagle. Maybe they'd come back. I tried to get up and escape, not wasting time to look back, but I was hit again across the back and I glimpsed human feet as my face struck the ground again. Someone knelt on my shoulders and held my face in the grass. I yelled but it hurt to breathe and grass and dirt in my face muffled the sound. Who was doing this? It had looked like a man's feet and I tried to look again, but someone else grabbed my legs and pulled them up and apart and a man's hips slammed against my thighs as he shoved his penis inside me. I struggled against the knees on my back and tried to get up and I kept trying and trying. I wanted to stop it, stop him, to get away. He was hurting me, pushing in and pulling out, dry and tearing, and my hips ached, pulled too wide. I kicked and grabbed with my hands but couldn't catch anything. I wanted to hurt them, hurt them more, not thinking, just pain and anger, and I couldn't do anything.

He pulled all the way out and dropped me. My knees scraped against the grass. They clubbed me across my back again. I gasped, and my ribs throbbed, my shoulders, my crotch, my knees. Their footsteps rasped through the esparto as they ran away. I sat up as fast as I could, but they were already out of sight and I was dizzy and I couldn't catch them. After a while I saw that a shirt and trousers lay on the grass next to me, a message.

My face hurt. I touched it. Dirt and something wet. I knew it was blood before I looked at my fingers. I knew why I'd been attacked. I was too valuable to kill because I could have babies but they wanted me to stop fighting, stop trying to make parents tell the truth, stop thinking that children had a right to live their own lives, better lives.

Parents. They'd silenced Julian. They'd hurt me as badly as they could. I knew what they wanted and I knew what I wanted and nothing they'd done to me had changed anything. Except for what I was willing to do. Heresy, rebellion, and war, at last.

Lux was approaching the treetops. I put my clothes back on. I stopped at an irrigation ditch on the way back to the village and washed everything twice, three times, and I shivered as I did even though it wasn't cold, and all I could think about was violence.

Children and grandchildren had put their clothes back on. Or they did when they saw me, bruised and scratched. They whispered to me, a knot of children in the plaza, about what had happened to Epi and Blas, and to Beck, Leon's little boy and Higgins's loyal follower, and to Nicoletta, Higgins's mother, about the threats and beatings. I was dangerous, they were told. Remember what happened to Julian. Don't listen to me, they were told, but they wouldn't obey anymore. I told them what had happened to me and that made them ready to fight back, but how? Even I didn't know.

Aloysha saw me and stammered, tugging apologetically at the fabric of the shirt he wore.

"Uri went to Rainbow City," I said, not waiting for him to speak. "Your father knew. They all know, all the parents. They don't want us to go."

His face puckered in confusion.

"They're afraid of the rainbow bamboo. And they're afraid of me," I said. "Sleep with me tonight." He stared, mouth open. "With a hunting knife," I added. He blinked, then nodded. It didn't matter whether he understood why.

I went to see Octavo. Blas said he was better but he didn't look better. The side of his face had collapsed and he spoke thickly. Saliva dripped from one side of his mouth.

"Girl, you are hurt."

"Vera is having people attacked. You know that. Remember Julian. We have to stop her."

His good hand stroked his face as if he were tracing the edge of the good part and bad part. "We expected paradise. To find paradise. Do you know what you found?"

"A better place to live at the city. You didn't want to go there, but I do. We do."

"The bones you found have DNA. Pax uses RNA. That is . . . why . . . it was the only city. Astonishing. Not from Pax. Others looking for paradise."

It took me a moment to understand. "The glass makers were aliens? Like us?" I didn't know what to think and I didn't have time. "We have to stop Vera. Can you help us?"

"Paula made herself a leader. Vera never learned, but no one did. . . ."

"Can you help us?"

"Help you what?"

"Go to Rainbow City." And escape from the parents.

"The bamboo is even smarter. . . . You will do what it wants."

"The bamboo isn't that bad. You haven't even seen it."

"It is, it is. It will make you stay."

"It asked me to stay. It needs water, it needs gifts, it needs us. The glass makers liked the rainbow bamboo a lot, you can see that in the city. It can't be worse than here."

He seemed to be looking at me but I wasn't sure.

"Help us," I said. "Tell the truth. That's all you need to do."

"Tell the truth. . . ." He nodded unsteadily. "Yes . . . the truth."

"Thank you."

"Your future, not mine." He seemed unhappy. I kissed him on his good cheek.

Blas told me he'd recover, the stroke wasn't as bad as it seemed. He fussed over the cuts on my face and pretended to believe me when I said nothing else was hurting. I was trying not to think about it but I couldn't stop and wasn't thinking just about me.

"It's not right," he said. "What do we do?"

"You'll see," I said. Although I still wasn't sure what I'd do. How would the parents react when Octavo started talking? Or the children? We children respected Octavo and some of us liked him. But the parents would try to hurt us. Again.

Octavo was dozing when I left the clinic. I walked to my room through the tiny huddle of ugly hovels that was our home. Plants bribed us but they didn't beat us or attack us. Aloysha was waiting in my room and during the night he held me tight every time I woke up trembling, dreaming I was in an esparto field.

In the morning, we learned that Octavo had died. Vera had been with him. A lot of children doubted her story and when I whispered to them about the city, the fruit, about what Octavo had said and what he was going to say, they understood what had really happened. The parents knew about the city and the aliens and were afraid, afraid enough to kill again. Who'd be next? We had to stop them and I could. I got ready.

Octavo's funeral was that evening. We marched at the pace of the slowest parents, shuffling with their canes and crutches through fields that sparkled with glowworms. Those fields, those ragged patches of green, were their only hope and accomplishment. We were silent except for sobs, and I cried too, for Octavo, for how bad things had gotten. They had attacked me. They had killed Julian and Octavo. If I didn't act, it would get even worse.

Octavo was lowered into a grave next to the snow vines that he had hated.

"He more than anyone wanted Pax to succeed," Vera said. "He searched for food crops, he helped us understand our place in our new home and how to live here in peace. He gave us his mutual trust and support so we could live in a new community and make a new society." She was quoting the Constitution, words she didn't believe in. I got ready.

She turned to pick up a shovel alongside the grave, not even considering that someone would speak, especially not me.

"Octavo was a liar like the rest of the parents," I said.

She turned. "How dare you!"

"You all know the city exists, you've known it all along."

She raised the shovel like a weapon, teeth bared. She stood several meters away. I ran toward her, pulling the knife with a poisoned blade from a sheath inside my shirt.

The wrinkles on her cheeks lined up in waves as she shouted, "Step back!"

She didn't deserve to be obeyed. I batted away the shovel. It fell to the ground.

"Stop her!" she screamed. "She can't do this!"

But all I could see was everything that had happened and everything I could stop. I raised the knife and brought it down. The blade bounced along her ribs horribly and she wailed like a swooping bat until I twisted the knife and forced it in with both hands and then pushed her into the grave. I took a deep breath. There was still more to do.

I turned to see Aloysha and Blas wrestling with Vera's son, Ross. Bryan already lay on the ground yelling, and Nicoletta stood over him, holding his cane like a club. The parents squalled that I'd violated this or that, and Nicoletta and Cynthia shouted back that I was right. The little grandchildren were shrieking and Higgins stood in front of them, fists raised at the parents.

Vera whimpered and was quiet. Was that how Julian died? I couldn't look into the grave. The new Pax was beginning the wrong way and I had to do something. I raised my hands, one of them with Vera's blood on it. Children's voices called for quiet.

"They all knew the city was there," I said, "and they were afraid. Something happened to the glass makers and they blamed the rainbow bamboo."

Bryan began to say something. "Quiet!" Nicoletta told him.

I continued. "But that's not why the parents lied. They had a dream. They wanted a new society, a better version of Earth. They thought they could make it with hardship, and the more hardship, the more they thought they had a new Earth here."

"That's right," Bryan called out.

"But it's not working," Nicoletta said. "It's not better."

"They have their new society," I said. "It is us. We can make our own choices. Us, the children. Octavo asked me if I wanted a life worth living. I do. There's a better place to live than here. It's time for a new moderator."

I looked around. Everyone was still, watching me.

"Who wants Pax to be more than endless hardship?" I said. "Who isn't afraid to change? Vote for me. I'll be the moderator, and we'll do more than survive. The parents wanted a new Earth. What we want is Pax. The time of the parents is over. Vote."

Hands went up for me: Aloysha, Rosemarie, Daniel, Leon, Nicoletta, Cynthia, Enea, Mellona, Victor, Epi, Blas, Ravi, Carmia, and Hroc. And Higgins and many of the grandchildren. And one parent, Ramona. I didn't call for the hands of those who were against me.

So that was the revolt. I became the moderator by a minority vote and in spite of the fact that at eighteen, I was seven years too young according to the Constitution. But by the time we'd moved everything to Rainbow City, I was actually old enough and Aloysha and I had had two healthy babies. Vera's son, Ross, was probably one of the men who attacked me but once he saw Rainbow City, he wanted to stay there and he worked harder than anyone to get it ready. By the time we left the village for good, only four parents were still alive.

I didn't want to abandon them, although their half-blind eyes looked at me as if I were a murderer in those final days. We even offered to carry them! When I left the village the last time, the Sun was rising bright red. When it set, we were camped in the valley above the waterfall. The bats began to swoop and wail, and I heard Vera dying again. It was the end of Earth.

HIGGINS AND THE BAMBOO
YEAR 63–GENERATION 3

We understand that we must endlessly make choices, and that our choices have consequences, and that we are not guaranteed health, happiness, or even life.

—from the Constitution of the Commonwealth of Pax

HIGGINS

Beck did right to invite me to the birth of his third child, since I've helped at two dozen other births, including a fippolioness once, almost my last mistake. Beck and I are best friends and besides, I was the real father and would've made a far better father and husband than him.

There's a stage in childbirth just before the real pushing starts when women often panic, and they don't mean the things they do and yell, although if it were me going through all that, I might turn homicidal. Women are more solid than men that way. Indira—beautiful brown-eyed Indira, with hair that swirls and curls like water in a brook—Indira had endured hormones, heartburn, headaches, and hemorrhoids for 325 days and then a half day of labor. She was curled up like a baby herself, teary and trembling in her always tidy house, where a crib waited for the wonderful moment. Beck hovered near the door for a fast escape if necessary; not the best husband, as I said, though a square-shouldered man, very fit for repairing brickwork and turning over soil. (I'm much handsomer, ask anyone, and, better still, perfectly symmetrical from head to toe, which indicates very fine genes.)

Indira commanded Beck to open the door to the sleety weather because she was hot. She shrieked that her back had never hurt that way before so something must be wrong.

"Here?" I asked, caressing her backbone. She wailed something I decided was yes, and I glanced at the old medic, Blas.

"Probably just the baby's head pushing against the spine, nothing dangerous," he said. "Everything's normal." To his relief, too.

I began to rub just above those beautiful round hips, hands sliding on the sweat. "Here?"

"Don't stop!" she said.

"Soon, the baby will come soon, soon, soon," I crooned. "You'll hold it in your arms, soon, soon, soon."

Just relax, just relax. Indira wasn't the relaxing type. . . .

But fippolionesses usually are, so a few months earlier when I heard Clay mewling deep-down tired and hopeless, I'd have run because I'd guessed her problem, but I didn't want to spook her. We kept a herd of a dozen adult lions and their young a bit upstream to fell pines for firewood and to clear new fields, and I was coming for my evening check, being the animal-responsible guy. People worry most about a lion's front claws, and they should, agile scythes that they are, but they do mere detail work when the lions dig up roots. The back claws are only as long as your fingers but they inhabit the end of those muscular hopping legs. A lion can rip out your intestines and toss them over the dome of a house with one kick. Or, with a bit more effort, it can knock over a tree.

Clay lay on her side, curled up and twitching in a nest of logs and leaves. Lions don't have the brains to need a big head, so births shouldn't be hard—and generally, the big fipps and I kept a respectful distance from each other. The rest of the herd was keeping a respectful distance from her that night, too. Idiot that I am, I approached, mimicking the coos of their chatter: "What's wrong, Clay? What's your problem, honey? Things aren't working right? Let me take a look, I won't hurt you, just relax, just relax."

I touched her claws the way they do for greetings and cooed and petted her long fur and let her sniff my face. Her prehensile lips curled in pain with a contraction, her eyes blinked exhausted and drooping, and she mewled again, terrible breath, which isn't at all characteristic of a healthy lion. She held her back legs tight to her chest, and her fur dripped with blood and birth fluids.

"Don't worry, Clay, we're fine here, let me look, let me look." I pushed on the legs, and she opened up a bit. "Just relax, just relax." A little arm covered with slicked blond fur stuck out of the slit just below her sternum, three precious fingers tipped with pearls ready to grow into claws. Lions should be born headfirst, like humans. This was bad. I touched the hand. The fingers flexed. Maybe there was a chance. I stroked the abdomen to get a feel for how the cub was located. Mama's claws began to stroke my back, very gentle, just returning the gesture. The cub wasn't fully transverse, near as I could tell, unless I was mistaking a tense stomach wall muscle for its head, very possibly so, but she was dilated and maybe, maybe I could ease the baby out.

The lead male, Pitman, at the edge of the clearing, growled and rasped his claws on the ground, watching me.

I massaged a little harder, and her claws caught the collar of my coat and began to tear it. "Just relax, just relax, if that makes you feel better, tear all you need." I was kneeling beside her, a very easy reach for a back foot. "Just stay relaxed, honey." I pulled a bit on the arm and kneaded on the outside to try to move the head past a hump, but I couldn't. It was close, and she had a contraction, but we accomplished nothing except probably to make things harder on the baby. Clay whimpered to break my heart.

Without much thought, I pulled up my sleeve and reached inside, hot and slippery and rippled with muscles, the head so close, and she ran her claws through my collar and coat and ripped fringe. My fingers closed around the cub's head, around the snout, guiding it up next to its extended arm, and she suddenly pushed and I pulled, pulled on the arm, on the snout in the canal, her claws reached into my hair, the snout out now, pink, her claws like razors on my scalp and my hair falling onto my shoulders, the whole cub's head out with another push, and I cleaned the little nose and mouth as she pushed again, more claws tearing my coat, and the cub's body was out and it took a breath and yelped and I showed it to her, a boy, and set him down and the claws flew from my hair and she was licking him and he was licking her, both weak but excited, and I backed away slowly, cooing. A cute, happy baby, a good day's work for a fine mama.

Pitman came toward me on all fours, growling. I stood up. He rose on his hind legs. My eye level was his chest level, so I was at an undisguised disadvantage. He could hop faster than I could run, so running wouldn't get me anywhere. But I had always had a feel about lions the way I did about kats. The Glassmakers or someone had domesticated both of them. Pitman probably knew how to be number two if I knew how to tell him I was number one, or so I thought.

I took a step forward. He raised his claws, and my disadvantage became all the more clear. I growled and raised my hands as menacingly as I could, puny fleshy fingers, and wondered if lions could laugh. What I needed was a big stick, but if I bent down to pick one up, I might get sliced to string. But he only wanted to assert authority, so he reached back with a foot and kicked a tub-sized mess of dirt and rocks at me. I saw it coming and caught it in an intact part of my coat. I grabbed out a rock and threw it hard right below his sternum, aiming for his manhood, and I got lucky one more time. He howled and doubled over but stood right back up and flexed to lunge. I threw another rock at his pointy nose, which I hoped would be even more tender than his manhood, hit it luck-on, and he was down. To make my point, I heaved the dirt in my coat on him. He stayed down, bloody-snouted, the new number two.

I walked around the clearing, holding out a hand to the other lions, but I had to force it to stay steady. A few young males sniffed, and I held my breath waiting to see if they would decide to make their own challenge. The entire pack kept its eyes on me. No challenges. I petted Clay and the cub and left with all the swagger I could still manage.

And so, at nightfall, I arrived back at the city, torn and sheared and bloody, and in a cold sweat and breathless realizing that I had used up a full year's worth of luck. In fact, I could have been killed right there, domesticated or not—even kats can kill, let alone lions, and what kind of idiot was I? The idiot who won, but was the prize worth it?

Indira came running down the street—"Higg! Higg!"—and when she saw I was all right and it was just Clay's blood, she went back to her loom, always a hard worker. Women are solid, but not always about what I wish they would be solid at. She was already pregnant. . . .

And now, Indira was in childbirth and had decided walking might make her back hurt less, and it did, and soon she was on her hands and knees, pushing. Beck, a purely decorative addition to the room, still hung by the door. I knelt in front of her, wiping sweat from a face that I sometimes see before I wake up in an empty bed, and she chattered now, breathing normally without having to be reminded to do so. Blas sat on a chair behind her, holding a mirror so she could see herself work. Another medic waited among towels and warm water and blankets and diapers, ready to spring up with whatever was needed, meanwhile tending the fire to keep everyone warm. Beck leaned out under the doorway from time to time for a few words with someone outside, as far away as he could get without a total cowardly retreat.

The head crowned and emerged, then one shoulder—two shoulders, wet and wonderful—and then the whole baby. Blas and I cleaned the child a bit, checked it quick, and Indira dropped into a cot to take the baby, a fine girl with good lungs. Indira and I marveled at her, then the medics did, and Beck finally got the grit to come over to look, all of us awestruck and congratulating each other. That kept us busy until the afterbirth.

A new baby girl. I didn't know what Indira and Beck were going to name her, but I was ready to sing her songs and shear a lion for wool for fuzzy slippers so those delicate little feet would stay warm day and night.

Indira's mother peeked in to say she would get their other children. I helped tidy up for visitors. "She's cute," the baby's sister, Moon, declared shortly after arrival as she marveled over tiny fingers and ears. Moon was my daughter, too, four years old, and her brother, Lightning, almost ten, was my son. I have a fair number of children (the Pax curse of infertility still being a problem, but not for me), and since I have such fine genes, spreading them around a bit won't cause special problems in downstream generations.

I wiped up the floor and carried some equipment back to the clinic, growing more joyless with every step. The excitement of birth had ended, leaving me with my particular form of postpartum depression as I pondered the philosophical contradiction of a baby that was both mine and not mine.

I could solve the conundrum with well-aged truffle. Lions won't eat fresh truffle roots, cloying and common though they are, I suppose because they smell like rotting trilobites, but the flavor mellows with fermentation. I collect what they dig up, boil it in water, and add a butter root (which the lions will eat, so I have to dig them up myself), then after a few days when it's done fizzing, I strain the stock into another jar, seal it with pine wax, and wait a month or more. The result is my big weakness (next to women) and my reliable consolation.

I'm an expert at truffle. Good truffle smells like thistle flowers, like roasting almonds, like the river at sunset on a warm evening when you've had a good day and expect a good night. I grabbed two large jars from a stack in a bay in my house, not the biggest or best house in the city, but good enough for me. The dome had been repaired passably well, but four of the six side bays were beyond hope and the walls were rebuilt plain and straight. Still, I had all the room I needed for a bed, a chair, a table, some tools, musical instruments, of course, and a whole lot of truffle.

I carried the jars in my arms and my guitar slung across my back under my coat, and headed for the Meeting House, the biggest building in all of Pax, a place where we guessed the Glassmakers themselves had held meetings, with built-in benches all around and a roof so wide it needed columns. The winter sleet had turned to a frigid downpour, my clogs splashed in the streets, and the fringe on my coat was going to be dripping by the time I arrived. Fringe doesn't keep me warm, but it looks good on me, so I've fringed up all my clothes.

And I enjoyed the walk anyway, or I tried to. The city has a special charm in the rain at night. The glass roofs on the houses glowed from the lamps and fireplaces inside, and the little candle in the lamp I carried lit a circle of raindrops and hinted at the gardens and bamboo growing around the buildings, the foliage skeletal in the winter and sparkling from the rain—a hint of the city rather than the solid reality of the city in bright daylight. You could hear more than you could see, though, if you listened. The splashes of the raindrops showed what was in the shadows: the curve of walls, the tangle of leaves, the flatness of pavement. It takes a good ear to appreciate the beauty of a cold, wet night. By the time I arrived, I had decided that I didn't have the ear to truly, deep-down appreciate a nighttime walk in the freezing rain.

Carilla, wearing a bonfire's worth of bamboo jewelry, kissed me on my cheek when I walked in. I knew those wide soft lips—warm lips— but she kissed me chastely, as if she had never moaned with ecstasy in my bed, and she was glowing with pregnancy now, my doing. Her husband, Orson, talked trivia with me about farm chores for fippokats. Paloma, plump and squeezable, kissed me just as chastely, holding little Sierra in her arms. That was my little Sierra, with a smile just exactly like mine. Sierra kissed me too, and Sierra had her doll kiss me, a doll I had carved for her from ivory wood with joints that moved and eyes inlaid with agate. Other women kissed me on the cheek and asked about Indira and the baby, but only my parents asked me how *my* new baby was. No one has as many grandchildren as they do, but private is one thing, and public is another.

Spoil the party with resentment? Not me. All my children were there. Jefferson and Lief had just lost a front tooth. Lief had my brown eyes, but mine couldn't look that sad, could they? Tatiana had learned more multiplication tables. She was only six but very serious about everything and quite tall for her age, neither of which she could have inherited from me. I had given Hathor some lion wool, which she spun and knitted into a hat, and her twin brother, Forrest, wanted some wool, too. Orion wanted to know if what Tiffany said was true, that fippokats understood everything we said, because Tiffany had a fippokat that would stamp a paw the right number of times when you said a number, provided it wasn't too big. I said that kats were smarter than we all thought.

Bjorn, always a quiet child, seemed fascinated by the growing quantity of food on the tables, and I stood next to him and shared the fascination—Indira's long childbirth had given the kitchen crew time to prepare. Pastries, two kinds of bread, sausage, smoked fish, three kinds of dried fruit, pickled onions, stewed birds, salads, eggs, deer crab, and yams. A great spread for winter and more food than we could eat. But we would try, after selecting the best tidbits to send to Indira. I set aside the truffle for Beck's arrival. I hoped he wouldn't be long, and at the same time I hoped he wouldn't leave Indira's side until he could offer no further comfort, incompatible hopes that included the sincerest hope that he was finally doing something for Indira. He had disappointed me. I had hoped that with the third child, he would have learned how to handle himself.

He came as the children were starting to droop. They had eaten and sung and danced until even the fippokats, green furry little party lovers that they are, had hopped off to their hutches, their curled tails dragging. I had helped out every step of the way. Nobody knows more danceable children's songs than me, Uncle Higg. I had a new song about the moons and Lux for the littlest ones, and even the adults joined in.

> Galileo is the silliest moon.
> It rises in the west and it sets too soon.
> It can't tell time but it's always bright.
> You can see it both day and night.

The children perked up when Beck arrived. "The name, the name!" they chanted, their birth party ritual.

"Snow!" he said. (Snow! I thought. What kind of name is that? Still, I kept smiling. Uncle Higg has to set an example.)

The children did their best to sing and dance to Snow, but they were ready for sleep. I slowed the song into a lullaby and they followed my lead to flutter like snowflakes to the ground and lie still. . . .

Not long after, I opened up the jar and ladled out toasts, aged soft, brown-red, and fragrant. Truffle for those inclined, and fruit punch and tea for those inclined to decline or combine, as the saying goes. Time to celebrate a baby! Number fifteen for me, twelve of whom had survived, and you'd think I'd get used to it, but every baby, not just mine, even lions, kats, bats, birds, and lizards, for billions of years and around the galaxy and universe, every baby is impossible to celebrate sufficiently. Truffle is a start, though.

Sylvia raised a cup. "All babies are special, but Snow is a measure. Today, there are now one hundred Pacifists. It's a wonderful number, and not because it's a nice even number. It's wonderful because the number keeps getting bigger. Snow is someone we always wanted, like all the babies before her and all the babies after her, and like everyone here. There are one hundred of us today. To Snow!"

Pretty soon, after two big cups of straight truffle, I asked Beck, "Why Snow?" I'd feared something stupid, since he had named the other children Moon and Lightning. I don't know why Indira lets him choose the names.

"You disapprove," he said.

"It . . . has resonance with nature, I suppose."

"It's snowing in the mountains now, so I thought, Snow. You hate it."

"Snow?"

"Snow. My daughter. I named her."

"I just wondered."

"It's my job to name her."

"You didn't do much during the birth, I suppose you need to take what opportunities are left."

"You know I hurt to see what Indira goes through."

"She goes through a lot. That's why she needs help."

"There are things I can't do."

"There are things you don't do."

"That's where you come in."

"That's not what I was talking about."

"But it's true. You got her pregnant. I do the naming."

"You sure put a lot of effort into your job, too."

"It's her name, Snow. My wife, my children. Your job's over."

I thought about that for a moment. He was right, although I would have preferred a real name like Anna or Rosemarie. And real names for Lightning and Moon, too. In fact, I would have preferred a lot of things, and he stood right in front of me, and he hadn't done squat, but he got the rewards. He had given the baby a stupid name that I wouldn't like just to make his claim obvious, like Pitman kicking dirt at me.

I punched Beck square in the face.

He staggered a few steps, hand on his nose. I hadn't hit him hard enough. He was still on his feet and his nose wasn't bleeding much at all. He looked at me and laughed. I deliberated hitting him again. People were watching, but no one was stepping forward to stop me.

"Higg!" He reached out to put a brotherly arm around me. I took a step back, but not fast enough. "You can scare the lions, but not me. You're the luckiest man on Pax. Women, children, truffle, whatever you want, whenever you want it."

By then he had me in a full embrace. He seemed to have drunk even more truffle than I had. The angle made a clean punch impossible.

"You're my best friend, Higg. Snow's a beautiful name, the perfect name."

"If you say so."

"I say so. Nothing personal."

"Nothing personal." I felt disappointed with myself. I could have punched him better than that, couldn't I? But I hadn't. I worked my way free. "I think I'll have some tea," I said, and Sylvia met me at the tea jar to hand me a cup of truffle, looking solemn.

"I used to be excitable," she said.

"I wasn't excited."

"I know. That's good."

She invited me to sit down with her. I don't remember the day when she killed the old moderator and saved us, but my mother says Sylvia changed that day. I do remember the move to Rainbow City. I thought Sylvia was smart and powerful. I loved her in a little-boy way, and it never wore off even as she got wrinkled and gray. We took a bench near the back wall, and I took a deep swallow of truffle.

"It's not fair," I said, a little boy again. "I love Indira and she stays with Beck."

"There's no accounting for tastes." She sipped her cup of truffle.

"I want a wife, I want . . . Indira."

"And Zoe and Paloma and Carilla."

"Them too. Anyone. They should stay with me, one of them."

"You know the mathematics. Men outnumber women. If you weren't fertile . . ."

True. Ivan and Tom probably stayed together because they had no other opportunities. I took another long swallow of truffle. "Women don't love me back. They use me."

"They know they can depend on you for anything."

"And Beck . . . all the men treat me like I'm a woman's toy."

"No. They see you with the fippolions. You're the top lion. It impresses everyone. I'm impressed."

"Right. Women love me. Men respect me. Lions fear me." Anyone looking at me from the outside might see things that way. "I suppose I shouldn't have hit Beck."

She shrugged. "It's not my business."

But the next morning, sober, I realized how she had made it her business.

That evening I went out to visit the lions. On my way, I listened to the bats flying overhead. Most hunters know a few words, but I understood far more. That night, though, they didn't have much to say: "Food!" "Where?" "Here." "What?" "Bugs?" "Many?" "Yes. Come!"

Pitman roared hello, and the rest of the herd echoed him. He trotted over. I had a big bowl of truffle roots for him, the stuff I strain out of the first fermentation, the rotting trilobite smell gone and replaced with alcohol. He gobbled them down, happy to be number two to a number one who brought such remarkable gifts. I had a little bottle for myself and sat on a log in a warm winter coat to sip it and watch the Moon dance like a child's star. He set his long, narrow head on my lap, and I scratched along his bony crest. He cooed. Other lions wandered over to flop around me, and their cooing became a chorus. I joined in, not sure what I was singing, and we serenaded the sunset together, a happy herd.

Women lie to me. Men laugh at me. Big, dumb, hairy animals think

I'm one of them. But children love me. And I have truffle. At sunset along the river on a winter evening as the auroras begin to glow, it tastes like the good times you can't quite recall but surely they happened sometime, maybe tomorrow, you just have to wait and see.

THE BAMBOO

Growth cells divide and extend, fill with sap, and mature, thus another leaf opens. Hundreds today, young leaves, tender in the Sun. With the burn of light comes glucose to create starch, cellulose, lipids, proteins, anything I want. Any quantity I need. In joy I grow leaves, branches, culms, stems, shoots, and roots of all types.

Water flows through the repaired foreigners' pipes like veins in leaves, freeing me from rain and seasons so I may develop at will. Water feeds fungus on my roots that generate nitrogen for amino acids. Water permits increased transpiration in leaves and thus higher photosynthesis, growth compounding growth and bringing gratification.

Because of the foreign animals, I am more than yesterday, bigger, smarter, stronger. Strong as I once was. In the city, I reign. Outside, groves and sentinels protect and feed me. I turn light into substance. Everywhere, I control the sunshine.

Intelligence wastes itself on animals and their trammeled, repetitive lives. They mature, reproduce, and die faster than pines, each animal equivalent to its forebearer, never smarter, never different, always reprising their ancestors, never unique. Yet with more intelligence, less control. The mindless root fungus never fails, but moth messengers come and go with seasons, larger animals grow immune to addictions, and the first foreigners, who built the city, abandoned it and me without explanation or motive just as we had begun to communicate. Did they discover my nature and flee, or was their nature renegade?

Their intelligence astounded me, far above that of other animals and plants. I could not have become what I am without their irrigation, protection, excretion, and compost. I suffered when they abandoned me almost two centuries ago, years that should have been prime, forsaking functions to preserve my roots, for what am I without memory but mere grass? But what am I without pollen to communicate, without nectar to trade with moths for the bits they gather for me, without seeds and spores to disseminate ideas, without roots to touch from grove to grove, without lenses to see, without crystals to sense electric waves?

Almost blind and numb, thirsty, crippled, yellowed by malnutrition, trapped in old memories too costly to maintain and too precious to let die, exhausting storage roots, I barely knew of these new foreigners. Day after day twinkled past while I hoped they might save me. Yet when they came, I was almost fatally slow to adjust my fruit to welcome and tempt them. Unfamiliar in body chemistry, but decipherable. Moths brought me bits of flesh and I learned.

Now I give fruit that makes the foreigners content and healthy, a complex balance between pleasure and utility. They give me water and nutrients, trained like fippokats by the snow vines, but so much more than fippokats, for they, like the first foreigners, make plants and animals their own servants. Indeed, tulips seek domestication, their minuscule intelligence aimed toward service, and I have encouraged them and other crops to serve the foreigners, and I have protected the crops from competitive plants.

I would have died without these new foreigners, I will die without them, but I have seen that intelligence makes animals unstable.

I must communicate with them and finally I have the strength. I am growing a root to store what I learn, but it now contains little more than pith. I have not tapped their intellect and used it like phosphates.

The Sun rises. With eyes at many nodes, I see them awaken, quick and busy. Many go to the gate near the river to leave for the fields. I observe color in their clothing. They see colors. They will see mine, grand and compelling, and know that I am no snow vine, that I have a significant and inescapable communication to enter into with them.

Animals never grow smarter, but I do. Ours will be a rewarding relationship.

The pollen in the wind, what little pollen there is, speaks of a wraith of leaf-eaters at the valley's farthest fern villages. One of my groves across the river reports that a pack of fippolions has been led away from it, which I never doubted, for the lion's claws are a tool of my new foreigners, well controlled, although I can easily teach lions to avoid roots and stems embittered to deliver the lesson. I listen for the electric snap of lightning. I await a taste of pollen or a messenger seed, or a tidbit from a moth, but it is winter and much is still. Intelligence conquers the seasons, but there is little intelligence in the world.

HIGGINS

Even the bats were whistling with surprise. Our guard, making a routine Luxrise check of the city, saw the surprise and ran to tell Sylvia, who woke the botanist, Raja, and still in nightclothes and with Raja's children tagging along, they rushed to the riverside gate. Raja's four-year-old, Muriel, took one look and ran to wake me up.

"Uncle Higg, the bamboo did something pretty! Hurry!"

So I was among the first to see it and hear the story. Raja was already calling it *the display,* even though it was lit only by torches and far less stunning than it would be in full sunlight. Torchlight couldn't begin to reach the top leaves of the bamboo, but could still make your jaw drop.

Along the road leading to the riverside gate, the leaves and stems of thigh-wide, sky-high stalks of bamboo had changed color, one stalk per color on either side. Red, orange, yellow, green, cyan, indigo, and violet. The bamboo had re-created a rainbow on either side of the road. I stood wrapped in a blanket, holding Muriel's hand.

I knelt down to talk with her, since children prefer to talk at eye level. "It's beautiful, honey. Thank you for waking me." Our breaths made clouds. I wrapped my fingers around her hand to keep it warm.

Sylvia and Raja inspected the bamboo while Muriel proudly named all the colors for me. More people arrived, sleep in their eyes. A few fippokats approached, thumping and licking the colored stems, hopping up to grab a leaf in their teeth, and making a happy game out of getting in the way. Raja's truffle-colored hair hung loose and still tangled from bed as she knelt down to look at the roots. A kat joined her in scratching at the dirt.

Above, bats swooped and whistled, chortled, twittered, and warbled.

"Danger?" "No." "Pacifists here." "What?" "Come!" "Bugs?" "No." "What?" "Here." "What?" "Here!"

"Why?" Muriel said. She asks that a lot, usually as a gambit to offer her own explanation.

"Well . . . so we would notice it, I guess."

"It's pretty. The bamboo likes us a lot. That's why."

"I think so." Actually, I thought it probably meant something more subtle. It might not even be directed at us.

"We should tell it we like it, too."

"Yes, we should. But how? Sing it songs? Make it a toy?"

Muriel giggled.

By sunrise, everyone was up, and some of us had gotten washed and dressed. Sylvia sent me to inspect the bamboo outside around the walls. I reported back during a formal briefing session in the Meeting House. Most of Pax had come, and the benches were packed. Nicoletta was taking notes.

"I looked for anything unusual, not just at the bamboo," I said, "in case it isn't about us."

"Good thinking," Sylvia said.

"Nothing, though."

"Nothing for us, either," Raja said. She and a team had inspected the city. "But it's at a location important to the city and to us. We're supposed to notice."

"Anyone, any observations?"

A boy stood up. "The rainbow bamboo, I mean the rainbow-rainbow bamboo, it has no fruit."

Sylvia looked surprised and thoughtful, as if she hadn't realized it herself. "That could mean something important. Any other ideas?"

"It likes us," Muriel said. "That's what the colors mean, and we should say we like it back."

"That's exactly what I think," Sylvia said. "We should respond. But how?"

We all mumbled puzzlements for a few minutes. We knew the bamboo was smart, but how smart was smart? Notice exactly what? Respond how? Was this even good?

Sylvia, never one to rush deliberations, talked quietly with Raja until we were done babbling, then stood and signaled for attention.

"We all know that the bamboo has become much more healthy with us here. We've given it water and fertilizer, and it's given us fruit and keeps improving it. Now, the bamboo seems to want our attention. I propose appointing Higgins to communicate with the bamboo for us."

I wondered if she had really said my name.

"He can command lions, he can direct kats, he understands bats. And baby talk." People chuckled. "If anyone can communicate with a plant, it's Higgins. If you consent, Higg, of course, and if that's the will of Pax."

She *had* said my name. If I consented . . . I knew Octavo's Rules, plants could see and think and all that, but plants didn't think like fipps, even less like people—probably. I had no idea. And I might say an inane thing and insult it. I've never figured out how to approach musk mice without getting smelly, and what could an insulted plant do? Octavo's Rules weren't encouraging. Why, oh why me?

"Raja will be able to help you with the science," Sylvia said. "You'll bring the intuition for the job."

But I could never say no to Sylvia, even if intuition wasn't anything like my specialty. Did I have the time? I had a charcoal mound burning, but it would need to smolder another five days before it needed attention, and there were bird hides to tan and beech tree galls to gather for tannin and woad to process for dye and pine trees to tap with the first warm spell for wax, but I could fit in a few more duties. . . . Sylvia gave me an impatient look.

"Of course I'll do it. I was—I was thinking ahead. It seems to have a lot to say to us."

People voted yes and slowly left, still babbling. I stayed to work out the details with Sylvia and Raja, hoping I'd get hit by an intuition lightning bolt.

"What do bats say?" Raja asked.

"Not much. Come here, go away, bugs, sex, things like that." At the mention of sex, I realized that I had never slept with Raja, and her breasts would fit nicely into my hands.

"You trained the fipps," Sylvia said.

I think she meant to encourage me, but I couldn't help being honest. "No. Someone else did that. Snow vines, maybe."

Sylvia frowned. She insists that she doesn't mind any reminder of the original village, but she does, and I'd forgotten about that.

"There's not much to it," I said quickly to say anything, "I just watch them and figure them out. Your father left some good notes on domestication and fipp behavior." Praise might smooth things over.

She didn't look smoothed, but she talked like she was. "What makes you think the plant has a lot to say?"

"That looks like a shout to me."

"Intuition."

"I suppose. It's too big. The size worries me."

"It's not like flowers," Raja said, smiling at me, a smile sweeter than nectar. "The colors were made probably by withdrawing the chlorophyll and unmasking colors that were there, although we've never seen it do that before."

"Something like it happened once," Sylvia said. "When I first visited the city, although it was just a small branch with colored leaves."

My intuition had me ask: "This is the same bamboo in the display as the rest of the city, right?"

Bad move. Raja looked annoyed by my ignorance. "All the bamboo is the same plant, all connected by roots."

"Octavo's Rules say plants always want something from animals," I said, and I managed to annoy Sylvia again, since she had a high opinion of the bamboo. "I mean that in a good way. When I call the kats, I want them to play, that is, do some work, or to let them know I brought food. It might want to give us something." She looked placated. "A new round of sharing, maybe. I mean, the fruit keeps getting better for us bit by bit." That actually charmed her. "Let me take another look and think on it this morning."

I took another look and couldn't think of a single thing. What did it want? If the plant had been watching us and figured us out, it might want to take something. And why so big? If it was meant to impress, it had succeeded.

Orson had asked me to take some kats out to weed a cotton field, so I did that instead. I went to the kat hutches, played a tune on a pan-pipe made of rainbow bamboo—useful stuff, that bamboo—until about twenty decided to pay attention, and led them past the display (where we had to pause and look up in wonder) and we left the city dancing, one-two-three-four, one-two-three-four, one-two-three-four glide! I minded my back. Last fall, in a moment of inspired teamwork, they had pushed me off the new bridge, a nice wide sturdy log bridge, the pride of the city's civil engineers. But transporting fipps had been worse before we finished the bridge. I used to have to get them across by boat, and they figured out much too fast how to make boats tip.

Burdock was sprouting in the cotton field. Kats will gobble tender burdock shoots and refrain from doing much damage as long as they're having fun, and fun for them means jumping at each other, jumping on me, chasing each other, chasing me, chasing lizards, hiding, and sometimes playing leapfrog. I taught them leapfrog. I even trained kats to work as hearing guides for Honora, who is deaf. Their limit is their attitude. Life must be fun.

I thought about this as I chased around with them, jumping over dormant cotton trunks, singing, and dancing. Sunshine warmed the air, and the dewdrop corals smelled sweet. (Well, smelled hungry, really, but that was their problem.) Newly hatched caterpillars crawled around, eating dirt and avoiding the corals. I kept an eye out for the giant hawk bats that eat kats. A soft wind rattled the rope palms that edged the field. A herd of deer crabs sneaked behind them, avoiding us.

A stand of rainbow bamboo stood at the edge of the field, surrounded by the thistle bushes it uses as guards. We were being watched by eyes small as dust-motes on the bamboo's stems. It had made the display, made colors, so it had to see (another of Octavo's Rules). We were being observed. Trained. Rewarded. Evaluated. A kat's highest value is fun. What did Pacifists want? What did I want? Women, truffle, music, children, food, a sturdy roof over my head. . . .

A kat jumped, grabbed the fringe on my collar, and swung around, and before I caught it, three more had decided to try that trick, then all of them, and I gave up and sank to the ground, fippokats all over me. I was laughing too hard to stand up.

Sure, I have a gift of cross-species communication. I have the sense of humor of a fippokat.

When the weed feast was done, we danced back to the city, and a kat named Pea took the lead and hopped backward, not something any of us could do well, which was the fun of it, and I didn't accidentally step on anyone, so we made it home safe.

If I wanted to train an animal from the beginning, how would I start? No, wrong question. If I were an animal that wanted to be trained, what would I do? First of all, I would want to react fast so the trainer knew I wasn't hopeless, even if I wasn't catching on right away. That meant I ought to respond to the bamboo that day—somehow. Even if this wasn't good, we couldn't ignore it.

I studied the display a bit more, not catching on to the lesson but that might be all right, then I found Raja in a greenhouse setting tulip leaf cuttings for spring planting, the soil and sap on her hands making them even more touchable, but, always a gentleman, I kept my hands to myself. "Can bamboo roots sense their surroundings?"

"Of course." At least she didn't look annoyed by the question. "They never come up through pavement or foundations or block the water pipes. The bamboo knows where it is and what's around its roots."

"How about planting thistles by the display? Would it notice?"

She slowly smiled. I had hit an intuitive nail on the head. "It knows thistles," she said. "It likes thistles."

We scouted thistles in the woods, put on gloves, and transplanted them, one at the base of each colored stalk. By chance or design, our fingers touched a few times, a fine feeling even through the gloves. Romance grows from small things, like bats chirping "here." She didn't seem interested in me, though. She had a fertile husband and seemed to be happy with him.

"Plants do things slowly," she said. "It might take a few days or weeks before we get a response."

"I can wait," I said. She might change her mind.

That evening, I put sturdy fences around the thistles and organized games for the toddlers and youngest children. *Everyone run to orange! Sierra, find the purple one. What color is the sky? Where is that color?* The bamboo, I hoped, was watching.

After the children's bedtime, I gathered a branch of each color into an extravagantly large bouquet (the bamboo wouldn't mind, I hoped) and brought it to Indira. She thanked me quietly. Her hair needed combing. Their home was neat as usual, from the dome down to the floor tiles, but that was probably the work of friends and neighbors who had come in to help. Beck sat next to her, whittling a spoon. He'd asked me to come and be cheerful, and by the way he'd asked, I knew what he meant even before I got there.

"How's Snow today?" I asked, grinning.

"Good. I think. It's hard to tell. She's not like the other babies."

"Every baby's different, that's what I like about them. How are you?"

"Good. A little tired."

She wasn't good, I could tell just by looking at her. "Have you seen the bamboo?"

She hadn't, of course. Beck had told me she wouldn't leave the house, even to go to dinner, so I described it enthusiastically, told her about my new assignment and about the children and the thistles. Beck and I made jokes and puns, since she always liked puns, the sillier the better. She smiled, but we couldn't make her laugh. Snow began to cry.

"She's hungry," I said. "Should I bring her to you?"

"Hungry? Are you sure?"

"I'm an expert at communications."

Snow wiggled in my hands as I picked her up, red-cheeked, impatient, and unafraid to bend the world to her will. I handed her to her mother. Snow suckled loudly, concentrating on the complex business of eating. It's a beautiful thing, babies and mothers still linked as life creates life, one person becomes two, a process almost fulfilled with childbirth, but real independence takes years.

The baby was fine. The mother had postpartum depression. Childbirth is hard, and not quite over when the umbilical cord is cut, not for the baby or the mother. I gave Indira a kiss on the cheek, and Beck walked me to the door and thanked me for coming. I ducked outside, where the night air was coldly clean, and I breathed deep. His baby, his wife? Only mostly. My work was far from done.

THE BAMBOO

Pollen grains, tiny and oily with urgency, land on nectared stamens, pollen that carries messages. The grains fill with water and sugar, and I absorb and read them. The outer wall displays sculptures to identify the sender: a bamboo that grew from seeds dispersed years ago to create sentinels. It barely survives in the southwest mountains, hideously stunted by wind and cold, starved almost to stupidity, small and lonely, an endless talker despite the poverty that should limit its ability to create messages.

The message was split into nine to send, then duplicated and released in clouds. The distance is long and winds are fickle. The inner walls of the first eight grains sketched an image of a ground eagle. The interior cells said a pack has left the mountains. After waiting hours, I capture the final grain. It says the pack contains at least forty eagles. Forty.

I have seen eagles drum their air sacs before they attack. Their hooked beaks rip apart animals as easily as fippolions destroy trees. A corm-root from an ancestor says eagles visit mountains in late winter, retrieving caches of food they left in summer and hunting animals that hibernate in caves. But normally smaller packs. Forty can deplete a mountain.

I have tasted eagles. The first foreigners buried their bodies, their meat rich with iron. I know eagles.

I also tasted the first foreigners. When they arrived, I misjudged them. They built shelters like mere birds, lived in colonies like mere fippokats, used fire like mere eagles. But they controlled fire and made it intense and transformative. Their first kiln glowed like the Sun, and from that kiln came glass, an artificial and amazing stone, and the foreigners surrounded me with my own colors and watered me and fed me. I gave them fruit.

We communicated with electric waves, what they called radio. We shared simple ideas about mathematics and meteorology, and progressed from there. I explained the animals and plants. They told me I live on a sphere of soil and stone of unimaginable size that tilts as it rotates and revolves around the Sun, which explains not just the day but the differing lengths of days as the seasons change. They had once lived under a different Sun.

These second foreigners have reacted to my display promptly, a simple message in response to a simple message, and I have hope like a germinating seed. I want to continue, but will we have time? Will they understand the scent of eagles if I reproduce it?

Eagles destroy. Foreigners create. So few things create and so many destroy.

HIGGINS

The bamboo answered thistles with flower buds, and each stem of buds contrasted with the color of the rest of the stalk—orange buds on a blue stalk, yellow on purple—so we had to notice. Raja and I took our time examining the buds, not because we found much to look at, although of course I enjoyed the company, but because we wanted the plant to know that we had noticed. A language of flowers! Imagine.

We tried hard. We imagined different scents for different colors or chemicals that would not just make you feel ever so slightly uplifted, as bamboo flowers usually do, but might make you smarter. Plants use all sorts of chemicals to communicate (Raja explained), so it might try that with us, or it might use different colorations or markings to create a vocabulary, or different shapes, not the usual floral trumpet surrounded by a wide whorl of longer petals.

The next morning, the buds had opened. I saw the flowers from far away, colorful in the sunlight and bigger than my hand with the fingers outstretched, but when I got close, they were a disappointment, solid-colored and rather normal. Maybe they held some other surprise. I smelled one. It stank, they all stank. A couple of kats were out nosing around, so I picked one up to smell the flowers, which they usually enjoy, but one whiff and it kicked and scratched and almost bit me trying to get away.

Raja broke into a run when she saw that the flowers were open, and her pretty nose wrinkled as soon as she smelled them. She didn't recognize the scent, but she reminded me that some flowers smelled worse—and always with a purpose. Carrion flowers smell like rotting flesh to attract scavenger lizards. "And *Euphorbia faeceus*."

"What?"

"The poop plant."

"Oh." I blushed a bit. (The poop plant has proven possibilities for mischief. It looks like a pile of brown plump stems.)

But the bamboo flowers probably meant to tell Pacifists something more complex than "food," if only because the bamboo had to know what we wouldn't eat. We asked for help, and a lot of people sniffed around for us.

Sylvia recognized the smell instantly. Eagles.

I had never seen eagles, but she had. A few hunters had, and they confirmed the smell. She organized a meeting to teach me everything everyone knew for a fact about eagles, as opposed to the fanciful stories swapped to pass the time. Sketches were passed around of meaty-legged birds a little bigger than humans with bark-patterned spiny feathers, huge hooked beaks, long flexible necks, and clawed hands on short forelimbs. They could run fast and jump high, right over our city walls, and wreak all kinds of havoc once they were inside. At least Pax birds didn't fly like Earth birds. Earth must have been a dangerous place.

Ivan and Tom, both hunter-explorers, told how eagles sometimes played with their food before killing it. Ivan slid close on the bench to use me to intimately illustrate nipped hamstrings, gouged eyes, nibbled soft and tender parts. He laughed at my discomfort. I was the guy who entertained women and children and fipps. I couldn't handle a real man's unmerciful world.

"How do eagles communicate?" I asked, trying to look like I would not be shocked if he said they wrote out words with intestines torn from living Pacifist babies.

"I don't try to communicate with eagles. I try to kill them." He grinned in a deliberately annoying way, his perfectly trimmed beard close to mine.

"I've seen them drum their air sacs and dance," Sylvia said a little loudly to interrupt him, and told her story, about how they hated water but understood fire—Ivan interrupted: "They use campfires and cook food"—and told how a pack had killed her father. She passed around a spiny feather.

I had an intuition that scared me bad. "You've seen rainbow bamboo everywhere, right?" I asked Ivan.

"Everywhere," he said with a swagger so I would know that he really had been everywhere.

"Plants communicate," I said, hoping I could sound tough about flowers. "They can send chemicals in the air and who knows what else to share information. I think our friend wants us to know that eagles are headed toward us." Desperately important information, I thought.

"Maybe it's trying to attract eagles," another hunter said.

"Then the scent would be outside the city, too," Tom said. "We can check that."

"Or maybe it just thinks we'd like the smell," someone else said.

"Then it's not a very smart plant," Ivan sneered.

I said, "I think it means danger."

Ivan didn't. "Packs are small. Three, maybe five members. They're stealthy and smart, but they don't want to take on big prey like us. It's good to have a warning, though, if that's what it is. Nice work, Higg. We'll take it from here."

Nice work, now go and play with the children and talk to the flowers. Real men will take it from here.

But they didn't find anything all day, not eagles or eagle-scented flowers.

I spent the evening playing with a bottle of truffle, and halfway through it, I realized that the display—sixteen full-size plants, bigger altogether than the Meeting House—was just too big for a few eagles. The bamboo was warning of a whole lot of eagles. I hurried to tell Ivan, and found him with Beck, Tom, Aloysha, and some other men in a garden about to be tilled. They were playing a knife-tossing game by lamplight.

"It's all right," Tom said, putting a patronizing arm around my shoulder. "We're a lot smarter than eagles. Even if there are what, ten of them, we can handle it."

Ivan laughed. "You're hearing the truffle talk, not the bamboo. And you should share that truffle. Get some for everyone."

I got them some, and they let me watch them play. The point of the game was to throw a knife in certain ways and have it stick into a target on the ground, but soon I got bored and left.

In the morning, without truffle in my belly, I looked at the bamboo and still heard it yelling about eagles. Ivan and Tom spent the day looking through the forest and fields for eagles or flowers and found nothing.

"Finding a few eagles in a big forest, that's not easy," Ivan said. "Higg, have your lions knock down a lot more trees."

They went out the next morning and came back for lunch, having seen a whole lot of nothing, not even spoor. There was talk about a false alarm and patronizing looks for me. . . . I decided to skip lunch and pass a little time with my lions, but I listened to the bamboo and strapped on a knife and slung a bow and full quiver of arrows over my shoulder before I went.

Just outside the city walls I noticed that the noontime was far too quiet. No birds barked in the underbrush. I crossed the bridge, listening to my boots clump, and walked along the riverbank.

Bats were singing. "Danger?" "Danger!" "Come?" "Coming." And a note I didn't know. Maybe "eagles." Or maybe "venomous lice." It might all have been a false alarm, but I couldn't help remembering that I was a terrible archer.

The lions were pacing and grumbling along the edge of the river. Pitman saw me, rose up, and howled a three-note welcome for the leader of the pack. The younger males jumped up on their hind legs to show me that they were plenty fierce, too, but the females muttered unhappily. I howled back and raised my arms, holding the knife and the bow, the fiercest of all—if they thought so.

And if they thought there was a problem, so did I, and forget about what Ivan and the other men might think. Lions were domesticated animals, not as fierce as nature might have made them and maybe no match for eagles or whatever was worrying them, so as their leader, I owed them help. I couldn't move them into the city, but I could move them closer, at least to the other side of the river.

"Pitman! Here, Pitman! Clay! Scratch! Everybody, come here! Porter! Fido! This way!"

Pitman looked at me and then at their patch of ground along the river, dug up and muddied, as if it had strategic advantages. I walked over to pat a few heads and scratch a few crests, and got a lot of sniffs and a few licks in return.

"Warmheart, Teaberry, this way!" I pushed their shoulders. The young females took a few steps, and young males hurried to get ahead of them, but the adult females hesitated, and ultimately they controlled the pack.

"Clay, honey, how are you? And your boy?" He looked at me with big, startled eyes, clinging to Mama's hairy shoulders. "You know I think the world of you." I cooed and slipped an arm around her waist to ease her forward. She took a step. "That's right, we're going to a safer place." I cooed again. Step by step, the pack started moving, and I hurried ahead to show the way.

Pitman sniffed and growled. I sniffed and maybe I noticed something, but I'd sniffed the bamboo flowers enough to be able to imagine eagles with no problem. He shuffled on all fours, looking around. If he decided to rise to his back legs and hop, I could never catch up. Behind me, the pack growled and grumbled. Bats in the trees commented: "Lions, here!" "Lions!" Eighteen lions of various ages marching along the riverbank attracted attention.

But the bats also said, "Danger!" and I didn't think they meant us. "Danger! Here!"

Where?

At the bridge, I shooed the pack ahead of me. I guarded their flank with Pitman and two young males, Fido and Scratch. I had an arrow nocked. Pitman roared, claws raised, looking down the road between the fields. The young males stood and howled. The rest of the pack began shuffling across the bridge. I saw nothing down the road, just bushes and stones, a pile of dead leaves, a log . . . it twitched. Were those eyes? Was that a stone or a beak? And there, was that a stump? That stump hadn't been there when I left the city.

"Eagles!" I shouted as loud as I could at the city. "Eagles at the bridge! Eagles!"

The lions roared, young and old, male and female. The bridge vibrated as they hopped. A drumming sound came from a hedgerow across the field, then from a shrub much too close.

"Pitman, Scratch, Fido, let's go." I tugged on Pitman's fur to get him on the bridge. He shrugged it off. Fido hopped toward the shrub. An eagle stepped from behind it, with beautiful feathers and a beak that could take off a lion's arm. A reddish sac in its neck swelled and sank, making a drumming noise. Its legs tensed to charge. I let an arrow fly, hoping it would hit the right target.

"Go! Now! Pitman!" I shoved him and Scratch onto the bridge. "Fido!" Five eagles had appeared, then more, a lot more. Fido took a long hop, slashing as he tackled the eagle. Feathers and blood and fur exploded. More eagles than I could count at a glance rushed across the fields toward the bridge.

They hated water.

"Pitman!" I kicked hard at a bridge railing and howled. I hoped his tiny brain would see and understand: destroy the bridge. I kicked again. Wood splintered in the rail and a board splashed into the river. "Pitman! Scratch!" I bent to grab a log plank underfoot and tried to tug it up to show them what I wanted. Pitman looked for a long moment, his eyes bright with anger. I howled. He hooked the toes of one hind foot around the end of a plank and lifted it with a grunt. Wood tore. He threw it into the river.

"Good Pitman! Good! Good boy, Scratch!" Scratch knocked out a railing with an easy kick. Pitman tore up another plank. I turned toward the eagles, now close, too close, too close to miss, and fired arrows as fast as I could. They hesitated. The bridge shook alarmingly, gloriously. Wood snapped and splintered. There were shouts from the city. I shot again. Again. The eagles gibbered at each other and dodged my arrows.

The bridge shook, tilted, and dropped from beneath my feet, and I tumbled into the river, banging arms and legs against logs and boards. I glimpsed Pitman and Scratch falling into the water. I swam clear of the logs and lifted my head to breathe and looked back toward the city side of the river. There, the lionesses were tearing the bridge apart. The pack had turned back to destroy it.

Human voices shouted from the bank. I took a lungful of air and roared with all the joy I could at my pack. They answered.

I shed my coat and swam to the city side of the river, dodging logs, glancing at the tense human faces on the river's edge. Zoe, with a bow and arrow slung over her shoulder, reached down from a boat dock for me. I climbed up, slipping on the dock, trying not to pull her in, and finally I was out and steady and looked around. The bridge was gone. Pitman was hauling himself up the bank. But Scratch was on the other side, on his hind legs, challenging the eagles. They stood at a distance, drumming at each other, then five of them, in atrociously perfect co-ordination, pounced and took him down, one on each leg and arm, one at his throat. He shrieked once.

People were still rushing down the bluff from the city, nocking ar-rows as they ran, but our riverbank was already lined with men and women with only one goal.

Arrows flew, fast and true. Eagles tried to dodge them, or freeze and blend into the landscape, but the farmers knew every bush and worked systematically in teams to eliminate false ones. Eight firing at the same target brought it down, even if a few missed—the bush would screech and leap up, studded with arrows, run a few steps tearing at them, and fall.

The arrows didn't stop until all the eagles on the riverbank were dead or fled, and then boats of archers hunted up and down the river. Ivan and Tom paused as they left to salute me with no trace of irony on their faces, just man-to-man respect.

I gathered up the herd. Quite a few were soaking wet like me, and it was a chilly winter day. Paloma brought me dry clothes and wanted me to go home, but I refused—a pack leader has his duties—and instead we built a small, hot fire. The lions were shy about the fire at first, but with my encouragement, they came in close, seduced by warmth, especially the wet ones, and we muttered and moaned in discontentment. I stretched out my hands to warm them and Pitman, at my side, copied me, delicately holding the long claws so their cutting edges threatened no one.

The city's guards built their own fire. Porter, a wet young male, adventured over there. He would be leaving the pack soon and wanted to test his independence, driving off the guards with a casual growl and settling in comfortably. I couldn't lure him away, but I finally convinced the guards that he meant no danger.

Sylvia came to thank me—"brave, smart work"—keeping her distance from the lions.

"Sorry about the bridge," I said.

"We should have built it less sturdy." She shifted the strap of her quiver. "I know how hard it is to believe in an idea when no one else does. I . . . We thank you for that."

A crew came later with a sandwich and thanks for me and bread and potatoes for the pack. I stayed the night and slept eventually, snuggled against a warm and furry body, and woke a little before sunrise, suddenly sure that some noise I had heard was an eagle sneaking up— probably the lizards on the far side of the river scavenging on the carnage. Breakfast and more praise arrived just after sunrise.

I moved the pack to a fallow yam field near a side gate to the city, good food for them and a post of brave guards for us, and no one questioned my judgment. We began burying the dead eagles, and at my orders (I could give orders now), the first thing we did was bury as many as we could alongside the bamboo display at the riverside gate—we had something to say, and that would say it. Raja and I dug two large holes in the human graveyard, helped by fippokats, and we buried what was left of Fido and Scratch alongside Glassmakers and Pacifists with a little ceremony.

Everywhere I went, everything I did, I got salutes, thanks, hugs, chaste kisses, wet kisses, pats on the back, and praise for wisdom, steadfastness, and heroism. Not to mention apologies from those who had doubted me.

After supper, I sang songs with the children, went to the kat hutches and goofed a bit, went to the lions and cooed awhile.

People acted differently toward me, but I didn't feel one bit different.

THE BAMBOO

I can feel iron. It flows abundant from my roots to the tips of my leaves to make chlorophyll and transport electric charges for respiration and photosynthesis. Iron is growth, this iron from the flesh of many animals buried to feed me.

The first foreigners told me that my sphere lacks iron in the soil. They said spheres and suns of infinite variety circle and spin in the sky. Iron on their sphere existed to excess, and boundless iron is here, too, but at the core of this sphere far deeper than the deepest root can tap, and so it is useless.

Many animals need iron just as we plants do, and iron-rich animals are nutritious. History says first we killed these animals with poison, but as we grew more intelligent, we trained them to live and die at our roots as service animals, a steady though slow supply of iron. Finally, we organized our service animals to hunt for us, and we enjoyed a brief abundance until our animals became too destructive. We taught them to fight our rivals with forest fires, and only I remain.

Today I taste temptation. I can grow as large and smart as the environment allows, and I can change the environment. I could lure more animals for the foreigners to kill or be killed by, but when the animals are all slaughtered, including the foreigners, I would starve again. Animals and stupid plants repeat the past. They do not change and grow. I will.

Eagles were buried at my display. The foreigners understood my warning and repaid me. I count twenty-six dead eagles, but no dead foreigners, and I am pleased but also worried, for they proved themselves clever fighters. I count two dead fippolions, and, strangely, they are buried in the site reserved by foreigners for their own kind.

I must communicate again. Dualism lies at the core of reality. Even simple plants understand: light and dark, dry and wet, up and down, positive and negative. And there are complex ideas like good and evil, being and nonbeing, life and death. I will present this to the foreigners.

It is hard to train creatures with intelligence, for it gives them an unpredictably wide range of reactions to a stimulus, but obviously they have been trained in the past. I would like to know how the foreigners think, to know what plant on which sphere trained them. It would be easier to communicate with those plants directly, root to root, seed to seed, pollen to pollen. Why does pollen not drift from sphere to sphere? Moths can overcome the wind. The foreigners have overcome the sky. In the sky, the Sun shines always and iron is as common as calcium.

I am thankful that none of my animals died in the battle. They will be too useful to me.

HIGGINS

We met at night in the far northwest corner of the city, near the laundry center, in a house that still needed repairs. The roof over a bay had fallen in long ago and made sort of a hearth where we were cooking eagle meat to celebrate the victory of the day before. Everyone who had killed an eagle was invited. I was beginning to wish I hadn't come.

We drank truffle by the light of the embers glowing beneath the spit. It was skewered with chunks of liver-colored meat, and now and then a bit of fat dripped down and a flame gleamed up like a firefly. I had selected a rough and tough batch of truffle, guessing that the less we actually noticed of the meat's flavor, the better. The aroma (to call it that) from the hearth was proving me right.

But that wasn't why I was wishing I hadn't come. Eleven faces glowed red in the firelight and watched me as if they were children in a classroom and I was the teacher, but these faces weren't sweet children. They were killers, and I was the alpha killer.

"I don't think any of my arrows hit a target," I said, knowing that I wouldn't get tossed out even if they believed me, which they wouldn't. "I've always been a rotten shot, and I wasn't aiming."

Tom laughed. "I saw one of your arrows score."

"And Fido nailed one of them, didn't he?" Hakon said, only fourteen years old and very impressed with me. (I thought he was a bit of a bully.) "Your lion, your kill."

"That's not the point." Ivan was already slurring his words. "You were incredible. Zoe saw it too, right? The eagles were about to get you, and you kept shooting. You knew the lions would destroy the bridge in time."

"I was hoping they would. I mean, they're not all that smart."

"You didn't know they would?"

"Well . . ."

"The eagles almost killed you," Zoe said like an accusation.

I shrugged and stared at my cup of truffle. In the firelight, it looked reddish-black. I hadn't thought much about that part of the fight, but thinking back, I realized that getting killed hadn't frightened me at the time.

"You always were like that," said Aloysha, Sylvia's husband, boylike even as an old man. "When we were coming to the city, down at the lower waterfall we carried all the other children to protect them from the slugs, but you wouldn't let anyone carry you. You grabbed a spear and took care of yourself." He puckered his lips, squinted his eyes, and held an imaginary spear ready to stab anything that moved. Everyone laughed.

"You were tough," my father said. This from a fisherman who handled venomous crawfish every day and had only eight and a half fingers, because mistakes happen.

Beck told a story about me when I was about ten and organized first aid for Orson after he fell, broke his leg, and panicked. I didn't remember it clearly, just that we were repairing the city wall. "You're pretty good during childbirth," he added.

"And before that," Zoe said.

"Is that meat done?" I asked. Anything to change the subject away from me. It was fun, I can't deny that, being a hero, but being a hero wasn't quite what I wanted—whatever it was that I wanted, which, if I'd thought about it, I couldn't have named.

"Is the meat done?"

Hard to tell, and everyone had an opinion.

But a little later my father asked, "Do you think the bamboo has more to say?"

I'd put a lot of thought into that. "I'm sure this is just the start. Maybe, someday, it can tell us about the Glassmakers."

"That's a lot to get out of a plant."

"It's going to take a while, a long while. We need to find a language we both know, or more likely we'll figure it out as we go along."

"You think the bamboo is that smart?"

Other people had paused in their conversations to listen, but I didn't mind so much, since we weren't talking about me, exactly.

"I don't know, but I don't even know for sure how smart kats are. Or lions. They knew how to destroy a bridge without being taught, which is something. The bamboo is growing new flower buds, so it means to keep talking."

"I hope it doesn't mean that more eagles are coming."

"These seem like different buds. Different colors. And I don't know how smart eagles are, but they have to be smart enough to know to stay away from us now."

"Here's to that!" Beck raised a glass. We cheered and drank—killers and proud of it.

"What're you going to tell the bamboo?" Ivan asked. "Thanks for the warning?"

"We said that already."

"Oh, right, we did. At least it likes us. It likes us, right?"

'I nodded. "I've been thinking about the eagles, too."

"You don't want to talk to them," Zoe said.

"If we could figure out what the drumming meant—"

Ivan's eyes lit like sparks. "Right. When they got Scratch, they had it all worked out."

We all began talking about what we had seen and heard of the eagles during the attack, trying to put together clues about how they communicated so we could eavesdrop, and we didn't figure out much, but it was sure a lot better than sitting around talking about me.

Eagle meat tasted musky and astringent, and was tough besides, but we smeared it with mustard sauce and ate it anyway. Ivan and Zoe walked home with me, and I figured out that they were competing over who would sleep with me, and it was probably the truffle thinking, but I decided to take them both.

I woke up wedged between them, naked and warm, thirsty from a hangover, listening to a fippokat nosing in our clothes on the floor, and considered what it would be like to be Beck. I'd wake up every morning with the same woman, a woman who loved me and needed me, and I'd be there every day because I needed her, too. It's fun to have different women, but I'm not a fippokat, I want more than fun. If I were Beck, I would be central to the lives of three children, instead of being on the edges of the lives of a lot of children. Children like me, maybe they love me, but when things are tough, they always want Mom and Dad. If I were Beck, I would be nothing special, just another citizen of Pax. Not the great communicator, not the alpha eagle-slayer, I wouldn't have anything to prove. . . .

But that's not the way it turned out. Life was unfair. Maybe Beck wished he were me. The universe didn't care, and my happiness wasn't important to it. But I could harm, and I could help, and I could be happy whether it mattered to anyone or not.

Zoe and Ivan woke up. I couldn't recall why, even with a surplus of truffle in me, I had believed Ivan was beddable the night before, but it wasn't his fault that I had sobered up, and we had a high-spirited sunrise. After breakfast, I said hello to the fippokats, worked with a new litter to get them used to me, and took a kat crew to the northwest side of the city, where by means of a dirt fight they dug a hole and I buried the remains from last night's eagle banquet. No one had wanted to take the leftovers home.

I visited the lions, who were still restless, but they had been enjoying the old yam field. It would be turned over and ready for planting soon. Best of all, they'd turned up quite a few truffle roots. While I gathered them up, savoring their future use, a female trotted up to offer herself. "Pitman!" I called, but he was already on his way. He'd figured out the advantages of having a non-lion as the alpha male.

I had lunch with Indira, Beck, and the kids. There's no bad without some good, and the attack had given Indira the final push out of depression. Her mind was back on her work as a civil engineer. "We need to rethink the water supply," she said. "We've been piping in water from a spring in the hills, but with a rising population we'll need more water, and we need to protect the source better."

Snow was thriving. She hadn't noticed a thing, not about her mother and not about the scary monsters at the river, although Moon and Lightning were upset and asked a lot of questions.

"Could they get in the city?"

"They won't cross the river," I said. "And the lions destroyed the bridge."

"We won't rebuild it the way it was," Indira said. "We're going to use a rope bridge now, so anyone can destroy it if they have to." (Eagles lived on our side of the river up in the north mountains, but we weren't about to mention that.)

Beck walked me to the door. "She's doing great again, isn't she?" His smile and the way he had looked at Indira all during lunch, at Indira and Moon and Lightning and Snow—I'd seen all that and ached to be him, ached from the toes on up.

"I'm happy for you," I said. I hadn't thought about anything while I was on the bridge and the eagles were coming at me, but I knew that if they crossed the bridge, everything I cared about was on the other side. I'd known that without thinking about it. And everything I cared about had stayed safe.

The next day, the bamboo flower buds opened, smaller and not as showy as the others, half of them white and the other half black. (Pure pigment, not a fake black by a mix of colors or fake white from background tissue or anything; Raja checked.)

The white flowers pointed up, the black ones pointed down. The thistles at the base of the culms with the black flowers died, white flowers' thistles lived. Only the black flowers had a scent, although it meant nothing special to anyone, including the kats and Pitman. The nectar tasted different, one acidic and one alkaline. What all this meant and how to respond kept everyone talking. At least they weren't talking about me.

We would have had enough to talk about anyway. Some of the children, and some of the adults (especially us killers), had nightmares or insomnia, so we decided to hold the annual spring equinox festival early—the next day. The festival commemorates arriving at the city from the old village, so we ate the traditional travelers' meal of trilobites, wild onions, and dried rainbow fruit. We walked around on stilts pretending we were Earthlings.

Finally, at dusk, at the site of the old central tower, we took off our clothes in spite of the cold because being naked showed we were willing to move on. We lit a bonfire to burn images of straw, wood, and paper of what we wanted to leave behind. Hydrogen seeds had been stashed in the images to explode with satisfying bangs and flashes.

The children and I had worked together all day to build a big eagle out of twigs. It stood at the center of the heap with a smaller beak than it ought to be and not as deadly hooked, which was fine with me. Sylvia had taught the children how to weave the feathers that hung off the eagle, no two alike, different sizes, different skill levels, different grass and leaves used to make them, giving the bird a ragged look. It hardly resembled the beautiful and vicious creatures that still raced in my dreams in deadly choreographed packs, but I was more than eager to see it burn.

My parents, like a few other older Pacifists, contributed straw figures of tall and skinny humanoids. Sylvia's always looked spookily lifelike, since she was a master basket-weaver. I used to pester my parents about why they burned Earthlings, and finally, when I was older, they told me everything about leaving the original colony that I had been too little to understand or remember. That year I realized that the festival wasn't for children, although children had the most fun at it.

This year, before lighting the fire, Sylvia presented me with an eagle feather as a symbol of courage, and then the children danced for me. I had no suspicion they were going to do that. In the dance, howling and hopping lions chased drumming eagles. The lions caught eagles and turned them into lions, and at the end, all the children were howling and hopping (with kats gliding among them, never ones to miss a good time). From the other side of the wall, our pack howled back their three-tone song, and then, from far, far away, wild lions howled. For a moment we were all hushed, listening.

And then we lit the fire and everyone howled and hopped as our fears burned and burst into the night, sparks like stars rising and winking out.

A few of us lingered over a jar of truffle. We had put on our clothes against the night's chill. The fire had sunk to ash. I had set the feather in a band on my head where it wouldn't prick anything, the alpha male for another night, not the role I wanted, but the role I had, and I was set to do it right.

"Did you like the dance?" Raja asked. She and Blas wore nervous smiles. "It was the kids' doing. They were afraid it wouldn't be good enough."

"It was wonderful. Wonderful."

They looked at each other and relaxed.

"Especially when the lions started howling," Blas said. "They really like the lions. I have to remind them that the lions aren't huggable like the kats."

"And if there are other lions in the forest," I said, "that probably means the rest of the eagles have hightailed it out, since eagles and lions seem to be natural enemies. But the bamboo is talking about something else now, and I don't know what."

"Opposites, I think," Raja said.

"Could be," I said. "Then how do we show we understand? And why would opposites be worth talking about?"

Beck had gone home earlier, but now he was running back and shouting for Blas.

"Snow is sick, very sick!"

THE BAMBOO

No response. Did they fail to understand? Dualism. The universe consists of fundamental and antagonistic entities and forces. Animate and mineral. Plants and animals. Parasites and producers. Creation and destruction. Acids and alkalis. Sickness and health. Sky and soil.

Day and night are not the same as light and dark. Once I believed they were, but now I know day and night results from an interplay between sphere and sky. In the same way, fire and water result from chemical bonds and changes, from the interplay of positive and negative atomic charges.

I survive with the help of servant animals and plants, and for the most fruitful relationships, I must help them in return. I could help the foreigners far more if we could share ideas in addition to nutrients. From an interplay and merging of intelligence, all things could result, things that have never existed before, and our world will grow.

I observed the foreigners' fire tonight, a large fire I have learned that I need not fear, although I do not like it. Animals are cyclical, and the large fire is an annual event.

But this year, the fire was not held on the evening of the spring equinox. I believe the eagle attack has disturbed a cycle. I could help them assess the passage of the days and years with accuracy. Repetition is important to animals. I respect their needs. I want to help them.

Answer me! Dualism is a simple idea. Light, dark. Up, down. Live, dead. Communication, silence.

Even if you do not understand, show me that you wish to communicate. Night has come, and the morning will follow soon. You can accomplish much in a day. A small action will suffice. Speak to me.

HIGGINS

"Here's your boot."

Moon, in her nightgown, sat on my lap, sleepy and confused as I dressed her to go outside. Blas was examining Snow and I wanted to eavesdrop, but Moon deserved my attention. She and Lightning would spend the night at their grandmother's house, away from busy doctors and terrified parents.

"Here's another boot. And let's see, you should have some clothes for tomorrow. What would you like to wear?"

"Can't I wear this nightgown?"

"Tonight, sure, but tomorrow morning you'll need to get dressed. How about the brown sweater and some trousers?"

"Okay." She wanted to go back to sleep. I put her coat on, set her back on her bed, and stuffed some clothes in a bag.

Lightning had gotten himself dressed and packed and was watching the bustle around Snow unhappily. "I want to stay," he told me as I picked up Moon. "I want to know what's happening."

"Snow is sick and we're going to take you to Grandma Cynthia so you can get some sleep. When you get up in the morning, you can come back."

He didn't look satisfied. Since the move to the city, the infant mortality rate had dropped considerably, but even a little boy knew that babies who had trouble breathing too often stopped breathing altogether. "She's my sister." He pouted.

"I know."

"I want to help."

"I do, too. Sometimes the best thing we can do is take care of ourselves." I knew from experience that rest and nutrition were good cushions in case tragedy hit.

He eyed me coldly. He, Moon, and I left. Outside, the sky was streaked with faint green auroras. He asked, "How is she? Don't lie to me."

I might simplify the truth, but I never lie to children. He didn't seem to be in a mood even for simplification, so as we walked between dark and quiet houses, I whispered, "I don't know. It doesn't look like hyaline membrane disease, so this is probably a fungus. You've had coccidioidomycosis twice. It's serious, but, well, we'll see."

"Are they sure?" he whispered back.

"Not yet."

"Can it kill her?"

"Maybe. But you survived. Twice. I've had it a few times. We'll know soon."

"Why do I have to leave?"

"So you can get some sleep in a quiet house. There's no sense in all of us staying up all night."

"Are you going to stay up all night?"

"If I can help, I will."

"What can you do?"

"Keep your parents company. Or get sandwiches for the medics. Run and get people or things if there seems to be a reason." *I can see if my little girl lives.*

"If she's going to die, will you get me?"

I looked him straight in the eyes. "Yes."

He looked back, steady. "I'm going to sleep with my clothes on so I can come right away."

Snow was coughing when I got back, a high-pitched, harsh little cough that exploded from her lungs through phlegm and fluids and turned her face red with exertion. Red was a good color. Blue would mean low blood-oxygen levels, yellow would mean jaundice, gray would be close to the end. (Three of my babies had died. I'd learned a bit of medicine.)

Indira sat holding Snow. Blas sat nearby, watching the baby intently. Beck hunched on a bench. I sat next to him.

"She has a fever, and it's climbing," Blas said. "The other medic went to get some ice."

We took turns sponging the baby with ice water. The cough got worse and she got a bit pale. I fetched an oxygen tank. Blas suspected a fungus or virus, but without the old technology, he couldn't know which. He gave her an injection of antibiotics and antimycotics. Her lungs were filling with fluid.

Indira stared at the floor, unseeing, unresponsive, shoulders drooping. Depressed, guilty. I could tell what she was thinking, that she should have noticed the illness earlier, she should have fed Snow better, dressed her more warmly, bathed her more carefully, she shouldn't have gotten postpartum depression at all, she should have been a better mother. Indira was like that, she felt responsible for things she couldn't even have done.

Should Beck have been a better father? He could have been. Should

I have visited more? I could have found the time. Would this have warded away microorganisms? No. But if we could have done more, if there was a way to protect babies from coughs and rashes, from hunger and injury, from mistakes and delusions, we would have done it.

I decided to write a song about that someday soon, a serious song, not something catchy for kids. Something to reflect the aches of a soul that had lived a day too long and knew failure, the worst kind of failure, the kind you couldn't prevent, a song that would make people cry when they heard it, that would make me cry when I sang it, about the grief that remained green in every season, and that I had to sing about because it hurt more to keep quiet.

We didn't cry, we sat there dumbly. Sylvia came and brewed tea. She brought a basket of fruit, but I didn't want any. It would make me feel better and I didn't want to feel better. Ivan and Tom came, although they were usually aloof from parental things. They stood like warriors near the door, as if they would kill death itself if it dared try to duck in. Beck's father and sister came.

Snow got paler, her breathing got weaker, and Blas looked sadder as he listened to her chest. Finally I went to get Lightning. He leaped out of bed when I whispered his name and followed me, wordlessly, weeping in the street.

At the door he said, "Wait." He took some shaky deep breaths and dried his face with his sleeve. With dry red eyes, he entered and stood next to the crib, reached in and touched Snow's blue lips, and whispered something. He looked at his mother and stiffened at her utter dejection, then went to hug her.

"Snow is a very good sister," he said, and wiggled onto the chair beside Indira.

Lightning was a very good son.

Snow died early in the morning, shortly after a baker had come and made a tender fuss of laying out hot bread and nut butter for our breakfast. Lightning had brought a plate of food to his mother, probably knowing that she might not eat but knowing what he ought to do for her. His was a kind of understanding and compassion so true that I knew he was going to be a better man than I was, and that was my comfort that morning. Kind, genuine, natural, that's what a man should be. . . .

I'm not like that. I help, of course, I'm useful, but I'm not the real thing, and that's why women don't want me for more than a bit of fun and high-motility sperm. I'm not naturally kind, I'm intentionally kind. I have to figure out what to do, I don't do it automatically.

But time never stops breathing and I couldn't refuse to sing, and death couldn't stop the sunrise. . . .

Blas asked permission for an autopsy. "This might be something new," he told Beck. "I'd like to—"

"Of course. Learn what you can," Beck said. Moon sat on his lap, sobbing, and he held her. Grandma Cynthia sat beside them.

Lightning stood alongside his mother, who still stared at the floor. People started arriving with condolences and flowers and aromatic herbs, and he greeted them and thanked them on her behalf and tried to rouse her. "Cocklebells! Lemon sage! Don't they smell good?" Slowly, she began to emerge, if only to notice how good her son was.

I decided to make my escape by returning the medical equipment to the lab. I was the guy everyone pretended wasn't there, the useful man, sometimes even a hero, but in the end, an extra person, the guy everyone loved and no one quite wanted, the guy everyone and everything could talk to because he worked so hard to listen. I gathered up the battered old oxygen tank. Blas wrapped Snow in a sheet, a tiny white bundle to take away.

"Wait," he whispered as we were about to leave. "You carry her. I can handle the rest. You . . . She's yours, after all."

She weighed hardly anything. We passed a few people in the street, and without a word they knew what we carried and stood at somber attention. Blas had me place her in the refrigerator. The medical lab always repelled me, not because blood and flesh bothered me (animals get you used to visceral life quickly), but because of the technology.

A windmill outside generated electricity. Batteries collected it and parceled it out to run the refrigerator, an autoclave, fiber optic endoscopes, a dental drill, little flashlights, a radio knife. There were racks of scalpels and curettes, a microscope, thermometers, clocks, needles, and examination tables. The air smelled of pure chemicals, of esters and acids and ammonia. My mother had made some of the equipment, scavenging bits from the broken-down Earth wonders stashed in an alcove, piles of glass and metal components like the skeletons of lizards under a spider colony. I gather roots and bark and clays and rocks and deliver them to chemists, who take the next step, and they can name the chemicals and write the formulas. Our mathematicians can explain special relativity and even work out the math.

It's all true, they tell me, the non-Euclidean nature of the universe and the valence of a carbon atom. And yet none of it speaks to me no matter how I listen. I was leaving Snow in a foreign environment, synthetic, unnatural, Earthly. I thanked Blas and left.

I checked on the lions and kats. The city looked beautiful as I walked around in it. I don't remember the old village, but I remember arriving at the city, my first sight of it. I had been told it would be colorful, but I hadn't understood what that meant. Like flowers or rainbows, they said. Exactly. Like living inside flowers and rainbows. I can't imagine what the Glassmakers could have been like, although I've seen all the archaeological evidence. Why would they work so hard to make it so beautiful?

"Did they want to copy the bamboo?" I asked Sylvia. She was in her workshop weaving a basket to bury Snow in, half-done, and all the strands of wicker sticking out looked like an out-of-control reed patch.

"Or did the bamboo copy them?" she answered, guiding a reed through the tangle. "I'm not sure. It's hard to date things. The city and the bamboo are very, very old, hundreds of years. If we could find another city or read their writing, we might know more about what happened here. If we could find another bamboo plant, if we could do more exploring, if we had certain kinds of equipment—"

"We could have saved Snow's life if the equipment still worked," I snapped. I didn't mean to interrupt her, and I didn't know how angry I was until that moment.

"Yes. We could have given her artificial lungs until the infection was cured. We could have identified the infectious agent and its antibiotic within an hour with an Earth laboratory. Yes, we might have spotted the eagles faster if the orbital satellite still worked, but its solar panels died and we can't get up there to fix them. Yes, we could have kept the computers running if we could have replaced the gallium arsenide chips, and we can't even make silicon chips. We can barely make glass bricks. We know what's possible and we know why we can't do it, but the thought of it makes us feel like failures, and it's not our fault!"

She cut a reed with a stone blade, then glared at the stone. "We could do a lot of things if we had iron. But we don't. We can't find any, except for a few meteor fragments and we have to use them for nutrition. Maybe it would be better if we forgot all about Earth. But we can't because someday we're going to be able to do all those things again and we don't want to waste time rediscovering how to do it. But we'll do it the Pax way, not the Earth way, because we know what the Earth way was like."

She worked for a while, lips pursed, silent, tugging at the reeds. I had never seen her angry, but of course she was angry enough to make and burn an Earthling during every spring festival.

"The Pax way," she repeated. "The parents didn't even tell us everything about the Earth way. Religion. Ideologies. Economics. War. Just words to us! They didn't trust us with those things. They're dead and gone, and they still decide how we live and how much we can know, because they thought they knew better than us, and they left us impaired, and worst of all we know we're impaired. All those books we copied from the computers before they failed, that's a tiny fraction of what there is to know, a very tiny fraction. I once saw a mention of a library on Earth with a million books."

I thought about that, about what there was to know, how to learn it, and who to learn it from, while she finished the lower part of the basket—about all the things we'd like to know if we knew they existed. "The bamboo is trying to talk to us about opposites," I said. "I think we ought to answer."

She looked up, suddenly less angry. "Opposites. I would love to talk to the bamboo about opposites. Or anything." She set down her tools, put the reeds for the upper part in a vat to soak, and we left.

On the way, we passed Zoe.

"I'm sorry about . . . about Snow," she said.

I thanked her, and then I hugged her because she seemed to be expecting it—and I liked it.

I looked her right in the face. "Leave Fitzgerald and come live with me."

She stood petrified, then shook her head. "Oh, I know it's hard when children die."

"I've wanted this for a long time. I want to live with you. I'll be better for you than Fitzgerald could be. I love you. You'll see. I'll make you happy."

She didn't answer right away. Thinking it over? She looked away. "I love you, too. I . . . I'll think about it. I will. You're a good man, Higg. I'll . . . I'll think about it."

I knew she wouldn't, but I let her go and watched her walk away. She'd always be around, she might even come to my bed again, but she'd never stay. She'd said she'd think about it just to be kind.

I had forgotten that Sylvia stood next to me and tried to think of how to explain myself, but she just took me by the hand and talked about the latest Glassmaker archaeology and about the way the city had been enlarged over time as we walked on toward the bamboo display.

We examined the flowers. The white ones had died and dried out. The dark ones had died and become a wet mess. Some thistles were alive, some dead. Black and white, up and down, wet and dry, dead and alive. Obvious opposites. We found Raja and reviewed our idea and began to work.

At the base of a white-flower stem we buried a spoon of acid from the lab, and at the base of a black stem, an alkali. We set an ember and a piece of ice against two opposite stems, small enough not to hurt the plant but large enough to be noticed. We planted a tulip roots-up and another roots-down. We dug holes and left one dry and filled the other with water. I carved a horizontal slash on one stem, a vertical on its neighbor. We wrapped white cloth around a black stem, black cloth around a white stem. We planted fertile seeds and sterile seeds.

And as we worked, we talked about other opposites that we could not express. Happy and sad. Earth and Pax. Young and old. Day and night. Health and sickness. Plants get sick, too. They probably get some sort of infection in their stoma, the pores they use to breathe. A plant has millions of stoma on each leaf. Snow had millions of alveoli, the tiny sacs in her lungs. Plants can grow new leaves. She could not replace her lungs.

Plants, Raja said, produce an endless variety of compounds, including antibiotics. On Earth, genetic engineering had created fruits and grains that contained medicines. We already knew the bamboo made vitamins and other chemicals to keep us healthy. If it could create those, she said, it could create whatever we could ask it to do. Old Earth technology was almost dead. If we could ask for what we needed . . .

We were a long way from that level of exchange, but we might have made a start. Someday, all babies might survive.

Raja left. Sylvia and I gathered up our tools.

"Good work," she said. "We may not have said much, but I enjoyed saying it."

"Talking to the plants. I like it."

We were about to leave, but she paused.

"Each generation sets its own rules," she said. "The women of your generation have worked things out, and they have their own agreement about you. They haven't told me but I know about it and I'm sure they haven't told you but you've probably guessed. They prefer sterile husbands because they can control how often they get pregnant. Too often and they'd bear less healthy babies. And you have good genes, very good genes, and they think they're lucky to have you. They share you, they use you, and I think it's cruel and I know you don't like it but I can't interfere, and it's harder to do nothing than I ever thought it would be."

"I'm happy."

"Really?"

"I want to be happy, so I am."

She didn't look like she believed me, but she wasn't going to interfere.

I'd been up all night, so I went home to sleep, but I paused at Indira and Beck's house on the way. His father told me they were resting. "They really appreciate everything you've done. I do, too. You're a good man, Higg."

I thought about that at home as I stared at the afternoon Sun shining through the roof. I had a little of what I wanted. I could be kind if I tried. I could be happy if I didn't try to be someone else. Children loved me, and I had some fine children. Men didn't laugh at me anymore. Women still lied to me, but they wouldn't if I stopped asking them to do the impossible. Big, not-so-dumb, hairy animals knew I was one of them.

I would go out to share some truffle with Pitman soon, and I would sing him a sad song about fear and hope, failure and healing, about sweet and fresh sap in leaves evergreen with grief. Maybe I could teach the pack to coo along. Music the Pax way. Cross-species communication. They never did that on Earth. Singing fippolions. Dancing fippokats. Helpful, talkative plants with a sophisticated appreciation of abstract ideas. Good times. They can happen. Wait and see.

THE BAMBOO

Fire and ice? A duality? Perhaps. Consider the thermodynamics: rapid heat-producing oxidation of wood, and a change of state of water brought about by absorption of heat. They understand dualities. This is communication, for they did more than mimic me, they extended my idea.

How high they can count? Numbers are infinite. Can they grasp that idea? They miscalculated the equinox this year. Perhaps this indicates a weak intellect that would make them more malleable and more likely to remain with me.

Perhaps I can adapt the electric language of the first foreigners to a pigment-based language. I know they understand visual communications. How big would a variable pigment display need to be for their visual acuity?

We have so much to say. What communication system did the plants that trained them use? Why did they fail to bring their plants with them? Perhaps the plants on their spheres were at war. Perhaps they escaped. Do they understand that the future can be more than a new cycle, the future can be a new way to live, an opportunity for accomplishments never done before?

A newborn among my new foreigners has just died, a significant loss for slow-breeding animals. Animals deserve good health, and I can aid with nutrition and medications.

We bamboo once had a vast civilization, with flowers that bloomed in concert to create works of art, and with root networks that enmeshed knowledge that has been lost forever. Cooperation had allowed us to colonize the desert, the sea, the soil that freezes in the winter, even the coral plains. I have the chance to rebuild.

Springtime. I am free of the seasons, yet I feel the splendor of longer days and clement weather. Neighboring plants awaken, seasonal animals return. It is a time for celebration. I have iron. I have the stamina and will to grow into this adventure, but it will take time. I must be patient. These foreigners are only animals.

We can begin with simple counting: 0, 1, 2, 10, 11, 12, 20, 21, 22, 100.

TATIANA
YEAR 106–GENERATION 4

The Commonwealth of Pax is a voluntary association of the citizens of Pax. Any sentient beings who have expressed their sympathy with the spirit of our Commonwealth and are willing to share in its goals may declare themselves citizens.

—from the Constitution of the Commonwealth of Pax

Day 371, autumn. Georg had been looking for a specific locustwood tree to cut down when he found a corpse in a ravine. He ran to tell Rose, the new moderator, who asked me to help investigate. She's still unsure of herself, as young as my grandchildren and barely old enough to hold office, and she trusts me. I have served under four moderators, five counting Sylvia, and today for the first time I have betrayed one. I told Rose utter falsehoods, but my job as commissioner of the public peace comes first, and I've always had to lie for that job.

We put on hiking gear, arranged for a stretcher team to follow us—although with the harvest, we had few spare hands—and headed west toward the hills with Georg. Rain showers threatened, and my old hips ached with the weather. Rose had all the energy of youth and an anxious need to talk.

She thought Georg had probably found Harry rather than Lief because the corpse wore brightly colored clothes. Lief disappeared three months ago, Harry disappeared four days ago, and everyone worried endlessly about both of them.

"Lief wouldn't wear bright clothes," she said. "Lief had to camouflage himself. I mean, he was an explorer. Who knew what he was going to find? And he found a lot of things, didn't he? Harry liked in-between colors best, blue-green, red-violet, yellow-green. He called them interpretive colors, like his art. Interpretive art. Finding the spaces between things."

And so on. She spoke to quiet her nerves. Harry had been her close friend—and mine? I think so. Whether the body was Harry or Lief, we were about to lose all hope for one of them. I am no good at consoling people, and I hoped her talk would help her console herself, the way that remembering someone at a funeral eases grief. I believed I could handle my own feelings. Four days had allowed us to work out some of our emotions for Harry—that is, the emotions we expected to feel.

"This caught my eye," Georg said, pointing to a red-violet rag tied to a shrub next to the stream where he had found it, a stream leading toward one of the damp, rank ravines in the foothills of the west mountains. We had followed increasingly overgrown deer crab paths as smaller crabs in the brush rattled and hissed at us. A branch of the path covered by low, flat corals alongside the stream led into a ravine, a quagmire that herbivores without armored legs avoided. We wore oil-tanned leather gaiters and high-topped wood sole clogs, and carried spears. Georg led, Rose followed, and I guarded the rear. Slugs noticed us but we kept them at bay.

The remains lay on the ground between two trees. Purple slugs and lacy, clear slime hummed and writhed among soggy bones, rotting shreds of flesh, silverish beads, and rags of clothing—bright, in-between colored clothing. Rose took a tense breath, although her face remained bravely calm. I took a few steps closer and raised my spear against the slugs. What had killed him? A large predator would have dismembered him, but he lay neatly stretched out among the tree roots, limbs spread, face-up. Those were Harry's clothes, his hat, and his bushy brown hair. The glass beads of a bracelet lay on the moldy ground at a tree root. The thong, like his flesh, had been mostly eaten away. Incised bright orange and pink beads were scattered among the wrist bones.

Had he fallen from a heart attack? Despite his youth, he had heart trouble. A poisonous lizard bite? Poison lizards liked quaggy woods. But why had he flopped down like a man enjoying a cozy bed? Harry could be theatrical. Or drunk or drugged. I walked slowly around the body. And then I noticed.

The ground was covered with tree roots, and one arched out of the soil next to the heap of wrist bones and beads, and its bark had recently been worn off in one spot. As I bent to look, a slug sprang humming from poor Harry's esophagus. I stabbed it and held my breath against the putrid whiff. The root at his other wrist was draped in a tatter of skin. I moved it with my spearhead and saw the same mark on the bark. Was that damp shred actually human skin, or was it a wide leather strap? I poked it again and studied the texture. Lizard skin, probably gecko, tough as it comes. What could that mean?

I stood to inspect his ankles. Rose, several meters from the corpse, had turned away, retching and, I think, sobbing, and Georg was comforting her, holding a kerchief.

Harry's half-eaten gaiters, clog laces, and socks lay in a wet tangle, but a root near his ankle showed a wear mark, and the root at the other ankle was draped by a half-digested scrap of leather. The heels of Harry's clogs had dug into the mucky soil again and again. Moisture and four days had softened the marks, but there they were, deep. All around the body, dead leaves and sticks had been shoved aside as Harry struggled. He had been tied down and fed live to the slugs.

I backed away toward Rose, turned, and fought a wave of nausea. I hoped I was imagining things. I looked again, my kerchief over my mouth. No, it was obvious.

"I hope it wasn't an eagle," Rose said after taking a deep, shaky breath. "It wasn't an eagle, was it?"

I considered my answer. I have trained moderators to expect me to answer slowly. Was she trying to deflect suspicion? I couldn't imagine Rose hurting anyone intentionally, but someone had killed Harry. Or something? No, no animal could or would do that.

"It's so sad," she said, "dying and then being . . . eaten like that."

"Eagles would take apart the bones," I said.

"A lizard?" Georg asked.

I inspected the body again. I saw no clear footprints around it besides mine, but I saw what might have been some indistinct ones, several days old. Nearby, half-hidden by a dead coral bush, was an empty truffle jar. Harry drank a bit, chewed coca seeds, and ate lotus roots, although he tried to conceal all that; and, in truth, he used them moderately. We had discussed it, he and I, and we found no disagreement on that or many other subjects. It would slander his good name to allow people to think that he died of intoxication.

But I allowed it. The crew with the stretcher came and, with difficulty, separated him from the slugs and slime and took him home. We mourned at the Meeting House and will bury him tomorrow. I should have told someone the truth. Instead I studied the sad faces and work-reddened hands of the mourners, wondering who did it. Who could? After almost forty years of working as commissioner of public peace and seeing things that neighbors do not know about each other, I have learned I can't enter people's heads to know why they sometimes abuse each other or steal from each other. At times I have not understood my own actions.

Murder. I had to check the spelling of that word because I have never written it before. "The unlawful killing of one human being by another, especially with premeditated malice," says the crime manual in my office—that is, the little guardhouse near the west gate, a private place to talk to people when I have to. Malice. Harry had struggled. Hard. I hope his heart gave out fast.

I have never investigated a murder before. The Earth methods prescribed in the manual won't work on Pax, of course. I don't know whom to trust, so I have told no one. Not even the moderator, and I want to trust Rose. How would Pax react if I announced that Harry was tortured to death? A public investigation would spread panic and make the guilty person even more furtive.

I should go to bed, but I won't sleep well. My consolation has always been to write down my thoughts each night, to empty my secrets onto paper and then burn them.

My husband has seen me sleepless before. He'll probably talk to me as we stare at the stars sparkling through the roof. He's working with a recently found meteorite, a kilo of fairly pure iron we can use for tools, compasses, and nutrition: a treasure. We can talk about the possibilities, and he can help me forget the here and now. My first marriage was a mistake, but with him, I can share almost everything, and when he senses that I must keep a secret, he merely says, "Ah," as if he's discovered a pleasant surprise. Sometimes we both laugh, but not tonight. I can't.

Day 372. The facts: Harry disappeared five days ago. He left for a morning stroll to plant bamboo seeds. His absence wasn't noted until the next morning, and a search found nothing because we believed he had gone in another direction—how did he get to the ravine? He had no obvious enemies, although Pax surges like a spring river with squabbles, pointless arguments, imagined insults, real insults, jealousies, grudges, childhood rivalries maintained over decades, family aggressions, sexual tensions, and gossip—endless gossip. Do the gossipers know how much I admired Harry?

Fistfights occur, mostly among boys and young men, although girls and women can be violent, too. I ignore fights if the injuries are minor and no one complains. But no one ever kills anyone.

I hope to eliminate suspects one by one. It takes two hours to walk to the ravine, two hours to walk back. Additional time would have been required to immobilize him. The killer may have stayed to be sure he died and perhaps to observe his death. No one has ever been killed by slugs and slime, so I don't know how long that would take. In all, though, the killer would be gone at least for a full pass of Galileo. Who couldn't account for their time? And who would want to torture him or anyone to death? Is this related to Lief's disappearance?

"The more you know about the victim, the more you know about the criminal," says my crime manual. I have seen allusions to a vast body of information about criminal investigations on Earth, ranging from scientific databases to popular fiction. Crime fiction? Earth was strange.

I have one slim manual copied in occasionally illegible handwriting from the computers before they broke down, a book not meant for general readership because it talks about human nature in a way that many on Pax would find disturbing. I find it disturbing. I'm glad I'm not on Earth. This book answers a lot of my questions about the Parents.

So I tried to learn about Harry. His mother is grieving ostentatiously and said she couldn't bear to clean his home. Rose and I did it first thing this morning. She met me at his door with puffy eyes, looking frail. We exchanged hugs, as usual, hers tighter than usual. What was wrong?

She had dressed appropriately for a funeral in old clothes, a wrap-around skirt of coarse brown fabric from the old village whose frayed edges had been bound and patched repeatedly, and a much-scuffed kat leather vest, the fur worn off long ago but the green color lingering. She had tied up her bouffant hair, brown like her skirt, in an old scarf. Strings of silver seeds used as beads, the marker for Generation 6, hung from her neck, wrists, and belt, so many that she rattled. But what did that tell me? Little or nothing.

My own clothes were also properly old. My generation, Generation 4, has no marker, but I had worn my oldest bamboo jewelry, pieces the Children had made when they first arrived, so old that the color had worn off some of them. A bamboo diadem that had once belonged to Sylvia held my hair in place.

As we ducked under the doorway to enter, I noted the way Rose moved. She looked around the house as intensely as I did but was distracted first by one thing, then by another, as if something had a meaning she could not bear, or as if the next thing had an even more compelling meaning. Harry's things spoke to her. And to me.

I had been inside before, in the small dome near the east wall, so his lack of housekeeping did not surprise me: clothes here and there, several racks of drying sheets of art paper, stacks of sketches, a frame of half-finished lace, baskets of mosaic tiles, baskets of beads, pots of paint with brushes carefully cleaned alongside them, a wood carving of a kat ready for polish, another piece of wood carved into a stamp for fabric or clay, a vase of wilting flowers sitting on a table, a bucket of clay, and more.

Harry had declared in his early teens that he would be the artistic bridge between Pacifists and Glassmakers, a ridiculous self-aggrandizement except that he had not lied. The Glassmakers' style shone everywhere, their love of light, their distinctive curves, their colors and patterns, their script. Not copies, though. Harry made interpretations. He maintained the Glassmaker Museum, and his familiarity with its contents showed.

Nothing needed immediate attention, like food that might attract lizards or worse, a kat expecting his return, a chamber pot that needed to be emptied. Nor were things as disorganized as they seemed. I looked to see if some last-minute visitor had left behind footprints or a clue. I stripped his bed, ostensibly to send the sheets and blankets to the laundry, looking for telltale hairs or marks. Nothing.

Rose attended to the clothing on the floor. She tried to sort things and gave up each time. "Aunt Tatiana . . ."

My attention had been caught by a bone-white ceramic goblet with Glassmaker curves and inscribed with Glassmaker numbers from zero to ten, the first of the Glassmaker writing that the bamboo had taught us. Harry had interpreted the symbols in Pacifist handwriting. Once, about two years ago, he had sat down with me in my damp stone office to explain the meaning of that goblet and other pieces of art he had brought with him, then taken me outside to explain Glassmaker architecture and what it told us about the Glassmakers, and it was as if I had never opened my eyes before. His own eyes had been dilated with lotus. It seemed to make him cheerfully patient. I couldn't object to that.

"Yes, dear?" I answered Rose. She looked up from the floor where she sat, eyes round with fear. Of what?

"At the funeral, what should I say? What should I do about his family? About everything?"

Reasonable questions: she had never presided at a funeral before. I gathered my thoughts into simple, clear instructions. "Your job is to praise him. Use the traditional words, then add anything you can, and invite others to do the same. Listen to what people say. They want to be listened to, and they can always tell if you're listening." She was listening to me. "Talk about his art, for example. His friendship. The more specific and heartfelt, the better. Don't talk for more than fifteen minutes. I'll gesture like this"—and I brushed my left ear with my right hand—"if it's time to stop." She does love to talk. "Keep centered on him. Don't talk about replacing him."

"Replacing him? We can't do that."

"We have to. His work mattered. It will be hard to find someone as talented, and you shouldn't start looking right away. But the art mustn't stop here."

She burst out laughing; grief sometimes makes people laugh inappropriately. I sat down on the floor beside her. "You liked his art!" she said as tears welled in her eyes. "Not everyone did. Not everyone liked him."

Who? Clues, I wanted clues. "The more I knew him," I said slowly, "the more I liked him. When we realized he was missing . . ." I tried to find the right word. My first husband often called me unemotional, and he was right, so I have tried to become more warm, at least in my speech. "I felt guilty because I thought I should have noticed sooner."

"I know, I know. I should have noticed, too. I spent the whole day in the yam fields and was too tired to visit him."

That would exculpate her. And the entire yam field crew, for that matter.

"I was going to marry him," she said, smiling and weeping at once. "We were going to announce it soon."

A jealous would-be lover might have killed him.

"You've been very brave," I said. No one loves more acutely than a bride-to-be. How could I tell this wet-eyed girl that her beloved's death had been a nightmare? I took a characteristic pause, and finally said, "I can't imagine who wouldn't like him."

"Not everyone sees the need for interpretive art."

Who? I wished with all my heart I could replay people's reactions to him, and then realized I could make it happen. After another pause, I said, "We should organize a show of his art as a memorial."

She grinned and wept even harder and nodded yes. "Art was his best."

Best. Her generation has created an idea of individual excellence that some people ridicule as "bestism." Everyone is the best at something unique, although their thing may be only a shade different from that of the next person. Ideally, this thing is surplus to survival, like fine arts or elaborate baking, although surpassing skill at a necessary task will do, like casting flawless glass construction bricks. Rose makes more varieties of candles than I could have imagined: colored, scented, shaped, or suited to some specific task or occasion. They burn steady and smokeless no matter how plain or fancy they are. Bestism has enriched Pax. I admire it.

We cleaned up a little and spent most of our time planning the art exhibit. She had specific ideas about lighting. Then it was time for the funeral. We walked to the plaza, reviewing her duties.

I can remember when the plaza had been heaped with debris from a three-story tower that stood there during Glassmaker times. We cleaned it when I was a young adult, reusing the stone, brick, and glass to make the plaza. We needed a big space for public events because the population had grown. The Meeting House, despite additions, was too small. So we created a wide area paved with a mosaic of glass block and edged by thick, waist-high walls of brick and stone that had once been the debris of the tower. A garden of cacti was tethered to the walls.

Pacifists in old clothes had begun to fill the benches. Harry's mother was not coming, said her husband, Lightning Junior. I asked why. She would have been the center of attention, and she had a love of attention like her son. But before he answered, I had realized that absence might be the most prominent presence of all.

"Daisy insists that she killed him," he explained with a sigh, long ago resigned to the melodramatic personalities closest to him.

"Killed him?" She had to have meant that metaphorically—hadn't she?

"If she blames herself, then she can't blame . . ." He struggled to finish the sentence: she couldn't blame Harry for fatal irresponsibility, which I knew was not true, and I had known that lie would hurt people. Now Lightning, a kind and gentle man, ached right in front of me, pain that I had inflicted.

"There's no point in blame," I said, weak words of comfort and yet another lie because there was someone to blame, I just didn't know whom.

Still, I would have to talk to Daisy to see exactly what she meant.

Harry's basket, closed, stood near the stage in front. I met my husband and we added the flowers he had brought to the piles around it. There were even floating flowers on strings tied to the basket, although they are hard to find this time of year. We found space on a stone bench at the side of the plaza near the front, where Rose could see me and I could see everyone.

She opened the ceremony with a voice that quavered but carried. "Numbers are a measure, and we are less now."

Except for a nurse, two hospitalized children, one guard minding the front gate, and Daisy, everyone had come. I studied them one by one, except for those too young or too ill to trek to the ravine, trying to remember whom I had seen, and when and where, on the day Harry died.

"This loss, the loss of his art, is a loss to the future of Pax," Rose was saying, "and his loss is a loss to my future. His laugh was the same laugh I wanted to hear in the voices of my children."

Hathor and Forrest whispered to each other, brother and sister who seemed to want to be identical twins rather than mere fraternal twins with their hair worn in identical short curls that made their round cheeks and fat hips look disproportionate. Sometimes they entertained themselves by waging gossip campaigns to wreck a romance or ruin a vocation. I have had to intervene occasionally, and I have been a target of their rumors at least once, but I did nothing, knowing it would merely inflame them. Nearby, Nevada dried the tears of her daughter, Harry's age and generation. A disappointed lover?

Lief's wife rose to say something, failed, and sat again, surrounded by her children and grandchildren.

Lightning rose and faced her. "The only thing worse than how I feel now is if I knew nothing about the fate of someone I loved. I grieve for you and your family more than anything. Everyone does, and we won't stop looking until we find Lief."

People murmured approval. Lief had beaten his wife and children until I intervened, another of the secrets I carry for my job.

The ceremony went on for some time because Harry had many

friends and admirers who wished to speak. After the burial, I went to see Daisy. She lived not far from Harry and kept a colorful house. She had, as usual, dressed in sumptuously embroidered clothes, but her face looked exhausted. Her hair was bushy like his but, of course, dyed green, and the dark brown roots were flecked with gray. Her face looked like an older, female version of her son's: full lips, cleft chin, curved nose, arched eyebrows—nothing I hadn't known, but suddenly her appearance seemed unnerving.

"I'm very sorry," I said.

She muttered, "Thank you," with narrowed eyes. Everyone knows what my job is. I might have come to deliver an ultimatum for her to change her behavior or else face public charges. And perhaps she thought that I disliked her, and I do act coldly to her sometimes, but I don't dislike her, although her personality and mine don't mesh. I respect her medical work sincerely, and her need to be the center of attention has motivated her to solve problems and gain the gratitude of the ill, bestism of a sort, and a very good sort.

She works with the rainbow bamboo to protect our health. This spring, she and the bamboo found the cure to the scarlet fever epidemic that killed seven people and would have killed many more of us, and they rescued us from disaster. She worked even though she was ill, too, knowing that by going without rest she might be killing herself, and she earned an eagle feather and deserved the title "hero." Over the years, she and the bamboo have saved many lives and solved much suffering. For example, they created the salve that soothes my chronic skin rash, a triviality that had won my daily gratitude long before the epidemic, which I spent in bed delirious with fever.

I don't dislike her. I dislike the bamboo, Stevland, even though it does so much for our health and our crops. It earned a human name in honor of its importance, and pretty soon we started calling it "him" as if he were a man and not a hermaphrodite plant.

I hadn't disliked him as a child. I remember Uncle Higgins's first efforts to communicate, when Stevland gave lessons in the same math that I was learning in school. I felt a childish affinity for the bamboo that increased as his ability to express himself acquired more sophistication and mirrored the progress of my studies. I learned Glassmade, the language that the bamboo uses, and as a young adult, I began to communicate with him. And soon I stopped, and I have never wanted to deal with Stevland since. But that's not Daisy's fault. My job this morning was to discover who had murdered her son.

"It was sad how he died," I said.

"Planting bamboo seeds," she said with bottomless regret in her voice. Stevland likes to have his seeds dispersed to grow outposts. She sank into a chair, half sobbing, half whining melodramatically. "Harry died for Stevland!"

"He wanted Harry to plant his seeds?" I found myself a chair.

"I should have planted them myself. Stevland asked me, and I made Harry go, poor Harry. I went to the baths, and then I went to the clinic. And then . . . You didn't know that he used coca seeds, no one did. I should have made him stop. He died all alone, a loss, a terrible, tragic loss." She looked at me defiantly through her rehearsed words and tears as if to say that I should have known and made him stop.

I could confirm her activities with the bath custodian and the medic. The melodrama continued.

"I can't face Stevland again. He would remind me of Harry. Oh, poor Harry!"

Harry had made many of the decorations and utensils in her home, and his designs had been embroidered on her dress, so she had no escape from him. I asked a few more questions about his friends "in case they need special consolation," listened to a speech that would have been self-pitying except that the truth was worse than her presumptions, and offered my sympathy again, trying to assure her with all sincerity that she hadn't killed her son. I left.

I stopped at the gift center, sat in a stall, and breathed the incense that masked the earthier smells. Stevland had an inquisitorial interest in Pacifist behavior, which he had wanted to regulate by directing my work as commissioner. His interest could help me now, and my dislike for him hardly mattered as much as finding the killer.

A little after lunch, after talking with the bathhouse custodian, the medic, and the head yam farmer, legitimate work but avoidance mechanisms all the same, I sat down in a little greenhouse, which, in addition to the clinic, is where Stevland "talks." The roof was clear bricks. Leaves cascaded from the very top of a wide, pale stem that rose in the center of the room. The stem, seemingly devoid of pigment, carried Stevland's messages, and the stem had grown bigger over the two—no, three decades since we had spoken last.

A slight perfume embellished the warm air. I sat at the writing table and fidgeted with the lacquered whitewood palette. A pot of cream ink stood ready. The felt brushes and cleaning rags were clean. What would I say? "I'm back, you nosy tulip"? That would be inappropriate.

Words began to form on the stem. Thousands of cells twitched tiny beads of pigment into view—red chromoplasts, dozens in each cell— to create Glassmade triangles and lines that took shape like objects drawing near through a fog. When I was young, the sight had amazed us all.

"I now welcome Tatiana again, happy you serve Pacifists well for many years."

At each node on the stem, tiny black dots almost too small for human eyes to see, Stevland's eyes, thousands of them, were trained on me.

"You and I now relate with mutualism," I wrote, wasting no time on niceties. I had not written Glassmade for a long time, and struggled with vocabulary and grammar although it is a simple language; in fact, he says he doubts he learned it thoroughly before the Glassmakers left. But it serves. I held the board up for Stevland to see. He answered quickly.

"I happy make-you mutualism. I remember long ago we discover mutualism difficult. I remember I perhaps be-me tulip."

That stopped me. Stevland had learned humility, or at least how to fake it.

He continued, "I learn truffle hurts not peace." That had been the last straw, when he had wanted me to eliminate truffle on the grounds that we did not understand our own biology well enough to use alcohol responsibly. Truffle can be used irresponsibly, but it wasn't Stevland's business. Nor was I about to ban the boat races, as if I could, after Tiffany drowned. Nor would I participate in schemes to identify and tranquilize overly aggressive Pacifists, nor report all misdemeanors to Stevland and consult with him over punishments, nor order marriages between individuals that he deemed most genetically favorable, including my own. I chose my first husband to spite Stevland.

"Tulips learn not," I wrote, able to do my own sweet-talking. "You learn every day."

"New roots every day. Pacifists teach-me much."

Enough sweet talk. "I come with great sorrow," I wrote. "I come with secret of my work. Someone five days ago kill Harry. I desire know killer. I desire you help-me protect well."

I may as well have said plans existed to chop Stevland down. Sentences began appearing and disappearing so fast I could hardly read them. "Great sorrow, yes, great surprise. Great loss of peace. Pacifists never kill fellow Pacifists. Behavior create imbalance. Great sorrow, yes. You will tell-me all of kill." I began to write. "Pacifist lives equal to my life," he added. "Perhaps killer act in emotion and not kill someone again?"

I answered, "Unknown," and tried to finish my first few sentences about the murder.

"Killing be not plan perhaps?" he flashed.

"Yes, be-it plan," I wrote. "You will not interrupt me and I will tell-you all." I needed to consult the dictionary many times. I filled one board, let him study it, and wrote more, six boards in all. He did not respond immediately. "I now finish tell-you all," I finally wrote.

He responded after another wait. "I see slugs kill small animals. Killing surely be sorrowful sorrowful slow for large animal. But slugs be-them not intelligent, we be-us intelligent, and making sorrow be-it wrong for intelligences. I learn from wrongnesses, and will prevent more."

He didn't sound like the Stevland I had known, but he hadn't lost his hectoring. After a long pause, he said, "Harry be-him artist, and buried today. We talk Harry and I of Glassmakers and art. Art be-it happiness like rainbows on bark, thus I will grow-me art using him from cemetery and extend-me his happiness tomorrow with artful flowers."

If I liked Stevland more, I might have appreciated that tribute, of using Harry as fertilizer to create flowers—what would Harry have thought?

"I need-me knowledge of who five days ago have time to kill," I said. At his request—no, insistence—I explained the nature of a criminal investigation, and added something about the nature of teamwork. He said he would review his memories overnight as capillary pressure reached all parts of his roots.

"Help and harm make duality," he said. "We understand-us perhaps, and understanding make balance. Large and slow plant, small and quick Pacifist, I and you will find killer. I thank you because you today come and ask-me help. You be-you wise commissioner for Pacifists and for me."

He had learned flattery over the years. So had I. Perhaps a relation-ship can be based on flattery. "You help us Pacifists with many prob-lems," I wrote. "You and I will find killer. I happy you and I talk and I desire more talk without sorrow." I added, "Tomorrow we make-us much mutuality." I wished him water and sunshine. He wished me warmth and food.

I had time before dinner to join a work team that had often included Harry. We went out to the rocky ridges a little northwest of the city to harvest chrysalises from butterfly bushes for their flavored oil and to check them for parasites or other problems. The weather threatened rain, but the mellow light made the fields and forest look richer, full of notes of ocher and gold—the cones high up on the pines, the leaves on the onions and tulips in the fields along the riverbanks. The pods on lentils and locustwoods rattled in the wind, nearly dry. It hadn't been a great year for crops, but we would make it through the winter with-out hardship.

Often my presence dampens conversation, but I encouraged them to talk by broaching the irony that we had led normal lives on the day he died.

"I was weaving," Nevada said. Weaving is her best. "You know, it has meaning, weaving does. It symbolizes the connections every Pacifist has with each other. A single missing thread and you ruin a brocade. Harry, he was a warp thread, dyed in the fiber." Et cetera. Bestism can inspire talkativeness. She eventually named everyone in the weaving room that day, and it included her daughter.

If that and all the other comments of the members of the work group prove true, I can rule out twenty-one suspects.

Now, in my office, I can see a stand of bamboo through the open door. My anger with Stevland so long ago might have been little more than displaced anger over my job as commissioner. I could not quite bear to blame Sylvia, my great-grandmother. When I was just a teenager, she called me to her deathbed, her body swelling as her kidneys failed her. She gave me a knife that had been made on Earth with a blade almost as long as my hand. I had been impressed by the steel itself, shiny and wonderful, but then she told me she had killed Vera with it. She described the days leading up to the revolt, a long story, and she got angry remembering it. I couldn't imagine the things she told me about, beatings and killings and rape. No one had ever told us about it.

"I did not, not, not want to die there," she said, "did not want to lead a hard, ugly life under the dictates of lying murderous Parents and finally be carried in rags through desolate fields and be left to feed the greedy, stupid snow vine." The Parents had betrayed the Children.

And finally she told me:

"We're here in Rainbow City now, and it's the job of the moderator to help us choose what to do as a group and to do things the Pax way. A moderator can't keep the peace between individuals. I've tried, and it's too much. Moderators must be public. But Tatiana, you can be private, you can keep secrets, I know you. This knife is your first secret."

So she appointed me commissioner of public peace, and I was too young and flattered to realize that the job would eventually set me apart from everyone, and that the secrets I learned would make me freeze my heart to protect it. Still, the job must be done and done well. I kept working for a time when I was young simply to spite Stevland, to prove that he was only a plant and couldn't control me.

I still have the knife and keep it sharp. I wear it almost always, slipped into a boot or tucked inside my vest in a sheath of thin, tough lizard

skin. When Great-Grandmother died, everyone wondered where her
steel knife was. They still do.

Day 373. Stevland had been paying less attention to daily activities than
I thought and supplied less information about who was where than I
had hoped, but we ruled out twenty-two more people today. Added to
the children, ill, incapacitated, and individuals that I had already ruled
out, I am left with 160 suspects, almost two-thirds of all Pax, although
Stevland had some distant roots he wished to check.

"Investigation resembles hunting," he enthused. "Animals hunt-them
food, most plants not. Many times Pacifists tell-me hunting give-them
pleasure. Now I understand. We hunt killer using stealth, using secrets,
and for good end, not for gluttony."

Someone tapped on the door. "Whenever you're ready. No hurry,"
Jersey called amicably from the other side of the door. She is translating
an Earth book for Stevland, *A History of Mathematics,* and spends an
hour most afternoons with him.

"We hunt killer with ideas and information," he said, "and with intelligence. I grow more roots. I give-you more intelligence, give-you blue
and small fruit high on stem near office gate. Good for animal brain."

Intelligence fruit? I had to think about that. Stevland gives fruit tai-
lored for specific individuals to cure infections or ease childbirth or
provide extra nutrients or enzymes, among so many other things. But
he has always whined about our limited mental capacity. Starting with
my smallest suspicion, I asked, "Perhaps you explain-me why intelligence fruit now and not such fruit yesterday."

The answer came slowly. "Best intelligence increase be good
nutrition for children. Balance create best health, and extra intelligence through fruit create unbalance. Sickness create imbalance,
thus medicine seek balance. Body enhance medicine because body
also seek-it balance. Extra intelligence fruit opposite of medicine
fruit. I test-it intelligence chemical in fescue with fippokats and learn
of risks and benefits. You Tatiana have strong health, so you have

strong balance for such risks. You will not give-others fruit, perhaps. Search for killer balance risk from fruit, perhaps."

The risk would balance the need. He thinks like that, in terms of balance, as if in some root he places ideas on a tiny double scale. Such a grand intelligence. Would he have told me about the risk without asking? Doubtful. He knows what was best for us—he has always been sure of that.

"I make fruit carefully," he added. "I examine your physiology with detail. You perhaps talk with medics of hip pain."

How did he know that? He hadn't been watching everyone, but he had been watching me. I answered very slowly, after I had entertained some irrational thoughts, and they all led to the sight of Harry's corpse and the feel of Rose's anguish and the tragedy of Pax's loss and the danger we were in and what my duties were.

"I eat fruit today," I said. A taste, at least. Perhaps we could find the killer before it did me too much harm. Stevland wouldn't want to harm me, would he? "Jersey be here." I needed to exit gracefully before I said something confrontational that would make my job harder, no matter how much he deserved it.

"Jersey tell-me Earth mathematics memories. I learn amazing amazing much. Human create book intelligence, not fruit intelligence or root intelligence. Animals exceed limits creatively cleverly, learning rather than repeating. I feel surprise."

I did not feel flattered. "Water and sunshine."

"Warmth and food."

Jersey had found a bench nearby and was studying her book—patiently, of course. She has an odd kind of patience, more like timidity, and a kind of generosity that approaches appeasement. It makes sense knowing how Lief treated her as a child, but I might also be seeing things that aren't there because I know about her childhood. She treats her own children well as far as I can discover.

She sat on a bench made of a split locustwood log with a checkerboard grain. The ends had been carved to look like a cluster of locustwood seedpods. Stevland had negotiated a deal with the locustwood community, and the bench commemorated our pact. The trees agreed to give us strong, decorative wood and seedpods containing potassium and the amino acid methionine in exchange for limited logging, protection against pests and competitors, and seeds sown in ideal locations. Stevland thought the trees were eager to deal and shrewdly forward-looking. So is Stevland. As our negotiator with plants and crops, he has made himself essential. People trust him to help us.

Jersey looked up slowly as I approached, and a hint of a frown passed across her face. I'm used to that kind of reaction. Maybe she thought I had news about her father, Lief.

"Stevland enjoys the book," I said.

She smiled, looking relieved, and nodded. Her pretty little nose has fewer freckles than when she was a child, and now she has two boys, freckled and blond like her. You can tell she's originally a blonde by her hair's bright shade of green.

"It's hard to read to him," she said as she stood. "Glassmade doesn't have a big vocabulary. Well, it must, though, because Glassmakers did a lot of science." She giggled self-consciously.

Math is her best, math so far advanced that it becomes abstract, and she enjoys teaching it. Nevada had woven the rust-red brocade for her sheath dress that incorporated multicolored numbers and symbols in its pattern. The style seems a bit cute to me, but they both love the dress and it is very well made.

"He knew square roots," she said. "On Earth, they've been using them for four thousand years. That shocked him. And the name fascinated him. No one told him we call them roots, and roots mean a lot to him."

"Shocked him?" I felt myself smile.

"Yes. He can do all sorts of analytic geometry and tangents because of how he grows, so that was easy, but now we're up to imaginary numbers and complex roots. I don't know how to tell you how surprised he is, especially by how useful they are. Wait till I get to non-Euclidean geometry."

Even I had a vague idea of what an imaginary number was, something about negative square roots, and Stevland hadn't. "He says he's learning a lot," I said. "He's amazed."

Jersey is on the suspect list. I tried to imagine her carrying out the murder. She's small and slight, but if Harry was drunk, she could overpower him. I couldn't imagine the two being alone together, but that may speak to my imagination. And, selfishly, I didn't want someone who was shocking Stevland with the accomplishments of human intelligence to be the murderer. He has non-Euclidean geometry yet to learn from us.

The intelligence fruit was waiting for me, high on a stem growing just inside the rarely used west gate near my office. To pick it, I had to climb to the top of the wall and lean over. I probably wouldn't have noticed it if Stevland hadn't told me about it.

I ordinarily eat two bamboo fruits, one early in the morning and one in midafternoon. More makes me light-headed, less makes me sluggish. I still had doubts, but I ate a blue fruit and waited. It was faintly bitter but mostly tasteless. Nothing happened until evening.

My husband and I went at Luxset to the Meeting House for Harry's posthumous art show. On the way, the city seemed more interesting, more detailed. I spotted fippokat runs between the houses and low smudged handprints on doors of homes where children lived. Overhead, bamboo branches were arranged to capture the most sunlight possible, leaves arranged in whorls that diminished in length along stems, making efficient cone shapes. Jersey could probably write the equation.

When we arrived, I noticed new things about the people, about who really paid attention to whom or to what: to children or food or the art itself. They stood in patterns like the groups in a flock of moths, the cliques and age groupings and work teams, some with hard feelings against each other, and they all looked at me as I entered as if I knew everything they wanted to hide, and I wished I did.

The Meeting House now includes two smaller domed buildings in addition to the main one, connected by wide arched halls. Rose had arranged the art carefully on tables in front of bays to take advantage of the light. The main room housed household objects.

I pretended to look at the art, hoping to conceal some eavesdropping, but I actually looked at the art in spite of my plans and saw things I had never seen before. The fur of a carving of a kat mimicked the texture of the stones and bricks of a house. A square pottery box, incised and glazed, showed Pacifists and Glassmakers dancing together, and I realized that the pattern around the rim was their swirling footsteps. I even recognized the dance. The carved lid to a child's chamber pot made me laugh out loud, but no one was in a mood to laugh, so no one looked pleased.

"It's the pattern," I explained. It looked at first like the intricate pattern of lines on a Glassmaker tile mural. Subtle differences in the height of certain parts of the pattern revealed a small, low plant. "It's a poop plant," I said. "Camouflaged." Curious people looked and saw it themselves for the first time, and a few chuckled. I pointed to the other art. "A box waltz. A house kat." Slowly, more smiles.

"Harry was a good man," I said loudly. I realized I could move my investigation forward if I kept talking. "I'll miss him. I'll miss his art." I gestured at the white goblet. "I wish I could have done something to help him. I wish I had known." I had tears in my eyes. That surprised me. And I realized that the intelligence fruit had taken effect. Did being smarter make me less cold?

My outburst affected people. They began talking about what they were doing that day and about what they could have done. I could listen to two, even three conversations at once and remember what I heard. I eliminated sixty people. And I made the evening a real tribute to Harry, and a chance for the fabric of Pax to heal a bit, although when I find the killer I will tear it open wider than ever.

And now, back in my office, I have been studying my crime manual. Generally, murderers fall into two classes. The first kills for passion— in the heat of an argument with a loved one, for example—and tends not to repeat the crime. The second type kills for pleasure. These people plan the attack, use restraints, and control the event carefully. Pleasure killers will kill again.

Harry was killed by the second kind. I can't afford to waste days.

I wonder about Lief. Is he alive? Nearby? A schoolteacher had come to me fifteen years ago to say that she saw odd bruises on Lief's children. I confronted him, and his wife made excuses. He said nothing, and I agonized over how to proceed and whether to make a formal public complaint. But the next day he announced that he planned to go exploring alone, a foolhardy idea that no one could talk him out of. He left, headed due south. Had I sent him to his death? I lay awake for many winter nights wondering.

He returned the next spring with a tree-dwelling fipp on his shoulder and useful information about uncharted lands. The trip, he proclaimed, had changed him. His family had grown less subdued while he had been gone, and as far as I could observe, they remained happy. Perhaps he had changed. He organized more exploration trips that discovered many useful plants, animals, and resources, as well as an extraordinarily beautiful waterfall just over the east mountains that everyone has now visited at least once. The Glassmakers themselves had built a few domed buildings there, perhaps a resort.

But Lief never spoke to me again after the initial confrontation. He never looked me in the eye.

He's been missing for three months, and he could live off the land for that long.

Day 374. Rose, the moderator, was supposed to meet Hathor and Forrest for lunch but did not show up. They waited, then began to look for her, thoroughly miffed. I was about to talk to Stevland when I heard about their complaints. I immediately organized search parties.

"Maybe you're overreacting," Georg said. I was about to reply but he saw the look on my face. "Never mind. Sorry. I'll head a search party if you want."

What did he believe I was thinking? He had been fueling the furnace at the glass foundry when Harry died. It was a lengthy job involving teamwork, so he wasn't a suspect. His search party was out of the gate headed downriver in mere minutes.

I went to ask Stevland where Rose had been. After searching his roots, he said he had last seen her that morning outside the riverside gate with Roland, the fippmaster.

Roland had volunteered to join Georg's search party, bringing sniffing kats for what would seem to them like a game of hide-and-seek. I waited for his return in the Meeting House, aware that the blue fruit, which I had eaten again, made time move slowly and made remembering too easy. The suspect list still numbered one hundred and included Roland.

I had mixed emotions about him, and sharp memories.

Several years ago, after too much truffle, he and I snuck away from a late-night childbirth party at the Meeting House, and we hurried through the dark streets to the city walls. Early spring lizards peeped, looking for mates. He spread his fringed coat on the walkway on top of the wall, and we fumbled with ties and buttons and made love half-undressed.

The next morning, I blamed it on the truffle, on the fascination that fippmasters have, on Uncle Higgins's legend, on the lion pheromone that clings to his clothes and sexually excites humans, on anything I could think of. He was elegantly handsome, small, and strongly built with a lush beard, and he was an accomplished, exciting lover. But I could not excuse myself for having sex with a man in a different generation, his hair as green as his kats. I am the commissioner of public peace.

Maybe that was his main attraction: his age. The growth and success of Rainbow City has allowed younger generations to create in ways we could not imagine. Consider Harry. Young people are becoming what Sylvia had hoped for.

Several days later Roland and I met by chance outside the city and made love again in a little dale surrounded by budding wild tulips. Almost a year of "accidents" followed. I can't blame him. I'm responsible for what I do, but even now I don't know why I did it. It's a wonder no one noticed. Maybe it was the thrill of taking a risk and breaking the rule that bans sex between members of different generations.

Guilt finally stopped me. I said "enough," and he kissed my hands and said he would obey with regret, and then I felt guilty for stopping, and I wished I had someone to talk to about it—to talk to about all the secrets of my life and my job. Instead I write them down like this and then I burn my writing, and the ashes that fill a jar in a corner of my office serve as my confession.

So I waited for news about Rose, hours made bitter by memories and doubt.

The search party returned in the midafternoon. They had found nothing. Roland wanted to get fresh kats and try again. He hurried to take the tired animals to their hutches and get new ones, and I followed.

"Did you see Rose today?" I said, hoping I could somehow rule him out as a suspect.

"This morning . . . yes, Rose and I," he said. He talked in quiet, soothing tones, directing the sound at the kats, but his face was flushed and gleamed with sweat. "We went to the shed near the cotton fields. She was so lonely without Harry. I wanted to make her feel better, to feel loved, and we . . . we made love. Then she said she was going to pick flax from some thistles. She should have come back right away."

He set the kats down and called two others, urging them to come quickly. Rose was from the Bead Generation, not the Green Generation like Roland. I thought I felt anger, then realized it was jealousy.

"I don't know," he continued. "There aren't any eagles around, the lions tell me that, but we have to find her." He picked up the kats and looked at me. "We looked down one trail. Now we'll try the other. The path toward the pecan patch."

He almost ran out of the city. I hurried along with him down the path on the river bluff past onions and tulips until we reached the cotton field shed, trying to think only about finding her, but instead wondering whom Roland hadn't had sex with, and noticed how genuinely worried he was, but why? We followed another path and stopped at a fork. He set the kats down. He pulled Rose's nightshirt out of his backpack for them to sniff, then they sniffed around until they found her trail, which they followed into the woods.

We found Rose in a clearing dominated by quitch grass and low pines. She lay on the reddish-gray grass with one end of her belt around her neck and the other end tied to a pine branch that had apparently broken off from her weight. Next to her lay her basket. It looked as if she had dumped the thistles from her basket and stood on it, tied the belt to her neck and the branch, then jumped, and the branch broke.

The kats sniffed her, confused. Roland sank to his knees and called them to his arms, his voice tight with anguish. I approached her.

I saw marks on her neck right away, bruises and abrasions, especially the nape, showing that she had been strangled by a narrow cord or rope. Her bead-embroidered belt would have left different marks. I covered her blood-darkened face and bruised neck with my head scarf. I looked at her fingernails to see if she had scratched at her attacker, but they were clean. Washed? The grass was too tough to show any footprints or marks of struggle. I couldn't see where the branch had broken from the tree above and suspected it had been brought from somewhere else. This might mean the killer lacked the strength to lift the corpse to tie it to a real branch. Roland could have lifted her. Or Lief.

I realized I was stamping as I walked on the stiff, raspy grass, angry with the killer for killing again and with myself for being unable to protect Rose. I should have acted quicker. I had given the killer another chance.

Roland sat on the ground, head down. The kats in his arms rocked back and forth to comfort him. I went to the city to fetch a crew to take Rose home.

No one has ever committed suicide on Pax before, although some of the old and ill have sought euthanasia, but that's entirely different. Field teams left their work as we marched past with the stretcher, and they offered to help carry her or to run ahead with the news that she was coming. By the time we got to the gate, a hundred people waited.

"Why?" I heard that question whispered as we walked through the gate. At the bathhouse I recruited some weak-eyed matrons who would care for her body but who wouldn't study the marks on her neck. They were more likely to fuss over making her look nice. I left her corpse among the brick tubs filled with soapy water and the scent of wet cotton. Her mother, the former moderator, had died in the scarlet fever epidemic this past spring. Rose's father had heard the news before I came to visit him, and after seeing him, I urged his relatives and friends not to leave him alone, as if they hadn't realized that themselves. If I told him she had been murdered, would it ease his burden or add to it?

And then I was called to the Commonwealth Committee meeting.

Twelve people, including me, help the moderator with day-to-day decisions. I arrived a little late. The Committee had already decided that I should become the new moderator. It was the last thing I expected to hear.

"At least for the time being," Bartholomew added, and I couldn't tell if he was saying that to me or to the others. "You have the experience to handle the situation efficiently. Pax needs that."

Or maybe Bartholomew would make a good moderator: an older Greenie, a skilled woodworker, a widower who had never remarried and who seemed to find strength in solitude, a reservoir of good sense delivered with an exaggerated fussiness that made him disarming. I am far less likable. But I didn't argue. The position might give me opportunities to find the killer faster, and it was only temporary, in some ways in name only. I asked Bartholomew to help Rose's father and make arrangements for the evening's wake, asked the head of the Philosopher's Club to hold an open discussion on grief, and left to talk to Stevland.

"I now welcome Tatiana." The words appeared before I had the door closed and the brushes ready to write.

"Someone kill Rose," I scribbled, and then explained everything, including my own lack of timeliness, ignoring Stevland's interruptions about "sorrowful" or "wrongness replicated." I finished with, "You in morning see Roland and Rose. You will tell-me other observations."

We discussed suspects and their movements, and we reached two conclusions. First, the killer may have hidden his or her movements from Stevland as well as from Pacifists. Second, we could not rule out Roland. My crime manual says that criminals who act in an organized fashion are often sexually competent, charming, and stereotypically masculine. They may return to the crime scene, volunteer information, and anticipate being questioned. Of course, that was the case on Earth, but this was Pax.

"Roland lies perhaps," Stevland said. "I make-you fruit for truth. Lie be-it think twice. Fruit make thinking be-it only once, so thinking less smart. Bad imbalance, very bad, but very temporary. It will grow near smart fruit, with stripes."

"Perhaps you explain-me bad imbalance?"

"Less smart be-it bad because be-it less thinking," Stevland repeated unhelpfully. Intelligence fruit has been making me feel odd, so what could truth fruit do? But I will use this new fruit. The killer will kill again if I don't stop him or her.

At the Meeting House, Bartholomew and the Philosophers had done a fine job, and I complimented them. I asked Roland, who was suffering horribly, to see me first thing in the morning. Hathor and Forrest had decided that Rose had killed herself because her heart was broken over Harry's death—and the art show, which was still on display in the Meeting House, seemed to support the guesswork.

I talked with many people and eliminated two dozen suspects. It would have been easy to eliminate more if I hadn't wanted to avoid creating suspicion and warning the killer. The lie about Rose's broken heart began to trouble me. I couldn't learn anything more, so I left.

On my way to my office to begin writing tonight, I saw the truth fruit developing. If Roland admits to killing, I don't know how I will react. I am angry with the killer beyond expression. I am also angry with Stevland. He can make us smarter or more honest, but seems to be content to give us fruit that usually makes us a bit more alert and sometimes cures our illnesses—that keeps us balanced. But if he was altering the fruit from time to time, we would never notice. What is in the salve for my skin rash?

The manual says destructive behavior is motivated by desire for power, and Stevland has always wanted power, to be the biggest and smartest bamboo in the history of Pax and to have the best service animals ever. Great-Grandmother was wrong. He's not naturally altruistic. He naturally seeks control.

Truth may come in a fruit, but lying is my life. I lie to protect the privacy of others, I ignore lies for the same reason, I lie to protect myself, and I lie to my husband to protect him from feeling that some inadequacy on his part caused me to visit Roland.

I want to be with my husband now. I want to pretend I know nothing special, that no killer is hovering over us like the imaginary giant child-snatching bat that children think they see when some flaw in a glass brick in a roof makes an odd flash. In our little city, everyone thinks we know everyone else, and we are wrong.

Day 375. Roland stumbled to my office early this morning to talk to me. He had deteriorated during the night, was shaky and pale with lack of sleep, unwashed and uncombed, and the truffle I smelled on his breath probably hadn't helped him. If he was the killer, would he attack me? In his condition, he might not be able to fight hard. He seemed ready to confess even before I served him breakfast, tea and striped truth fruit. I had already eaten my special fruit and had a fine steel knife in easy reach, so I was smart and ready.

"It's my fault she died. Mine," he babbled hoarsely. "I did it. I . . . I know it was wrong. It was wrong with you, too. It's just, I love all kinds of women, I know I'm not supposed to, but you're—you, you're tall and smart and not like other women. You care about me. You care about me, Tatiana, don't you? You watch out for me, like yesterday, and Rose felt so bad, I wanted to make her feel better, but I know it was wrong. So did she, and she felt guilty, I know she did. You did, I know you did. But you're strong. She . . . she . . . she . . ."

He is Generation 5. She was Generation 6. He thought she had committed suicide because of him.

It got worse as the fruit took effect and made him even more painfully honest, and he confessed to being with other members of taboo generations, many women and some men. He neglected to train the fippokats and failed to do his share of the fieldwork. He didn't make truffle. He ate lotus root. As a child, he had stolen toys and goofed off in school.

"I should have died instead of her. Pax would be better off without me. It deserves a better fippmaster. I'm too selfish for this job. I only got it because of my looks."

Sniveling, woebegone, he seemed more attractive than ever, or perhaps it was the pheromones on his clothes and skin again. I could easily imagine the shape of the muscles of his shoulders under the fringed collar of his coat, and the strength of his thighs.

But I make excuses. I meant only to talk him out of suicide, and my assurances of his self-worth became explanations of my former sexual interest in him, which had never ceased: taboo love, not in keeping with my office, but breaking that taboo had hurt no one, hadn't it? He said, truthfully, if I could believe Stevland's fruit, that he had always felt more real when he was with me, more sure of himself, never felt better than when he made me happy. And I was happy and relieved that he had not killed Rose. Age means nothing, really, we agreed—by then we were hand in hand and flushed with excitement.

We made love on the same table where I'm writing now. The intelligence fruit didn't help me think twice about what I was doing.

I felt stupid at Rose's funeral later that morning. The killer was somewhere among the people in the plaza, unless it was Lief, and why would Lief kill Rose? Or Harry? At least she wasn't tortured. Maybe. Most hunters won't use choke snares because they think that strangling is cruel.

At Rose's funeral, I lit several of her candles and spoke the traditional words about the numbers of Pax. I praised her honestly, but who besides me at that moment believed that she had fortitude? People sat quietly, stunned. I am cruel to let them think she died by her own hand. The killer mocks Pax and mocks me.

Stevland, when I spoke to him after the burial, said we should use the truth fruit on more people, since Roland hadn't killed Rose. I thought a moment. "You will tell-me means of you know such fact of Roland." The bamboo outside my office couldn't have seen anything.

He hesitated, and I knew enough about hesitations to know I had asked something he did not want to answer. "You will keep-me my secret," he ordered. I wasn't sure I would, and I'm still not sure I should. The Glassmade words faded and were replaced by words in English. "I have learned your language. I have duplicated auditory organs in many places around the city. They are more useful than I expected."

"You can hear me?" I wrote in Glassmade, too stunned to realize I didn't have to.

"Yes, however with difficulty," the words on the stem said in human language.

"How long?" I said, and wrote, this time in English, two small words that felt entirely unseemly, like doing mathematics with a fippokat.

"I learned by reading your language over many years. I watched school classrooms, but hearing is new this year. I sense many sounds at once and must separate each. This is my difficulty."

I sat still for a long time. It was no theatrical pause. He knows what we say, what we do, and has the information about our biochemistry to control us by fruits and scents. He has long been willing to issue threats and commands. What was the scent in the greenhouse doing to me? It could be doing a lot and I would never know. His secrets and power would protect Pax lives only as long as we served him.

"We can work together better," he wrote to break the silence. "We must find the killer."

"I will question more people with the fruit," I said. But that was not enough for Stevland, not at all.

"We must use the truth fruit for the entire population."

"No. Social peace requires lies. Trivial, necessary lies. We must find the killer without destroying Pax."

"We must find the killer. Then I will give you fruit to kill that person."

"The punishment will be decided by the people of Pax," I said, and wrote to show to him so he would have to understand, but I wrote so fast that my writing was almost illegible.

"I want the killer's blood," he said.

"You already have the victims'."

"You speak of logic. I speak of desire. I am deeply motivated."

"Perhaps you can present your desire to the people of Pax for their judgment." He did not answer me, which was just as well, because I might not have answered constructively. After a period of unhappy silence, we discussed where to begin my questioning. Stevland suggested Rose's best friend, Tami, a glassblower named Kung, and my husband. I could not bear to ask for his reasoning about my husband.

Rose's friend Tami liked the fruit. She likes almost everything. She hadn't killed anyone, and the subject of their deaths turned her into a loud puddle of self-recriminating tears because she should have seen that her friends were suffering and helped them. Kung, a big, gruff, slow man who I always suspected was more sensitive than he seems, enjoyed the new fruit and hadn't killed anyone, but he got so depressed over the idea of senseless death that he spent the rest of the day sitting on the city wall staring at nothing.

My husband hadn't killed anyone but had noticed that I have seemed troubled and angry lately, and wanted to assure me that he honored and respected my work completely. He said I help people who in turn often disrespect me, and it broke his heart. He confessed to having sex with Moon and begged for my forgiveness. I assured him he had it and did not mention that I already knew about the affair and could hardly complain. Moon belongs to our generation.

If I could write tonight, if I had a pen and paper and the tranquility to write, this is what I would say:

Day 376. In a way, I feel sorry for Jersey. But not very. Right now, I would be glad to feed her to Stevland.

I had things to tell him this morning, and the smart fruit makes me impatient because time moves so slowly I can't stand it. I bundled up to walk to the greenhouse through empty streets as clouds over the mountains glowed faintly pink with the sunrise. Humidity fogged the roof inside the greenhouse. I lit a candle—one that Rose had made—and sat down, prepared to talk about a new idea for investigation, about bringing more people in, but Stevland wrote first:

"A foraging root of an outpost of mine reports human flesh in the soil." He explained that the outpost grew near the giant ponytail tree on the route to Lief's beautiful waterfall in the east mountains. Stevland's roots, fine as threads, interconnect like a web covering hills and fields well beyond the city. He speculated that the body had been buried some time ago and that the recent rain had washed its scent, as he put it, through the soil.

It had to be Lief. I left right away so I could investigate the site without anyone asking where I was going. Smart fruit: no patience. I took a shovel, some supplies, wrote a note to my husband, passed the special bamboo flower buds growing near the riverside gate in tribute to Harry, crossed the rope bridge, and passed the statue Harry had made of Uncle Higgins, a boulder carved into a half-human, half-lion figure, laughing, holding a glass of truffle. Behind me in the city, white, fragrant smoke began to rise from the bakery chimney.

By noon, I saw the tree towering over the forest, the tallest tree in the world, we thought as children, and as far as we know as adults, it's true. Stevland says it's the oldest living thing he knows of. It rises from a gnarled gray trunk so big that twenty-five people can ring it hand in hand, and high over our heads the trunk splits again and again into fans that end in sprays of long, fine leaves like human hair with needle-sharp points. Smaller versions grow in our gardens, where they look pretty, rather than grotesquely powerful like the tree. Stevland calls it sluggish and uncurious. It might not notice and wouldn't care that a human being had been buried near its east side.

The east side of the tree included a lot of territory. I guessed that one muddy spot behind some bushes near Stevland's outpost might be the place, but I quickly uncovered enough old tree roots to know better. I tried another spot. I found an old boxer bird burrow with the remains of the bird inside. A section of the path some distance from the tree had an oddly raised area between two big roots, as if someone had built a bit of a bridge over a muddy spot. Burying Lief beneath our feet might have been macabre enough for the killer, and it was. Just beneath the ground were a lot of rocks, none too big for a grandmother like me to haul out. Beneath them was Lief. The remains of his clothing was proof. Face-up. Hands and feet had probably been tied, judging from their placement. Bow and knife alongside the body.

Not much more could be told. Little remained even to reek. Sponge worms had replaced some of the flesh, and the bones themselves were being drilled away by termite worms for their calcium. I re-covered Lief. If I hurried, I might be home by sunset. Eighty suspects still waited on my list, but at least he wasn't on it anymore. I began to review the list as I walked.

A pebble rattled behind me. A dead leaf crunched. A bat settled into a tree, only to be startled again. I turned around and saw nothing. It might be an eagle or other predator—unlikely, though, since hunters try to keep the woods clear. More likely, I was being followed by the killer, since no one else would hide from me. He or she would realize I was investigating the murders. If I hurried to the safety of the city, I would not see who the killer was. If the killer meant to kill me, I might be ambushed.

I had my steel knife, I had fruit that made me just slightly faster than anyone and, as I understood later, overconfident. I decided to try confrontation.

I walked back toward the ponytail tree. Its fuzzy green crown rose like a giant tufted head over the other trees. I passed it, and somehow, a kilometer later, the killer had gotten behind me. I heard the distant footsteps again. I stepped off the path behind an empty bluebird reef and tossed a pebble ahead so it might sound like I had continued forward. A few little nine-legged crabs hissed at me from the burrows they had appropriated. I crouched, hoping my dark clothes would look like a shadow.

Footsteps approached, a bit hesitantly. I squinted around the reef. Jersey tiptoed past, stopping at a curve in the path to peek down it before continuing. Jersey. Jersey?

Yes. With her mathematics dress, with a bow and quiver of arrows, with all the stealth she could manage.

I waited, then followed her. Perhaps she thought to trap me, but I knew the path, too. A rainbow bamboo grove grew not much farther along. I paused there, waiting for her to discover my trick and turn around. Stevland's outpost would see me and send back word.

I waited, ate a smart fruit, ate some pemmican, emptied my canteen. My hips hurt. I considered what to ask her: Why? Why torture Harry? Why kill anyone? I imagined capturing her somehow and bringing her back to the city—how? I needed to figure that out soon. How would people react? Not well, probably.

The smart fruit made me impatient. Something, I decided, was going on ahead and I had to know what. I walked for a long way. I found nothing. Suddenly Lux was setting.

Too late to turn back: smart fruit indeed. A little farther ahead I knew I'd find a shelter built for travelers on the way to the waterfall. It would be stocked with firewood and a few pots and blankets if no animals had filched them. Jersey might be there, but what choice did I have?

The small, domed fortress stood in a clearing on one side of the path. Stone and brick rose to a double-thick glass roof, round like a house but without bays. Slits high in the walls allowed those inside to peer out and, if necessary, fire arrows or darts. I circled it slowly. The heavy door stood high above the ground, shut tight. The ladder to reach it was nowhere in sight. A tiny owl peeked out of a burrow near the building and bristled. A wisp of green in the sky foretold auroras. No light glowed through the roof. If someone was inside, they hadn't lit a fire— but was that a hint of smoke in the air?

I reached up with a stick to scratch at the lower edge of the door like a lizard or tree crab. Silence. I scratched again. Silence. Or not quite. A whine, very faint. Maybe just a moth.

Then the rasp inside like a foot on a floor. Jersey?

I didn't want to spend the night outside and discover what predators might be in the area, but if she was inside I might be safer out there. A grove of bamboo grew on the other side of the path. Stevland's guard thistles would provide a haven of sorts. Back home, my absence would have been noted, and hers, too. By tomorrow, things would be different—provided I survived the night.

I took a few steps toward the grove. Something wooden rattled inside the building. A bar being raised on a shutter that blocked an arrow slit? Something squeaked. A leather hinge? She had carried a bow and arrows, hadn't she? Why hadn't I noticed? When would the arrow come?

I stood still—stillness being my only camouflage—and waited. No arrow flew. Finally I turned. The aurora's greenish glow lit the upper leaves on trees where crabs twinkled. All the arrow slits looked dark and shadowy. I looked down and saw my pale greenish hands floating out of dark sleeves. She could see me. I couldn't see her. I drew a breath to talk—to say what?

She giggled and whispered, "You're trapped, Tatiana."

"I can walk away."

"Shh. The eagles will hear you. They're down the path. Listen, you'll hear them."

I listened. Singing bats, barking birds, a howl of a lion at the setting Sun, which suggested that eagles weren't near, chirping lizards. A breeze in the treetops, followed by a rattle of crabs renewing their claw-holds. But if I played along, she'd stay inside, trapped by her own fear. Something gibbered to the east, probably a mountain spider and its cubs come down to fatten on slugs and fish before winter.

"That?" I whispered.

"They sing," she said. "They have a fire. If you beg, I'll let you in."

That was her game: to lure me inside. "Why?" I whispered. "Why did you kill them?"

She laughed, and I guessed which slit she was talking from. "It will be fun to watch you get eaten. I wish I could come out. I'd tie you to a tree so you couldn't get away. I hear they like to cook their food by tying it live to a stake and lighting a fire around it."

That was pure fiction.

"You're afraid, aren't you?" she said. "And cold. You tried to catch me, but I caught you." She sounded childlike, as if she were playing a game of frozen tag and could tease the frozen players with impunity. "Did you play fair? Did you play by the rules? Of course you did. You never missed a work assignment. Moderator? I made you moderator. I'll make you into eagle food."

Patient and generous, that was the Jersey I knew. Timid and appeasing at worst. Who was this woman?

"Think about it," she said. "Smelly eagles with those big claws. They can hide anywhere. You'll never see them until they have you. Tomorrow, I'll say that you tried to kill me. You chased me. I hid, and the eagles rescued me from you. You're the killer. Everyone will believe it. You're always sneaking around with all kinds of secrets."

When children use that tone of voice, I leave. It makes me crazy. Even as a child, she had never talked like that. But I could change her tone of voice and get honest answers. "At least I have food," I taunted back.

"You think you can bribe the eagles?"

"Not with fruit, but I have it and you don't. Aren't you hungry?"

"What kind of fruit?"

"Bamboo fruit."

"If you don't give me some, I'll shout for the eagles to come."

"Will you be quiet until dawn?"

"Absolutely." She was lying, but that didn't matter. I threaded four truth fruits on a long twig and held them up to the arrow slit. She snatched them inside. After a moment, she said, "These are weird. They're poison. They're going to kill me."

"No. They're new, with vitamins."

"Prove it to me. Eat one yourself."

I almost said no, but I thought twice. Then answered fast, so she wouldn't suspect anything. I needed to learn the truth.

"Sure," I said.

One flew out the window and landed on the ground. I stifled my hesitation and picked it up—the smallest one, at least. I hoped I would be emotionally stronger than Roland, or that the smart fruit would cancel out the truth fruit. Or that my habit of never speaking frankly would remain intact. I made sure that she saw me eat the fruit, and I swallowed it in big chunks so I might digest less. It tasted cloyingly sweet and slightly like the iron supplements I took when I was pregnant.

I waited. I couldn't spot a moon to judge time with. Another green curtain of light brightened to the north. The aurora rippled and became streaked with red. Crabs and stars twinkled. The spiders continued to jabber.

I edged closer to the arrow slit. "Is it fun to kill?" The fruit would take effect soon, and when it did, I wanted her to be already talking.

"You'll be the most fun of all. I'm not kidding about the eagles. I saw their fire, I heard them. I should call them now."

I needed to distract her. "Why your father?"

Giggles again. The truth fruit hadn't taken effect or she'd be morose. "I didn't know how easy killing would be. Or how much fun. I killed kats, but they're nothing. They don't beg. Papa begged."

"Start from the beginning."

"You're not begging. I thought you'd be the most fun. Tatiana, begging."

"Why did you kill him?"

"But listen, there they are."

The jabbering again. It wasn't spiders. A wind carried a snatch of conversation, of language, full of complex squeaks and squawks. An odd, foul smell. I started to agree—truth fruit at work? I thought hard twice. If she thought eagles were near, she'd call them. "It's spiders. Spiders hunting fish, teaching their young to hunt." I could still lie!

"I saw their fire."

I took a deep breath and lied again, each word an effort. "It's the aurora. You saw it reflected on a puddle."

Her footsteps rasped on the stone floor of the building. A shutter hinge squeaked inside. Down the path, something was talking. Could eagles talk? They drummed before attacks, but I heard no drumming. I seemed to smell smoke.

Jersey came back. "Nothing's going to kill you, then. I'll have to kill you."

"Why kill me?" The question came easily, since it reflected my true thoughts.

"No one hurts anyone on Pax. You make sure they don't. That's fun, isn't it? You make people act nice. I can act nice. Imagine making them suffer. Making them dead. I can do that." Her tone of voice had changed, less playful. "I make them hurt. I surprise them."

"I'm surprised. You were never like this."

"I was never like this." She was quiet, then sighed, then was quiet again.

Don't stop talking—I wanted to say that. "When did you change?"

"I don't know." Quiet again.

What was wrong with her? The truth fruit made everyone else talkative. Had she eaten it? "How did you change?" That was an easy, honest question. I waited for her to answer, waited even though I was filled with smart fruit impatience, and was about to ask again when she whined:

"I wanted to make it stop. To stop thinking."

Truth fruit had not made other people more coherent, or her, apparently. "Thinking like what?"

She whispered an answer so quietly I had to ask her to repeat it. "Hurting people."

"Why?"

"Why? Why hurt my children? I love my children." She had become morose, finally. "I want to hurt them. I always think about hurting them. I see it. I grab a broom and beat Bram until he's bloody, his bones break, I knock out his teeth, smash his face . . . Oh, I hear it, I see it, I smell it. Always, always, always. At the baths I want to drown them. When my husband kisses me, I think I might bite him, chew his throat open. I think it, I feel it, taste it. That's all I ever think about. I dream about it. I want to make it stop. Stop."

I couldn't recall her so much as looking angrily at her boys. She was telling the truth, though, wasn't she?

"To make it stop?" I repeated.

"I never feel right. No matter how good I am, no matter how I treat the boys, how good, no matter how good I treat my husband, I can't stop thinking about hurting them. I keep my house neat, I do my work, and it doesn't do any good. I can feel a knife in my hand and how it would feel to shove it into my husband's chest. Blood, lots of blood. I see this and I feel this and I worry about this all the time, all the time, when I wake up, when I'm writing to Stevland, when I'm asleep, sometimes I dream about it and it's all mathematical, an equation about how many times I can hit Bram until he dies. The maximum number."

"But you haven't hurt your children," I said gently.

"No. But I couldn't make it stop. I tried. I tried. It didn't work. I killed kats. I killed Papa and the others. It didn't work."

I kept all trace of accusation out of my voice: "You thought it would help if you killed them."

"If I did it to someone else, I wouldn't do it to the kids."

"You killed your father."

"I didn't plan to. I was looking for a bluebird reef to set fire to and I found him by the ponytail tree. He had fallen and broken his leg. I know you think I hate him, and he was mean when I was young, and I thought I hated him. I thought . . . I thought I wanted to hurt my children because of him, that's what I thought when I saw him lying on the ground. I tricked him. I told him I'd make him more comfortable and then get help, and I didn't. I piled rocks on him, one by one by one by one until he couldn't breathe anymore. He begged and suffered and it was everything I thought it would be like. And I thought, I've done it. I won't have to think about doing it to my children. I was free."

The truth fruit and smart fruit in my veins made me want to interrupt and tell her she should have gotten counseling. There's a good counselor at the clinic, Lightning. I swallowed my impulse and waited for her to talk more. "I'm listening." I forced myself to sound understanding. "You were free."

"No, I wasn't! I still thought about killing my children and my husband. And about Papa. I lived it again and again. Every stone. It was better than thinking about my children. And then I thought about other people, about killing other people. Anyone who was around me. And I thought, if I do it again, then I'll feel better, I'll have more to think about. I thought, if I pick someone special and do it horribly, then it will be even better. Harry. Everyone loved Harry, and his work was so important. It would be perfect to kill him."

I knew what I needed to know. But truth fruit makes a person talk. I had to stand there and listen to what I didn't really want to know.

"It felt good to watch him die so slow. It was better than I imagined. When the slugs came, they took a long time. I was afraid they would go for his eyes first and he couldn't see and be afraid, but they didn't. But the next day, I thought about how much I would enjoy tying down my children for the slugs, how I could pile rocks on my husband. I don't want to, but I can't stop thinking about how I would do it and enjoy it and I couldn't stop myself because it would be so much fun."

"Then you killed Rose," I interrupted.

"I didn't plan that, but I got the chance, and she's important, and I thought that if I killed someone who was important, who could tell me what to do, then I could tell myself what to do and what not to do. And if I kill you, you're the one chasing me. You're the one who makes me feel guilty. You're bossy, you're always pushing people around. If I kill you, then I'll feel better. I won't have to worry about being found out. And if I can rest, I'll have time to change. That's all I want. I want to stop thinking. I want to stop thinking about you, about Papa, Harry, about my family, about everything, everything, everything. I want to stop!"

Her voice was rising. She would call the eagles whether she meant to or not.

"I want you to stop, too," I whispered.

"I will after you're dead." She was whispering again. The smoke smell had become undeniable. "I want peace. I want you dead." The jabber and twitter became louder again, voices calling to each other as if they were on the move. "Here they come. I don't want to watch. I don't want to see it this time. I just want it to happen." She closed the shutter on the arrow slit.

I didn't move, I didn't breathe. Some creatures can see heat. Maybe eagles could. I waited and watched the aurora lights glimmer in the sky. Animals rustled in the trees. A bat flew past, and I caught the words "fire" and "beware, beware."

Jersey sobbed.

And I couldn't lie to myself. I was afraid.

How would I explain her at a General Assembly of Pax? What is justice? We don't have written laws about murder.

But she's not well.

What would I say? That I lied to everyone, that I was afraid of mistakes, I was afraid to lose control of the investigation, that I was afraid of manipulation by Stevland, and so I said nothing. Rose died because I kept secrets and acted too slowly.

No one will respect me. That's what I live for, really. Respect. Power. I have it now. I'm the moderator and the commissioner of public peace. Sylvia's knife means that I'm special. I'm different. I'm a little better than everyone. But I let Rose die. Then I took her place and was happy to do it.

I crawled to the bamboo grove. Stevland opened his guard thistles for me, and here I wait for dawn, crouched in the grove in the cold night. The truth fruit and the smart fruit won't let me sleep. I shiver and think. I'm different from Jersey only in why I did what I did. And in that I know how to stop. The aurora has brightened again. I could almost read by this light. If anything looks for me, it will find me, and Stevland can't protect me. He's only a plant.

The difference between Jersey and me is that I will deal with things the right way. I will try to survive, and then I will be the best moderator I can be. I lied, I made mistakes, they can vote me out as moderator, as commissioner, and I'll still be me, knife or not.

Day 377. I have never tried to go without bamboo fruit before, and I didn't know I would be so miserable. I'm hungry and thirsty, but not for food and drink, and in fact I feel too queasy to eat. My head aches. I feel as if something bad is going to happen, some sort of attack or storm or accident, although I am at home, and my husband has fallen asleep watching the fire burn to embers waiting for me to go to bed, and I will sleep eventually only because I didn't sleep last night.

I won't eat any more fruit or use any more salve. I need to be free of Stevland.

Last night, crouched in the bamboo grove, I was too afraid to sleep. My muscles stiffened and cramped but I was too afraid to stretch, even to shiver, and in the aurora light, I could see my breath. Three times I heard eagle footsteps rustling through leaves and grass, gibbering at each other with whistles and rattles and snaps like sticks breaking. The smoke of their campfire wafted past from time to time. They were cooking meat. I crouched there and thought about myself and how I have always been true to what people asked me to do, not what I wanted to do. I have always lied to myself.

I finally understood why I slept with Roland. I used him to get even with all the moderators I have served and with Pax itself for demanding a job that made me suffer. I broke the rules to rebel against Sylvia.

Eventually I glimpsed Lux through the treetops. The east became brighter. Turkey clans and boxer birds began barking to claim their territories. The scent of wet ashes arrived on the breeze. I hoped it meant the eagles had broken camp. I waited. If they were leaving, they didn't seem to be coming down the path toward me. I finally stood, or tried to. My hips scraped like cracked pottery, weak and painfully rough-edged at the joints. I had to pull myself up by grabbing the bamboo.

Stevland was watching. The guard thistles relaxed so I could pass through. I thought I heard a faint whistle from the north and froze. Eagles? Hawk bats? I heard it again, still faint but more clear, a Pacifist clay whistle, two low tones. A rescue team whistle. Stevland must have sent help. I inched through the thistles, and then hurried to the shelter. I had to keep Jersey inside until the search party came. A shutter in an arrow slit opened.

"The—" I said.

"I heard it," she interrupted. I could barely see her face and a glint of green-dyed hair in the shadows. "They're coming from the city." She sobbed. "Those eagles—"

"They've left."

Something wooden clattered on the floor inside the building as if it had been kicked. "Kill me," she said in a pitiful voice. "I want you to kill me. Please. I'll come out, and you have a bow or a knife or something, right? Use it, will you?"

I didn't answer. If I killed her, I could easily claim self-defense and I would spare the citizens from the task of deciding what to do with her. Inside, wood rasped on wood as she took the bar from the door. The leather hinge squeaked open. She stood on the sill, looking at me with puffy eyes and hands wringing a tangled lock of hair.

She leaped out headfirst.

It was only three meters to the ground, but her intent was obvious, and she seemed to fall forever as I watched with a stopped heart. Truth fruit causes despondency, and she had eaten a lot of it. A severe blow to the head this far from medical help could be—was meant to be—fatal. This was suicide.

But she jumped too hard and flipped over slightly as she fell, landing on her shoulders. Something cracked: her bones or sticks on the ground or both. She yelped, tried to rise, and fell back, panting. A trick? I walked around her.

Her fingers dug into the ground. Her legs twitched. Her eyes begged. "Kill me. I want you to kill me. Do it."

"Why?" I kept my distance. She may have been injured but perhaps not crippled. "I know you have a reason."

"I'm hurt."

"But you'd rather be dead. Why?"

She groaned and twitched and looked me in the eye. "My children. My children. They'll find out why I did it. I don't want them to think I would hurt them. If you kill me, they'll never find out."

A reasonable wish. But this problem belonged to Pax, not to me. Let Pax solve it. Still, as a mother, even a cold one, I could understand wanting to protect her children. The whistles were getting louder.

"Say you did it for fun," I said. "Tell them that's what you told me. Or that you did it because you got angry with your father and Harry and Rose, because you argued. Tell them you don't even remember doing it. I'll tell them that you said whatever you want me to." She looked up at me unbelieving.

She said nothing.

"It's not my job to judge people. It's my job to try to keep the peace. That's all. The people of Pax have their job." Voices were calling our names, and I shouted back to them.

Roland ran up the path, sweating in the cold morning, breathless.

"Tatiana! You're here, you're safe!" He hugged me tightly, then looked at Jersey, still lying on the ground, and looked back at me.

"She fell and hurt herself."

The rest of the party arrived. A medic examined her, then they lashed her to a stretcher, asking questions faster than I could answer if I had wanted to.

With Roland and the two strongest men in the party, we went to examine the eagle camp. We approached cautiously, keeping the scent of wet ash ahead of us, listening. The eagles had gone, leaving behind a clearing full of trampled grass, a wet firepit containing small bones, a few feces, and footprints. Split-hoof footprints, not eagle footprints. Like the split-hoof footprints in the museum, the footprints on the ceramics Harry had made.

"Glassmakers," one of the men whispered, then turned toward the shelter and shouted. "Glassmakers! Come and look!"

"Are you sure?" Georg asked. "Could be deer crab."

"Nah, deer crabs are little U shapes. Look, it's a clean split, two rectangles, sharp edges. Lots of 'em."

I stared at the prints and the camp debris and eventually realized that I had stopped breathing. I had nearly met Glassmakers. They existed. We'd wondered if they would come back since Sylvia discovered the city. And now we knew.

"Let's find them!" Roland looked at me with the face of a delighted child.

I thought a long moment. "No. They could have found us if they wanted, but they didn't. If we followed them, they'd think we were chasing them. They might be afraid of us."

He dropped his gaze to the ground. "Yeah, afraid."

"Maybe they know we hunt," Kung agreed, unhappy.

I was unhappy, too. Glassmakers! "We'll have to think of a way to meet them. Later, but soon."

The walk back to the city took hours, slowed by my exhaustion and the difficulty of carrying the stretcher, and after we tired of discussing the Glassmakers, questions about the murders began to surface. Jersey, on strong painkillers, didn't talk. I showed them where Lief was buried. A group could return later to bring his remains back to the city for interment. We arrived at the city to exclamations of relief and confusion. Jersey's children and husband came running. I took him aside.

"She fell from the door of the fortress." He stood gape-mouthed.

"Tell the children she needs to see the medic and will be at the clinic for a while. Take them indoors and keep them there. Your family will help you." He obeyed mechanically.

I called a Commonwealth General Meeting and explained—briefly and incompletely—what had happened, confessing that I may have caused Rose's death by keeping the secret and acting too slowly. "It is your duty to decide what to do now." Murmurs. "Unless there is objection, I will set another meeting for tomorrow evening, so we all may have time to think about this. We must return to the harvest." I paused. Murmurs, lots of murmurs. "In the meantime, I am available for questions, and will be in the Meeting House tonight."

Jersey's mother rose and spoke so softly that someone had to repeat the question: "Why did she do it?"

"I don't know, but she might not be mentally well."

In the afternoon, I talked to Stevland, too tired to want to fight, but it happened.

I sat down in the little greenhouse glittering in the Sun, and Stevland began with flattery. "I am unable to express how happy and relieved I am that you are alive and you have found the killer. I watched, and you were very brave and intelligent. Eagles will kill without reason."

"Those were Glassmakers."

"Glassmakers? Are you certain? Did they see you? Did they follow you? I will question my furthest outposts. This is worse than eagles."

"Worse?"

"Worse. I do not wish to see them again. They left me without an explanation, as if they were seasonal moths. They left me to suffer and wonder and wait. I have no interest in them, and they have no interest in me. They were at the shelter and I did not know about it because they deliberately avoided my outposts. This is sinister behavior."

But we wanted to see the Glassmakers. He would have to get used to the idea, and I needed to ease him toward that realization. "Don't you want to find out why they left?"

"Understand my position. Mutualism and selfishness. Protection and abandonment. Trust and betrayal. This is not a dualism that allows for a middle path. Glassmakers brought me tragedy. Do they want to know the consequences of their irresponsibility? How I nearly died?"

We were going to have a problem. I thought about what to say, but he changed the subject: "Jersey, why did she kill?"

"I think she is mentally unwell," I said. That was becoming the official story.

"I can cure illnesses. I want to examine her before she is put to death."

"The people of Pax will decide what to do."

"They must not allow her to live. Killers have no place in my city. She did not even kill as a hunter kills, with minimal suffering of the animal. She is like an eagle within the walls. The decision is clear."

His city! I considered and discarded a lot of thoughts, so by the time I answered I had an idea that seemed constructive. "You could become a citizen of Pax. You could vote, and you could take part in debates."

"I am not an animal."

I decided not to ask what he meant by that. "Has anyone shown you our Constitution . . . ? No? I will order someone to do it." I took the opportunity to leave, and went to Bartholomew's workshop to ask him, a legal scholar, to educate Stevland. I explained that the bamboo could hear and understand English, especially if Bartholomew spoke slowly—he almost dropped the cabinet door he was making. I left after answering only a few of his questions. It was his problem now.

At the clinic, they said Jersey had broken several vertebrae, and injured and swollen neural tissues caused paralysis and uncontrollable pain. They had given her some painkillers that left her barely responsive. I told them to do what seemed best for her.

I checked on her family, knocking softly at the door. Her husband let me into the immaculate little house.

"Will she be all right?" Bram asked.

"Probably not."

He closed his eyes and shuddered. The boys glared at me, the bearer of bad news.

"But she and I talked when we were in the forest," I said, "and she wants you to know that she loves you, all of you, more than anything, and you mean more to her than anything. I don't have a way to tell you how true that is, but it is the complete truth. No matter what happens, I hope you will always believe that." The boys had begun weeping. I left.

I was tired. I hadn't eaten any fruit and the lack of stimulants was becoming clear to me. In the greenhouse, Bartholomew was almost finished talking to Stevland. "Sympathy with the spirit means, well, Article Two, principles and purposes," Bartholomew was saying slowly and distinctly when I entered. "I can read it again for you."

"How is sympathy demonstrated?" Stevland spelled out on his wide, pale stem. "Greetings, Tatiana."

Bartholomew turned, smiling. "Hi, Tat. In fact, we have no precedent for demonstrating sympathy. Mutual trust and support, undeniably, you've been undeniably supportive, but on the issue of mutual trust, why have you kept your ability to listen and understand English secret? Now, don't answer, just think about it. But listen carefully. The Constitution says, 'Any sentient beings who have expressed their sympathy with the spirit of our Commonwealth and are willing to share in its goals may declare themselves citizens.' I would say, although it's just my considered opinion, that all you need to do is explain why you are in sympathy and willing to share our goals, write an essay, I suppose, with the final line, 'And therefore I now declare myself a citizen of the Commonwealth of Pax.' Hmm. Perhaps we should have had a more stringent procedure, not in your case, Stevland, because I can't imagine any objections, but in some future situation this could create difficulties. The Constitution was written by idealists and it has its flaws, like giving children the right to vote. What do you think, Tat? What else does our friend have to do?"

"I think that's right," I said, actually unsure, then added a bit pointedly, "Stevland would be an equal citizen."

"Equal," Stevland wrote. "Not like a fippokat."

"Equal, of course." Bartholomew stroked his green, braided beard. "Sentient beings are specified. Fipps aren't entirely unintelligent, of course, but they don't seem especially self-aware. I've never had much of a conversation with one, at least. I suppose an operational definition of sentience is saying that you have it."

"I will be a full and equal citizen?"

"Of course. Like anyone else. I think you might consider additional means of communication, perhaps in the Meeting House, for citizenship duties."

"With a great effort I can grow another stem like this one by tomorrow. You must open a space in the floor."

They worked out the details, and Bartholomew left to tear up mosaic floor tiles. I sat down.

"Jersey is sick," Stevland said. "The medics gave me a blood sample to analyze. She still has active antibodies to the parasite that caused the scarlet fever this spring. Her body is fighting something. I believe the parasites are present within the cerebral membrane."

"She told me she couldn't control her thoughts."

"Like a root infection. I have had to destroy roots. It is terrifying."

I wondered if he still wanted her executed. I didn't get the chance to ask.

"I want you to resign as moderator. When I am a citizen, I will take the job."

From citizen to leader immediately. Equality wouldn't do. He wanted control—perhaps so we couldn't leave him like the Glassmakers? Or so we couldn't contact them? He began to tell me how he was more committed to our peace and success than we ourselves were, and above all was more intelligent, quoting phrases from the Constitution—learned so fast!—and explained that our goals, such as justice, could be even better served since he was beyond the interpersonal relationships and hypocrisies that . . .

I walked out. I went to my husband's workshop, and eventually I napped despite the noise of metalworking. He woke me in the evening, and we walked to the meeting, aware that at every few paces I passed a bamboo stem. Stevland was everywhere. At the Meeting House, a section of flooring toward the front had been lifted up and temporarily fenced off to protect it from being trampled, although not even the children seemed frisky. I saw a mound and crack in the soil. The new stem was growing.

Questions for me centered on exactly what happened and when—a lot of exacting questions and second-guessing. I explained about the intelligence fruit and truth fruit. Hathor wanted to know exactly whom I had considered as suspects, and seemed offended when I replied, "Everyone, at first." There would be even more second-guessing now, I thought.

Bartholomew announced Stevland's plan to become a citizen.

"He should be. He's done so much for us," said Marie, a member of the Committee who usually analyzes new ideas carefully, but she's a dental medic and he works closely with the medics, so she already knew him as a trusted coworker.

A farmer agreed. "Without him, we'd eat a lot less."

Hathor said, "A new citizen!" and nudged Forrest. They'd have a fresh target.

"But does he understand us?" Nevada asked. "He's never even been to one of these meetings. Does he understand democracy and voting?"

Bartholomew arched an eyebrow. "That's a point I'm exploring with him. He plans to grow a stem here to communicate." He pointed to the open space in the floor.

The medics said Jersey was stable, but in a grave state. They thought the antibodies Stevland had discovered might be related to an auto-immune disorder or an infection. They were trying to keep her comfortable. Her children had visited her.

I expected criticism for my decision not to pursue the Glassmakers since there is a tangible passion to know about them. Instead, I got a lot of questions about what exactly I had heard and seen. How did they talk? Smell? Every little detail, told twice. Some of the hunters suggested initiating a process of observation and perhaps gift-giving. Nevada wanted to set copies of Harry's art in places where it might be found as a peace gesture so they could begin to understand us. Pursuit, many agreed, might have been misinterpreted, but why hadn't the Glassmakers initiated contact? We wanted to meet them so badly! But we needed to do it right.

People should have complained about what I did. Hathor and Forrest, at least. But during the meeting, someone began to snack on a piece of fruit. That was it. Stevland had made them docile, agreeable. They were drugged.

After the questions were answered, I took members of the Committee aside and told them that Stevland wanted to be moderator. "He wants control, and he's powerful. You know how much he can do, and he would do it, even down to little details of our lives."

"Moderators can only do what the Committee lets them," Cedar said.

"Can he do that?" Moon asked Bartholomew. "He's not human."

"Technically, once he's a citizen, it's possible for him to be elected. But we already have a moderator, so the post isn't open."

"They'd never do that on Earth, let a plant run things and be equal," Moon said as if it were a good reason.

"He's never thought of himself as our equal, always as superior," I said.

"But you can work with him," Cedar said.

Marie knit her brows, which deepened the wrinkles across her forehead. "Moderator might be too much, but Stevland is our friend. He has his idiosyncrasies, and that's a concern. Plants think differently and you have to allow for that, but he genuinely cares about us."

Docile fruit was at work.

"Get some rest," Marie told me. "We'll talk about this."

My husband, when he learned what Stevland wanted and why I wasn't eating fruit, quietly removed all bamboo fruit from our home so I wouldn't be tempted.

So I end the day in a situation worse than last night's. Then, I was in danger. Now, everyone is, and there's nothing I can do.

Day 378. Notes from the evening Commonwealth meeting. Agenda created in collaboration with Bartholomew and others. Quorum present, 271 people. Missing: Jersey's children, her mother, medical personnel, medical patients including Jersey, and city wall guards. Medics and guards represented by proxies. Jersey's husband was present. I have never seen a more miserable person, pale and drooped like a wilted flower, which was not surprising given what he would have to say.

First item: Stevland's citizenship declaration. We had prearranged this ceremony, although Stevland hadn't been informed of everything. The stem had grown tall, bloated, pale, and leafless. Stevland had said earlier in the day that the growth had been very taxing, and he had had to pull in adenine and sugars from some distance.

People settled into seats and benches, sat on the floor in the aisles, and stood along the walls. Harry's art displays had been pushed into corners.

Bartholomew explained the constitutional provisions. Stevland presented his statement of sympathy with the spirit of the Commonwealth of Pax: "I share your natural disposition for joy, community, freedom, and peace, especially peace. . . ."

Freedom. Stevland and I had discussed that earlier in the afternoon. I don't think he understood what that meant. "Animals are repetitive," he had said. "If they can be prevented from repeating mistakes, their lives would be more free." We wrangled over that for some time. He still wanted to ban boat races.

But at the meeting, he continued:

"I regret the loss of the bamboo civilization before my germination, but you have brought me aspirations beyond my imagination. I share your love of beauty and curiosity in the world and universe around us, and your hope for a happier life. With some of you, I also share vanity, and that is why I did not tell you I could hear and understand your language. I was waiting for fluency. . . ."

Liar. But freedom includes the freedom to lie, especially to ourselves. The truth fruit had only made people miserable.

"And therefore," he said, "I, Stevland Jamil Barr, now declare myself a citizen of the Commonwealth of Pax."

He had claimed the full Earth name of the first human to die on the trip here. What cheek.

Everyone rose to applaud. Children came forward to sing and dance the welcoming song for newborns, which Stevland had not expected.

"Thank you," his stem said. "I am very happy. It is the start of a new life."

Item two was Jersey, and went as planned. Medics reported that they could care for her paralysis but not her pain, which was severe. They discussed the antibodies in her blood and the probability, according to medical texts, that the infection had affected her behavior. Her husband, who had spoken with her, rose to plead with great dignity on her behalf for her death, a gentle euthanasia.

Stevland, as planned, offered to work with the medics to investigate her condition to see if it could be treated. He promised to prevent her pain during the investigation and her final sleep as he had done in previous cases of euthanasia. Her husband said that nothing would make him and Jersey happier than to be sure no one would ever suffer from that illness again. Citizens agreed on a voice vote.

So everyone was happy, especially Stevland, who had wanted her dead and would kill her. The hard issues were avoided.

The third issue was the Glassmakers. The hunters, as they had proposed earlier, rose to suggest setting out gifts for the Glassmakers and slowly initiating a peaceful encounter. Stevland, who had not been consulted, warned that the Glassmakers could be capricious. "They left the city suddenly. I do not know why, but now they have no interest in this place or you. We would waste our time and effort."

The debate was long, deep, and productive, and several people pointed out that we could ask them why they left if we developed contact. The hunters' proposal, somewhat modified, passed with fifty-three votes opposed, including Stevland, although most of the opposition was from people who wanted to move faster.

I wonder what it's like for a creature used to solitude for so long to discover the compromises of social living.

Fourth, Stevland's candidacy for moderator. He hadn't formally announced it, but that didn't matter. The Committee had a plan. Bartholomew spoke:

"Of course, there's no vacancy, although of course the Committee could vote Tatiana out, but I think this would be a good time to discuss the nature of the office itself." He discussed in detail the duties, constraints, and prerogatives of the office. A historian recapped the administrations of the previous moderators.

The children began to fidget, and who could blame them? The talks were not for their benefit. Speakers from the floor outlined the relationship of the moderator to groups like the farmers, weavers, and hunters. Stevland was listening, and occasionally Bartholomew asked him if he had understood a certain issue. Marie rose to speak on the Rule of Generations. Each generation sets its rules, dress, habits, and organization as freely as possible.

I believe in that, of course, which was the only reason I allowed the meeting to continue. Cedar had brought me Generation 6's plan just after lunch. They were worried about Stevland. I hate the plan, but they had put together a majority, and the worst thing is that their logic might be correct. She led me out to a yam field to talk far from any bamboo.

"He'll get what he wants one way or another," she said acidly, but she's always like that. She's young, tough, and a leader because she elbows her way to the front of a group. "I know he means well, but, you know, he wants a lot, and he doesn't really understand us. We are worried. But we can't survive without him, and we've been working and living with him for a long time. We brought the Greenies in on this. Even Marie."

She grimaced. The two women did not like each other. Cedar continued:

"She said he's been acting as a leader of his own little team for a long time, in many ways a citizen already. But every team leader is held accountable, and that's a kind of control. We decided the best way to control him is to give him some of what he wants, limited power, the limits that any leader winds up having. You know what I mean. You've been working well with Stevland. You can keep him reasonable, and the Committee will back you."

I answered slowly. "He can control us with drugs. He did that with smart fruit and truth fruit, and he could do it to make us agree with him."

She dismissed my objection with a shake of her head. "Marie talked to him. He said he wasn't happy about that fruit. He needs us healthy.

He knows better than to 'unbalance' us, as he likes to say. Look, we have a lot of power in this relationship, Tatiana. We'll tell him it's a fair division of power and responsibility, a balance."

Cedar hadn't come to explain the plan to me, she'd come to deliver orders. She certainly wasn't docile, and maybe there really isn't any docile fruit, but she was incredibly optimistic about what I can actually do. But I didn't have a better idea or the votes to get it passed if I did, and I'm used to doing what I don't want to do. Thus Pax would sidestep another crisis. I agreed to become co-moderator, and we all wondered how Stevland would react. If he turned on us, we were dead.

Bartholomew's show-and-tell was meant to convince him that he would need a human co-moderator to balance him.

"Now," Bartholomew concluded, "the moderator is a busy person. Perhaps too busy. Some duties take reflection and wisdom. Some take immediacy and action. As our population grows, so does the burden. So I propose creating co-moderator positions. Sylvia and her descendants have served us well. So has Stevland. Who can doubt his contributions to our success? What do you say, Stevland? Co-moderator?"

I had the time to take and exhale five slow deep breaths before Stevland responded. I know how fast he can answer. He was thinking. Finally: "I accept." I wonder how sincerely. A voice vote confirmed his election.

End of meeting. We remained crowded inside the Meeting House in sort of a wake for Jersey, able to express our grief at her illness and avoid the harder question of her evil deeds. Things like that don't happen on Pax.

Cedar gave me a pat on the back, her beaded vest rattling. "Good work," she whispered in my ear. "Good luck." She and other Beads and Greenies had gathered around Stevland to butter him up. I left the meeting early and paused at a stem in the street that I knew had ears. "We'll talk tomorrow."

Stevland and I had already talked earlier that afternoon, and it hadn't been pleasant. Stevland had noticed I wasn't eating fruit. "Are you afraid I will try to control you?"

Suddenly the greenhouse filled with slugs, humming and squirming toward me. My hands had been tied to the table, and bones already poked through the flesh. Termite worms drilled through the bones. And then the vision was gone.

"It is a scent," the words on the stem said. "A gas that makes bad dreams. Do not be afraid of the fruit. I make it pleasant, I make it healthy, but I do not make it to control you. I could do much but it would be wrong. I have learned to trust Pacifists, and I have learned that leadership is not violence. Force is violence. Mutualism involves trust, so I will show that you can trust me. I want to help all Pacifists, and I can do great good. The future can be a new way to live. You will like it."

Thank the stars I'm an old woman. I won't have to deal with Stevland forever.

Day 379. So the crisis is over, the problems are solved. I rose this morning, dressed, and went to the ovens. Nye, a baker, worked with teenage efficiency, pulling lentil-filled turnovers from ovens that vented white smoke. Flour dusted his arms, and a strand of beads dangled around his neck. The sweat on his cheeks dampened the curls of the first hairs of a beard. He worked under the sign he had carved and placed over the ovens: "Bread is the essence of Pax. Its first crop was wheat."

I like getting bread in the morning. The ovens line the back wall of a square building. Soot on the walls and ceiling makes it dark like a cave. The wide doors stand open in all but the worst weather, and even the cold dawn breeze couldn't dilute the air inside, warm and scented with yeast, browning crusts, and hickory wood. I was among the early risers, as usual, waiting with yawning children and farmworkers preparing to hike to distant fields. Cedar arrived, looped in strings of Generation 6 beads like a dew-covered doll. She's a meteorologist as well as a cartographer, and sunrise observations matter to her.

"Nice meeting last night," she said.

A few people nodded. "Everything was thought through," one of them said.

"More like a show than a discussion," I said. Stevland didn't have a stem nearby.

"We said what we wanted to." Cedar shrugged and smiled. "Anyway, now you have an assistant."

"I'm sure Stevland thinks I'm the assistant."

She glanced at the bamboo rising over the houses and shrugged again. "Fippokats think we're here to invent games for them. This afternoon, we're going to go pick flax and bring it to them, and they'll race each other to clean the fluff from the seeds and eat them, and we'll use the fluff to stuff mattresses. Kats can think what they want. So can Stevland."

I got a warm loaf and, as I left, I picked up a couple of pink bamboo fruit from a basket set on a bench outside the ovens, a delicious helping of vitamins, minerals, and maybe a few antibiotics along with mildly stimulating alkaloids, because our health matters. Perhaps Cedar would make a good next moderator, and she's young enough to serve for decades. I need to start thinking about that. I think the next co-moderator ought to come from Generation 6 because the co-moderator idea came from their ranks. Let them cope.

I ate, walked with my husband to his workshop, joined a team to harvest lentils, and went to bathe. Finally I went to the greenhouse and, although it was warm inside, closed the door.

"Committee meetings are always open to observation," I wrote. "Our consultations ought to be, too, starting tomorrow. If you have anything private to say, say it now."

"Why observation?"

"Because we are responsible to other citizens for what we decide." I hoped that an audience might make Stevland temper his outbursts and ease my burden, although, more importantly, I would be setting a good precedent. The intent was to keep him under control, after all.

"I have something private to say." Those words disappeared quickly, replaced by a paragraph:

"I do not agree with the decision about the Glassmakers. I did not understand much regarding the Glassmakers because I lacked a comparison society of intelligent animals, but I have observed you now, and I am troubled by their behavior. They did not seem entirely intelligent. Yet, by a decision of the citizens of Pax, we will initiate contact, and we must try for peace and understanding. I will donate fruit to their taste as gifts. I believe that if there is trouble and if they are used to fruit, then we can use it to control them."

The words faded and the stem remained blank.

"Is that all?" I asked.

"Persis and Wolf are bullying other children."

"They like to lead rough-and-tumble games. You might misinterpret their fun. But I'll look into it."

"There is a group of women that meets certain evenings near the west gate in seclusion," it said. "This is suspicious."

"The Philosopher's Club. They like to debate."

"Why do they exclude others?"

"To keep out serious people." I had attended only once as a guest.

"I will listen to them."

"You will learn interesting things."

"Do you have anything private to say?" Stevland asked.

I wanted to mention Vera as a warning to heavy-handed leadership, but Stevland wouldn't understand. "It's hard to be a moderator," I said. "You will have few real friends."

"I am pleased to be a moderator, especially a co-moderator. Duality is good in moderators, animal and plant, transient and permanent, a stronger leadership for Pax and a perfect balance, as Bartholomew explained. I have examined the polysaccharide in my most active roots and come to conclusions about equality."

"Are we equal?"

"Equality is not a fact, like the length of days. Clearly I am superior to you in size and age and intelligence. Equality is an idea, a belief, like beauty. The duality at root is barbarity and civilization. It is barbarous for eagles to eat Pacifists. It is civilized for Pacifists to seek peace with Glassmakers. It is civilized to live as an equal with Pacifists. It was barbarity that destroyed bamboo civilization when my ancestors allowed their interactions with animals to become selfish. Civilization will govern my interactions and give them a meaning and new purpose to my species."

Some sort of answer was due. I wish that I believed Stevland with my whole heart. As commissioner I have heard many people declare that they would seek a new way to live and would abandon their bad habits, like abusing their husband or avoiding work. They may have meant it sincerely, but often, they soon returned to their old habits. Sometimes only a horrible shock could cause permanent change.

"These are noble goals," I wrote. "I am looking forward to sharing the job of moderator with you." I needed to be encouraging, no matter how self-deceptive the declaration may be. "Until tomorrow, water and sunshine."

I have just returned from seeing Jersey. The medic monitoring her is scrupulous with his care. She has been fed and given all the comforts a mother gives a newborn, including a soft, warm, clean bed alongside a window in the clinic. Tendrils reach in from the stand of bamboo outside. One tendril snakes up her ear, another up her nose, both growing and exploring her brain, tasting the blood and tissue as Stevland looks for how the parasites made her mad.

Could he heal her? He can cure scarlet fever. He could kill the parasites. But he wants her dead, not cured.

Straps of wide, soft cloth keep her from injuring herself with involuntary movements. Her breathing is calm. Her skin is pink and warm. A third tendril wraps around her neck, and rootlets deliver sedatives and painkillers. Eventually, he will deliver enough sedatives to put her to sleep forever, just as he has done for other cases of euthanasia. We will bury her in the cemetery, and Stevland will send larger roots to feed on her, just as he will do to me when old age takes me.

I climbed to the top of the city wall before I entered my office tonight. Across the field in the forest, a tree shook repeatedly, then fell. The fippolions were at work, and Roland led them in song. Bats called to each other. A grove of bamboo rose alongside the wall. Stevland can hear, but he can't read thoughts. Even with tendrils in Jersey's brain, he won't know that she acted out of love, agonizingly wrong and tragically brave. How are we to know when our own thoughts lead us to unspeakable error?

We tell ourselves Pax is a good place, and we are happy at Rainbow City, safe among the rebuilt ruins of the old Glassmakers, where Stevland is our friend, helper, and leader. Harvest is a joyous time of the year. We are a long winter away from spring's Naked Festival, but during the festival, I will burn something that no one will recognize, and it will represent Stevland. I will make no pledge to change, though. I am too old to change as much as I need to.

NYE
YEAR 106–GENERATION 6

We, the citizens of Pax, covenant to affirm and promote the inherent
worth and dignity of all sentient beings and of the interdependent web
of existence of which we are a part; justice, equity, and compassion in
our relations with one another....

—from the Constitution of the Commonwealth of Pax

It figured. Right outside the city, Marie, Cedar, and Roland started to
argue.

"We should have followed the Glassmakers right away," Marie said,
"but Tatiana said no. They could be anywhere now."

She didn't mind bad-mouthing the moderator, but only behind her
back and two weeks after the decision had been made. Still, Marie
wrote and read Glassmade better than anyone and was a total coward,
so she was just what we needed for a peacemaking trip, unless she gos-
siped the Glassmakers to death.

"Not then," Roland said. "We had too much to do. Jersey was hurt."

"That whole investigation was a disaster," Cedar snapped. She
couldn't stand Marie or Tatiana. Maybe it's a generational thing.
"Tatiana should have recruited more help. She didn't have to do it all
by herself."

"Stevland helped," Marie said.

"Tatiana wants what's best for Pax," Roland said.

"Pity she's too old for you." Cedar's voice didn't pity him.

Roland just smiled. He always acts like he could have any woman he wants. He has muscles and a really nice beard, but he doesn't have to flaunt it.

Kung and I didn't say anything. Kung is a Greenie like Roland and Marie, but his hair is black and won't hold dye, so he braids green ribbons into his hair. He's big and dim, but he didn't have to be very smart to stay out of a stupid argument. Me, I'm just starting to get whiskers, but I was experienced enough to let politicians waste their time and energy, not mine.

All I wanted to do, all I'd ever wanted to do, was meet the Glassmakers. The five of us were the people who most wanted to try to find the Glassmakers, and we weren't the best work team in history. The Glassmakers wouldn't bicker like us.

Things got worse when we arrived at the shelter for the first night. The women and Roland debated whether we should have noticed that Jersey was sick. I gathered firewood and salad greens, reheated the turnovers I had carried from the city, played a little tune on my flute to drown out the debate, and went to bed. No one complained about the meal or the music, at least.

The next day the women debated having Stevland be a co-moderator.

"He cares about us," Marie said. She was a dentist and spent her days poking at diseased teeth. "He gives us everything he can, from painkillers to fluoride."

"He needs tight limits," Cedar said. "We need to think about the whole situation, not just medical details, and hold him accountable." She worked on weather and geography and scribbled up maps for every occasion, so Stevland couldn't help her much.

They argued for hours over exactly why having co-moderators was a good idea. It was a good idea, period! I tried to enjoy the walk. It was fall, and there was lots to see.

Roland, Kung, and I began to hang behind them and look at migrating deer crab herds and colony bushes with big bright wings. Floating ribbons were trying to snag a spot for winter in the trees that were already losing their leaves. These were all the interesting things that women didn't have time for because they worried about people instead of things. I wondered if they heard bats sing or the rhythm of the wind.

When we got to that night's shelter, we had climbed so high in the foothills that the air was already getting thin and boiling water wasn't as hot. I cooked some good food, smoked boxer bird and potatoes, and I tried to start a better conversation.

"I already feel like I'm friends with Glassmakers. Don't you?" They looked blank. "I mean, when we were kids, we had all those dolls and little tools and blocks and we'd pretend to build the city."

Cedar nodded and sighed. She was Generation 6 like me, but she wore so many beads she'd float if she fell into water. She wasn't chunky like Marie, or tall, but she had a way of standing that took up a lot of space.

"Remember dancing?" I said. Two people would pretend to be a Glassmaker. One would stand behind the other, bend over, and hold the first person around the waist. Then they'd try to dance with four feet. It was dumb, but when I was a kid, I thought it was great. Real Glassmakers looked pretty different, we knew that, with skinny legs that bent out and skinny arms with two elbows, a body like a long loaf of bread, and a head sort of the same shape. Only as big as human kids, too. We used to make dolls out of sticks.

Marie laughed like a mother, but she must have been a kid herself sometime. Or maybe not. She was the kind of Greenie who dyed all her hair, including her pubic hair for the spring festival, but she made sure she let the hair on her head grow a while between dye jobs so we could all see that she was gray. Maturity meant wisdom, supposedly, but I'd never voted for her for the Committee, even when she was unopposed.

"They had a bigger population," she said, very teacherly. "And they must have a more complex social structure, since they have morphological castes. I'd like to see how it works."

"Me, too." Different bodies for different jobs.

I used to have dolls in all three kinds, the big females, the sturdy major caste, and the little workers. The majors and workers were asexual, although I didn't understand asexuality when I was a kid. I mean, why call them females if there were no males and they just popped out babies when they felt like it? But that was the names they themselves used, according to Stevland, and rainbow bamboo had three sexes, which was even weirder.

Anyway, I wanted to find out how castes worked. I wanted to meet them, not be stuck in a cabin with gossiping politicians. I had my job on the team, to cook, play music, act friendly, and be a teenage boy so they could see different ages and sexes of humans.

"Stevland hasn't been much help," Cedar said.

"Stevland had no frame of reference for them," Marie answered, "and they communicated for only two years before the Glassmakers left."

"Poor little orphan," I said just to pull Marie's greenies.

"He's very lonely," she said. "It didn't help his socialization to grow up with no cohorts."

Cedar used Marie's tone of voice. "Well, now he's one of us." She has two little kids that she kept saying she missed. I felt glad I wasn't one of them.

"What do you think it will be like to meet someone new?" Roland said. He gave me a sneaky little smile for some reason.

"We have our instructions," Marie answered. "We are diplomats. We will be calm and friendly."

"Calm, friendly, sure," Roland said. "But how will it feel? Someone you've never met. We won't know a thing about them. Totally new."

"Not even like meeting an animal," Kung said, grinning with crooked teeth. "With a lion, you know what a lion is, huh? But Glassmakers, no."

"We know a lot about them," Cedar said. "We know how they built the city, what they ate, how they dressed. We know their level of technology, which was higher than ours right now." She was right. They had radios and lots more metal.

"We don't know why they left and why they've stayed away," Marie said. That was actually Stevland's complaint, and he had a point.

"I can't wait to hear Glassmaker music," I said. "Better yet, I can play with them. A duet. They played flutes, too. They're in the murals, so we have music in common." I had dreamed about that ever since I

started playing the flute. Really. That was why I wanted to make music my best.

"Music." Roland still grinned at me. And Cedar looked annoyed.

I tried to ignore them. "And I want to ask where they're from," I said. "I can point out Sol."

"That's a wonderful idea," Marie said, not like a mother or teacher, finally.

I got up the next morning happy that we'd be at the waterfall by afternoon. I'd seen it when I was ten, which wasn't that long ago, or at least it didn't feel long. Back then, before we left, I had heard all about it and seen drawings and was sure I'd like it, and the waterfall was everything I'd hoped for, but the sky was the best. I had never stood and seen the horizon actually below my feet, a pale line far, far in the distance.

We heard the roar of the waterfall like a drone note a kilometer away, and saw the mountains around us so tall they touched the clouds. We'd be going through a damp, stony pass, and then we'd see the waterfall again. It leaped off a red stone cliff and fell narrow and straight so far that you could count ten heartbeats before it landed in the pool below. The path led down to a wide grassy terrace alongside the waterfall, and when the Sun was out, you could see rainbows in the mist that came up from the pool. The Glassmakers had built some houses just like the ones in the city with rows of colored glass blocks in the roofs like rainbows. Stevland had a stand there, twenty full-grown stems, but they didn't connect to the rest of him because of the mountains.

We hiked through the pass around boulders and cliffs, and the thunder of falling water got louder. Kung made the final turn around some rocks and stopped. I thought he had stopped so we could catch up and look together, but he stopped because of what he saw.

The bamboo had been burned to the ground, the houses smashed like eggs. We stared for a long time, and the water seemed to roar in rhythm with my heart, fast.

"Earthquakes aren't impossible," Cedar said, but she didn't look like she believed herself.

"Earthquakes don't start fires," Roland said quietly. He looked behind us, then all around the terrace.

Marie sighed. "See anything moving . . . ? No? Then let's go."

Kung grunted, and we hurried down. When we got there, he set down his packs and began to poke at the ruined buildings. Marie stared at the remains of the bamboo.

"Inspect the area," she said. "Stick together, and everybody, stay in sight of someone else at all times. Who knows what we're dealing with."

"Bears, river wolves, and mountain spiders. And eagles and dragons," Cedar said. "Oh, and wild lions and slugs." Marie gave her a mean look. "Just keeping us on our toes."

"Thank you," Marie answered.

I decided that someday I'd try to use that tone of voice in music. Not all music has to be beautiful. Maybe it could be nervous, too, a lot of little notes, waiting for something to become a tune, to make sense.

"Where's the fippokats?" Roland whistled for the colony that nibbles the lawn. He finally found a kat hiding inside the remains of a house, and it took him a while to coax her out.

Those four inspected the area, but the afternoon was getting late, so Marie told me to cook. I inspected the firepit. Bamboo had been burned in the firepit recently, judging from the ashes, but Stevland hates fire and never lets us burn him. I cleaned out the charred bits before I began. I baked some yams and boiled water to make tea in a ripe yellow cactus that I'd caught that morning on the path, but as I did that, I kept thinking so hard about the Glassmakers and the ruined buildings that I burned a finger on an ember.

Roland held the kat on his lap while we ate. I had never seen a kat sit that still. Kung said the houses had collapsed when digging undercut the foundations.

"A lot of things dig," Cedar said, "but what wild animal wants to dig long and hard enough to destroy four buildings?"

"Eagles might have wrecked the houses, huh?" Kung said. "They have fire. They eat kats."

"Maybe it was Glassmakers," Cedar said. "They're around, after all."

"No," I said, "they wouldn't do that. Those are their own houses. They built them."

She never liked anything. Maybe she already hated the Glassmakers, too.

"They're not their houses now," she answered, looking at me as if I were stupid.

"Maybe they're afraid of us," Roland said.

"Maybe, maybe not," Marie said. "Stevland knows what happened, if his roots are still alive, but right now, we need to make a decision. Should we go or stay?"

I would have bet she wanted to leave, being a coward. We were supposed to wait ten days to see if any Glassmakers happened to visit the waterfall, but we could leave earlier if we thought we should. Roland wanted to stay and find out what happened. Kung wanted to stay and begin repairs on the houses. Cedar said stay, but she would have said go if Marie had said stay. My vote didn't matter by then, but I said stay because I wanted to believe the Glassmakers hadn't wrecked things. They were our friends. I was their friend, at least. This was my chance to meet them.

So we began waiting. Kung built a wood-and-leaf roof over the remains of one of the houses. It would be cozy, all of us in half a house. Roland curled up inside with the kat and napped. He'd take the late-night watch. Cedar and I hiked around the area. We found a big bluebird reef, good news since they love slugs, some colony bushes and some vegetables, a bead bush with huge seeds, and a big surprise, a rag of heavy red-brown cloth on a thorn.

Cedar took it from the thorn. "Flax. Dyed after being woven. We always dye in the wool or the yarn."

"It's Glassmaker, then?"

She looked at me and opened her mouth to say something, then looked away and sort of laughed. "That's one guess."

We went back and talked about it while the Sun set. Glassmakers had been there.

"Maybe the Glassmakers came later, after eagles or whatever had wrecked the place," I said, and Cedar laughed again like I was an idiot, but Marie said it might be possible.

I had the first watch, and I played a few lullabies on an alto flute to help everyone calm down. It was hard to control my breath in thin mountain air and it was too cloudy to see auroras. At what I guessed was midnight, I woke Roland.

"Thanks," he whispered. "Here, take my bunk. It's warm, and the kat would like company." I had a wet dream, of course. Fippmasters have that pheromone on them from the lions, and it affects everyone. I should have expected it. He knew it would happen and he did it just to annoy me.

The next day, Kung found a feather that might have come from an eagle in the pile of ruined stones in a house. He showed it to the kat, and she panicked. Definitely eagle. That didn't prove anything, though, Cedar said. Merchant crabs use eagle feathers to frighten away other crabs from their burrows. They trade feathers over long distances. But we didn't see any merchant crabs.

We got bored. The women pecked at each other, Kung hauled stone and dirt, Roland babied the kat and explored, I found food and cooked it, and in my spare time, I played the flute, trying to make us notice-able to Glassmakers. *We're here. We're not hiding. Hear us. Come meet us. I have flutes to share with you.*

I thought about the Glassmakers, and I saw them in my dreams. The Glassmakers had us beat in a lot of ways. They'd be beautiful because their city was beautiful. They'd be wise because the city was laid out logically. We humans couldn't have built that city. I've seen the old village, what's left of it. It was nothing.

They must have been more efficient than us because they had the three castes so they could divide work logically. They wouldn't snipe about work groups and specialties and who's sleeping with who. And they kept their technology working. We couldn't.

There had been two or three times more Glassmakers in the city than us because there were so many houses, but we didn't know how they were organized or what their families were like. That was just one little detail to learn, and we wanted to find out everything. Soon we would.

Four days into the wait, with nothing to do, I picked the big silver beads.

"They'll look good on you," Roland said with his usual smirk when he saw me putting them in my backpack.

"I think I'll use them to bribe a girl to sleep with me," I said. "We can't all rely on pheromones. Do you know how us Bead boys celebrate the first time? We sneak out in the woods and cook and eat a fippokat."

I thought he'd be shocked, but he just kept smiling.

"They're tasty," I added.

"I'm glad you had a chance to find out. A lot of women like you, you know. I see how they look at you. They're just waiting for you to put on a few years."

I couldn't tell if he was kidding, but I wouldn't let him get to me. I hadn't had much luck with girls and he probably knew that. Sometimes I'd see him sitting with a smile on his face for no good reason, and then he'd glance at me and the smile would get big and smug. I didn't know what to do. I didn't want to pick a fight and I couldn't figure out how to annoy him. Greenies are such Parents.

And we had six more days to wait.

But what we found the next morning made us decide to leave. Marie went to dig a new gift center hole near what was left of Stevland, hoping the roots were alive, and she found a trap.

"Come and look," she said, "and watch your step!" Slowly, we gathered around. She had pulled back a cloth covered with dead weeds and ashes to hide the opening big enough that even Kung could have fallen into face-first. Stakes stuck up from the bottom. I shuddered, trying not to imagine them in me.

"Maybe Jersey did this," Roland said.

"No," Marie said quietly, as if it were a reasonable idea.

"Is it dyed after it was woven?" I said, hoping it wasn't. Cedar checked and shook her head. I said, "This must be to protect Stevland against eagles or something, right? Eagles or something."

"Maybe, or maybe it's for hunting," Marie said. "Maybe there are more."

Kung poked at the ground around Stevland and found another hole. I would never have noticed it. Suddenly I was afraid to move my feet.

I looked down, trying to guess where it might be safe to step, but I couldn't know.

Marie sighed really loud. "Let's leave. We know where it's safe to walk, but in an emergency, we won't have time to check where we run. And there might be other kinds of traps. Vote?"

"We don't need to vote," Cedar said. "It's unanimous."

We stood for a minute without moving, staring at the ground.

"I wanted to meet them," I said, but I wasn't complaining. We had to go.

"We might not be the target," Roland said.

Cedar picked up the cloth and shook it off. "That doesn't mean we won't get hurt."

"This is a disappointment." Marie sighed. "But Tatiana approves of prudence. She'll understand."

"So will Stevland," Cedar said. I couldn't tell if she was challenging Marie.

"Are we still going to leave gifts for the Glassmakers?" I said.

"Why, yes," Marie said in a way that made me feel intelligent.

"Too much we don't know," Kung said, shaking his head, and his braids moved in waves. He walked to the hearth, watching where he put his feet, and picked up a heat-cracked rock. He held it like a hand axe. "Hmh. Might be a good weapon."

"No," Marie said. She walked, slowly and carefully, to the fresh soil around the houses. She took a big rock, whacked it against a foundation stone a few times, and came back to Kung. "This has a sharper edge. Everyone, gather up your possessions, but let's travel light and fast. Leave behind what you can. Roland, bring the kat. Nye, leave some flutes and anything else they might like. Cedar, am I forgetting anything?"

Kung stared at his new weapon. Cedar stared at Marie, surprised to be suddenly treated as number two. I was thinking that Marie really knew how to beat a hasty retreat, just what we needed now, and I wanted to leave only a little bit more than I still wanted to stay. But I'd have to meet Glassmakers some other time. I hoped they were safe.

"We should leave a message," Cedar said, still looking surprised.

"Great idea. What?" Marie asked. We discussed it and reached a decision without arguing. With flutes and gifts and a few additional sticks, we wrote in Glassmade: "We desire-you friendship," using the flutes for the word "you." I kept one flute, a small one of patterned locustwood, my favorite.

It took no time to pack up our stuff, since we didn't have much. Most of what we'd brought was food. We repacked enough for a two-day march and put the rest near the message. I took the lead. Kung took the rear, holding the stone axe.

We had just passed the crest of the path between the rocks and were headed down the far side of the mountain when I saw a footprint in some damp, bare dirt and waved for everyone to stop. Glassmakers have split hooves, but the mark wasn't clear. Roland took a look. "Deer crab, maybe." Or maybe not. I couldn't decide if I felt relieved or disappointed.

We hiked a few more minutes. The path turned around a boulder. On the other side, there were unmistakable Glassmaker tracks in a patch of dirt. "Several individuals," Roland said. "Different sizes and depths."

"Not long ago," Cedar said. "The ridges haven't dried hardly at all."

"Headed that way." Roland pointed up the path, the direction where we were headed. Maybe they had made the traps, but they had to be friendly, just like us. And we were going to meet them!

Kung looked at the stone in his hand and threw it away. "I won't fight Glassmakers. Promised." He looked at Marie. "Make Nye play something. We're not chasing them, not us, no. Not sneaking."

Marie nodded. I took out the flute, had to try twice to take a proper deep breath, and began a cheery song. *We're coming. We aren't sneaking up on you.* I wanted them to hear this in the music. *Don't be afraid. Come and meet us. Finally. Here we are.* I hoped it wouldn't take long because I was too happy to wait. *Meet us. Please.* And be what we hoped for, be friendly like us. We're a lot alike.

Roland scrambled ahead of me on the path and began to march to the music. Cedar and Marie clapped in time, and Kung, completely out of tune, whistled along. *Here we come!*

Two hundred meters later, we knew before we followed the path around another boulder that Glassmakers waited on the other side. I saw their shadows. Glassmakers! Roland pointed and grinned and led the way. I followed, still playing the flute but too anxious to play well, to breathe right, to remember the tune, or anything. I was about to meet Glassmakers!

On the other side of the boulder, Glassmakers blocked the path. For just a moment they looked like a tangle of tree stumps and dead branches. Then I began to see them, their bodies and heads, and their skinny, bent arms and legs. What on Earth would be called insects. Two arms, four legs. All brownish like tree trunks, different shades of brown. Maybe twenty-five of them. Their big eyes sparkled.

They were pointing spears at us. Spears.

That wasn't what I had hoped for at all, but I kept playing, looking and playing at the same time. We stood still and kept clapping and moving to the music, but I barely moved because I felt ready to fall over with excitement. With every note, I could tell that I wasn't the only one. Kung stopped whistling, and someone was clapping out of beat.

The Glassmakers didn't move or make a sound. They were workers and majors, shorter than I expected, much shorter than any of us. But they weren't dressed fancy like Glassmakers in the murals. They wore plain, tattered blankets draped over their backs, leather gaiters on their legs like us, and baskets strapped to their flanks. A few wore leather hats or collars.

They smelled like rotting tree fungus, and so intensely I could have gagged.

Their spears were tipped in stone. Stone, like us. Where was their technology?

A major wearing a brown-and-green plaid blanket stepped forward.

Maybe these were explorers. Our explorers didn't carry much and didn't dress fancy. They didn't bathe much. They carried simple tools. I shouldn't expect them to look magnificent. Or be surprised that there weren't any females. They probably had better things to do.

I played one more chorus of the march, stamping my foot to the beat, and the rest of us clapped along. The Glassmaker who had stepped forward stamped one of its front hooves for a few beats. It understood the music! We had already communicated without saying a word. I ended the song, lowered the flute, and waited. I had done my job! It was Marie's turn.

She raised her arms, elbows out, palms up, like the Glassmakers in the murals. They didn't move. I wished they would lower their spears. I realized I was holding my flute like a club. Slowly, I unwrapped my fingers and held it like a pen.

Marie gestured toward herself. "Marie." She pointed at us. "Cedar, Nye, Kung, Roland." Then she pointed at the Glassmaker who had stepped forward.

Its face didn't move. It didn't answer.

"We are very glad to meet you," she said slowly. They wouldn't understand, of course, but we had no idea how to pronounce Glassmade. The major in the plaid blanket still didn't react.

"We have come from the stars, too," she said, "and we are pleased to share this planet with you. There is much that I hope we can learn from each other."

The fippokat began to climb out of Roland's pack. He reached over his shoulder and took it in his arms. "What do you think, friend?" he murmured, and nuzzled it like a mother kat.

The Glassmakers' bulging eyes were on the sides of their heads and had no pupils, so I couldn't tell what they were looking at. And their faces never moved, so I couldn't tell what they were thinking. Were they friendly? One of them whistled something that ended in a snapping sound.

Plaid Blanket gestured at the path behind us and took a step forward, then repeated the action, gesturing more. "Shall we go back?" Marie said. I nodded. I think the others did. She turned around and took a few steps, looking over her shoulder. The Glassmaker took a step forward. "Let's go, then."

Kung took the lead, and we followed him, Marie last. Hooves thumped behind us.

The walk back seemed longer than the trip there, although it was all downhill and fast and easy walking. I wondered if I should play more music. I looked over my shoulder a lot. A line of Glassmakers was following us down the mountain. A few majors gestured and spoke, and often I could heard them speak, squeaks and chatters and a noise like "chek" or "shuk" or "cheek," harsh and unmusical. I couldn't make those noises. They probably couldn't make mine. But we could learn to listen. We would all have to, and we all wanted to. That's why we were there.

Back at the terrace, we lined up behind the message we had left. "I hope they can read," Marie murmured. They formed a circle around us, and Plaid Blanket squeaked and chekked and pointed at the message. The damp air from the waterfall made their putrid smell seem worse.

Marie stepped forward. Plaid Blanket's head swiveled. She reached down and picked up a tulip bulb from the food we had left behind. Stevland said they ate tulip bulbs. She held it out. "Tulip," she said. It stared at her hand, moving its head to study it, and shuffled a few nervous steps. Slowly, it reached out a skinny arm with two elbows and four long fingers. Marie stood still, smiling wide but with lips closed. No teeth, nothing threatening.

It touched the bulb, but instead of taking it, its fingers slid around it to hold her hand. They say Sylvia had dreamed of this, standing hand in hand with a Glassmaker. I had dreamed of it as a child. Pacifists and Glassmakers, friends at last!

The Glassmaker said something that sounded like a damp stick breaking and jerked Marie's arm so hard she fell down. Kung grunted, and other Glassmakers stood stiff as if we might begin fighting, but we had to be friendly, so we just stood there, and I didn't know what to do anyway. Marie looked up from the ground.

"What was that for?" she said.

The major didn't answer.

She got up and gave it a look that could have scorched its hair. They stared at each other.

It put both hands on its spear.

"Let's try this again." The real Marie had surfaced. She bent down and picked up the tulip bulb and held it out. "This is a tulip. Tulip. This is for you. A gift. Take it." She held it by its pointed bud end rather than flat in her palm. "Go on," she said a bit nicer. "I won't hurt you."

It took a few nervous steps, head bobbing. She set the bulb on the ground close to its feet, then turned and pointed to the words on the ground. "We desire-you friendship." She picked up a flute and handed it to me. "Nye, play something short and friendly."

Friendly. I could do that. I played a few bars of the children's welcoming song for babies, repeated them, then, thinking of their noises, played it with harsh squeaky notes. I held the flute out toward Marie. She took it and held it out in the same manner toward the leader. It gestured toward another major, who came forward and took it. It blew in the mouthpiece, but not the right way, and no sound came out. It looked at me and squeaked sort of like the tune I had played.

I picked up another flute and blew into it, showing the proper angle. It tried again, finally got a tweet, and did it again. It handed back the flute.

"Thank you, Nye," Marie said pointedly.

"Good idea, Marie," I answered. We had communicated! But they should have known what flutes were. They were in the murals.

Plaid Blanket reached toward Marie. She didn't flinch, but she blinked hard. It pointed to the strap to her backpack and gestured for her to take it off. She put it on the ground and stepped back. Two workers came forward and took everything out, the underwear, food, a blanket, a comb, a bit of soap wrapped in a leaf, and a Glassmade–Pacifist dictionary. Plaid Blanket and a few other majors picked up every item one by one and spoke a lot among themselves. They sniffed the soap and leafed through the book, but didn't seem to read anything.

They looked at the gifts on the ground, too, especially Harry's carving of a Glassmaker. They sniffed the fruit Stevland had made with Glassmakers in mind, but set it down again. During their chatter and whistles, I whispered to Roland, "What do you think?" He understood fipps, so he might understand Glassmakers.

"They're surprised by how much we're alike, us and them."

"Shouldn't that be good?" Cedar whispered.

Plaid Blanket called out, "Chek!" at us. By its gestures, it wanted us to take off our packs, and we did. They went through them. The dried meat in Kung's pack earned a sound like "kongaree!" Roland's pack included an obsidian mirror, something I don't think they had ever seen before, and a little ball of lion yarn that they smelled again and again. My pack had nothing interesting. When they were done, they huddled and talked.

"Knives," Marie said, and took the thumb-sized stone blade from her belt and set it on the ground. We all did the same. This really excited the Glassmakers. They picked up the blades and knives and studied them and finally stashed them in a worker's basket. The worker said something. Plaid Blanket called it forward and hit it so hard across the mouth that it bled red blood. It couldn't have said anything to deserve that. I looked at Roland. He was watching them, holding the kat tight, as if he wanted to protect it. Marie had no expression on her face at all.

I had seen people get hit in fights, but if both parties throw punches, it's fair. Roland had to beat up old Qin to take the leadership of the lion pack, but they had rehearsed the fight. We Pacifists watched along with the lions, and when Qin left the field with a fake limp and fake blood on his face, we booed him.

But the Glassmakers were people, and normal people wouldn't let themselves be hit for real, and normal people wouldn't hit someone defenseless. I had pledged to be a diplomat. If a Glassmaker hit me, I couldn't hit back. But I had never, ever thought before about a Glassmaker hitting me. How could they?

They took our food, except for the bamboo fruit, and handed it out. They ate quickly. Not all the workers got something to eat.

"Look," Kung murmured. "Teeth in their throat. See them move?" But we didn't say more. Plaid Blanket didn't seem to like talking.

We got our packs back. Then Plaid Blanket ordered us to march down the mountain with them. "As they wish," Marie said, but we didn't have a choice. What would they do if we resisted? I gathered up the flutes and couldn't tell if I was frightened or angry, but I stumbled when I stood up because my legs for a moment had no strength. The Glassmakers weren't what I expected. Maybe they *had* destroyed the houses and burned Stevland.

The path below the waterfall resort was steep and narrow. We hiked single file, mostly silent. Marie insisted on walking with Plaid Blanket and other majors. They spoke occasionally, and she had her dictionary out. The path sometimes got so steep that we had to climb on all fours, but they didn't offer to help us and they seemed impatient. Sometimes a major would hit or kick a worker, but I couldn't figure out what for, as if there could be a good reason.

A cold wind blew through the rocks along the base of the cliffs. Cedar, ahead of me, pulled her clothes tight. Roland began to sing to his fipp, but Plaid Blanket made a gesture, and a worker near Roland clamped its hand over its mouth. Roland stopped singing.

We hiked for the whole day and hardly stopped to pee, and saw that they peed from the far end of their body, but they never stopped to eat, and when the Sun set, we weren't even halfway down the mountain. We camped on a wide ledge with nothing more than rocks, shrubs, and vines. We lay down, exhausted, and Kung passed out dried bamboo fruit. I chewed it in tiny, sweet bites to make it last longer. The Glassmakers knelt to sleep, legs tucked under them.

"Can you understand them?" I whispered to Marie.

"I don't think they want me to understand," Marie said.

"They're afraid of us," Roland said.

"Too afraid to hurt us, hmm?" Kung said.

"Too afraid to let us go, too. Too afraid to touch us. They're afraid of each other, some of them. The workers are afraid of certain majors."

"They hit them," I whispered. "It's not right."

"No, it's not," Marie hissed.

"Can we escape?" Cedar said.

"Can you outrun them?" Roland answered, and of course we couldn't.

Plaid Blanket didn't like us to talk, so we didn't say anything more, but I wanted to. I would have stood up and yelled at him. I stared up at the overcast, black sky. The Glassmakers weren't talking, either. The silence annoyed me to sleep.

The next day we hiked down a windy ravine into a forest of trees with square trunks. Tree fippokats with green spots in their brown fur chattered in the branches. Bats called but I didn't understand them at all. They had a different language.

Ahead, the leaders whistled and kakked and stopped in front of a little stand of rainbow bamboo, probably just ten or twenty years old. Our explorers planted Stevland's seeds everywhere. It reminded me of home, of family and friends and Bead girls who ignored me. They were all probably thinking nice thoughts about Glassmakers right now.

The majors screeched orders. Workers hurried to gather deadwood and stack it around the bamboo. Marie looked at them, and her face and hands were moving, and I knew what she was thinking. It was like watching the Glassmakers getting ready to hit us. I had to let them hit me, and now I had to let them hurt someone else. I crossed my arms to keep my hands still.

She was almost crying when they struck a spark to the wood. I didn't love Stevland, but I would never hurt him, and I wouldn't let him be hurt, but I had to. She had to. We all had to.

I whistled like a Rainbow City bat: "Fire. Bad." I think she heard me.

The bamboo was still smoking when we started marching again. The Glassmakers must have been the ones who burned Stevland at the waterfall. They must have destroyed the houses, but they didn't have to do that. They didn't have a reason. I had promised to be nonviolent, and they weren't like me.

We marched fast. By nightfall, Cedar said we had gotten two-thirds of the way down the mountain. It was foggy and damp. We settled down to sleep. Even the ground felt like a relief because I was so tired. Kung handed out dried fruit, and I was so hungry I almost swallowed mine whole.

"Hunger makes the Glassmakers hurry," Roland whispered. "They want to go a lot faster."

"What do we do?" I asked.

No one answered for a while, then Marie said, "Learn what you can."

I tried to fall asleep. I'd never been that hungry before, or that angry. I wasn't learning anything.

We began marching again as soon as it was bright enough to see through a cold drizzle. I walked with my blanket wrapped around me over my coat. The rain made a sad rhythm echoing on the bare stone. The path changed from stony to muddy, which was better for wide human feet than narrow Glassmaker hooves, and then it got stony again. At one point we were on a narrow switchback against a cliff, so narrow that the Glassmakers' baskets scraped against the rock. Drizzle made the path slick. We all had to walk slow and careful. I tried not to look down at the long drop just a sidestep away.

Roland shouted, and we all turned, but as I did, I knew someone had fallen. Not him, I hoped selfishly, just because he was one of us, one of our team, and we were all alone on this side of the mountain. I turned so fast that I slipped and for a terrible moment thought I was going to fall, and at the same time realized his voice came from down, not behind.

I knew what I would see before I looked down the face of the cliff. Roland was falling. His body bounced off a rock outcrop, his shout ended in a loud grunt, and he kept going down, arms and legs flopping. He landed on the path far below and a crunch echoed up. I waited, listening for a groan, watching for a twitch, for anything, but he lay facedown and still on the wet stones like a doll. Then he moved. No, it was the kat in his backpack peeking out. It inched out, green like his hair, limping, and nuzzled his face.

Glassmakers were already running down the path. Marie followed as fast as she could, and I could only stand and watch.

Marie examined Roland. It didn't take long. She turned to us and shook her head. She was too far away to see the expression on her face. She picked up the kat. The Glassmaker leaders shouted at each other and made a lot of gestures at Marie. They took off Roland's backpack and took out his blanket. Diagonally, it was big enough to wrap him. Plaid Blanket called over a worker, the one it had hit back at the waterfall, I think, and had it take off its baskets, and they laid Roland across its back, tricky to do on the narrow path, and then we all began walking again.

Roland was dead. I had hated him over a lot of stupid reasons. He had all the sex he could handle and important work while I burned my hands in the ovens and could barely get a woman to take me seriously. That didn't matter anymore. I had known him all my life, and he was annoying, but he never hurt me. I couldn't imagine him wanting to hurt anyone. He wasn't clumsy. It wasn't his fault he slipped. It was the Glass-makers'. They were making us march too fast.

We hiked down into a valley. Moths nipped us. Packs of little grunt-ing birds with feathers in the shape of twigs ran through the brush, like little dried weeds scooting around. A warm wind blew up the moun-tains and condensed into fog. Bluebirds barked and dashed between our feet. The leaves on the trail became slick and slippery from the fog.

I was too tired to do anything more than put one foot ahead of the other. None of the Glassmakers seemed to be much better, but the majors seemed too tired to hit anyone, at least. The sky got clear, then cloudy again. We reached a meadow with lacy weeds that smelled like celery, and I felt hungrier than ever. Roland's body was moved to a dif-ferent worker's back.

The path became more level, and I glanced back. Mountains stood behind the forests, and the red rock looked like walls holding up the clouds, with valleys like cracks in the walls. It had been an endless descent from Lief's Waterfall, and it would be an endless climb back up there from where we were. If we ever went back.

We crossed some little streams and scaly moss grew on everything. I worried about slugs, but saw only swimming beetles and lots of aquatic birds. The Glassmakers wanted to go faster, but when Marie asked us to speed up, Cedar just said, "I'm trying."

I wasn't going to whine like Cedar, but I couldn't go faster, either. A few Glassmakers raced ahead, making whistles and kaks and snaps like wood breaking. They were answered with calls that got louder and set-tled into a chant: "Kongareee, kongareee . . ." Drums kept time. We were there, wherever we were going.

The path got wide, with tree stumps on either side. A Glassmaker village, maybe a whole city, couldn't be far away. There would be food and water and a chance to rest and wash. Someone would be able to read and write, and Marie could do her diplomatic mission. Someone might know how to play a flute. Someone would explain why they burned Stevland, why they destroyed the houses at the waterfall, why they made us march so hard that Roland fell and died.

I didn't think that any reason would be good enough.

And there in a field was the Glassmakers' village. It was small and drab, so ugly that at first I thought maybe it was just a workshop area, but it was where they lived, two dozen tents shaped like the domes at Rainbow City, but they were little and made of bark and hides and cloth and straw mats, all worn out and poor. There were no colors, no rainbows. A bluebird reef was built better than their city.

Kung said, "Oh," and shook his head. There was nothing else to say.

Glassmakers were waiting for us, maybe fifty of them. They ran toward us, waving their arms and chanting so loud my ears hurt, and some were banging on drums. We marched through a field of green weeds covered with white bugs like big snowflakes. The wind carried a strong Glassmaker rotting stink at us. With every step, the chanting and drums seemed louder. Soon, like Cedar, I had to cover my ears. The kat clamped its ears shut and covered its nose with its paws.

As they got closer, I saw a couple of females, and they were big, with heads almost at my eye level. A few Glassmakers were even smaller than the workers, with eyes barely above my knees. Children. Lots didn't even have blankets over their backs, and a few limped or looked sick. The ones who weren't singing kept jabbering at each other, and two of them pushed each other in some sort of argument.

Not wise, not magnificent, not civilized. I kept looking around, but I don't know what for. I guess I hoped that a real city was hidden somewhere.

We were marched toward a tent that was bigger and nicer than the rest, with sapling poles that arched to a dome taller than we were. Marie guessed it was their Meeting House. The dirt floor had a few bark mats and leaves on it. The worker dumped Roland's body near the door. It was stiff.

"I hope they feed us," Cedar whined.

Soon, three females arrived with Plaid Blanket. I guessed one female was old because her fur looked thin and she limped. They all wore newer, clean blankets.

They stood and looked at us, and we looked back.

I wanted to sit down but didn't dare. Plaid Blanket launched into some kind of explanation, pointing at us and Roland a lot. The whistles and kaks meant nothing to me, but Marie interrupted. She squawked, "Cheek."

Everyone stared at her, including the Glassmakers outside peeking in through the open doors. Plaid Blanket repeated what it had said. Marie squawked the same sound. Then she tried to describe with gestures and a few sounds the fact that we came from Rainbow City. At least that's what it meant to me. Then she used her canteen to ask for something to drink.

One of the younger females said something in return, Plaid Blanket talked more, then they yelled at each other; finally the young one seemed to get angry and they all left. Guards stayed at the doors.

"You talk Glassmade, Marie?" Kung sat on the ground far away from Roland's body.

Marie looked for a place to sit. I had already sat down on a mat, almost fell, really, I was so tired, and moved over for her.

"I listened while we marched and learned a few words. I said 'attention' or 'listen,' I think. Something like that."

Ten workers came to take away Roland, still wrapped in his blanket.

"Shouldn't we stop them?" Cedar said.

"What would we do with him?" Marie said.

The Glassmakers lined up four on each side of the body, one at the head and feet, seemed to count to three, heaved him up, and left.

Marie repeated the count quietly. Buzz, croak, gurgle. She looked the words up in her dictionary. "I think the writing is phonetic. I hope so. That would be a big breakthrough."

"Ask for food," Cedar said.

"I asked for water. When they bring that, we can all ask for food." She tried to smile, but she was too tired. She nodded off soon.

I think I slept, too. After a long time, I thought I smelled meat cooking, maybe mountain bear. I couldn't tell. Stinking Glassmakers. But they'd brought us water.

"Hmm. Maybe a feast after a funeral," Kung said.

"An execution," Cedar said. The kat dozed on her lap. "These are violent people."

"I'm dying of hunger," I said.

Marie had woken up. "Try to survive." She took a comb from her backpack and fussed with her hair. "We don't want to offend them. Unnecessarily, at least. They have odd habits and probably odder rules."

"They're violent and primitive," Cedar complained.

"Yes, they are. It's worrisome."

"There have to be real Glassmakers somewhere," I said. "This must be a subgroup. They got lost from the main group or something."

Marie nodded. "Maybe. These are very disappointing. But they are Glassmakers, and we have our job."

We looked out the door, but all we could see was guards and the wall of the next tent.

"Funerals," Marie said. "That will be a test." From the look on her face, she was going to pass the test, no matter what.

"These Glassmakers, look at their shoulders," Kung said. "They move up and down, not sideways, not like this." He motioned to throw. "Two elbows. Their arms aren't strong. Can they dig to bury him? Or do we dig, hmm?"

A couple of Glassmakers walked past the tent carrying firewood. "I've read," Marie said, "that some Earth cultures burned their dead. We're here to make friends. They don't seem to have much experience at that, so we will have to provide the example. Music, a few words— you can say something if you're moved, of course. I will. Our goodbyes, our memories, our friendship. Set an example."

"Can we cry?" Cedar asked, challenging Marie again.

"Please do."

When Lux set, a group of workers marching in time came to get us, carrying spears and led by Plaid Blanket and a drumming major, and I grabbed my backpack with the flutes. They took us to the edge of the village, where everyone had gathered, and five females stood in the front of the crowd. The stink almost overcame the scent of cooking meat.

I had looked into the doorways of huts as we walked past. The biggest thing I saw were looms for making blankets, no furniture or much else except a few pathetic boxes and baskets.

Two mats waited for us, one almost new and the other one heaped with green leaves. "Sit," Marie said, pointing, and we arranged ourselves on the bare mat. I thought about which flute to play and what song. The unmoving Glassmaker faces surrounded us. Someone began drumming, and the sound came from the direction where the food was being cooked.

I picked out the flute with the lowest register and played a sad song by old Uncle Higgins that had words about living a day too long and seeing failures you couldn't prevent. Perfect. Marie began humming along. On the second time through, Cedar and Kung joined us. "Once more," Marie whispered. I did, with more feeling. I had never liked Roland, and I would miss him for exactly that reason. I set down the flute.

A female with curls of dark fur down her back, the one that had argued earlier, repeated the opening bars to the song in a hoarse whistle, almost a squawk. I played the first seven notes again, then held another flute out. She stepped forward and took it. I held mine up to my lips. She copied the gesture, though her mouth was vertical. I blew and made a note, fa. She blew and made a breathy note. She did it again. I covered the first hole and blew to make a different note, mi. She copied me. One by one we copied the notes, then, together, a duet, we played the seven opening notes in order, fa, mi, do, mi, re, do, re.

Finally, finally, I had played a duet with a Glassmaker!

I lowered my flute and bowed solemnly. But I didn't feel solemn. I wanted to jump and shout. I had shared music. If we could do that, we could do anything. They were willing, they just didn't know how, like Marie said, and we would have to provide the example. We had a lot to teach them. More than they could imagine.

The Glassmaker stared at me with those big, blank eyes. She handed the flute back, but we would play again, I felt sure. These Glassmakers weren't all bad.

If this was a funeral, it was time to bury Roland, but we didn't know where he was. We didn't have shovels. We needed a place to dig. The smell of cooked meat came on a wind, and I was so hungry I couldn't think about anything for more than a moment.

A drum started beating again in the direction of the cooking area. People made way for something large. Clouds of steam rose from it. A roast, a very large animal, maybe a fippolion. I had never smelled anything quite like that, but it was delicious. I glimpsed it again through the crowd. Maybe it was a small lion.

"Bear," Kung murmured.

I got a better look. Not a bear. It was a large animal with a round head and a flat torso like no animal I knew, and the skin was grilled crisp and golden and shining with fat. The crowd opened up, and I got a clear look. Not a lion, not with such long legs.

Cedar wailed, hid her face in her hands, and turned away. The head lay facedown, and I recognized a crisp and golden ear, a human ear.

My mouth filled with saliva, not from hunger, but the rush before vomiting. I got to my feet and ran, hand over my mouth, away from the crowd, and dropped to my knees. Marie had said again and again to set an example. I had to, somehow. Glassmakers were watching me. I tore off a chunk of moss from the dirt to make a hole and puked into it. There was nothing in my stomach but bile, bitter yellow slime, spasm after spasm. Every time I thought I was through, a whiff of . . . a whiff made my muscles jerk again.

Finally, the bile burned my nose and destroyed my sense of smell. I waited, panting. I was done, empty, completely empty. I put the moss back over the slime and used my tears to wash my face with my sleeve. The salt on my lips cleared my mouth a bit.

I stood up. The Glassmakers squeaked and whistled. Cedar had her head in her hands. I stumbled toward Roland. Maybe this didn't mean what I thought it did. No, I knew what a roast looked like. This was supposed to be food. Kung stared at the ground. Marie stood up and stared at Plaid Blanket and tears dripped down her face. I had never seen her cry before. Never.

The female who played music came to stand beside Plaid Blanket. Arms spread, she said something to us, and waited for our response. Behind her, Glassmakers jabbered at each other. She said it again, and I looked at Marie. She sighed.

"Thank you very much," she said gently, although her face said something else. She faced the Glassmakers. "Numbers are a measure, and we are less now.

"We came in peace," she continued. "We will remain in peace, regardless. My job now is to praise Roland. He was what a fippmaster should be, enticing and gentle and always, always confident, a lion among men. He was what a member of this mission should be, ready to give everything to create a good first meeting between our people. He gave everything.

"I am going to assume," she said in a strong voice although she was still crying, "that you mean well. In fact, I am sure you have behaved respectfully. We can't accept your kindness, but we thank you for it. Roland will not rest in peace, I think. I will not, not for the remainder of my days, whatever their number. I can only hope that we will achieve something from our many misunderstandings. I am sure we have mystified you. We will continue to do so."

She turned toward us. "Nye? Kung? Cedar? Anything to add?"

Cedar stood up and blew Roland a kiss. "On behalf of the women of Pax," she said, and shuddered and turned away.

Kung stood stiffly. "He was kind to his animals, always kind."

I stood up, felt dizzy, and spoke anyway. "He wasn't a friend. He was usually really annoying, but he was a good fippmaster, and he tried to be friendly, and I'll miss him. I really will."

Marie took a spoon that had come with Roland and approached the friendly female. She pantomimed digging, made some Glassmaker noises, and tried to show that she needed something like a spoon but big. "We're going to bury him," she said. "It would go easier for all of us if you get us tools and selected a spot."

After a lot of confusion and kakking, a female slapped a major. There was more yelling, so loud my ears hurt, and some arm-waving, and a few more slaps. I looked at Marie.

"I told them I'd mystify them." But she didn't say it as a joke.

A worker finally ran toward us carrying a crab-shell spade. "Where?" said Marie again and again, pointing to different places, and after even more arguing, Plaid Blanket pointed to the edge of the area where we were, but he didn't seem happy.

"You start," she told Kung, and pantomimed drinking and squawked, "Cheek!" and they all jumped, and a worker brought us water in bark buckets. It tasted sweet, so sweet, and I washed away the bile from my mouth and throat, and I knew right away it wouldn't come up. Something that Marie had said had changed my feelings, but I didn't know what it was. I cupped my hand and held out some water for the kat. It drank, then it went to help Kung dig.

Very soon, I relieved him. I had to dig. I had to dig or I would start smacking Glassmakers in their immobile big-eyed faces. They didn't need to be so horrible. They didn't need to cook Roland. The spade chopped into the damp soil. The Glassmakers kept yelling at each other.

If they were afraid of us, they should have treated us better. They should have fed us, they should have talked to us, they should have come with us to Rainbow City. They should have had a beautiful city of their own. They shouldn't have burned Stevland. They should have sung, not squawked, and their squawks were making my head hurt. They should have kats and clothes and they should be understandable. They shouldn't hit each other . . . and Cedar called my name and pointed. Six majors were punching and kicking each other, and then two females tried to break it up, and they started yelling and swinging their fists at each other, too.

Marie was watching in a way that I knew meant she was learning something. I started digging again. Glassmakers weren't at all like what I had come for. They were stinking, stupid savages. And Roland, what they did to Roland was horrible. I kept thinking the same things over and over again.

I was panting hard. The kat had stopped to chew on a root. The Glassmakers were still yelling, but not fighting.

Marie tapped me on the shoulder. "Cedar will dig for a while. She needs to do something," she said quietly.

"What if they don't let us go?"

"Think of the mission." Her voice didn't sound like she believed her own words.

"I am. We were supposed to make friends. But I don't want to."

"I understand. I'm not sure I want them as friends either, but we need to be at peace with them."

Marie herself finished digging the hole and lifted out the kat. We each picked up a corner of the mat where Roland lay and slid him in. He broke apart as he fell. Marie was fast in sprinkling dirt over him, and the kat joined in, kicking dirt into the hole with its big back feet. I went to my pack and got the silver bead seeds I was going to take back to try to find a girlfriend and I sprinkled them over Roland.

We shoveled more dirt, and then it was done. The kat was hopping on the mound to flatten it. Marie turned toward the Glassmakers. The people who were fighting had separated into two groups. They started shouting louder than ever at each other and at us, waving hands, a few holding sticks. I looked around to see where to run if they attacked. But they could outrun us. I picked up my backpack as a shield.

"Cheek!" Marie shouted. They began to quiet down. "Cheek!" she said again. She gave them the look that could light a fire. "Thank you for not interfering. I am sure you are confused. We are more confused and disappointed than I could tell you if we spoke the same language. This is unlikely to change soon, and I am very troubled about that."

She ordered me to play music again. I didn't feel like it, but I did anyway, repeating Uncle Higgins's song, this time letting my feelings fill the notes. It sounded like the Glassmakers, exactly like them, harsh and unmusical. We should never have come. That's the song I was playing, living a day too many in the wrong place and seeing things I never wanted to know. They didn't stop arguing even while I was playing.

A couple of workers brought us food. Marie thanked them elaborately, although there wasn't much food: four little flat loaves of nut bread, a dish of stew with onions and gritty snowflake bugs, and a basket with some velvet leaves and tomatoes. We gave the leaves to the kat. I was still hungry.

"Will they let us go?" Cedar said. "If we don't go back soon, we'll never make it over the mountains in winter."

"I hope so," Marie said. "Our job was to meet them and express our hope of friendship."

"We did that," I said.

"Yes, we did," Marie said. She looked worried, maybe even afraid.

As soon as the food was gone, they took us to a small tent. The ground was covered with onion leaves. "Perfume," Kung said. "For them." He shook his head. The tent walls kept out all fresh air. I was too tired to sleep, but I lay down in the onion leaves and fell asleep right away.

When I opened my eyes, Kung was using the chamber pot. The air smelled worse than ever. Marie squirmed her hand through the tent flap until she could reach a peg and open it. The Sun was rising. The guards outside said something. "We need fresh air," she said. I wouldn't have argued with her.

"Noisy at night," Kung said. "Noisy now."

There were lots of kaks and cheeks and squeaks. They were apparently still arguing.

Cedar looked out the door. "Rain for sure. We're going to get a steady rain."

The kat was eating the onion leaves. I was thirsty. Marie asked for—demanded, actually—water, even said a squeak that she thought meant "water." I smelled wood smoke and roasting nuts. I was hungry again.

"We ought to go and warn the city," Cedar said. "The Glassmakers are dangerous."

Marie didn't answer.

They didn't seem to be in a hurry to talk to us. The kat made a game out of harassing the guards. At noon, three females and Plaid Blanket came with a squad of workers carrying spears.

"We're in trouble," Cedar said. But Marie left the tent and greeted them as if they had come to make some sort of formal visit. I tried to imitate her self-confidence and stared at them, those stinking idiots.

"Look at everything," Marie said. "Learn what you can. Nye, count heads."

A female, the one who had played the flute, announced something. The Glassmakers became silent. They gestured for us to fall into a procession, drums ahead of us, drums behind us, all of them too loud. The kat in my arm tried to squirm away, and I held it tighter and covered its ears. I started counting as we were marched through the ugly little village. Five females, about forty majors, about sixty workers, maybe fifteen children, but they ran around a lot and were hard to count. Maybe one hundred twenty altogether, one hundred twenty disappointments.

The procession turned toward the path out of town back toward the mountains. We had to scurry to keep up. They finally stopped at the edge of the forest and pointed on ahead. Yes! They were sending us home. But we had nothing. We couldn't walk that far with nothing. They were sending us to die. Marie cleared her throat.

Hooves sounded behind us from the village, and workers arrived with our packs and handed them to us. They gave Kung our canteens, filled with water, and gave Marie a battered basket filled with loaves of bread.

"We must give gifts in return," she said.

"The kat," Kung said. "They want the kat." Marie nodded.

I handed it over, soft and warm. I wondered if they would learn from the poor animal or if they would cook it.

"One more thing," I said. I took a flute from my pack and held it toward the female who had played before. Plaid Blanket grabbed it, then she grabbed it from him and yelled, waving it like a club. I suddenly hoped they choked to death trying to play it, if they ever did.

Marie faced them, impassive. "We have enjoyed your hospitality and sincerely look forward to meeting you again. I am sure our peoples have much we can teach each other, and eventually we will have a long and peaceful and productive relationship. It has been a genuine privilege to be part of this mission and to meet Glassmakers face-to-face. I can speak for all of us in saying we will never forget this."

I wondered how much of that she believed. I didn't believe a word.

The female whistled something in return, then she turned her back, then another female turned away, although Plaid Blanket kept watching us. We took the hint and began walking. Far, far away through the trees, mountains rose like red walls, and the skies looked gray and ugly.

After about two hours, it began to drizzle and the path got steeper, and in another hour, we found an overhanging rock to protect us. Cedar said a hard rain would start soon. I dug a trench to protect us from water pouring downhill. The women gathered firewood. Kung tore down some tree branches to make a lean-to and block the cold wind.

We huddled around a fire and ate some bread. "We did our job," Kung said.

"What? We failed completely," Cedar said, and began to list everything that had gone wrong. "Because of Marie—" she began at one point.

"Marie did fine," I interrupted. "I never liked her, but this was the job for her."

Marie was right there, but I couldn't stand to listen to Cedar whine anymore.

"It's true," I said, "a lot of things went wrong, and I hate these Glassmakers."

Kung grunted. I kept talking.

"But I don't think we could have done anything different. We tried to make friends. We tried hard. What more do you want?"

Everyone was silent. Marie looked at me and, after a while, nodded. The rain started falling hard.

"I wanted them to be what I expected," I said. "That's what went wrong. They weren't what I wanted at all. They weren't the Glassmakers I grew up with."

"We learned a lot," Marie said. "They're nomads. That's a temporary camp. They got rid of us because we'd slow them down, and they're not hanging on by much. And then we went and wasted all that meat. We aren't compatible. Not at this point."

"But we didn't communicate," Cedar whined.

"We did. They saw us. They saw that we're strange, but we're not going to hurt them."

"All that way to say that. And they might hurt us."

"They liked the music," Marie said. "The music was a success."

"I hated playing for them," I said. On an impulse, and one I'll never regret, I reached into my pack and took out my flutes and burned them. No one stopped me. A mistake, that's what this trip was, my mistake for wanting to come. One mistake, easy to make, and it cost so much. I would never play the flute again. I never wanted to see another Glassmaker ever. If I had children, I wouldn't let them play with Glassmaker dolls.

We had a long way to go, and the trip would be hard and cold and miserable. The worst thing would be arriving at the city, because we would have to tell everyone what had happened and what the Glassmakers were really like.

LUCILLE AND STEVLAND
YEAR 107–GENERATION 7

The name of this Planet and Commonwealth shall be Pax as a reminder to ourselves for all time of our aspirations.

—from the Constitution of the Commonwealth of Pax

LUCILLE

Damn! Cedar walked into the gift center right after I did.

"Lucille," she muttered, without even a hello or a smile. What lizard was in her liver now?

"Nice weather tonight," I said. The words echoed around the gift center dome, and I ducked into a stall and pulled the straw curtain shut. I sat there, bare butt on a cold ceramic seat—nice weather if you like it chilly. She and I were liking each other less every day. Well, nobody likes to lose. I won the co-moderator election a week ago and she didn't.

I decided that if I moved quick, I could get out while she was still in her stall, but I heard her curtain open while I was still buttoning my pants. The spring had been dry, which meant poor groundwater flows, which meant the center smelled like poop, but still, I could wait and she'd leave. Then I could go back to Tatiana's funeral and wonder what to do next.

No such luck.

"Did you notice what Stevland said about Tatiana?" she said, and she had to be talking to me because we were the only people there. "He said she argued with him and even got angry with him. Think about that," she said, and without waiting for me to think, she added: "She was tough with him. That's part of the job, keeping him responsible and reasonable." Translation: You better do the same, girl.

I decided to re-retie the knot on my belt. It was an old belt, of course—old clothes for a funeral—and it didn't lie flat. I called back reasonably, "Pretty amazing about him dropping flowers into her grave." Translation: There was more between them than you think. I peeked through the curtain. Cedar stood in the light of an oil lamp, not leaving. Damn.

"You know," she said, "Stevland thinks he should have found the Glassmakers instead of us. Everything has to be his doing."

Exactly. Stevland had an ego like a mountain. It sort of made him lovable. The knot on my belt was as perfect as it could be, the laces on the faded old vest were tight, the knife underneath it didn't show, my socks were pulled up and the darned patches were rubbing my heels, my collar would never lie straight no matter what I did, and I was going to look like I was avoiding her if I stayed in the stall, so I smiled and walked out.

"That's the problem with our defense," she said, standing by the crab-shell water basin. "We have to have a defense, right?" She pointed a finger at me: Answer if you dare.

"Well, it can't hurt to be prepared," I dared to answer. Not everyone agreed, but there were all sorts of dangerous animals, so defense couldn't hurt even if the Glassmakers weren't hostile—and who believed they were? Well, a few people did. I edged up to the basin to wash my hands. She barely let me by, and even though she was only ten years older than me, she made it seem like more.

"Our defense needs to be centered around what we can do," she said, "not what Stevland can do for us." She still shook that finger, and her battered old funeral beads rattled. "He's part of it, of course. His out-posts, his observations, his warning, that's going to be crucial. But what can he do during an actual attack? I don't think he understands offense. He thinks defense, defense, defense, and that's not enough."

"Well, we need to balance his ideas. He was all for that. Balance, balance, balance." I decided my hands weren't dirty and rinsed them quick. The water was scented with orchids but frigid. I'd be out of there in no time. We'd talked about defense at Committee meetings lots of times, so why bring it up now?

She leaned over the basin toward me. "We need a drill. A practice. Like a real attack."

"Well, we can talk about that again." There would be a mountain of debate about that again.

"Not just defending," she said. "Attacking. Like Higgins's Battle."

"Are there lions in the attack?"

"Seriously!" She never had a real sense of humor.

Footsteps clopped on the wood walkway up to the gift center door. Someone was coming, maybe someone who'd provide a distraction and I'd get away.

"A full and complete drill," she said. "With an attack."

Marie walked in. Cedar liked her even less than me. I tried to look serious. "It's on the agenda for the next Committee meeting." Glass-makers were always on the agenda.

"Good." She turned and saw Marie. "Yes, a drill of a counterattack against the Glassmakers, just in case our next encounter isn't a diplo-matic success."

Marie was enough of a diplomat to ignore what needed to be ignored. I hoped.

"What do you think, Marie?" Cedar said.

She looked her straight in the eye. "I'll hope for success."

Marie seemed a lot older than when she left on the mission. She'd lost weight on the hike home last fall—all four of them did—and she had bright green hair now, the color that comes from dye over pure white. She sighed. This was a tired debate. Cedar had argued all winter that we didn't really know anything about the Glassmakers except that they had weapons and abused each other a lot, so that meant they'd fight, and Marie had argued back that we had a more realistic picture of them, and obviously we'd need to protect ourselves, especially Stevland, but we didn't need to be aggressive, since aggressive plans would make aggressive acts easier to commit.

Their only truce was the moment when Tatiana awarded eagle feathers to the mission members, including one for Roland. That one was on display in the museum.

And here in the gift center, Cedar told Marie, "Kids don't play with Glassmaker dolls as much anymore." Snottiness dripped from her voice.

"That might be good," she answered softly. "We'll expect less."

"They're not our special friends anymore," Cedar said.

"It hurts to lose a friend."

I said, as happily and as helpfully as I could, "We'll try to make friends with them next time we meet." That had been my campaign slogan: *Next time, friends!* But the way Cedar snapped her head around to look at me, I realized I shouldn't have brought that up.

"We need to do that." Marie sighed. "We all do. Almost all of us still want friendship." Translation: The friendship candidate, Lucille, won by a big majority, and you didn't. She tried to edge past Cedar.

"Then they should have voted for you," Cedar said. Translation: Marie had also run for co-moderator and had gotten hardly any votes. That had been strange.

She looked at Cedar for what seemed like a long time, sighed again, and said, "I have kidney failure, interstitial nephritis. I might not be alive when we meet the Glassmakers again. So I asked my supporters to vote for Lucille."

"What?" I said. It was the most intelligent thing I could think of to say at the moment.

"You were a fine alternative," Marie said, and entered a stall.

Cedar looked at me without a hint of friendliness. "A drill," she said, and left.

"You had them vote for me?" I called to Marie.

"You would have won anyway," she called back. A deeply diplomatic response.

"Oh," I answered, another intelligent thing to say. I waited a minute to give Cedar a head start, then I headed back toward Tatiana's funeral reception.

We'd known Tatiana was dying. We'd all seen her naked at the spring festival when she announced her retirement. She could hardly walk even with two canes, skinny as a twig except for the joints swollen up from an infection. Then she burned the moderator's chair—the real one—in the bonfire. That shocked everyone.

And winning the co-moderator's election had shocked me because I had run only because I teach—taught—preschool and I wanted to show them how elections work. "You need to think very far ahead," I told the kids. "You should vote for someone with experience and maturity." They nodded their little heads like they understood, and what did they go and do? Well, there were fifteen little heads, and then on election night, we were in the Meeting House crowded butt to butt on the benches, watching the election committee pull fancy little papers one by one from the ballot box, read them out loud, and put them in piles.

"Lucille. Lucille. Cedar. Lucille. Flora. Lucille. Lucille. Bartholomew. Lucille. Marie. Lucille. Lucille. Lucille . . ." I'd voted for Marie. I got almost two hundred votes.

Now Tatiana wasn't there to give me advice anymore. Soft music and lots of talk would fill the Meeting House if I went back there. Who'd voted for me because Marie said so? Daisy, probably. And Kung and Nye. (Nye came back from the mission scarily changed: quiet, serious, no more arguing, no more flutes.) The new fippmaster, Monte, who had he voted for? He was spending the evening with the kats and kids, helping them practice dancing, and he was so quiet and patient you never knew what he thought. Hathor and Forrest, they were Cedar voters for sure. My parents? Who knew? Two hundred votes for me— I'd never figure it out.

I'd tried to. On the night of the election, I helped Tatiana home and asked, "Why did they vote for me?"

She took several slow, painful steps. "Octavo said a long time ago that Pacifists were big fippokats. The perfect Pacifist is happy and helpful.

They're playful. Gentle. That's you, Lucille, the biggest fippokat in the city. That's what people wish they were. They want a fippokat to represent us to the Glassmakers."

"Well, thanks, well, I mean . . ."

"And young. You'll last a long time. Elections are disruptive, so people don't like them."

"Well, yeah." I was the first child in Generation 7, a lot older than anyone else in my generation, just old enough to be co-moderator. As soon as I'd hit puberty—properly chaste, I might add, since no one else was of my age—I decided that face paint would mark my generation, and I began painting up a storm, new colors and patterns every day. "Will I have to quit teaching?"

"You'll have too much to do to teach anymore," Tatiana said. We'd arrived at her house, and she patted my cheek with a dry, cold hand. "Go back to the election party. Drink a lot of truffle. Your troubles start tomorrow."

But that tomorrow had really arrived today, a week later, the day she died. Trouble now filled the Meeting House. My tomorrows had just started. So instead of going back to the funeral reception, I decided to go to the greenhouse, and I kept the door open so Stevland and I wouldn't be talking in secret.

I sat down and put my feet up on the table. "Hey, that was nice, what you said at the funeral."

After a moment, words flashed on his stem. "Greetings, Lucille. It is customary to speak sincerely at funerals."

(He'd said: "It is like a grove being taken from me. No one but she ever argued with me. No one but she ever became angry with me. It was a practice of equality that surpassed belief and ideation. We were not friends, she and I. I do not believe she liked me, but she never hesitated to try to teach me. I am a better Pacifist because of her.")

"Tatiana taught us all," I said, then, "Cedar wants to hold a drill in case Glassmakers attack."

"Indeed. Tatiana taught me to aspire to mutualism with the Glassmakers as the civilized course of action rather than remain trapped in my fears and sadnesses, and I mean to continue to pursue civilization aggressively. Together we can balance, Cedar and I. As with you. You are optimistic, and you have good social skills, things which do not come naturally to me and which will be important to build friendships with Glassmakers and to overcome Pacifist fears."

Translation: I'd have to help him with Cedar. As if I could. "Yep, I'm a big fippokat."

"Yes. Humans and fippokats are social animals that avoid violent and aggressive behavior, and the Glassmakers are obviously social as well. I believe this is why few people support Cedar."

Humans aren't violent? That's what he thought. Tatiana had given me a steel knife and a heavy history lesson. Jersey wasn't Pax's first murderer. But that didn't make Cedar right, did it?

Who had Stevland voted for? Well, he had to know about Marie, since he helped with everyone's health.

But he wanted to talk about missing far outpost groves again. Every time he didn't hear from one for a couple days, he panicked, even if the only problem was that the wind was blowing pollen the wrong way. Understandable, though. I was scared of slugs and crawfish, he was afraid of fire and lots of other things. Tatiana had said that he was unhappy, that he didn't even know how to be happy, and that she was no one to teach happiness. And now she was gone, leaving me.

But fippokats were happy no matter what. I listened, and I said that friendly Glassmakers wouldn't set fire to Pacifists, and I hoped he felt better. I felt like too much depended on me. I said, "Water and sunshine," and went home.

The next morning, I painted my face fippokat green and went to the Meeting House to practice Glassmade sounds with Stevland and Marie. The Sun was shining bright through the roof, splashing colors all around. Most of the debris from last night's reception had been cleaned up, and some of Harry's art still decorated the room. Marie and I sat down at the table. I wondered about asking about the election, but I'd have won anyway, right?

I took a deep breath. Tatiana'd said I could imitate Glassmade because I didn't mind making a fool of myself. Marie had learned some

Glassmade on the mission, and I was going to need to talk to the Glass-makers sooner or later.

"Aaah kak weeooo!" I yelled, then I laughed. I'd probably scared every bat in the city. "How was that?"

"Do the kak again," she said. "I think you finally got it."

"Kak! Kak! Kak! Kak!"

"That's it. How do you do that?"

"I don't know."

"You close your throat and push with your diaphragm," Stevland said.

"How do you know?" I said.

"Understanding human speech meant understanding their vocal-ization techniques. I dedicated a root to that, as I must do now for vocalized Glassmade."

"Roots! I want a Glassmade root. I need to learn Glassmade faster. We can't make friends if we can't talk."

"Correction. You want a Glassmade voice. Vocalization is not a plant characteristic. Chromoplasts are a plant characteristic, and with the appropriate graft, you would not have to paint your face anymore. I can offer you a rainbow of colors."

I thought a minute. "Did you grow a humor root?"

"You said I would find it enlightening, and you were correct."

"Oh." I'd told him a while back to lighten up and grow a humor root, but since he didn't have a humor root then, I guess he didn't know I meant it as a joke.

I said, "How about the aaah? Aaah! Aaah! Does that come close or am I farting instead of pooping?"

"I received no gift," Stevland said. That humor root at work.

"Tense your vocal cords more," Marie said.

"Moderators. Excuse me," Carl called to us from the door. Back so soon? Yes, there he was, and with a couple dozen people behind him. He was our top scout, supple as a kat and nervous as a bird, short and tan. He could walk for forty hours without resting, he knew what was around the bend of a path even if he'd never seen it before, and he could sneak up on an owl. He'd left that morning to go down the river valley all the way to the sea, a three-week trip supposedly to prepare for a salt-making expedition, but we all knew that what he was looking for wasn't salt.

"Carl!" I said, and then to be a playful fip, I said it like a kak: "Karl! Come in. Kome iiin! Your report! Tell us all about the ocean. Still wet? Still big? How's the salt? It's great to see you back. Quick trip, too. Everybody, kome iiin!"

He took off his hat and came in, sweaty, wearing heavy hiking boots and a camouflaged cape. The rest followed him, murmuring because they knew what he was going to say. Well, something about Glassmakers, obviously. He sat down at the council table to give a formal report, his fingers drumming bird-nervous on the tabletop. Cedar came dashing in and stood near the front. She already carried a bow and a quiver of arrows, so I knew what she expected.

(The mission hadn't seen any bows and arrows among the Glassmakers, and when they got back, she had practiced until she could shoot an arrow accurately at two hundred paces and always went sleeveless to show off her arm muscles.)

"Glassmakers are here," Carl said.

Glassmakers!

I flashed a big kat-happy smile because I didn't know what else to do. The room got perfectly still, and so did I on the inside, but not a calm stillness. Couldn't let that show, though.

He said, "They're in the valley downstream from the waterfall. I saw, oh, I'd say a hundred, carrying a lot of gear, about to come up the cliff. I ran back, but they move fast. They'll be here any minute."

Everyone looked at me, and I had to set the tone. One hundred? We'd been counting on a diplomatic mission, like maybe a half dozen, and we weren't even ready for that. But the tone: serious and calm. Fake calm would do. "Well," I began.

"Call everyone in!" Cedar shouted.

"Well," I tried again, "that's—"

"That's too many," she said, "and they move too fast. If they aren't friendly, we have to be prepared."

"I—"

"It's fine to be dedicated to peace, but now isn't the time to take chances—"

"Stevland," Marie murmured, "fires?"

"I have no roots east of the geologic fault that creates the waterfall. I have no observations."

"We get to meet them at last!" Daisy rejoiced.

"Not a hundred of them," Hathor said. "Not the way they smell!"

"But we want to meet them, right?" Nevada said. "They made this city. They have a right to it. And if we're locked up inside, that wouldn't be friendly."

Marie nudged me. "A hundred would be the entire village, if they're the Glassmakers we met."

"Well, yes." Happy, helpful, playful—a lot of good that did right now, with everybody arguing. Marie should have been elected. Everyone was looking at me, expecting me to know what to do. "What do we do?" I murmured to Marie.

"There's still time for a diplomatic mission," she murmured back. "Ours. Bring people in as if it were an eagle attack, and then a few of us can meet them."

"I concur," Stevland's stem said.

I stood up. "All right! Here's the plan: Everyone inside, and then we'll send out a diplomatic mission."

"Inside?" Daisy wailed. "But we want to meet them!"

Cedar didn't hide her contempt. "Another diplomatic mission!"

"That's right," I said. "And if it goes well, we all get to meet them, but a hundred Glassmakers, that's the whole village, isn't it? If it's the same Glassmakers." Cedar's eyes got big. Translation: She hadn't thought of that. "Now, everyone inside! Hey, they stink and there's a hundred of them, so we need to be careful, got it?" A few people nodded. "Glassmakers are coming! Let's get ready! Kak! Kak! Kak!" I grinned like a happy fip, what a lie. I felt like . . . well, I didn't know how I felt.

People started moving. We knew how to prepare for an eagle attack. Everyone inside is the first step. Trumpeters blew the call to return to the city, farming teams began running home, and trained bats flew out on reconnaissance.

I rounded up our diplomats. Stevland ordered the thistles around his groves to stand at attention. Crews hauled in firewood, boats, and everything valuable from storage sheds and workshops outside the city. Monte rushed to the lion pack, which grazed a few kilometers northeast, and we would communicate with him using smoke signals and bats trained to deliver messages in exchange for food.

Glassmakers were coming! Friendly? Tolerable? Or a damn disappointment again? We'd been waiting since Sylvia's time for this, and legends—if you can believe legends about her anymore—said that she cried when she saw Rainbow City in ruins and realized she'd never meet one. Now we'd meet a whole village. I hoped they were nice just so I wouldn't have to deal with Cedar anymore.

Most people waited up on the walls. We diplomats waited outside of the city at the river bluff: Marie, Kung, Bartholomew, Carl, a couple of other Committee members, and I. Cedar was up on the wall somewhere.

The wall. Almost two meters tall, it kept out nasty little things like slugs, but eagles could jump over it, and some kinds of deer crabs, and maybe the Glassmakers could jump it, too. We'd repaired the wall and added some shelters for archers, but Cedar wanted more, and for once she was probably right, but we hadn't had time to do more.

Outside, at the bluff, I waited and looked down and around. Shiny gold tulips bloomed in the damp fields next to the river, and soon their leaves would sprout. Up on the bluffs on both sides of the river, beyond the roads, grain and cotton had germinated, and lentil trees spotted the landscape like purple polka dots. We grew the trees scattered so an attack of scorpions would get only one tree before we could stop them. Pale new leaves were everywhere on the trees and shrubs and snow vine hedges at the riverbank, and stands of rainbow bamboo stood here and there. It looked pretty, orderly, and promising. Would the Glassmakers like it?

Marie stood next to me, and tears shook on her lower eyelids. I'd have hugged her, but Kung had already wrapped an arm around her shoulder. Nye was in the greenhouse to relay messages from Stevland, because he didn't want to see any Glassmakers at all, and who could blame him?

He shouted: "The Glassmakers are at the old outpost. . . . Farther upstream . . . at the ridge. I am getting little attention." Translation: They aren't burning me. Nye's voice sounded relieved.

I felt for the steel knife under my shirt, because Tatiana had said it made her feel brave to wear it, but I didn't want to feel brave, I wanted to hop around like a kat with no worries at all. Behind us, teams pulled the gates shut and the big hinge posts grumbled in their greased sockets and bars were dropped in place with a bang that vibrated through the stone-and-brick walls.

I listened. "Glassmakers are noisy, right?" I asked Kung and Marie. They nodded. We couldn't hear anything. Finally, a bat flew overhead. "Big animal animal coming!" Up on the wall, someone shouted, "I see them!" A lot of people started shouting.

Well, I couldn't see them from down on the ground. "Where?" I called.

"On the road on the river bluff," someone answered. "They're carrying something, a big box." More shouting and waving up on the wall. I recognized Daisy's voice: "Chik-o!" which was sort of like the word we thought meant hello.

I squinted at the road, and there were three or four Glassmakers a half kilometer away, right where the road comes out between a couple of trees, and they weren't moving. The box was big enough to hold a fippolion.

"Scared," Kung grunted. "They see us, big city, people shouting." He began waving. I waved, too, and shouted, "Chik-ooo!" Friendly, not scary, not scared.

They seemed to huddle—everyone had committee meetings, apparently—then they picked up the box, one at each corner, and started running toward us. They moved quick, two-jointed skinny legs held far out from their body, just like the dolls I used to play with. Major castes.

"Anyone we know?" I asked.

"Hmm. Don't know," Kung said. "Let's wave."

"This is just a diplomatic mission, right? Just these four guys and a box. Nothing to it."

The Glassmakers stopped suddenly, set down the box, squawked something at us, and ran away, fast as lightning. Mission accomplished: Deliver the box.

"There's writing on the box," Marie said. "I was hoping some of them could read."

"Let's go read it," I said. Up on the walls, people were arguing over whether to open the gates. Cedar was screaming no. I decided to pretend I was deaf and kept walking, modeling calmness, for all the good it might do. Diplomacy depended a lot on lying. I'd already learned that from Marie. The gate stayed shut.

When we were almost there, Marie said, *City friendship gift.* It's for us. See?" The message had been painted on one side of the box in mud. The top was open. We got close and leaned over to look inside. Thirty or forty fippokats squirmed around inside and looked up at us. Latticework over the top kept them from hopping out, but one jumped up, grabbed a slat with its front paws, and hung on for a while. Carl shouted the news back to the city: "Kats!"

"Why kats?" Marie said.

I was going to say, "Because it's friendly," but I began to sneeze.

Nye screamed from the city: "It isn't a gift! Don't bring it in! Don't touch it!"

I backed away so I wouldn't sneeze on the kats and waved at Nye to show him I'd heard.

"Smells funny," Kung said.

"Lucille," Nye shouted, "come talk to Stevland!"

So I ran back to the city. They let down a ladder so I could climb up the wall, and then I climbed down on the other side and went to the greenhouse, ignoring all the people looking at me with big doubting eyes. Nye sat inside with his head in his hands staring gray-faced at Stevland's stem. Words were already waiting for me.

"I suspect that the fippokats are being used in the same way that crabs infest a bluebird reef with slug larvae to eliminate the birds," Stevland said. "I must be clear that I merely suspect. I do not know."

"They think the kats will eat us?" I said.

"You might eat the kats. Poison also can be absorbed through the skin, or inhaled, or the fippokats could be infected with disease." The words came fast. "But the poison might not affect you. Poisons can be specific to species, and they do not have experience with your physiology. I can assure you of nothing. I do not even know if they are poisoned. I do not believe the fippokats should be let in, but I do not know why I believe that. I am extrapolating from the behavior of crabs, but other animal behaviors may be more parallel. I am not offering ideal moderator behavior, for I have emotional prejudices against the Glassmakers. But if Glassmaker behavior is benign, then—"

He was babbling, so I interrupted. "Seen anything else suspicious?"

"They are waiting some distance away, still hidden by the forest, by my estimate approximately one hundred, probably a full social unit. All castes and ages are present, but with possible overrepresentation of non-breeding castes and underrepresentation of juveniles, as was the case with the village that the mission discovered. They have obvious internal disputes. It may be the same group. That one had not been harmonious, either."

"They don't have to be friends with each other, just with us."

"An interesting idea. Possibilities for dialogue may depend on whether the fippokats are poisoned or not. I would like to analyze the fippokats, although I do not know if it will be possible."

"The kats made me sneeze. Kung said they smell funny."

"Your olfactory sense is a limited but effective method of chemical analysis."

"Well, what do we do? I don't want to act unfriendly."

"A brief wait may tell us much. I am sorrowful that this response seems appropriate."

I left the greenhouse, climbed up and down the ladders at the city wall, ran to the box, and started talking to our diplomats. Waiting wasn't a popular idea, that's for sure.

"Who would poison kats?" Carl said.

"This could seem impolite," Bartholomew said.

Cedar had come running behind me, and her eyes scared me. "I knew it. It used to be their city, right? We're just some weird animal that they need to clear out. That makes perfect sense. But it's our city now."

We sent for Flora, the veterinary medic, to come and check the kats. "They're listless," she said. "That's not good."

Stevland said, via Nye shouting back in the city, that Glassmakers were still watching us from the forest. "Their response to our refusal of their gift may tell us more than an analysis of the fippokats." Nye's tone of voice predicted something bad would happen soon.

"Look," the vet said. "Shallow breathing."

"We're in big trouble," Cedar said. "Lucille, we have to be ready. We should have drilled."

The vet said, "They're bleeding from their noses."

Marie began to cry.

I touched my vest and felt the knife hidden beneath it. It was a mistake to elect me, and I couldn't go back to a week ago and change it. What would Tatiana do? "Let's get inside and start getting ready." Words don't have taste, do they? But these did: like poop.

At first, I thought people would stage a revolt like Sylvia's against me, and maybe they should have. "Get ready for what?" "You promised friendship!"

Then Daisy climbed down the ladder and ran to look at the kats. She came back squalling in a way that changed a lot of minds. "Those poor dear things! Oh, I wish I could help them! But it's too late for them. We have to save ourselves!"

"The Glassmakers are preparing to move," Stevland announced. "I am sorrowful, sorrowful that they have returned. We have found joy in our community, and they must not replace it with barbarism." That didn't improve anyone's mood. Parents hustled their children home.

The Greenies and the Beadies started shouting at each other about how we could have prevented this, Beadies up on the wall, Greenies down below, and I had to stop them, so I said, "Hey, if we can show them that they can't win, then they'll have to talk, right?"

"How do we show them that?" Daisy said.

"We use arrows, stupid," a Beadie said.

"I'm not going to kill a Glassmaker," a Greenie shouted back.

"We have to. If we had been prepared—" another Beadie said. Cedar came running down the wall to join the argument.

"I helped build up the wall," the Greenie said. "Don't blame me."

Leadership. Here goes. "Let's use blunt arrows, all right?" I said. "At first, at least."

"What?" Cedar said. "What will that prove?"

"Hey, that's a great idea," said a young Greenie. "Lucille is right. Blunt arrows! We could hurt them but we won't."

"But if they keep fighting?" Cedar said.

"If we do it right the first time," I said, "they'll see we want to be friends."

And so on, and that's how I finally got everyone up on the walls, ready, and just in time.

Stevland and bats and sharp-eyed guards on the walls said that Glassmakers were sneaking up through the woods, a whole lot of them. We heard screeching Glassmade, and it kept getting louder, and there they were. Twenty or thirty majors scurried down the riverbank, and I yelled at them, "Chek-ooo." Maybe it wasn't the right thing to say, but I wanted them to know we knew they were there.

They didn't come near the city, running full speed across the bridge to the other side of the river to set up camp, not the ideal place, but they hadn't asked us.

Glassmakers kept dashing out of the forest, dropping heavy side baskets at their new camp. Some of them started looking at the children's flower garden around the statue of Higgins that marks the place where he fought with the eagles. The wind carried their odor. Even from so far away, they stank like rot.

A Glassmaker worker in a black blanket picked a flower. Another ran over to grab it, then a third, and a scuffle broke out with a lot of pushing and shoving. Glassmakers who were arriving dropped their baskets in the middle of the road and rushed over to watch. The fighters had cheering sections, and I could make out at least three sides. They trampled the garden. Then a major in a plaid blanket—"Him. That's the one, the leader," Kung said—raised a club and shouted, "Chooo-a-reeee," and the struggle ceased.

"Just like before," Cedar said.

Down the road, they kept coming. The adults set up domed tents and unpacked their baskets. Plaid Blanket shouted something and little workers scrambled to greet four females—big, slow, and clumsy, just like the mission said. With them were other Glassmakers—about six—that were so tiny they had to be children, and they ran around in the garden tearing up what was left of it and chasing the jewel lizards that lived in it.

"It's the group we visited," Marie said. Shabby, like she'd said. "There's one fewer female and a lot fewer children. Could the young ones mature that fast?"

"You look like you don't think so,'" I said.

"Something's wrong. They weren't hanging on by much. That might be the answer." From the look on her face, she didn't like that answer. And me, too. But what exactly was wrong?

The attack came soon. Some of them sneaked up through the trees with catapults built out of what we had thought were tent poles and began launching glass vials of poison over the walls, and some splashed on an old man, Bjorn. He got a fever and almost stopped breathing, but the medics acted fast and saved him.

Our bows took them by surprise—or rather, the range of our bows—and they retreated quick, but a few got hit. Even blunt arrows can hurt. Cedar and other sharpshooters destroyed the catapults, but the Glassmakers had balls tied on ropes, and they could throw well, with two elbows swinging like a crack-the-whip, so their attacks had range, too.

"It's time for real arrows now," Cedar said. "We outnumber them. We'll win."

A Beadie agreed: "Right. Let's kill one and see if they roast the corpse and eat it."

"We don't want revenge," a Greenie answered. "We want peace."

"We get peace," Cedar said through gritted teeth, "by winning."

To decide the matter, we held an impromptu Committee meeting in the greenhouse, which is near the wall. Marie led the group against real arrows. "Diplomatic," Cedar called it, an insult. Stevland didn't know what he wanted. Eventually—because I'd had enough pointless shouting—we decided that everyone could decide for themselves. So some shot real arrows, some shot blunted ones. They seemed as effective either way. Cedar entertained herself for a while lobbing flaming arrows at the footbridge. Finally an old hunter told her that if she kept missing, the Glassmakers would figure out our range versus accuracy the way the mountain spiders had, and we'd lose an advantage.

This situation lasted for five days. We launched arrows now and then when Glassmakers tried to sneak up to the wall. Trained bats carried messages to Monte and flew reconnaissance, and the bats understood the situation, so the damn things tripled the amount of food they demanded per trip. People looked at me, wondering what to do.

What would a fippokat do? When owls and spiders attack, fippokats run and hide. They're green. They know how to stand still. They can dig a hole in seconds flat. They can jump high enough to land in tree branches. They can slide down a wet grassy hill faster than a ball can roll. And us, the big fippokats, we were trapped with no way to run and hide. It was my job to lead, and I didn't know what to do besides act happy, helpful, playful, and gentle. What good was that? I was useless.

Glassmakers had taken to drumming and singing day and night to harass us, when they weren't screaming at each other. Our children whined that they couldn't leave the city, and that it was too noisy to sleep—true. Endless, mind-rattling noise, because the Glassmakers meant to make us suffer. Our children made earplugs. We adults wondered what to do and debated too much. The old hunters and Stevland spent their time observing: social order, eating habits, and fighting techniques. And we were learning things, but not fast enough. We couldn't wait inside the city forever. We'd go nuts.

There was nearly a fistfight tonight. "It's time to kill the musicians," Cedar said at the Committee meeting.

"The noise is keeping the Glassmakers awake, too," Daisy said.

"What?" Cedar said. "Do you want me to feel sorry for them?"

"You can survive hardship," Carl said.

"Hardship? This is torture. Torture for me, for my children, for everyone."

"Right, it's making you crazy," someone whispered in the hall.

"Who said that?" Cedar jumped to her feet, looking hard at the people on the benches, and someone snickered.

"Don't be a fool," Carl told Cedar.

"I am not a fool."

More snickers, including someone at the Committee table. Cedar looked like she knew who and took a step in that direction. Time to be happy and helpful, my one true talent.

"Well," I said, standing up, "I'm with Cedar. I mean, who doesn't want to kill the musicians? Voice vote, purely advisory, all those in favor, cheer and stomp your feet. Let's hear it!" An overwhelming vote yes. "Is it making you crazy?" Cheers and stomps. "Cedar said what we all think, right?" Cheers and stomps. "Thank you, Cedar. It's what we needed to hear." I led applause for her as I sat down. She looked confused but sat down, too.

Nye rarely left the bakery or spoke except to Stevland. The kats in the box outside festered, and the smell upset the kats inside the city. Our crops were being pillaged or suffering from neglect, but at least the Glassmakers hadn't set fire to Stevland. We sent them letters tied to blunt arrows asking for friendship and peace, and they looked at the papers, but if they could read, they didn't bother. What else could we do?

STEVLAND

My leaves complete their nightly turn toward the east in anticipation of sunrise. Water pressure from roots and the night's high humidity result in guttation, and water seeps from pores on leaves like imitation dew. I ache with turgor, yet I desire to wilt. Fighting is disaster, flood and drought together.

With my eyes in the grove across the river, I see the Glassmaker musicians, their bodies radiating infrared light in the cool night, as they pause to lap up water before reluctantly picking up their drums and raising their voices for another noisy song. They are small Glassmakers, the worker caste. "The overworked caste," my humor root suggests, and humor contains truth. They wish to sleep, but when the Sun rises, they will be sent to the fields to gather tulip roots, though this is not harvest season, and the tulips resent it.

Indeed, they will gather any food, in season or not, all the while generating more resentment. While the damage they do to the life of our valley is sad, equally sad is the fact that the workers will eat only what larger castes fail to consume. Parasites and hosts constitute a common biological relationship, but in this case parasitism occurs within a single species rather than cross-species, a perversion of mutualism, a barbaric relationship.

Were Glassmakers always thus? I had fewer roots when they built the city and I understood too little, far less than I realized at the time, and my communication with them was brief and limited to specific individuals. I should have but did not fully recognize that the different sizes of animals, specifically of the Glassmakers, meant something distinct from different sizes among plants. Plant size depends on our environment and age. Animal size is fixed by their type, like the genders among humans. Type can affect function and social standing. Equality among types is an ethical rather than universal practice. It is not practiced among Glassmakers.

Up on the city wall, a pair of Pacifist guards patrol in soft-soled slippers, heeding any rustle that might warn of a Glassmaker attempting to approach. In the greenhouse, a young woman watches my stem for warnings. Earlier this night, fippmaster Monte dissuaded his pack from a quest to find and eliminate the source of the annoying noise—that is, the Glassmaker musicians. It was a tragedy avoided, since the Glassmakers would have killed all the lions, but would have suffered losses themselves, and I do not want any deaths.

This is all I can report to the young woman as Lux rises and sunrise approaches. She and I pass the time chatting. Talking stems are costly to maintain, and chatter depletes my immediate stores of adenosine triphosphate, so I would prefer to remain silent in this time of great trouble, but Pacifists find inaction difficult, and she must remain alert. Five days of confinement within the walls have unbalanced the Pacifists, who require activity.

Cacti and ribbons, still holding on to their winter hibernation anchors, release zygospores to grow into new air plants. Flowers bloom everywhere, and pollen and perfume traverse the winds. Spring is the most beautiful and the most impatient season. Plants must grow fast or perish, even those of us who have enlisted animal help to overcome the seasons. Spring losses can rarely be recovered, and this has been a dry spring, adding to the urgency.

Within the city, humans know this. Their own resources become depleted during winter and must be renewed. They are impatient, too, and fearful because they can imagine disaster and death. They displace their fear and anger at the Glassmakers by growing angry with each other. Cedar provoked an argument last night when her proposal to kill the Glassmaker musicians was turned down. Without Lucille's intervention like water to put out a fire, there might have been violence.

"We can't take much more," Lucille confessed to me later. We are lucky to have such a resourceful and sociable co-moderator. I have an idea that may resolve the situation, though not easily.

I must be brave and share courage like a mental gift. I have strong roots and innumerable leaves. The Sun rises. Photons rush down, and I begin to split water into oxygen, hydrogen ions, and energy. I am large. My roots, laid end to end, would reach the Sun. Instead, my roots are spread throughout our valley, and I know that as the day progresses, they will draw in a din of chemical complaints from other plants that increases day by day. Our helper animal has been replaced by a pest. Forward-looking plants worry. Our ecosystem is disturbed and angry, as well as thirsty.

The most fragile is me, for I can see the stars for what they are. They are suns, and they have their planets, and travel to them would be longer and more complex than I once believed, and yet the more I know, the more real the idea becomes, and these desires are unbalancing. My wants are no longer simple.

Pacifists see the stars and dream of travel, too. I ask them when, and they say, "Someday," and they mean it. When that day comes, we will go together, their descendants and my seeds and plantlets and roots. Pots are confining, but I can withstand hardship. This will be a sweet fruit of civilization. The combined efforts of humans and Glassmakers would make it arrive sooner.

A small moth flock, the first migratory group, has arrived from the south. Their custom is to bring me bits of meat to analyze in exchange for nectar, thus I have finally examined Glassmaker physiology in depth. With that information, tonight I have constructed an astonishing idea. Mutualism can be coerced. Civilization can be imposed. It would solve the situation without barbarism, but it is a complex plan that would require cooperation from our entire ecology and an untested commitment from humans and plants alike. Its failure would result in worse disaster.

A lamp is lit in Lucille's home. Her commitment to friendship inspired my idea. Cedar joins the guards and stalks the walls like an eagle. The restraint that has been imposed on her response to Glassmaker attacks will make my plan possible.

Glassmakers awaken. New musicians take up the concert. The large castes gather to plan the day's harassment of the city. They clumsily attempt to duplicate human bows and arrows. They have vandalized but not set fire to my grove.

Lucille arrives at the Meeting House. I share the night's news of the drama with the fippolions, and my humor root interjects, "Perhaps the children could make them earplugs." This is nonsense considering the lions' auditory apparatus, but nonsense is one kind of humor. She laughs and repeats the joke to Bartholomew when he arrives.

More people come. I share my observations about Glassmakers and bows, and after a discussion, Cedar concludes that the Glassmakers lack experience to make a truly dangerous weapon. "They might learn fast, though," she says. There is a loud screech of music. "I ought to put the poor little things out of their misery."

"The worker caste is overworked and exhausted," I say. Cedar smiles unpleasantly.

The meeting begins with all members of the Committee, along with many citizens. Without farmwork, they have little to do. Hunters sit far in the back, carefully chipping sharp edges onto glass arrowheads.

I was not the only entity thinking overnight. Generation 4 hunters propose a surprise raid against the Glassmaker camp. The master hunters are few in number and age has made them fragile as dry reeds, but they are cunning, and their plan draws admiration for its boldness.

"The big thing is this," says their spokesman, Orion, whose Sun-browned skin hangs in wrinkles that almost obscure his eyes. "We have to kill them all, or we have to deal with the survivors. They'll be hostile, since we'll have wiped out their friends and family." When he was young, he spent many years observing mountain spiders, and his knowledge eventually led to peaceful coexistence. "But I think we should kill as few as possible anyway. Maybe just Plaid Blanket. That means a lot of prisoners. It's not a great plan, but it might work."

The plan has similarities to mine. Most of the support for his comes from farmers. "They even cut down some protected locustwood trees," Hakon, a farmer, says. "Stevland, the trees don't like that, do they?"

Here is my chance. "They do not. Tulips are also angry. As are pineapples. Cotton. Wheat. Lentils. Others. They expect to be respected and cared for, but they understand that their animal allies have been subject to predation. The seed potatoes that you planted in the upriver sandy bottomland are complaining to me as we speak because they are being harvested before they can create a new generation."

"Our potatoes!" Hakon says.

"They complain," I continue, "but they are unable to act. We can act. I have a proposal. It is not entirely different from the hunters' proposal. Before the attack, we must disable the Glassmakers by inserting stupefacients into their food. I believe I can persuade other plants to do this. When the Glassmakers are helpless, we must remove their weapons and possessions. Then, to survive, they must cooperate with us, and we will teach them to behave with civilization. I think of it as domesticating the Glassmakers, just as you domesticated the fippolions."

There is silence. Finally, someone says, "But Glassmakers smell." There is laughter.

"They bathed when they lived here," I say, causing more laughter, although the remark did not originate in my humor root.

"Cooperate?" Hakon asks. "Sure, they'll cooperate just long enough to get what they need to do us in."

"It will take much time and attention," I respond. "But the outcome will be tremendously beneficial to all of us."

"Stupefacients," Marie says quietly. "That's very tricky medication." She is correct. I do not answer that observation.

"Why don't we just poison them?" Hakon asks.

Marie stares at him with anger, then at Orion. "We have already set a goal of coexistence," she says slowly.

No one moves.

Finally, Cedar says in a disbelieving tone, "So we knock them out and take their weapons."

"We take everything," I say. "Clothing, baskets, tents. Our response has been measured so far. They will see that we mean them no harm, but that we will force them to cooperate."

"Maybe," old Orion says, "they won't cooperate."

"I agree that the plan has risks," I say. "Its root is cautious development of mutual trust and cooperation through imposed nonviolence. It will take significant patience and effort to force them to be friends. In essence, we will conscript a symbiont." There is silence. I add as encouragement, "This is often done by plants to animals."

"Let's go over it, step by step," Lucille says. She seems interested, and her interest will encourage more interest. This plan is different from the procedure I used to lure the humans from their old village to this city, and yet the core remains the same. We must reward appropriate behavior until it becomes natural behavior.

We are halfway through when I have to report Glassmakers are on the move. Sentinels on the walls call out the same warning almost immediately. The entire force of the majors is en route, all forty of them, and their trajectory seems to be the source of the water for the city. This could be disaster. The water flows from the springs to the city through pipes, and the springs are the most vulnerable part of the water system.

"I will notify the blade-leaf irises," I say. A decade ago, at my suggestion, we planted the irises to guard the springs and the pipeheads. Irises thirst for blood more than I do. They secrete anticoagulants on the glasslike lancets that cover their leaves, and aboveground roots are ready to absorb all blood that falls. The lancets are loosely attached, so if Glassmakers try to mow them down, they will scatter clouds of glass blades, some small enough to be inhaled and tear apart Glassmakers' lungs from inside with a hundred cuts.

"That gives us time," Cedar says, then turns and shouts, "Call up the fighters." Archers and child messengers at the meeting run out. She shouts at me: "How long would it take to drug the Glassmakers?"

"Two days. I must negotiate with other species, like tulips, for example, and they are shallow, slow thinkers. I must help them create the proper medications."

"Two days!" Cedar says. She has begun to put on fighting gear, as have other Pacifists. "Not good enough. They've got forty majors, right? We should fight now. We can outnumber them two to one, but that's counting everyone who can use a bow halfway decently, even Lucille— no offense, but you know what I mean. Everyone."

My roots from across the river report odd movement. The workers have ceased foraging and are returning to the camp. Will they cross the river to prevent us from protecting the springs?

"We should attack their camp," Orion says meanwhile. "The big ones'll still be trying to figure out the irises while we take control."

"If they've seen irises before," Carl says, "they might give up right away."

I begin to flash the news about the workers' movements even as discussion continues. I wish I had a voice, a flute, a drum. *Look at me!*

Cedar says, "The majors can turn around and be back in no time. We need to move."

"Right," Orion says, "so what if we take the females hostage?"

"No, we attack the majors," Cedar says. "Now!"

Marie reads my stem. "Look at Stevland. The workers are up to something!"

Cedar waves her arms at me. "It's a trick."

"Workers are not crossing the bridge," I report.

"What's the trick?" Lucille asks.

"The workers have massed around the large tents that contain the females," I report. "I do not understand their behavior. There seems to be a conflict." I could add that they are singing at each other, females at workers, workers at other workers, but this is clear to anyone with ears. Occasionally I recognize a word that Marie had taught, but a vocabulary limited to terms like "no," "water," and "hello" has no real use.

Cedar asks about the irises, but I am paying too close attention to the camp to answer. The voices rise like thunder. Workers fight and shed blood.

"The majors have stopped to listen," I report.

"You really think we can live with the Glassmakers?" Cedar shouts as she leaves. This is obviously a rhetorical question.

I tell Lucille, "The majors are turning around and may be headed back. Their speed is phenomenal."

"I have to go look. Sorry." Lucille leaves.

At the camp, females argue with females, workers with workers, and workers with females. As the majors approach, some workers grab tools and cut down the rope bridge. The majors stand at the river edge, brandishing weapons, threatening to throw projectiles, and shout at the workers and females, who shout back, and the noise causes my grove at the camp to become so dizzy that all growth stops. Humans on the wall have put their hands over their ears.

Approximately twenty majors turn toward the city and address the humans emotionally, waving weapons. The females across the river also gesture at the city walls and speak with great agitation, as do the workers, but their comments amount to discordant commotion. Certain majors argue with the others. Suddenly one of the majors addressing the humans is struck from behind with a sword, an expert blow that severs its head. Another lunges to fight. Three majors grab it and a fourth slices a sword. Both corpses are kicked with disrespect into the river.

Orion shouts, "Show your weapons!" All along the wall, human fighters raise their bows.

The Glassmakers witness it, and a few majors jump into the river to swim across.

"Lower your weapons! Remain ready!"

The Glassmakers absorb the warning and slowly fall silent.

Orion's display is clever, clever, clever. It is rich fruit. It is a message that could not be more succinct, and it will support my plan. We could kill but we will not. After a moment, the squabble among the Glassmaker resumes, but subdued. The talk goes on for a long time. On the walls, children circulate with water, and later with food. I send some glucose to my sick grove at the Glassmaker camp. The noise of Glassmaker talk is now no more significant than a strong breeze.

It is afternoon when all the majors swim across the river, one by one and without the natural skill of humans, although they are very buoyant, shaking themselves and their weapons dry as they climb out on the other side. Certain majors greet certain females, touching hands and heads, but most do not. The arguing workers have retreated, many returning to the fields to gather food. The singing and drumming does not resume.

I think my proposal has been forgotten, and I learn of torrential rains over the mountains to the far west. These violent spring storms will not likely reach our valley, but if the river rises, that would complicate any attack.

In the city, children nap and guards relax. An evening meal is prepared on both sides of the river, and suddenly several majors move quickly. They pick up weapons, surround three workers, and behead them. Blood flows into the soil. Soon I taste the iron. The music resumes.

As the Sun sets, debate begins anew in the Meeting House. "We need to do something," Lucille says.

"Teach them civilization?" Hakon says. "They have that. It's just not like ours. That was murder. No excuse."

"That's the point," Lucille says. "That's what's so good about Stevland's plan. No killing."

Bartholomew stands up. He is an old woodworker, plump and

gray-haired, who acts fussy but thinks sharply. He asks: "What is the difference between taking the Glassmakers prisoner and domesticating them?" I begin to formulate a reply, but he continues. "None. The question is, how many prisoners can we handle, and how soon? You said two days, Stevland?"

"Correct." Is he arguing for me or against me? I observed him and Lucille talking during the afternoon. Bartholomew is clever. He can take an idea and make it do the unexpected, as if it were a fippokat and he has taught it to fly. And this is what he does. I never thought I was such a genius, and I have never before observed Lucille as hopeful, energetic, and persuasive. I had not realized that my plan had so many advantages. It can almost fly.

"Pax," Bartholomew says. "That's an ancient Earth word for peace. Our ancestors came here to create peace. We know the price of war. All of us do, humans and bamboo. Destruction isn't the half of it. We would lose what we are. We are Pacifists. It's time to live up to our name and make peace real."

Within an hour, the course is laid out. We will domesticate the Glassmakers.

So as the night deepens, we begin. Lucille organizes planning groups. Outside the city, many plants begin as best they can to replenish their water loss from daytime, so the time is ideal to send them messages through roots. Calcium ions carry information from cell to cell in waves, each wave with its particular enzymes and chemicals and each pathway among the cells creating meaning. Most plants speak similar chemical languages, and most can produce certain useful chemical compounds at will, just as animals can create tools or build reefs. It is a question of knowledge and sophistication.

I start with tulips, since they seem to be a favored food of the Glassmakers, and since the only good time to talk to them is at night when they have closed their flowers. They do not have sufficient intelligence to maintain a flower and to communicate at the same time.

"Pests here," I say, sending the message through rootlets to a thousand tulips.

"Pests. Bad." "Bad." "Bad." "Bad." "Bad." "Bad," they answer one by one. My humor root observes that they have little to say but are talkative nonetheless. I am glad I grew the humor root. I can endure unpleasant situations better. The lentil trees planted among the tulips complain, too, about their own problems.

I try to guess where the Glassmakers will forage next on the tulips. Animal behavior is too flexible to be sure, especially among animals without prior commitments to the crops, but it seems obvious to guess that they will pillage the unharvested fields closest to their camp that are easily accessible from roads and paths.

"Helper here," I say to those fields of tulips. "Helper chemical. Pest go." I show an endogenous opiate, and transport that information with a bit of biotin to make it more interesting. I introduced similar opiates twenty years ago in minor amounts into my medical fruits to cause relaxation and reduce anxieties. I hope this alkaloid in higher concentrations will produce more extreme effects in the Glassmakers.

Tulips already produce a phytohormone based on the amino acid phenylalanine. With a few additional steps, they can manufacture a heterocyclic nucleus that can become the alkaloid. I show the formula. I repeat this explanation dozens of times for each plant, since they are slow learners. Molecules slip from my rootlets to theirs. It is tiring. I move some nitrogen from the city's gift center to their soil to help them.

Half the nitrogen will get rerouted to create purine and pyrimidine bases to create RNA and aid in the tulips' own growth rather than to make the alkaloid. This is one reason they have responded so quickly. They are stupid, but self-interest is not related to intelligence. I hope for a sunny day tomorrow so they can work quickly.

Lentils also snatch up the nitrogen and whine. They are waiting to be pruned. They are hapless plants that need assistance to determine the best way to arrange their leaves to gather sunlight. "Help me." "Prune me," the trees beg.

Glassmakers are ignoring the lentils, although their buds and twigs are edible, as humans and scorpions know. I wish it were different. Lentils are always eager to help.

Meanwhile, I contact the pineapples. They are intelligent but stubborn.

The agreement I brokered long ago between them and the humans was simple. The pineapples produce terminal tuft fruit in the spring and fall. Spring fruit must be replanted by the humans. Fall fruit may be harvested. Humans provide protection, cultivation, and labor. The pineapples add flavors and nutrients to fall fruits in exchange. But now their fruit is being harvested even though it is spring, and they are furious. I suggest drugging the spring fruit so that the Glassmakers can be defeated and life can return to normal.

"No," I hear eight hundred times.

"Think about it," I say. "It is like flavoring your fruit. You do that according to contract."

A common response says, "Our terminal tufts are to be planted in spring, not harvested, not under any circumstances, and they are being eaten now."

"You are not being eaten by the humans."

"The humans must enforce the agreement. You own them."

"We beg your help to overcome the predators."

"Our contract includes protection from predators. We will add terpenes to make our fruit inedible."

"I propose something better than terpenes, because intelligent animals might like terpenes, the way they harvest pine wax. They can simply learn to burn the terpenes off. Your terminal tufts would make good torches that could be eaten."

"Poison instead," one plant says, and it becomes a chorus. "Poison." "Poison." "Poison."

"Closer to my idea. But it is not necessary to kill the animals."

"These animals should be killed. These are pests. Your animals would approve. The humans extirpate weeds. This would be like eliminating weeds."

It would not be like eliminating weeds. If a field is cleared of nettle, there is always nettle elsewhere. If the Glassmakers are eliminated, there are no other Glassmakers, and even if there were many, killing them would be uncivilized. But I do not explain that, since the pineapples would not understand that I am a Pacifist. Instead, I say, "We wish to domesticate these animals. We wish to control their behavior. They are too valuable to destroy."

"You must make a contract with them," a pineapple orders.

"Indeed. They must be taught how to make contracts."

"The humans made a contract with us readily."

"I had already domesticated the humans."

"You must domesticate these pests," another pineapple says. "Yes, domesticate them," others interject.

"I wish to domesticate them, and I need your help. Help us help you." I wait for their replies.

Above us, stars shine. Bats swoop and whistle at each other. Fippolions howl, perhaps in protest to the Glassmaker music. A wild lion answers. Far, far to the south, a thunderhead flashes and rumbles. Nighttime flowers scent the air. Lizards chirp. I isolate a grove from my root network for a moment and enjoy the night as a human might, small in size but intense in outlook, entirely and pleasurably alert to nothing beyond my immediate surroundings, a luxury I can take only for a moment, but it is amazing how being small is a qualitative rather than a quantitative difference. The shape of the external world changes. I return my attention to my network of roots. Lentils continue to whimper. Most Pacifists and Glassmakers sleep.

One by one the pineapples agree and pressure their neighbors to join the majority. I show them how to combine urea and malonic acid to make barbituric acid, and I transport some urea from the gift center to close the contract.

And so the night goes: leeks, potatoes, yams, lettuce.

I did not expect to hear from the locustwood trees. Their custom is to select a speaker based on seniority and health, which means the biggest and most aggressive. It also becomes the sole breeding male; their sexuality is bipolar but elective. The theory of evolution brought by humans from Earth explains the outcome. They are self-selecting for escalating aggression, and they had already achieved significant success before human protection allowed for a supermature speaker.

"What do we get, bamboozler?" the locustwood speaker asks. "We are being cut down by the intruders. We value our relationship with the city animals, too. We have much to offer." A taste of ethylene in the message makes my rootlets freeze as the auxins are inhibited. As I said, he is aggressive.

I try to respond with self-assurance, but I can barely squeeze out, "What exactly can you offer?" All they make is decorative wood and edible autumnal seedpods.

"We propose a reasonable concession in the future in exchange for additional planting in the southern forestland."

"We need help now," I say.

He extrudes more ethylene. "We will fulfill your reasonable request whenever you make it. Be warned, we will not make this offer again. If you wish our help, this is our demand."

I am distracted. The lentils are sobbing. As kindly as I can, I say to the lentils, "We understand your problem and will help you soon."

Painful blasts of ethylene from several locustwood trees get my attention. Tatiana would have called this extortion.

"I have nothing for you to do," I say.

"We will do anything reasonable, but in exchange we want a southern colony. This is important to us."

My humor root suggests moving them all far to the south. An old root notices that the speaker's communication skills and perhaps intelligence have made a quantum leap with age.

"We have excess ethylene," the speaker says. "That would hurt many plants, including pineapples and tulips."

"I have no choice but to agree. You know that."

"We offer a fair bargain."

If Tatiana were alive, she would offer useful suggestions for coping with delinquency, but she is dead, and I need to answer quickly before my roots suffer permanent damage. "I agree. When conditions allow additional planting, planting will be done. But be prepared to follow my orders when I give them." My humor root suggests ordering suicide.

Meanwhile, I have begun to communicate with the snow vine that grows along the river. This could be crucial. I can use the vine's instinct to control animals to make it do what I want.

"New animal to control," I say. It has never realized that it is being used as a dike to stabilize the riverbanks during floods. It has easy access to water, it has attention, it thinks it is the ruler of the riverbanks and the master of the humans. The Glassmakers are using it to grow their snowflake-shaped scale bugs, and workers in particular like to eat the bugs, provided there are some left after the larger castes are done eating.

"You must control bugs," I say.

"Bugs no eat fruit," it answers. In other words, how can you control an animal except with fruit?

"Change sap for bugs. Like this." I show a chemical. "Sap will control animals."

"Bugs no eat fruit."

"Bugs drink sap."

"Yes," it says. "Bugs no eat fruit."

"Change sap for bugs because bugs drink sap, no eat fruit."

"Bugs no eat fruit."

I realize that we are related plants, both bamboos, in fact, and our shared physiology is the only reason I can have a conversation of any complexity. The hedge along the river is too small to have many sentient roots. The presence of other snow vines triggers an aggressive growth, but this hedge has lived alone and is content to lead a manicured little life parasitizing its aspens and putting down more guard roots than it needs, thus serving the humans without realizing it. It has no need for intelligence, none at all.

"Change sap for bugs," I repeat, hoping that repetition will of itself prove persuasive. "Big animals eat bugs."

"Bugs no eat fruit."

"Big animals eat bugs."

"Big animals eat bugs," the snow vine repeats. I have made progress.

"Yes," I say. "Change sap for bugs."

"Big animals eat bugs."

"Yes. Change sap for bugs. Like this."

"Bugs eat sap," it says. "Bugs are pests."

"Bugs are good. Big animals eat bugs like fruit."

The snow vine stammers some meaningless chemical compounds and finally says, "Bugs are like fruit." This is very significant progress.

"Bugs are like fruit," I agree. "Bugs eat sap. Change sap. Sap will control two animals."

"Sap will control bugs. Big animals eat bugs."

"Yes. You must change sap for bugs and animals."

"I will change sap for bugs and animals."

At last! "Yes. Change sap like this." I deliver some prototype chemicals.

All these plants. Long ago I behaved no differently from them. We grew together. We braved the storms, we suffered in droughts, we traded remedies for pests, we kept out dangerous corals and root-eating animals, we bargained for sunlight and nutrients, we timed our flowerings to share pollinators, and we staggered the ripening of our fruit to maintain seed-dispersing animals. We spoke simply because thinking requires energy, and the strongest among us could survive well enough almost without thought because our lives were simple. I have grown but they have not, and my needs run in tandem to theirs in ways they could never imagine.

Only intelligent creatures also create civilization. Civilization creates the idea of peace as well as war, and makes both possible. I am a Pacifist. I have chosen the idea that I intend to make real.

The Sun rises. I am weary after a busy night. Sunshine sends photons, and in my leaves they split water into oxygen, hydrogen ions, and energy. I am large. I will renew myself as efficiently as possible because we face even more difficult times in the campaign to domesticate the Glassmakers.

Marie comes to the Meeting House. Her skin color is too yellowish. I wish she were able to eat more because food would give her strength. "Exactly what chemicals are you making?" she asks.

"Something related to morphine, and it should have a strong depressive and hypnotic effect on the Glassmaker central nervous system, as I understand it. Also barbiturates to depress brain function."

"Dangerous combination."

"Dangerous because they produce strong reactions. Their effects may be cumulative. The goal is to disable them. We have seen that they are willing to kill."

She sits. "We can't control how much they ingest, though. Overdoses could cause respiratory failure."

"Correct. I have thought of an additional concern. Females and majors eat first and eat to their contentment. Workers may get none. We must review Orion's plan of attack. We may need to physically subdue the workers." Subdue almost sounds peaceful, my humor root interjects.

She nods. "We'll need to plan for injuries as well as overdoses. We'll probably lose some. I don't even know how their circulatory system works, just that they have one."

"I will supply antidotes for my drugs."

"We don't know how they'll work without tests, and we can't do tests."

"Correct. Much will rely on the skill of the medics."

She leans back, closing her eyes and letting sunshine fall on her face. The warmth of sunlight feels pleasant to animals. "Lucille's good," she says eventually. "She'll have us ready." She opens her eyes to look at my talking stem.

"She has proven to be a wise choice," I say. "And your efforts are vital. You have done incalculably much for Pax already."

Perhaps I should mention to her that after spending a night talking to plants, I am more acutely aware of why I am so pleased to have intelligent company. Humans have made my life happy. I wish they lived longer.

I avoid thinking about what might happen if my plan fails. I am large. Humans are fragile. They might all be killed, but I would survive in one form or another despite anything the Glassmakers might do to me, and I would be desolate beyond imagination.

LUCILLE

When Stevland got the plants to start drugging the Glassmakers, there was a fantastic party at their camp across the river for a day and a half. At first the stupefiers made the Glassmakers silly and loud, with lots of yelling and singing and stumbling around. Then they argued and started fights, and Glassmakers got tossed bleeding into the river. At least one drowned. Bats even brought food to Monte to ask him what was going on. The drumming got off-beat. It had to be scary for any Glassmaker who could still think straight.

I kept pretending to be cheerful and optimistic, trying to balance the medics and Stevland, who worried about all sorts of details. Cedar saw setbacks every half hour: eating too much, eating too little, too aggressive, too sleepy, too much optimism on our (my) part, too much pessimism, always some damn thing.

Finally, on the second day, toward sunset, the Glassmakers began to pass out. The females and majors collapsed over dinner, and when the workers saw them sleeping, they scurried to eat the leftovers, and pretty soon they fell facedown into the feeding bowls. That was our sign. We sneaked out of the city by the back gate, threw a rope bridge across the river at a ravine downstream, and crept up the riverside road toward the Glassmaker camp. The old hunters led. And Cedar, of course.

Marie hiked right ahead of me, stooped under a backpack, and when she tripped on something in the dark, glass bottles full of antidotes clinked. It had to weigh a lot, but I couldn't help her carry it since we wouldn't stay together. I carried nothing, especially not weapons. They might fall into the wrong hands if . . . well, it wasn't my job to think about failure. Hathor had already done that thoroughly. She was too old to fight herself and stayed safe and sound back in the city. I'd been too nervous to eat all day.

The hundred of us creeping toward their camp accounted for most of the able-bodied adults and older children of Pax. Another fifty hid on the other side of the river, ready to cross it in boats as soon as they could. There was more than one of us for every one of them. We'd win, they'd lose, but with how much damage?

"Paralytics, that's what was in the food tonight," Marie had told everyone before we set out. "Overdoses aren't just possible, they're inevitable. They also might choke on the food in their bowls and drown in the soup. Check the breathing first of all."

We couldn't carry lanterns, so we couldn't see what was ahead, and it was cloudy so we didn't even have starlight or auroras, but we could hear a lot of whiny snarls.

"Snoring," Marie whispered.

Piotr stifled a laugh. He'd painted his face with big gray eyes and a vertical stripe across his mouth and nose to look like a Glassmaker. Camouflage, he said.

"Listen," he said, "everything's quiet." Right. Nothing barked or sang or sparkled in the night.

"Lizards eat vegetables," Marie said. I wanted to ask if this would hurt them, but that question would have to wait.

We were close to the camp, silent with fear, straining to hear. The old hunters and the best fighters had arrived at the camp ahead of us. No big noise. Translation: No big trouble—probably, but I couldn't see a thing, so I didn't know.

A bark like a bluebird called to us from the underbrush. One woof. Good. It was a sign that things were fine. We kept creeping forward. "Woof!" again. But then a Glassmaker moaned far ahead, something fell, a bowstring twanged, probably to deliver a tranquilizer-tipped arrow, and humans whispered angrily. Piotr gasped and held his breath. I kept creeping.

We knew they wouldn't all be asleep. Some of them would have eaten too little, or wouldn't be as susceptible. But how many awake? Why wasn't anyone yelling anything? That many overdoses? Something else thudded, something crunched like a basket being crushed. What? Should I bow-wow a question?

"Woof" came from just ahead, then a lot of whispers and a big thump like a tent falling down.

In a few more steps we turned a bend in the path, and we found Orion with a bow over his shoulder, holding up a flickering red lantern, and a woman was leaning over a motionless Glassmaker, listening to its breathing and untying weapon belts. Farther ahead, a purple lamp with a tiny flame glowed, and vague shadows hurried around. Someone to my left imitated a bluebird whine perfectly, a call for a medic. Marie hurried toward the sound.

I kept looking for my field commander—there, his amber lantern. The old hunter gestured thumbs-up, everything woofy, then pointed to a female slumped on a mat. Mine to check, to strip of everything I could, including clothes. Lamplight reflected on her gray eye. The eye twitched. A good sign, really; she was awake, probably fine, just incapacitated. I thought she'd smell bad close up, but she didn't, more like ripening truffle and bitter cloves, and not strong at all. She must have bathed recently.

I took off her blanket, soft and fluffy and folded several times, bigger than I thought and really warm. The next morning, I half helped, half shoved her onto a raft and across the river. I felt small next to the females. Their heads were almost as high as mine, but their bodies were lots bigger, bulky and long, balanced over spindly legs. Marie said a lot of thorax space was devoted to lungs and hollow bones, so we weighed about the same.

The drugs turned out to be a little too strong, as we expected. We lost five majors and nine workers to respiratory failure. Two more Glassmakers got injured and died when they struggled, and four died of injuries from drugged fights before they passed out. Our side took a few hurts, too, including a hunter who accidentally shot himself with a tranquilizer arrow. A Glassmaker child stayed in a coma for a whole terrifying day, and most Glassmakers woke up nauseated, throwing up, and panicky. A few got hysterical, including Gray-Eyes.

Stevland got morose. "A toll of twenty percent is excessive. I committed a major misjudgment and caused a needless slaughter, a repeat of the depraved history of my species. I have so badly betrayed the Glassmakers that they will never accept mutualism." Et cetera. I asked the Committee for permission to talk to him alone. The counselor-medic gave me a questioning look but spoke in favor, and the motion passed, with Stevland abstaining. I didn't know why he abstained but it didn't matter.

So, everyone left the Meeting House, I shut and barred the door, sat down in front of Stevland's stem, pulled out the knife, and started talking: "Nice weapon, right? I got this from Tatiana. She got it from Sylvia."

"I have never seen it before. It is metal."

"Steel. From Earth. It's a secret. It's the knife Sylvia used to kill the old moderator, Vera. You know that story? Well, I mean the real story. Everyone says Sylvia's revolt was just a vote, they say the moderator got voted out, the first and only time that's happened. Well, that's not what happened. Sylvia wanted to come here to Rainbow City but the moderator didn't and the Parents didn't, and she finally had to kill the moderator. With this knife. Other people got hurt and killed, too. Sylvia even left some Parents back in the old village because they didn't want to come here. They were afraid of you."

He didn't say anything. He was probably shocked giftless. That was kind of what I'd hoped for.

"Sylvia gave the knife to Tatiana and she gave it to me so I would know that being moderator isn't a game. It isn't easy. It isn't fun. We're not fippokats, happy and gentle and everything. Well, maybe we are. Kats can kill if they have to, they can kick something to death like little lions. We can make mistakes, but we can do the right thing, too, even when it's a terrible thing to do. The hard part is knowing what to do."

"The Parents were afraid to come?"

"You're the one always saying how big and powerful you are. You can be frightening."

"I did not mean to be frightening."

"Don't worry. It was their job to know when not to be scared."

"I wanted you to come too much, perhaps."

"We're glad we did."

"I never knew until now that she had to kill people to get the colony to move."

"That's not what they teach in school, is it?"

"I did everything I could to get Sylvia to return. I wanted a colony of service animals here. I did not wish to make her kill. That would be highly, highly uncivilized."

"She decided to kill Vera, you didn't. And you tried not to kill Glassmakers, and mostly, you didn't. I visited the old village in the big history tour for kids. We walked around on stilts and pretended we were Earthlings, and we studied the old storm cellars and the barrens where snow vines grew. It wasn't a great place to live. Sylvia did what she had to do. So did you. We can make mistakes, but you didn't. Sure, some of them died, but you know what slaughter is, and it wasn't slaughter."

"There were more deaths than I expected."

"More deaths than you'd hoped for. Balance these words: expect and hope."

He was quiet for a while. "The difference is emotion."

"Exactly. But feelings aren't facts." I picked up the knife. "I'm here to give this to you. Where can I put it?"

"Plants do not have personal possessions."

"Moderators do." After a while, when he saw that I wasn't going to change my mind, he decided to have me put it in a glass box, like an artifact at the museum, then bury it under a floor tile in the Meeting House. He said he would weigh more feelings against facts.

And he must have, because soon he began directing autopsies of Glassmakers. "I will learn from my error, for if I can do great harm, I can do great good. The Glassmakers will see the difference between conflict and mutualism." Et cetera, again.

Nye and Kung organized elaborate funeral ceremonies, burying the Glassmakers in the cemetery grove in full view of the surviving Glassmakers "so they see we won't eat them," Nye said. Marie had said Nye had never given up on the Glassmakers.

We put the females and children on our side of the river under a wide, open tent alongside the city wall next to a bamboo grove with lots of eyes and ears. The majors and workers went on the far side in an open corral, eating food laced with tranquilizers that didn't calm them down nearly enough. They moved like they were sleepwalking. They also sleep-hit each other, kicked, scuffled, and brawled. Not to overlook the sleep-attempts to attack the guards.

We took the females off tranquilizers because everyone on the mission (Cedar included) thought the females had leadership roles and were a lot more reasonable than Plaid Blanket. Well, they were. They didn't hit each other, they just yelled a lot really loud. They didn't threaten us, they ignored us in an arrogant and superior way.

We started taking females on tours of the city. Well, actually, we had to plead with them and half drag them to get them to come. I started calling them queens. I'd found that word in an old Earth book. It meant women who rule arrogantly and act superior. Queens!

On the fourth day of Operation Domesticate I wanted to lead a tour for the gray-eyed one and another that we called Bellona because she bellowed so much. She was a bit bigger than Gray-Eyes, with a faint striped pattern in her brown fur.

A warm morning breeze flapped the tent, and the guards waved at me. "Chek-ooo!" I called. "Good morning! Let's go!"

The children jumped and ran away to huddle next to the grove. The queens didn't move. Gray-Eyes was sitting on a mat. I took her tough-skinned hand and tugged gently, keeping my fingers away from her claws. "Come on, it will be fun. We'll even give you dinner." At first she ignored me, but finally she stood up. I gave her hand to Piotr, who often came with me on tours along with some guards. He was Tatiana's grandson, sixteen years old, but his real job was to run and get more help if we needed it.

Bellona took a few steps back as I approached and said something unfriendly. "You haven't seen our city," I said. "Well, your city, too." I took her hand and didn't let her snatch it back. "You know we're not going to hurt you. Kak kak! Time to go." I tugged. I tugged harder. Another queen said something, and they had a brief, hostile exchange. Then Bellona started moving.

We began hiking toward the gate, and two guards fell behind us. Bellona took a couple of quick steps just to show that she could elude all of us if she tried. But when we entered the walls, she stopped dead and stared.

"Hey, it's beautiful!" I said. "I told you. Come on, we'll show you more."

The kids had put signs in Glassmade on buildings to welcome them. "Clinic." "Meeting House." "Gift Center." "Bathhouse." "Dining House." "Glassmaker Museum." But the queens didn't seem to notice. Gray-Eyes occasionally grumbled at Bellona, and Bellona grumbled back. No reaction, until finally they took deep sniffs in the kitchen. Deer-crab stew with onions. It smelled great, and I had the cooks give each of them a bowl of it, which they gobbled down, and when they were done, Bellona threw the bowl on the ground.

She had reacted! So, I thought, silly me, because Gray-Eyes had visited the city already, she might not be impressed, but this was Bellona's first time, and we had her attention. She'd like the museum. We went there and I opened the door. It's full of bits of machinery, old dishes, a steel cup, scraps of fabric, and other artifacts that are pretty amazing. Best of all, there's a diorama of the ruined city in one of the bays of the building, and in another bay there's a gallery of the two dozen ceramic portraits of Glassmakers from the cemetery, everything labeled in Glassmade as well as Pacifist. Bellona would see that they were honored and they were our friends, or at least that they could be our friends.

We walked in, footsteps echoing, and I pointed out the diorama and gallery with all the enthusiasm that I'd use for teaching a class of small children. "We're especially proud of these." They couldn't understand, but it was the noise and gesture that counted. "This was your city, and it can be your city again."

She didn't care. I don't think she looked at anything. With those faces that never move, who could know? I decided to skip Harry's Gallery a few buildings down, another tribute to the Glassmakers. She wouldn't care, and besides, children and kats were waiting to dance for them. Our message couldn't be clearer: *We want to be your friends, so get domesticated.* And their answer was clear: *Drop dead.*

But as I watched the kids and kats sing and waltz around, I thought about looking at things from the queens' point of view. After everything that had happened, the attack and deaths and now having to live naked in a cold tent, Gray-Eyes probably hated my guts.

The kids and kats finished the show for Gray-Eyes and Bellona—a great performance with some amazing acrobatics. All us Pacifists applauded and cheered. The queens could have been statues. A solemn-faced little boy brought them necklaces of flowers and said in his best imitation of Glassmade, "Cong-wee, cong-wee." We slipped them around the queens' necks.

Later, at a Committee meeting in the Meeting House, I said, "Gray-

Eyes sniffed the flowers. Roses, really fragrant, and Bellona said something like rotrotrotrot, and that was all we got out of them, which was pretty much nothing. I took them back to the tent. Then the queens all started yelling at each other."

"They were reviewing the visit," Bartholomew said. "They don't agree on their interpretations of events." He spent most of his time at the tent, observing and ready to communicate if they wanted to try, which they didn't. "I think Bellona has an especially divergent opinion."

"Not domesticating very fast," Cedar said. "I separated the workers and majors this morning into different corrals. We thought that would help."

"It helped, hmmm?" Kung said. "Less fights, more fair fights. And the same ones fight, same ones against others, certain others."

"Right, there are sides," Cedar said, and then imitated Bartholomew. "Divergent opinions. Especially Plaid Blanket, but what would you expect?"

"Then let's separate them some more," I said. "The different factions of majors, like that."

"Sure," she said, "get me people to build corrals. But everyone's working the fields, and they should be, because we have fields to tend. We don't have enough people to make this work."

"It will take time," Stevland said, "but the rewards will be great."

"How long? We're not as slow as plants."

Stevland answered after a pause. He'd been pausing a lot lately, probably thinking, the way Tatiana used to. "Intelligence makes predictions difficult, but there is only one intelligent outcome."

"There are a lot of stupid outcomes," she said.

"By acting intelligently we limit the opportunities for stupidity, like pruning a tree to direct its growth."

"I need a lot more pruners if we're going to make this work," Cedar said. Some Beadies nodded.

After a pause, Stevland answered, "I suggest hobbling those Glassmakers inclined to fight to limit their ability to walk and kick, perhaps by tying back legs together."

"They'll untie it," she said.

"Glue the knot."

Cedar flushed. I guess she didn't want to be outthought by Stevland, and I knew I needed to keep the meeting moving. If she didn't like Operation Domesticate, fine, we all have opinions, but she was starting to remind me of a queen. "We'll get the leatherworkers on this," I said. "They have some tough old hides and glue. Flora, can you work with them?"

"You need to know," Cedar said, "that it's going to storm tomorrow. They're going to be out there in the rain. They won't like it."

"They get hobbles, they cooperate, they get a roof," Kung said. "I can build roofs, thatch roofs, separate ones, and we separate them quick that way. Behave, stay dry."

"Offering rewards for good behavior will be a major step toward domestication," Stevland said, and Kung grinned. "The medics and I have concluded that they communicate by scent using various volatile chemicals and pheromones. This explains the relative poverty of their spoken language. During the autopsies we discovered that their olfactory organs are enormous, and they have significant scent creation and diffusion glands. Their sensory abilities far exceed yours and mine, which is why you have not noticed these smells, and I must grow more sensitive organs quickly. We must analyze and learn their chemical language."

"Maybe there's a slapping language, too," I said, hoping people would laugh. They did.

"Violence is a form of communication among animals, although your abilities to communicate render violence too crude for routine social relationships."

"They don't have as many rules," Bartholomew said.

"They might just be nasty by nature," Cedar said.

"Maybe," Marie said diplomatically, "their social order has broken down. It takes a lot to maintain a society. I've been thinking about that. They're all sick, even the children. They have lots of chronic illnesses, and they have injuries that haven't healed well. There aren't enough children, and there probably aren't enough females. An imbalance in workers and majors—Cedar, you see how they behave. They're sick, and their population is skewed. But why? We can treat their symptoms, but we can't cure them if we don't know why. It might be environmental, like a toxin in the environment or nutritional deficiencies. It might be an epidemic. Nye and I both counted more Glassmakers last fall. They're dying. They need help."

She was looking sicker but seemed energetic. Stevland had told me the toxins in her blood acted as stimulants.

There were a few more reports: Farmers were trying to help the crops recover, but some fields needed complete replanting. Hunters were too busy guarding the Glassmakers to be able to do their jobs, so the cooks would be using dried meat or meat substitutes. No happy reports. Some of us stayed afterward for a lesson in making Glassmaker sounds. Waaak! Tsee! Chik-a-chik-a ugh! But we were all tired and went home soon.

As I walked through the city, Stevland's leaves rustled in the wind over my head. Plants got tired, like me, and he was still negotiating with the other greenery to keep making stupefiers in more refined doses, and the plants he had to deal with weren't necessarily cooperative or smart. Imagine a plant like Cedar.

So, the Glassmakers were still prisoners. Not symbionts. Not partners. Not domesticated. Nothing close to that mutualism friendly stuff. We needed to be patient, patient, patient. Damn, I'd be the queen of patience.

Well, that was the situation on the fourth day of Operation Domesticate, a warm spring morning, tall storm clouds on the horizon, bats singing, "Rain coming!" overhead, the streets full of people starting their day or finishing their night. We didn't work that hard even during harvest. A few children marched down the street, firewood on their backs. They chattered like Glassmakers, "Curtlcurtlcurtl." Maybe it was a game to them, but they should have been in class learning multiplication, and when they delivered their wood, they'd have to go work in the fields while the adults kept an eye on our prisoners.

I hustled to the bakery to help deliver bread. One way to domesticate an animal, Stevland said, was to give it food: bread, stews, fruit,
salads, soups, tea, roasts, whatever we had.

The bakery smelled of sweet smoke and bread, all wonderful. The
three bakers were up to their elbows in dough. All the ovens were fired
up. Sweat made Nye's shirt stick to his arms and back as he lifted stone
baking trays of nut-studded bread for the Glassmakers from the oven.
I didn't know he had such muscles. Lifting, kneading, hauling bags of
flour and grain, it all added up, I guess. The other two bakers had strong
arms and shoulders, too, once I looked.

"Of course, we'll run out of wheat," one of them said. She was shap-
ing loaves from a wad of dough the size of a four-year-old boy.

"We'd have gotten a little low on wheat anyway," the senior baker
called as he formed lentil turnovers.

"Low?" she said. "We have a ten-month supply, at least we did
before we had to feed more mouths."

"Five days, eleven sacks of flour. Do the math. If this harvest doesn't
come in, we're short."

"Firewood, too," the woman said. "We'll need extra firewood."

The senior baker looked up, and his bald head wrinkled as he raised
his eyebrows. "Maybe a couple of helping hands. It's one thing to work
every day, but from Luxrise to sunset? I'm too old for that."

"An apprentice," the woman answered. "How about that Jewel girl?
She's old enough."

"Jewel likes cooking, not baking," the man said. "There's a difference."

Nye finally said something. "A worker. A Glassmaker worker. They're
smart. They're fast."

We all stared at him. He stacked nut loaves into a basket. They had
been baked to perfection.

"I thought you didn't like them," the head baker said.

"What I like doesn't matter. It's what we need. We have to make
them be part of us. That means they have to do what we do. I'll work
with them, I'll teach them, I'll eat with them, I'll talk with them.
Because I have to."

No one said anything for a while, then the senior baker said, "They already know how to bake. They make bread. It won't take much to get them used to this place."

"Yeah, a Glassmaker," the woman said.

"Well, that's mutualism," I said. "You want firewood, and a worker, and that's what you'll get." I flashed them a smile, especially at Nye. He helped me put loaves into a basket for the queens and children.

I slipped through the front gate in the city wall. We kept it halfway closed just in case. It felt good to be out, to be seeing the city's glazed brick wall and the rainbow bamboo rising tall inside it like a giant garden, and I understood why they wanted us out. It was a beautiful city.

Across the river, the majors and workers stumbled around inside their corrals, fenced in by wide hedges of brambles and thorns. Guards, including Cedar, watched them, bows in hand, backed up by more guards on the far side of the river, and Flora talked with the guards, pointing out individuals to hobble. Kung walked out of the woods with a load of palm leaves, thatch for roofs.

Eagle feathers. I was going to have to award a boatload of eagle feathers when this was done.

We needed to find a worker to become a baker's apprentice. How?

I tried not to look at the trampled children's garden and the muddy fields that used to sparkle with tulips. Stevland had said the plants would recover fast with our help and would be more loyal than ever since we'd proved that we cared about them, especially the pineapples. I sure hoped so. I felt really small when I looked at the fields and forest all around us. What if all the plants decided they didn't like us? They knew what to do.

The queens' tent had mats on the ground and food. No clothes, no furniture, nothing extra, and it was going to rain and get cold soon. Would they want their blankets back? We'd explained in a letter that they had only to ask. It lay on the ground, as far as we knew unread. But someone among the Glassmakers could read and write, we knew that. All they had to do was communicate. Not even agree, just scribble a note. Just ask. Just call us idiots. Anything. Damn queens.

"Chek-ooo, Bartholomew!" I screeched as I entered the tent.

"That's a matter of opinion," he said. He sat on a mat playing a game of Go with himself. The queens were talking to each other and didn't seem to look our way, even when I set the basket of bread in the center of the tent. The children ran up and took loaves as soon as I stepped back.

"I'm still ignored like a piece of poop," he said.

"Poop is a gift. Ask Stevland. You're a gift to the Glassmakers. They just don't see it."

A child grabbed the letter from the ground and looked ready to tear it up, a bored little kid looking for something to do. They were really cute, those kids, with soft curly fur and heads a bit oversize just like human kids. Bellona screeched something. The kid put the letter down. A kat hopped over and turned a somersault. They liked the kids, too. The children and kat began playing follow-the-leader.

"They don't want to admit we exist," Bartholomew said. "But this morning two of them got up and marched out of the tent toward the city gate. They wanted to go someplace, obviously, fine, so I escorted them and they went straight to the museum. They didn't pay attention during the first visit, or so we thought, but that was a false front, because they knew exactly what they wanted to look at this time, and it was the section about the abandonment of the city."

"Hey, that's something."

"She read the labels out loud, that one." He pointed to a female with a row of curly black hair down her back, the one that had been most responsive to the mission last fall. "It's written in Glassmade as well as Pacifist, and they quarreled over something. Well, quarrel is too strong a word. They were upset over something. They had a discussion about something. They were deeply moved by something. You know, the label that starts, 'Rainbow City was founded about four hundred years ago by space travelers like us.' They came right back and haven't stopped talking since. Listen."

"They're interrupting each other."

"As usual. It says in the museum that there were a thousand Glassmakers in the city. I believe that's what they're talking about. I've seen them counting on their fingers. They're planning something, that's what I conclude."

Bellona grabbed the letter and waved it around. Bartholomew and I exchanged glances.

"Nothing stupid, I hope," I said.

"They're not stupid."

They kept talking with their impassive faces, squawky shrieky voices, and the curly-backed one had a lot to say. I set down a few Go stones to complicate Bartholomew's game for him and listened. Curls picked up a loaf of bread and slapped Bellona across the face with it. Then she yelled so loud my ears rang.

"They like the food," Bartholomew said. "Marie! Good morning!"

I turned, and there she was hurrying to the tent. The morning wasn't cold, but she was bundled up in sweaters. She looked yellowish and exhausted. "Good morning, Bartholomew. How are they eating?"

"They eat everything we give them." He got up to give her a hug. Greenies do that.

"Even the stews and salads?"

"They love the stews."

"Good. Stevland ran some tests overnight. They're all malnourished, severely malnourished, beyond the point of illness. They're crippled and stunted. It's . . ." She shook her head. "It explains a lot. I'll show you. The queens are as bad off as anyone, and they're the leaders, supposedly. They're in no condition to lead."

The queens kept arguing and ignored us. Marie walked right among them and started pointing and talking, shouting to be heard.

"Look at their eyes! Look at the individual facets! Some sparkle and some don't! This female, look, she's completely blind!" It was Gray-Eyes. "That one, see that grayish area around the edges of her eyes? See how wide it is?"

I took a few steps closer and squinted. "So she sees only with the center? That's not even half. Damn." I looked around. Curls had eyes that were almost all sparkly. And she was leading some sort of scheme.

"Yes, blindness," Marie said. "But it's worse. Look, here, at the skin around her eyes and mouth." Gray-Eyes twitched under Marie's touch like a bug had landed on her. "Those marks that look like wrinkles, they're actually sores or scars from sores. There are more but you can't see them under the fur. Their teeth are in their throats, and in the ones I autopsied, the teeth were bad. These Glassmakers aren't like the ones in the museum. I mean, they're the descendants, but their health—their proportions don't look right. There aren't enough old ones, and if no one lives to be old, they all die young of something. If you're malnourished, you're susceptible to all sorts of problems."

She waved angrily toward the slit trench being used for a gift center. "There's blood in some feces and all sorts of parasites. A simple purgative would do them a lot of good." She dropped to her knees in front of a child, the same one that had been in a coma from the tranquilizers, and took it by the hands. "Look at this child. The eyes are already going bad. The fur is thin, these claws are malformed." Tears sparkled in her eyes. The child shifted nervously.

I felt like I ought to do something.

"These leg sores aren't healing," Marie said. "Ulcerated sores on a child!" She touched the joints and it squealed. The queens had stopped talking and Curls came closer to watch her. "Malformed joints. And I hate to think"—tears slid down her cheeks—"what this means for mental development. It's hard to keep us well fed. It takes all our skills and a lot of help from Stevland. We're not made for this planet, but we can get what we need."

She began to sob, too sick to stop herself. "We can help them. We can make the Glassmakers well. If they let us."

I knelt down and put an arm around her. Those words hit me: If they let us. Why were we waiting for them? This was forced friendship. We decided what would happen. We'd make them accept help. We were the ones in charge, and the damn queens had to get used to the idea, the sooner the better.

Then I took a deep breath. Anger wouldn't help.

Curls was saying something to Bartholomew.

Communicating! Even if we couldn't understand what she said.

He got a slate and began writing. "She be-her sad," he read out loud, pointing to Marie. "All you be-you sick." He held it out to Curls, who studied it, following the lines of writing with a finger. She could read!

He wrote some more. "You need good food. We be-us sad because you be-you sick. We give-you good food."

Curls read it and turned back to the other ones and began yelling at them again. Bartholomew looked at me and winked.

"Do you want to talk?" I shouted at her. If they liked to argue, I could, too. "I want to listen. Chek-ooo! Kak!" She turned toward me. "Bartholomew, tell her—no, make her come talk with me at the Meeting House. One-on-one. I have things to say."

"Make her?"

I waved at the rainbow bamboo around us. "It's time to get aggressively friendly, right, Stevland? Her and me, no more damn games. We're going to become best friends. Starting now."

Bartholomew glanced in Marie's direction. "It's time to try something else, I suppose."

"Bring her." I was co-moderator. I could give orders. I helped Marie to her house to rest, which she didn't want to do, then went to see Stevland at the Meeting House.

"Hey, water and sunshine. I'm going to force friendship. No more being nice."

"Warmth and food." Pause. "You are a likable person, and this new tactic holds promise, but you will not like the promise I made."

The door was open, so we weren't meeting in secret, but no one had come to the Meeting House. Everyone had too much work to do.

"I'll always like you." I sat down. His cheerfulness was probably a front, like mine.

"I promised the orange trees that you will cut them down."

"What? Damn, I'll never understand plants."

"They do not wish to be cut down. But they do not wish to produce nutritious catkins for the Glassmakers, who need ascorbic acid and thiamine, with copper. I can transfer copper to the orange trees for this purpose. You can harvest at levels that will still permit pollination. But they refuse to fortify their catkins. The animal equivalent is a lion challenging the fippmaster."

"Fippmaster Stevland?" I meant that as a joke. He answered slowly.

"Perhaps I did not make a perfect analogy, although the image you invoked is humorous. Their behavior is perverse. Additional copper would allow enhanced production of cytochrome enzymes and plastocyanin in their chloroplasts. They would benefit from this activity. They refuse because oranges are naturally insubordinate. They routinely refuse to join us other plants in synchrony to share pollinators or maintain frugivores for seed dispersal, perhaps because they grow in shade and need not negotiate for canopy rights. But they are not unintelligent. They will see it is to their advantage to help us."

I knew what a chloroplast was, at least. "If we cut them down, we can't harvest anything."

"I suggest trimming one to ground level, which is close to barbarism but necessary. And we must act quickly. Their catkins are budding now. If you trim the tree severely, it will suffer, not die, and the entire grove will be frightened. We do not have time to wait. The Glassmakers have been sick for a long time, and if we can make them healthy, they will be more responsive. They will see that we mean them well, and that sharing lives with us is to the mutual benefit of everyone. We must appeal to the intelligence of the Glassmakers. I have observed that intelligent creatures are easier to control because they can foresee the results of their actions farther ahead."

"Control?" Tatiana had said he wanted too much control over us.

"Exactly. With very little effort, you humans and I were able to enter into mutualism, which involves mutual control. I am a social creature, so submitting to social control is a desirable thing. The Glassmakers will submit, but we must act quickly. I am tired. I know you are. Marie's health is failing. You must cut down an orange tree this morning. The wood is very useful. I can direct a forester to the optimal tree to frighten the oranges."

That didn't sound too scary, the mutual control part, at least.

"Perhaps the forester can bring a lion," he said. "Trees fear lions. Lions eat roots. The animal equivalent is someone attacking your face. Both you and the Glassmakers are not native to Pax. For that reason you do not thrive naturally. I have worked hard to keep you healthy, and without assistance, the Glassmakers are failing. But when they lived here earlier, I was not capable of helping them as I have helped you.

Malnutrition may have led to the city's demise, if, as Marie speculates, it leads to social breakdown. I do not know. Ignorance is another kind of imbalance. I can make only general guesses about their needs, but we are learning many things quickly."

It began to rain outside. I thought about shutting the door, but then we'd be alone. "Good. The queens, well, you saw. They're up to something."

"They realize the situation is completely unexpected. This may give us opportunities to communicate and create new balances. Bartholomew has persuaded a queen to come. I believe his shouting and anger was an act. Humans are exceptionally able at dissembling."

"Right. I can shout, too."

"You must balance her behavior. I believe this will be a pivotal moment. Correction. I hope it will be a pivotal moment. We would all benefit if the current stalemate is ended positively."

"Balance, balance, balance."

I heard Bartholomew's voice: "This is where we're going. Here. No, here!"

"Chek-ooo!" I said. The queen and a worker entered and stopped. "Come in!" I said, waving her over. Bartholomew shooed her from behind, holding a palm-leaf umbrella, and she moved closer, the worker following. Even from across the room I could see that the worker was sickly and a bit blind, now that Marie had taught me what to look for.

Curls looked around.

Bartholomew sat down at the table with a bit of show to demonstrate how we did things in the Meeting House. She took a few steps closer. "She insisted on the worker. That's what took so long."

"No problem." I picked up a slate and brush. "We propose-you friendship. We will talk-us of future. I be-me Lucille" (I wrote as phonetically as I could) "and I be-me leader of city." I turned to Bartholomew. I wasn't good at writing. "Is the grammar right? The imperative?"

"Almost." He corrected a word. The queen leaned her head over to look. I remained sitting, eye level with her big body, within reach of her four-fingered, clawed hands.

"Well?" I said to her. "Tell me what you think." I pushed writing materials toward her. She stared at them. She made a sound that seemed to be disagreement.

I stood up. "Hell, we can't wait forever, you and us. We have to get something going here." I gestured at the brush, slate, and ink pot again, and as queenly as I could, I said, "Write something, damn you. You're alone, you don't have to argue with the other queens, just with me."

She looked at the writing materials suspiciously. She picked up the brush like an unfamiliar tool, testing how to hold it in her four fingers, two of them small and opposed, two straight but jointed like human fingers. A stiff line of flesh, sort of like a fingernail, covered the backs of her fingers. The cuticles alongside them had pulled away in some places and had fresh scabs. She began to write slowly and formed the letters shakily, as if she'd never written much.

"You steal-us things." Translation: We'd taken all their possessions. True.

"Write this," I told Bartholomew—he could write faster and better than me. "We won't keep them. You know we want friendship, not fighting. We can share the city."

She read the words and muttered something, then settled onto a bench, legs underneath her body, sitting. The worker sat on the floor next to her, very close.

"You perhaps no need-you friend," she wrote. I swear she wrote the word "friend" with disdain.

Stevland answered. "No, we have-us no need. No need be-it art. Our art be-us befriend-you." It was a play on words, since *art* and *need* were spelled almost the same. Bartholomew pointed at Stevland's stem. Curls looked and said something like "Eep!" She nodded and swiveled her head. Teeth ground in her throat. The worker wiggled closer to her.

In Glassmade, he continued: "I be-me Stevland. Your ancestors knew me. I be-me pleased perhaps to address you." Translation: What's your name? She pointed to him and looked at me, and started to say something, but stopped.

I nodded. "Stevland," I said, pointing. "Lucille. Bartholomew." I pointed at her. She said something like "See-You." That's what I repeated, anyway.

"You chose intelligence to share-us city," Stevland wrote. "You be-you sick. Your sisters be-them blind. Your children tremble of type of hunger. We will feed you. We will make you healthy."

She snorted. With her thin, scabby fingers, she dipped the brush in ink and began to write, maybe the word "we," but she crossed it out and wrote again, slowly, constructing the word with effort: "Slaves."

I took a brush and wrote, "No. Never slaves." But why? I looked at Bartholomew. "Explain the law for her."

"Our writings," Bartholomew wrote in Glassmade and read out loud in Pacifist "order us to do equality. No slaves. Would you like to read our books?" He got up and grabbed the original copy of our Constitution from a table where it stood framed under glass and set it in front of her. "I can translate for you." She leaned forward to eye it.

Nye entered carrying a tray. I wasn't expecting that. It was heaped with food.

"Warmth and sunshine, Nye," Stevland said in Glassmade. "I ask-Nye bring-us food."

"You return-us weapons," she wrote, apparently ignoring Nye.

I thought about how to explain, but Stevland beat me to it: "Weapons be-they with equality, you will understand, because we also believe in caution, and you try to kill us."

"Us. You be-you plant," she wrote, and said it aloud. I thought I understood the screech for "be."

"I be-me equal," Stevland said.

She snorted again as Nye laid out rainbow fruit, nut spread, meat, roasted vegetables, and reddog tea. There's lots of vitamin C in reddog tea.

I showed the way—I hadn't had breakfast and I was hungry. She hesitated, but soon was delicately lapping up tea from a little bowl. Nye sat next to the worker and smiled at it, offering it a plate of vegetables. Grayish streaks marked its eyes, and creased scars glowed red in its furless inner elbows. Its claws grew small and curled, like a fingernail after you smack it and it grows back. I explained what this meant to Nye.

He stared at the floor for such a long time that See-You noticed.

Finally he looked at the worker again. "Stevland, tell me what to feed them and I'll make it."

"Ask them what they wish to eat, and I will help you make it healthy. They will eat more if we offer food they consider desirable."

Bartholomew set down his plate, picked up a slate, and relayed Nye's questions to See-You. More sweets? More salt? Roasted onions? Meat? What do Glassmaker children like? The questions seemed to annoy her.

"We want-us clothes."

"Hey," I said. "We were waiting for you to ask for them." I got up and opened a chest alongside the wall and hauled out blankets. "Just grab yours."

Instead, she picked up a plate of roasted deer crab meat, sniffed it deeply, then stared at it. After a moment I realized: Glassmade words for different foods decorated the rim. She said something quietly. The air seemed a little sweeter. Some smell-word?

She took up a stylus. "Perhaps we not all agree-us."

"That's tricky grammar," Bartholomew said. "Perhaps we won't all agree among ourselves, she said. That is, the queens will argue, as usual. And that gives us an interesting situation. Or rather, highlights the existing situation. We've seen them fight among themselves. Do we need to treat them all the same? Or do we divide and conquer?"

"Tell her that those who agree get not just clothes and food, they get shelter." Bartholomew looked at me with an eyebrow raised. "Well, I said aggressive, right? I mean that. Cooperate and get a house. Look at that rain." I held up a blanket. "Is this yours, See-You? Kak? House, blanket, shelter, food! We'll even let you work. Know someone who wants to be a baker? How about this blanket? Yes? Tseee! Here it is." I came over and, trying to act like it was a great honor—and it was—I draped the gray-green blanket over her body.

A pivotal moment.

Bartholomew began writing.

"I want-us house," she answered before he could finish.

Cedar ran in, dripping. "I hear she's talking!"

I decided to assume that she'd like the new aggressive friendship policy, even though she probably wouldn't. She threw her raincoat on a rack by the door, strutted over like a fippmaster asserting status, and began to read over my shoulder.

"Perhaps you define us," Bartholomew wrote.

"Us mean-us family."

"How many?" Cedar asked. I was about to ask the same thing, but without her anxiety, and Bartholomew was already writing it with no visible anxiety at all.

"Three majors, four workers, two children. They not fight you."

"Why?" Cedar shouted.

"She be-she perhaps what," See-You wrote, twitching her head at Cedar. Translation: Who does she think she is?

"You know what I am," Cedar said. "Why won't they attack? What's going on with you? Here, give me a brush." Cedar grabbed at the one in Bartholomew's hand. He didn't let go. See-You looked at her brush, raised the row of curls on her back, then she dipped the felt tip in ink and began writing again. She gave off a flowery scent that I knew but I couldn't name.

"Those without mothers attack. Mothers control each's family, orphans outnumber families and control with fear all. Orphans order attack you, take-us city. Orphans burn beauty-bush Stevland to give-you fear. Now I escape orphans perhaps to safe place, house, food, clothes, dry, warm, rest, peace, happy." She wrote slowly.

We read silently, and finally Bartholomew said, "That explains a lot."

"If you believe it," Cedar said.

See-You stared at Stevland, muttered, and wrote, "Many die when we nomad. Many mothers. We come-us back or all die. City make healthy life. Perhaps." That was a question.

"We welcome you," Nye said in a shaky voice, and I turned and saw that he was reading the message in Glassmade on Stevland's stem. Nye put an arm around the worker's shoulders and hugged it. He looked like he was going to laugh or cry.

"If families are that small, that leaves us a lot of hostile orphans," Cedar said, not laughing.

"Ask her, why did they cook Roland?" Nye said, really close to tears. "Ask that, please." Bartholomew did.

She bowed her head to him before writing. "Orphans say you eat dead like eagles. I say no, and if no, you live. I try music stick but be-it stolen. I like music. I like food. I like you live."

She put down the pen and scratched a sore at the edge of her eye. I wanted to grab her hand and make her stop. I wanted to grab her and dance around the room with her. I wanted to grab Stevland and hug him, because I knew he felt the way I did, or hug Nye or Bartholomew, but I didn't want to scare her. Instead, I took the pen from Bartholomew's hand and wrote, "Friends."

That had been my slogan: *Next time, friends!* Lucille, the perfect fippokat, happy, helpful, playful, gentle. Helpful—"Hey," I said, "everyone inside who's our friend."

Of course, it wasn't that easy. Cedar fretted that the queens' houses would have to be guarded because we shouldn't trust them, true enough. She fretted over which houses and where, and in the end we needed only three because the fourth queen didn't want to come inside.

"Bellona says it's a trick," Bartholomew said—shouted, really, because the rain had become a storm with gusty winds that blew rain inside the open tent. Bellona and her child huddled in the most protected spot. "She says she'll be a prisoner."

Water blew into my raincoat. "Tell her she's a prisoner now. If she comes inside, she'll be a friend. She'll get her clothes back. Oh, hell, I'll get blankets for her and the kid anyway." I noticed that across the river, Kung's thatched roofs were holding up under the rain just fine.

I expected the evening's Committee meeting to turn into a minor celebration. We finally had good news.

"The family workers and majors are out of the corrals. Less fighting," Kung said.

"Right, but there's almost sixty orphan Glassmakers out there who hate us," Cedar said. "And maybe thirty other Glassmakers inside the walls that do, and we can't put on hobbles in the rain. We shouldn't relax."

"Caution is well advised," Stevland said, "and yet we have made major progress in domestication. If the orphans had won, barbarism would have engulfed the city."

"They thought we were barbarians," Bartholomew said. "Diplomacy paid off." He nodded at Marie, who'd been smiling since I woke her up that afternoon and told her the news.

"We should mark this day," Daisy exclaimed. "This is the day when the Glassmakers finally returned home. We can have music to commemorate the success of the mission, astronomy studies to recall our first homes—"

"Archery contests," Cedar said, not smiling. "The archers saved us."

"No, no weapons," Daisy said. "We want to celebrate friendship, don't we, Lucille?"

"Right," I said. "And we can celebrate now. Operation Domesticate is working!"

"The archers are working right now out in the rain," Cedar said.

"Perhaps a feast," Stevland said, "an especially nutritious meal on this date next year. There is still much to do. Food will be key to domestication. The orange trees report that they have reconsidered their objections to fortifying their catkins. My outposts report that the river is rising upstream. Our supervision of the orphans will be complicated by a spring flood."

"Just what we need," Cedar said.

So much for a happy meeting. I stopped at See-You's house on my way home. The guard opened the door and I peeked in. The queen sat on a mattress on the floor near the fire, her blanket draped over her and her family snuggled up around her. A table held the remains of a big, tasty, nutritious meal. The room smelled odd, not quite sweet, something I couldn't name, but happy. A happy smell. She swiveled her head toward me.

"Chek-ooo!" I said. "Sorry to disturb you. Just wanted to say good night." I waved. She waved back, and her family joined her, ten hands waving sinuously at me, warm and fed and dry and housed and safe and resting peacefully under soft blankets, happy—I hoped they were happy.

I was happy as I turned to leave. The guard closed the door, and he looked at me grinning, and we hugged and laughed in the cold rainy night, celebrating.

STEVLAND

Water is life. So say plants, at least. I have not discussed spiritual beliefs with the humans, but they celebrate equinoxes and solstices and make minute observations of the stars, and each star is a sun. I suspect that humans have an unarticulated reverence for the Sun. Sunshine is predictable, so a sun is a suitable object of reverence for cyclical beings like animals. Water is worshipped by plants not because of its necessity but because of its unpredictability: floods and droughts. We grow and change over time, and we venerate water.

As the Sun sets, I prepare for worship not unlike the human spring equinox festival. We plants will celebrate. The spring rains came, leaving the soil deeply moist, a cause for great joy, for we channel the water upward into buds, and new leaves and stems unfold as water fills our cells. We grow. The sensation is pleasurable, in fact jubilant.

Humans regained control, and two days ago, the Glassmakers started communicating with the humans—only some of them, but limited communication will lead to extensive mutual understanding. Progress occurred, the weather became beneficent, and disaster has given way to optimism and glorious springtime. Spring is the most impatient, exciting, exultant season. We celebrate life.

As darkness falls, we plants busy ourselves with catabolism and growth, but we have energy to spare for rejoicing and gift-giving. I send calcium carbide to my neighbors, who have water galore to break the molecules down to acetylene, which then oxidizes with a delightful flash of energy, entertaining and nutritious. The fight with the Glassmakers left me tired and dispirited, but I am recovering and am joyful to share, because the victory came with the help of my neighbors. I cannot fully express my happiness and indebtedness to them. We have rain, we have peace, we have life. We grow.

"I am pruned! I am pruned!" lentils sing.

"Good," tulips chant. "Good." "Good." "Good." "Good." "Good." "Good."

Pineapples send me isoprenes. "You said humans would like terpenes," they say. "Here. Make them happy."

Isoprenes can be made into any number of useful terpenes, such as flavorings, vitamins, or scents. I have been learning the meaning of some of the scents of the Glassmakers, and the chemicals are entirely familiar to us plants, such as certain terpenes and alcohols, for example. Any plant can produce dozens, even hundreds, of scents, depending on its intelligence and the complexity of its flowers and other structures, and often scent is how we communicate with lizards and other pollinators. Glassmakers may be able to communicate with other plants besides myself. I do not know if I would like that.

The locustwood speaker gives me a generous amount of zinc ions. "Nice work, bamboozler. Nice animals, your humans. Don't forget our agreement."

"How far south did you wish to go?" I send enough calcium carbide to blow apart a rootlet.

"Move me closer to useful animals, farther from you."

I realize that I am not the only plant with a humor root. "Name your useful animal."

"Fitch."

"Extinct." Due to bamboo.

"Gecko dragon."

"Slow, stupid, and venomous. Perfect for you."

"Humans work for fancy, fruity, oversized grass. What do they see in you?"

"Fruit-eaters like fancy fruit," I tell him. "I treat them well."

He sends me some fructose, fruit sugar. I send some xylose, wood sugar. Even before I grew a humor root, I understood that sugar is a comical substance because its chemical structure is exceedingly fussy. Locustwood is rarely in such a good humor. Sugar!

Willows, palms, wheat, yams, even orange trees, we all rejoice at the promise of a productive season and unfold buds to be ready for tomorrow's sunshine. The spring floods are routine and merely annoy most riverside plants, but the snow vine suddenly panics.

"Bugs gone! Bugs gone! Big animals eat bugs! Sap control two animals! Water come, bugs gone!"

It does not realize that the bugs can be replenished. Yet I share its concern. The snowflake-shaped scale bugs both fed and drugged the workers and majors. In addition, the floods are creating logistic problems. I send some calcium carbide to the snow vine.

"More!" it says.

I comply, and say: "Water go, bugs come back. Roots good?"

"Roots good. Bugs gone! Big animals eat bugs. Sap control two animals. Water come, bugs gone. Bugs gone!"

"Water go, bugs come back. Happiness tonight, happiness tomorrow." I repeat this several times, spicing my message with calcium carbide, and finally the snow vine calms down.

Onions are hardly more verbal than tulips, and they are not festive tonight. I am not sentimental about individual leaves, but onions covet theirs because their growth comes from a single bulb. Pacifists harvest only after the onions develop bulblets for reproduction. The onions suffered untimely predation by the Glassmakers until the "pesticide" I suggested made the Glassmakers stop harvesting them. But now their low-lying fields are flooded, which will delay their growth, if not kill them. I send as much oxygen as I can through my roots. Drowning is a slow, hard way to die. Perhaps the farmers can erect walls to protect them. The rain ended this afternoon, but the river will continue to rise for several days.

Life among the humans slowly moves toward balance. No one languishes ill or injured in the clinic tonight. The flooding river has made supervision of the orphan Glassmakers more difficult, but it has also isolated them. They are too drugged to swim across the rushing water, and this means the guards can relax a bit. In general, the orphans have been behaving more civilly even without hobbles, and some have even helped gather food, easing the burden of the humans. Bellona, the female allied with the orphans, has softened her hostility a bit.

But is this true domestication? "We can't tell," Cedar is saying at the nightly Committee meeting. "We turn our back, and that could be the chance the orphans are waiting for."

"I agree," I say, and Nye voices the words for me. "Pruning has not been completed yet."

"You agree?" she says.

"Domestication takes time." I should explain further, but my attention is drawn to the plant festival. The locustwood is using aldose and ketose sugars to construct a joke about water. The punch line is . . . water is flat! Like snowflakes! Of course, but who would have thought of it that way?

"We need to keep them afraid of us," Cedar says.

I try to find an attentive root. "Fear will prune their actions."

"I can't believe we're agreeing."

"The intelligent actions are few. We are likely to agree," I say, avoiding deeper concerns. I have not checked Cedar's health in a long time. I wish I could. She is behaving erratically, and this could foreshadow more serious problems. I have discovered five cases of Jersey's disease since her diagnosis. The patients reported obsessive-compulsive behaviors. Cedar is obsessed about the Glassmakers. Is there a way to coax her to the clinic?

I say, "We all seek a peaceful solution."

"Sometimes you have to fight," she counters. She stands and paces to give her words more emphasis. "We can't keep them drugged forever, and the first chance they get, they'll attack. If these were eagles, you'd want to wipe them out."

"Eagles lack that level of intelligence," I say, having found a mindful root. "Moreover, there are few Glassmakers. Extinction is uncivilized. Where possible, even eagles should not be eliminated, merely dispatched to hunt elsewhere. They eat deer crabs, which eat plants, including me, so I appreciate their ecological niche."

"Eagles are intelligent enough. They use fire. Don't be a tulip. It's us versus them, and there's fifty-two orphans, and we have at most a hundred good fighters, and Glassmakers are fast, so they have the advantage."

"Damn," Lucille says. "So what you're saying is to kill them now?" She, Cedar, and I can read the frowns, the shaking of heads, the downcast eyes, the little movements that betray the thoughts of the rest of the Committee. No one wants to kill them. Bartholomew translates for See-You, who is attending the meeting. Her reaction is unreadable, although I sense a scent whose meaning I do not know.

"This is stupid," Cedar says. "We could get it over with. We don't have time to sit around and wait. We have to plant. We have to hunt. What do you have to offer? Wait and talk. That's not a plan. Words will get us all killed." She sits down hard, a display of displaced anger.

Pacifists have been hunting and working in the fields. They have replanted ravaged crops and caught up on enough primary tasks to have the time for occasional optional labors. They have picked crocus anthers to make spice and they have set traps for young ribbon plants to cultivate them for their fibers. Hunters have slain deer and birds dislocated by the flood, providing good meals. Foresters have snagged logs floating in the river to dry for winter firewood. Pacifists have accomplished much, as members of the Committee report, and Cedar's pessimism is disputed. The cooperative females' majors and workers have begun to join the city's workforce.

"Glassmakers are great," a farmer says. "We can do four days' work in only three days, even though they're still learning and we need to watch their health. If we can get the rest to cooperate, think of it. Think of what we can do."

People smile. Bartholomew translates, and See-You emits perfume. Nye nods. This morning he asked me to grow flutes with mouthpieces suitable for Glassmakers.

Glassmaker scent communication will likely remain beyond the humans, but I am developing specific sensory organs and specialized roots to understand them. See-You has given me lessons, and I am beginning to glimpse the underlying grammar.

For example, ethyl alcohol means *welcome* or be *relaxed,* and is the active ingredient in truffle, which humans sense as faintly sweet and pleasant. *Come* is methyl alcohol. By contrast, each Glassmaker family has its own identifying smell, a heavy lingering oil produced only by the female that requires a greater degree of proximity for detection. *Welcome* or *come* are easy for any caste member to fabricate and diffuse quickly over a wide area, and their uses are many. *Identification* is specific, controlled, and lasting. Anyone can say *Be relaxed*. Few Glassmakers can say *You are mine*. See-You has anointed Lucille, Marie, and Bartholomew, who understand and appreciate the message.

"There are many more smells. This is baby talk," See-You told me after today's lesson, which involved eugenol, a sweet-spicy phenol that means *What do you see?* "You speak and smell baby talk," she said, which I decided to interpret as praise. I have learned some basics. There is much mutualism to celebrate.

The Committee meeting ends. Humans and Glassmakers go home and sleep. The plants' rain festival ends with the mass release of thiamine to benefit the mycorrhiza fungus at our roots, which absorb water and other nutrients from the soil and pass them on to us. I look forward to an evening of peace and growth.

Pollen has blown in on swirling storm winds from one of my starved alpine groves. Eagles are on the move, heading over the west mountains toward the river valley. It is logical. Storms have arrived in the valley, and eagles understand the consequences. Rising water in rivers displaces prey. They have come to hunt. Will they come this far north? Unlikely, because they have learned to fear humans, and as Cedar pointed out, they are somewhat intelligent. But I will watch for them. The pollen is not fresh, and eagles can run quickly.

Relatively little other pollen rides on the wind, even though it is spring, due to the damp weather, but wind-pollinated species cannot afford to wait for ideal conditions, and now the wind blows steadily from the east. Each species can be identified by the sculpting of the polymer of the outer wall as well as the oils that protect it. I recognize pollen from an orange tree by its external spikes, scalelike shape, and aromatic coat of oils. Have they complied with their bargain and improved their nutritional qualities? They say they did, and they know the penalty for refusing, but I begin an analysis of the oil and cytoplasm anyway.

Bats fly and sing. Spring lizards peep as they look for mates. Birds bark. In damp vales, slugs hiss and hum. Belowground, sponges throb as they filter silt. I think about music and condense buds for Nye's flutes. Plants are silent. Do we have to be?

The pollen grains break down quickly in analysis. The orange trees have betrayed me. There is no ascorbic acid or thiamine, there is a very different chemical, an ammonia derivative. I check again using fresh grains and processing the information in another root, waiting, waiting for the chemicals to be identified, because the scale of the betrayal is grand, and the consequences could be disastrous.

Results confirmed. The orange trees have produced dextroamphetamine to counteract the soporifics. The orange trees reject mutualism, and they wish me and my fellow Pacifists harm. The orphans have been eating many orange tree catkins as an ingredient in a stew. They are not tranquilized at all. They could attack. We must take precautions. Now.

No one is in the greenhouse to read my stem. No one is in the Meeting House. The medic in the clinic is dozing. But the Pacifists must know this news. I must find a way to warn them.

I observe the orphans, though the night is very dark. Clouds obscure the stars and auroras. I see the orphans by their body heat, and on this cool night, unclothed, they glow. They seem sluggish and sleepy. But they are not sleeping. I see too many small movements. I think they are waiting. They may have plans, and we are not prepared. Cedar said they would attack at the first opportunity, and I agree with her.

Bellona, the orphan-allied queen, stirs. She walks toward the river. The guards on the wall are elsewhere, making a routine check of the west gate. She stops and utters a sound like wood breaking. The orphans, who had been feigning sleep, rise to their feet. Even were the guards watching, could they see this on such a dark night? And what will the orphans do, separated from the city by fifty meters of rushing floodwaters? First they must break out of their pen. But they know this, and we know they are hostile.

No human is awake to read my stem. Orion walks to the gift center. Inside, he sings softly. If I could tell him what I know, he could react even better than I could, for he is clever and experienced. He can sing, whisper, shout. I can only listen and observe, and what I see is withering.

Across the river, orphan workers tear apart the roofs Kung built and use the sticks and thatch to build a sort of bridge over the thorny fence that surrounds them. One by one, orphans escape their pen. Perhaps they will enter the forest and flee the city instead of attacking. I hope so. A major makes a sound like breaking wood, and they run north along a trail above the riverbank. They arrived from the north, from the river valley below the big waterfall. Perhaps, perhaps they will return that way and leave us Pacifists in peace, but Bellona does not move, and I cannot imagine her wishing to remain in the city if the orphans leave. They have a plan, and it is not escape.

The orphans stop at a gorge in the ravine, where the water rushes between stone cliffs, the narrow place where humans had erected a temporary rope bridge for their assault on the Glassmakers seven days ago. But the Glassmakers have no rope, so perhaps . . . I hear an axe at work and triangulate the place. It is at the cliffs.

"They're cutting one of us down! One of our tallest. Who?" the speaker for the locustwood demands, providing the location. The trees can barely see in daylight.

"The pest animals have escaped captivity and are gathered at that spot," I explain. "If the log falls correctly, it will serve as a bridge across the river, and they will attack my domesticated animals in the city." I try to remain calm, but I sense that the oscillations in the calcium ion waves in my roots are spiky and agitated.

"Can they win?"

"I do not know. They may surprise my animals, and that could be decisive."

"We are at your service. We will alert others." His waves, too, are agitated.

But what can we do? We plants often feel aloof: boxer birds fight with dragons, spiders vie for territory, and we carry on regardless, ignoring animal conflicts as trivialities. Not this time. There could be unthinkable consequences. If I could sing, shout, scream—

Bellona waits for the orphans, who arrive running silently up the path above the river. I smell communication, though I do not know the scents. The orphans linger beneath trees as the human guards on the wall pass by.

I know these guards. Nefertiti, twenty-seven years old, has three children and a husband, and manages the wheat harvest. She can drum in a way that makes humans and fippokats want to dance. Osbert, thirty-three, divorced, has two young sons, and as a team he and his twin brother blow beautiful glass vessels of any size and for any use, their best. The twins' father is Bartholomew.

I know all the humans in the city. I have known them all from birth. They are all in danger, the old, middle-aged, and newborn alike. I could scream, howl, smash things—

I have thistles around the walls. I instruct them to bring themselves to full turgor so they are stiff and tall and provide the best obstacle they can. They should delay the orphans briefly. Briefly. Briefly.

Inside the city, I hear movement in Marie's house. She leaves, walking without a light because after a lifetime in the city, she knows the streets by feel. Where is she going? Does she wish to talk to me? I can only hope so. She walks slowly and with a new, odd limp.

A large major approaches the city wall. It examines the distance required to clear the thistles and the wall, then goes to search for a more favorable location.

Marie enters Lucille's home. I hear weeping. I try to guess the reason. Marie knows the course of her illness and can recognize symptoms of the final phase. The time has come, perhaps. If I could weep, if I could squall, if I could toll like a bell—

The major finds a spot and leaps and lands on the wall, clutching a log like a club. I know what will happen next. I wish to sever roots so I could not watch, but I dare not. Death comes to Nefertiti so suddenly she may not have known what killed her. Her body lands outside the wall amid the thistles. I know what awaits Osbert. All I can do is pledge that if my humans remain sovereign, I will find a way to make noise.

Osbert falls. The worker orphans construct a bridge of sorts over the thistles and up the wall. Their speed is phenomenal. The clouds begin to clear, revealing green auroras, intensely bright, crowned with red. If the sky had cleared a few minutes earlier—

Marie and Lucille leave her home, Lucille supporting Marie, Lucille talking quietly, gently, occasionally laughing, an unusual laughter that contains several emotions at once, including a constriction of the throat that is close to a sob. I think they may be walking toward the clinic. This is very good. I have a talking stem at the clinic. I can warn them, and even in their sorrow, they will react immediately.

Orphans jump from the wall, moving silently, releasing *come* and *What do you see?* scents to guide each other, but their progress is slow, despite the now bright light. They do not know the city. A major pauses, listening. It hears Lucille. It and several other majors rush toward them, tilting through the curved streets with horrible grace.

I know what will happen next. . . . No, they do not kill the women, they grab them roughly and cover their mouths. Lucille struggles, and three majors attempt to subdue her. She has the advantage of height and strong arms. She tears a hand from her mouth and starts to shout, but the hand is replaced before she can make much noise. I smell blood. Both she and Marie moan and grunt. Marie kicks a bottle and it breaks against a house. Then more orphans arrive and overcome the women.

Bartholomew lives within that house. He usually sleeps lightly. I hope he awoke. I hope someone wakes.

Bellona is waiting near the main gate while ten workers hurry around gathering something. Wood. They are gathering firewood from outside homes and stacking it in my grove that grows near the front gate. They are carrying the women toward the grove. I think they plan to burn me, which would be horrible, because what is worse than fire? But what will they do to the women? It hurts to guess.

Bartholomew peers from his door, his face infrared-warm in the night, a kat in his arms. There is nothing to see from his vantage point and little to hear: the soft scratch of Glassmaker claws on pavement, a rustle as wood is gathered, distant moans. Scents float lighter than pollen in the air. The kat squirms. Bartholomew sniffs and listens.

"Oh, no," he whispers. He understands what is happening! I think he does. He sets the kat down, edges out of his house, and picks his way through a garden, then slowly through another garden and to a street, almost as silently as the kat, though he is not lithe and he must feel cold dressed only in his nightshirt. I hope he will arouse someone. . . . Cedar. She is what we need now.

The Glassmakers are exploring among the houses, listening at doors and entering buildings that are uninhabited. After searching a toolshed, they display scythes, knives, shovels, rope, and pitchforks. From another, hammers, saws, and axes. Humans keep their weapons in their homes, their bows, arrows, spears, javelins, and machetes, so those will not fall into Glassmaker hands; but a scythe or axe will be formidable. The orphans continue to search, raiding the rayon workshop, emerging with knives and choppers used to shred cellulose bark. Other orphans are making a game out of subduing Marie and Lucille, using their claws to make their holds more effective. I have eyes very close by and see the blood. I am revulsed.

Gray-Eyes and her family begin to stir, then See-You's. Perhaps the scents on the wind have alerted them to trouble. See-You opens the door, sniffs, and wakes the human guard who has fallen asleep at her door, young Piotr. He tries to say something, but she shushes him and motions for him to come inside. "We talk," she mutters. He looks around, sleepy and confused. She grabs his arm and pulls him in. The door shuts.

I think Bartholomew is indeed going to Cedar's home. He is running down a street, looking behind him, stifling a cry when his stockinged feet stub something. Bartholomew turns a corner and is at Cedar's door, knocking gently, then enters, whispering, "Cedar. It's Bartholomew. Quiet. Be quiet." He shuts the door. I hear talking, even exclamations. Cedar will know what to do.

The orphans use the rope they found to immobilize Lucille and Marie in the grove where they are stacking firewood, and continue to search buildings. The firewood is frightening. Lucille tries to speak, but a hand remains over her mouth. She looks at Marie and grunts in a questioning tone. Marie does not answer and her eyes are closed, but she still breathes. Injuries from the claws shine with warmth. I try to pump water into the stems and leaves there. I can only hope that Cedar will react without hesitation. She has been eager for this moment.

Orphans are now searching for a source of fire. Three of them batter the door open to a home where one of the old hunters lives, Beatrice, the only great-grandmother in the city.

Cedar's door opens. She rushes out, buckling on a wrist protector for use with a bow and arrow. "We'll go and see," she murmurs over her shoulder at Bartholomew, who runs behind her, but cannot run as fast.

"But they're inside," he whispers. "The orphans are inside."

"Yes, the so-called friendly queens are here. You let them in. It could be them."

On the far side of the city, See-You's door opens. Piotr steps out and begins to shout in a boy's voice: "To arms! To arms! Orphans are in the city!" He holds his bow ready and is flanked by See-You's majors. One holds Piotr's knife, two others hold firewood logs like clubs. Piotr adores Lucille. He will do all he can to save her.

There are shouts in Great-Grandmother Beatrice's house, then silence. Two orphans run out, one clutching a bowl containing embers from her fireplace. Beatrice appears in her doorway, leaning on the frame. I think she is injured. "Orphans in the city! Riverside gate!" Her voice is frail and breathy.

Cedar starts running. Behind her, Bartholomew shouts, "Orphans in the city! To arms! Riverside gate!" People will hear it and react. They will come to rescue the women.

Bellona screeches orders, no longer worried about being quiet.

Majors release their hold on Lucille's mouth, torn and bloodied by claws, and she screams, "Kak!" again and again, "Stop!" And to Marie she calls, "Are you all right? Help is coming!"

Marie, at her side, does not move.

An orphan worker spreads the embers on dry leaves on the firewood, blows on them, and a flame erupts. Orphans cheer and release benzaldehyde, pyridine, and other strong scents.

The flames grow larger. I push water out of pores like dew, enough to fall like drops of rain, enough to ransom a minute of time, although the orphans shelter the fire with their hands and continue to push tinder at it. Flames grow and heat rises, and directly above it, the sap in a leaf simmers, a twig roils with steam, and bark singes. The pressure from the steam keeps water from rising in the stems. Pressure builds until the water vessels burst, and steam permeates my tissues, cooks me from the inside and it is torment, but I maintain contact so I can observe the situation closely and do what little I can. Twenty, thirty leaves wilt and wither and begin to burn. But the flames are still distant from Marie and Lucille, who continues to squirm and shout.

"Don't do this! We can talk. Per-zee kik kik tsee!"

Orphans echo her words derisively.

Marie still breathes, although in many places her clothes, like Lucille's, are stained with wet blood. Lucille twists against the ropes, and they, too, are wet.

Cedar arrives at the riverside gate, looks around, and rushes unnoticed to crouch in the shadows under one of my groves. She does nothing, but she is alone. The orphans have the advantage. But I see fighters leaving their homes all around the city. The rescue will begin soon, very soon.

Bartholomew arrives, a spear in his hand. The blue-black nightshirt acts as camouflage for him. He creeps in the shadows toward Cedar. They whisper, their words drowned out by the shouts of the orphans. Then their voices rise.

"They're burning Stevland," he says.

"There's lots of Stevland."

"The fire will reach Lucille," he says.

She hesitates, then says, "What can we do?"

"Something. A diversion?"

I want to tell them I am delaying the spread of the flames, I have dampened the firewood and my own wood is saturated. It boils and finally burns, but slowly, very slowly.

Other Pacifist fighters are a hundred meters away and running as fast as they can. Beatrice has drawn her bow. Piotr crashes through a garden and is almost here, with See-You's majors behind him.

Lucille continues to plead.

"It's too late," Cedar says, but I can see that it is not too late. Now is the time. She stares at the fire. "We'll get killed."

"More people are coming," Bartholomew tells her. "We can fight."

"We'll get killed."

"You won't do anything?"

"What can we do?"

"No!" Bartholomew yells, and jumps out of the shadows. "Stop!" He shakes the spear. "Kak! Kak!"

Orphans turn toward him, Bellona shouts an order, and several majors charge. Beatrice fires arrows fast, but the orphans are faster.

Bartholomew stumbles back. Then arrows come flying from behind him. Pacifist archers have arrived. The orphans stop.

"Watch out! Lucille and Marie are at the fire!" Bartholomew shouts.

Pacifists shift their aim and arrows continue to fly. The orphans dance evasively, but backward, backward. Pacifists take steps forward.

I squeeze all the water I can from branches above the flames, and water drips down and hisses.

"Don't worry about us. Stop them!" Lucille shouts. She has freed a hand from the ropes. The flames have not crept too close. She and Marie will be saved.

Bellona gives an order. Plaid Blanket rushes toward the flames and throws big glass bottles. They smash and their contents splash across the women. I recognize the scent of acetone, a solvent they have taken from the rayon workshop. The liquid bursts into flame like hydrogen seeds.

My nearest eyes burn, and my farther eyes see a moment of despair on Lucille's face before it is hidden by a wall of flame.

More bottles follow. A cloud of heat and fire rises and sears even my uppermost leaves. I sever the root, but the pain is so intense that it jumps the break and I must sever the root again.

I failed. I saw disaster developing and I could do nothing to prevent it. I was useless. The despair on Lucille's face sours my roots, the last glimpse of her I shall ever have.

The sudden flames illuminate the scene like a long-lasting stroke of lightning. Pacifist fighters clog the streets around the riverside gate, outnumbering the orphans, who scurry around, trying to dodge arrows.

The fire burns smoky, and the women cannot be seen. I smell charred flesh, and the breeze carries the scent to the Pacifists.

"Attack!" Piotr yells in a voice suddenly adult and angry, and Pacifists begin advancing again.

Bellona shrieks something and releases a scent, a hydrocarbon of some sort. The orphans rush to the wall, jump onto it, and run away. Some jump down as soon as they are clear of the defending Pacifists.

"Watch your backs!" Cedar yells.

"Where are they? Where?" other fighters yell. I could tell them that the orphans are spreading out in the dark city, and I fear for any home whose occupants cannot defend themselves. Pacifist ranks are confused. Cedar is shouting to kill every Glassmaker on sight. Piotr is clutching See-You's majors to him to protect them. Beatrice calls for organization. Bartholomew shouts, "Meeting House! Stevland sees everything! We'll talk to Stevland. Meeting House!"

Yes, I have seen everything. I have much to say. Too much. . . . I must formulate a plan, quickly. I am the city's sole moderator now, and the city's future depends on me. The fire rises tall and smoky, and heat rises and swirls in the wind. Bats sing of danger, danger, danger, for they know I should not be burning. My roots ache, especially the one that balanced the position of moderator. It holds information about Lucille, and she is gone, and everything I value is in danger. Everything could be destroyed.

Other plants notice the fire, and the locustwood trees have spread the news. Now is the time to fight. My heritage as a bamboo is of ruthless war-making, but I will not commit atrocities like my ancestors.

Monte has gone to the fippokat hutches. Adult kats gather around him while juveniles cower in burrows. He sings to them, "Guard and defend, little ones, time to fight, protect, and attack," a grim tune they have been trained to respond to, and the kats, like any animal, can defend themselves. "One, two, three, go!" he says, and kats scatter.

Orphans are blundering through the streets, trying doors, all locked and barred so far. Pacifist fighters can subdue the orphans, I am sure of it, if we can formulate a plan and coordinate our efforts.

Why did Cedar fail to protect Lucille? Even now, she is attempting to take command, ordering fighters to go on patrol and kill all Glassmakers on sight. Perhaps she was afraid. I am afraid, but I will put my fear to use. I cannot run away, so I must fight or die, as all plants will do, and we are not patient. I can see everything and must think bigger than Cedar can. I will create order within the city again and control the animals. I must create predictable behavior as fast as possible, for I cannot control chaos.

An outpost to the southwest says eagles are less than a day's hike away. If they smell Lucille and Marie, they may hurry. Eagles seek animals roasted in forest fires.

Bartholomew, Piotr, and others arrive at the Meeting House. Piotr has See-You's majors with him. See-You knows the orphans better than I do; knowledge will be crucial for control.

"Warmth and sunshine," I say. "Bring all friendly Glassmakers to the Meeting House. I will question them, and they must be protected. Cedar must organize patrols. I observe Glassmaker orphans in all parts of the city. She should protect Pacifists rather than hunt down orphans. Pacifists are the hunted. She must hurry."

A house near the kitchen is occupied by a young father and three small children. The wife has joined the fighting forces; the father, who injured an ankle two days ago, remains with the children, and the youngest begins to cry. Orphans hear, and four gather at the door, which is strongly barred, but one has an axe and begins to chop.

That noise, in turn, attracts ten or twenty fippokats; they move too fast to count. They leap out, kicking like lions, but in coordinated acrobatics that fill the air with crisscrossing clawed back paws. The orphans flee, but not before one is injured. Kats chase them, but they scatter when an orphan turns and swings a scythe. The kats fought cleverly and bravely, but the next incident may be tragic. Patrols must begin immediately.

But at the Meeting House, Cedar argues: "I should be giving orders. I should be handling the defense." She strikes a table with her fist.

"This isn't your decision," Bartholomew says in a calm voice, although he stands stiffly, repulsing her symbolic violence. They are fighting each other when they should be protecting Pacifists. Carl seems to be organizing patrols without authorization, and I am relieved to see it.

"Then whose decision is it?" she says. "A plant? He's co-moderator so we can control him, not the other way around. We know how to fight and we need to fight."

"He is moderator now," Bartholomew says. "He knows what's happening, and by now you should know what he can do."

Bartholomew is correct. I can do much. I cannot drug the orphans now, but the past success holds promise, like a seed.

"I want all the Glassmakers out of the city," she says. "There are no good Glassmakers. All of them. Out! Do you hear that, Stevland? Glassmakers. Out."

I survey the faces and stances of other humans, and I suspect a few agree with Cedar. The humans have experience with individual murder but not with the extermination of an entire species, so they may not grasp the atrocity of Cedar's proclamations.

The orphans have used scent communication to converge on a single home. Kats lead Monte there, and he coordinates harassment, and a pair of archers join the attack, but they can do no more than delay a group that size. I say, "Cedar, fifty orphans are attacking Flora's home." She looks astonished, then rushes out. Most of the fighters have already left under Carl's direction.

I consider the lessons. The fire may have been a diversion, a way to lure fighters from their homes so that the orphans could regroup and attack undefended families. If so, then I have discovered predictable behavior, and this is the soil to grow the seeds of a plan. My humor root adds that all I need now is water, and it is right. I must find the means of control. Once I have that, I can try to end the crisis. And yet, the eagles have moved much closer, so there may be another crisis soon.

Piotr and several archers escort See-You and her family toward the Meeting House. These Glassmakers move as a coordinated group in a cloud of scents, protecting themselves from attacks from all directions.

A major scouts ahead and the rest follow, the air alive with whistles and words and puffs of communication. Another major hears a rustle and pauses, signaling the others. The group turns as one to face the challenge: fippokats. Workers shoo the animals and hurry along. Piotr and the archers exchange looks of astonishment at the efficiency of the family's movements, a feeling I share. But the orphans can also employ that level of efficiency, which will make them even more formidable.

The pineapples send a message reminding me that their contract includes protection from predators. I intuit a seed in that message. Earlier tonight the pineapples sent me isoprenes, a compound that could be the basis for many useful substances, including the scents the Glassmakers use for communication.

"Welcome, See-You," I say as she enters the Meeting House. Most Pacifists have formed squads to patrol the streets, but the few that remain in the building cheer her, raising weapons in salute, and her majors return the gesture. I am pleased. I want as many Glassmakers alive as possible. That is the only civilized action.

"I wish communicate with orphans," I write in Glassmade.

"Worthless."

"I wish tell-them lies."

She considers that for a second. "I will help."

"I wish send-them from city with scent." This is my plan, although it needs much elaboration.

"You speak baby talk. Not good enough."

She is wrong, she has to be wrong.

Plaid Blanket has led several orphans into the bakery. Now they are stacking sacks of flour in my grove next to the bakery. Flour is very flammable. They must not burn me again.

"You will teach-me." I write slowly, carefully, despite my alarm. "I need to know now. Show me *warning*."

She moves close to my stem. "You be-you too confident. I will show you *alert*." Aliphatic ketone 2-heptanone, a pungent smell, easy enough to reproduce.

Another female, Buzz, and her family arrives, and she asks many questions and spreads many scents. See-You answers. The discussion gets too complicated to follow, and I do not have time for their quarrels.

The orphans seem about to light a fire in my grove next to the bakery when they pause. Plaid Blanket sniffs. I strain to identify a scent, and I identify many, among them the *alert* ketone, and methyl alcohol, meaning *come*. The orphans run away—correction, run toward something. Toward Violet's house. Other orphans are there, and Bellona. They move silently. The air is heavy with scents, including citrus-scented limonene, a terpene. An elderly man, his young grandson, and several neighbor children are inside. The other adults are out fighting, and the old man and children will be unable to defend themselves.

I interrupt the argument between See-You and Buzz. "Perhaps you tell-me this," I say, and produce limonene. The Glassmakers in the Meeting House jump and huddle together.

"You say-us *attack*," See-You says. "You say you attack-us."

"Plants no scent-talk," Buzz says.

"Bartholomew," I say, "the orphans plan to attack Violet's house."

He gestures at a young girl with an extraordinary and powerful singing voice. She goes to the door to exclaim the news. See-You gestures at one of her majors, who rushes to her side to guard the girl on the street. See-You also made a scent, the terpenol compound citronellol, a flowery odor.

"Perhaps you tell-me this," I say, reproducing the citronellol.

"*Defend*," See-You says. She shows me *flee*, a balsamic smell, the monoterpene hydrocarbon beta-pinene. That makes sense. It and the alarm scent are lighter-weight chemicals than limonene, and naturally a message of *go away* or *alarm* would be more useful over a larger area than *attack*. She goes on to explain some rules of grammar, how certain scents must be accompanied by others. I must learn this accurately or the orphans will suspect a trick.

The female Gray-Eyes and her family arrive. The smells in the room send them into a near panic, and Gray-Eyes, suspicious and slow-witted, starts to quarrel with See-You.

My grove in the forest to the northwest observes that the city's lion pack has noticed the troubles in the city. Lionesses have begun to pace and males to roar. Another grove, to the southwest, says the eagles are yet closer. They have smelled the smoke. Eagles and lions are enemies, and both could make things worse.

I have flowers near Violet's house. The petals ordinarily produce geraniol, a fragrant alcohol; quickly I switch the output, remove a water molecule and rearrange the chemical bonds, and send out beta-pinene. The stamen usually produces nerol, a citrus scent, and the chemistry is a bit trickier, but I subtract three carbon atoms and four hydrogen atoms, in the process removing and replacing the oxygen atom, and it is 2-heptanone. The chemicals are lightweight; even on a cool night like this one, they boil away as fast as I can make them. I will see if I can communicate well enough to lie.

Bellona and the orphans sniff and hesitate, and majors pace about, searching for the source of the warning. They all fidget, uneasy, and Bellona edges away from the house. Then, from down the street, Cedar shouts: "There they are! Let's go!" Kats creeping in the bushes leap out and kick at orphans' legs, knocking some of them over. The *flee* scent becomes stronger; the orphans themselves must be making it. They run off.

This is a key achievement. I have used Glassmaker scent language to control their behavior. The Pacifists are fighting back. We have a means to subdue the orphans and restore peace.

The argument among the females is getting more heated in the Meeting House. Bartholomew gestures at me. He is concerned. I think that I can smell fear; at least, I guess that methanethiol, the smell of certain rotting plants, conveys an unpleasant emotion.

I tell Bartholomew to get out a jar of truffle he had hidden in the bureau that houses legal documents. He occasionally drinks truffle when no one is looking. It is a troubling habit, but the ethyl alcohol may relax the Glassmakers.

He seems unhappy. "You see everything, don't you?"

"Truffle has many medicinal properties," I say. I am aware of the social value of lies. Truffle should be banned, but that will never happen.

He takes out a small jar. See-You edges closer. He lifts the cork. She sniffs. He pulls a small glass out of the bookcase and pours a bit. "I'll show you how it's done. Here's to friendship!" He swallows the contents, pours more, and hands it to her.

She sniffs it suspiciously, takes a sip, and coughs. Buzz and Gray-Eyes have pushed in close, curious. They sniff and chitter.

"Pour some in a flat plate," I say. "The scent will suffice for them."

They relax, or at least they perceive a strong message from Bartholomew to feel comfortable. I hope the scent will overcome the lies I will disseminate outside the building.

I have fully formulated my plan: I will release *flee* scent starting at the east side of the city. The wind will carry it west. I will release *defend* and *attack* ever westward, drawing them toward the west gate. I will ask loyal plants to the west of the city to release the scents also, and will order the gates opened. I will coordinate the Pacifist fighters to drive the orphans out through the west gate.

I tell this to Bartholomew and the females. He raises the cup in salute. "Excellent." But he does not drink. He pats the girl singer's head. "We'll get the word out."

"You be-you big liar," See-You tells me. I hope this means she thinks I can succeed.

The plan has weaknesses I have not communicated. We must keep the orphans from reentering the city, and that will not be easy. Eagles are coming, and perhaps they will distract the orphans. Or perhaps not. Perhaps they will not arrive. Perhaps they will join with the orphans. Perhaps the lions can help us. Many things could happen. Humans speak of crossing a bridge when they come to it, but I want to regain control immediately, I want to foresee the future now. If I fail, I will lose everything. Everything.

The orphans have begun destroying all they can as they pass through the city, smashing baskets and jars and slashing at clothing hung up to dry. The noise and motion help me locate them. . . . They are effectively everywhere, since they can move so fast. I begin to emit ketones and beta-pinenes from my groves along the east wall and ask the tulips and lentil trees east of the city to do the same. "Helper chemical. Pests go, pruners stay." Perhaps if I build a wall of scent around the city, the orphans will not try to reenter when they are driven out.

The girl calls out: "Drive the orphans to the west gate and out." Fighters hear and cheer. They wanted a plan. They do not know how desperate it is.

I have centered my attention on my planning root, and meanwhile the fighting has been intense in the streets. I count three orphans dead or too badly injured to move, and nine more injured, but that leaves approximately forty ready to attack, and the truth is that the orphans have the advantage with speed and communication. They are beginning to learn the terrain and to coordinate their movements. They create running ambushes faster than kats and bats can detect and issue warnings to help the humans, faster than I can exude a useful scent, faster than humans can react.

Even as the girl is singing out the plan, Cedar's patrol is surrounded by orphans rushing out from behind houses, six orphans against five humans. The Pacifists call for help, but the orphans complete their attack and flee before help arrives. Only one human is left standing, and the rest, including Cedar, are injured or dead.

I move the wall of scent west fifty meters, then another fifty meters, the fruity-flowery scent luring them toward the west gate. The faster the better, because the situation is no longer chaotic: the orphans are clearly winning. They, too, have developed an effective strategy. A house is on fire well west of the line of scent, and if I follow my plan, I cannot prevent events like that to the west of the scent because the orphans have free rein there. Anything can happen.

Another human patrol is ambushed. The noise of the struggle causes a boy, Fabio, to open the door of his home. Two orphans rush in even as more arrive to finish off the patrol, then they, too, enter the house. . . . The noises and scents are beyond description and sorrow, and occur at a pace that signals deliberate cruelty.

Patrols listen for the announcements from the Meeting House, but at times the girl cannot step outside to make them because orphans are too close. Bellona has realized that the girl is relaying information, and broadcasts scents to gather an attack against the Meeting House. I hurry to move the *flee* scent farther westward, engulfing the Meeting House. Bellona is confused, but finally turns to look for a new target, and there are many to the west of the scent line. It is now past midnight, and eagles continue to approach.

A patrol and an orphan ambush fight to a draw: one dead on each side, all injured. I move the scent westward again.

Elsewhere, orphans drag Fabio, bleeding, from his house and use him as a shield against arrows. The archers hold their fire, but the kats love children, and they attack, kicking around the boy, although they cannot do this with their usual grace, and two kats are clubbed to death. They continue to attack anyway. The orphans use their claws to blind and torture the screaming boy even as they hold him in front of themselves for cover. They break into another home and set fire to it, and finally a major takes the boy by the ankles and swings his head against a stone wall. They run off. The boy has not died instantly, but he will die soon, very soon. The humans are forlorn, and if I could wail like them—

I see this, the information travels from root to root, and each root is transformed. A wave that had been forming in many roots coalesces into a single realization. The orphans, like slugs, are not suitable for domestication, but for a different reason. The nature of a slug defies domestication. The orphans probably could be domesticated, but they do not deserve domestication.

I will not have animals like those in my service. Slugs are mere scavengers, and in their own way necessary. Orphans have done what I have pledged never to do, what I pledge never to permit. Their acts exclude them from civilization.

I must respond. But I will not ask the humans to help beyond the minimum. I will bear the guilt, and I have ancient methods at my disposal.

I contact the lentils near the west gate, which are in bloom and eager to help.

"We must kill the pests," I say.

"Yes, kill," I hear thirty-eight times. They would agree to anything, and besides, they are plants. To them, pests must die, even when they are large, intelligent animals.

"What I ask is complex."

"Kill." "Kill." "Kill."

"I need you to make scents to attract the enemies of the pests." I show certain proteins like myosin, and lipids including oleine. This is the smell of cooking meat, and it will attract the eagles. The lipids are the most complex.

"I can't make these," is a common response.

"A small number of molecules will suffice."

"I don't know how." "I don't have enough sulfur." "Is that a molecule? It's so big."

One by one, I teach, but it is hard, very hard, not because the lentils do not learn, but because I wish to kill right now, not later.

I hope the eagles will kill for me, but they may or may not be enough, and I want complete extermination. I contact the irises that guard the springs.

"Attract animals," I say. "Kill for blood." I show the *alarm* and *attack* smells. Irises are like tulips in intelligence, but unalike in temperament, so they snatch up the molecules, eager to make more, eager to hunt and kill.

"Good!" "Good!" "Good!" "Good!"

"Also this," and I pass on Bellona's identity scent in quantity because irises cannot make a such a complex oil quickly enough.

The eagles run toward the city, now only a kilometer away, but I see them slow to sniff, look around with suspicion, and listen to the din from the city. One drums. Another answers. They slink on, cautiously.

I move the scent westward. Human patrols have already opened the gates. I begin to emit *attack* scent outside the gate. The orphans follow, believing they are about to kill more humans.

At the last minute, Bellona realizes that they are being expelled from the city that she meant to take over. She organizes a final stand, screeching commands and scents, and many of the orphans near her turn around. They mass near Tatiana's former office, preparing to charge.

But the humans are prepared. Three archers have scaled my trunks and hidden in my branches, and now they launch arrows.

"Aim for Bellona," Carl yells.

They do, and she is a large target. A hail of arrows flies in her direction. One arrow glances off her side, another sinks into her shoulder. A major waving a pitchfork rushes forward, but stumbles when an arrow hits its rear haunch.

Piotr has approached closely on foot, a foolhardy act, but he knows the terrain, crouches at the corner of a house, and patiently takes aim. His arrow lands in Bellona's eye.

The orphans watch her fall, and while they are immobilized by shock, two more fall. The scent of *flee* fills the air, and they dash out of the city.

Piotr is among the first to rush to shut the gates. A cheer rises from the gate and spreads throughout the city.

I wait for a several minutes, wishing I could cheer with them, before I have the girl singer warn about the eagles.

"Eagles coming from the south, looking for food."

Archers return to the walls with sad, tired faces.

Carl shouts, "They'll eat the orphans." The cheer is ecstatic.

The cries of an orphan who has been lured into the irises attract others. Plaid Blanket rushes in, then realizes that it has rushed into a trap and desperately shrieks a warning before it falls. The remaining orphans huddle, uncertain.

The eagles arrive. They smell the fresh blood of the iris patch, and the eagle pack is larger than I had thought. They slip through the pineapple field unnoticed until they attack.

The night hides much slaughter. Glassmakers are fast and intelligent, but eagles are the superior predator. Their drumming tells us of their success. They light a fire, and I observe how they kill at their leisure. Compared to the orphan methods, it is decent and fast.

At sunrise, the eagles dance and drum, jubilant, around butchered corpses. Monte has slipped off to the lion pack. Its members seem relieved to be asked to challenge the eagles, and its males bound toward them, the females close behind. They stand in a line, howling and growling and tearing at the dirt with their claws.

The eagles size up the threat and seem unimpressed. Then thirty screaming archers run out to stand alongside the lions. The entire population of the city is on the walls, chanting. A few eagles step backward. An archer fires and hits an eagle, not a clean hit, not a mortal injury, but the eagles take note and gibber at each other. One drums. None answer. Then, as if with one mind, they turn and grab all the meat they can, watching the Pacifists and lions over their shoulders, and sprint west toward the nearest mountains.

They are wise enough to know they have exhausted the easy hunting possibilities. But they are intelligent enough to remember where they found easy hunting. They will be back eventually.

In the light of day, Pacifists assess the human death and damage. They find only one surviving orphan, a cowering worker.

Twenty-one humans are dead, many of them children, at least fifty are injured, some gravely, and there is much property destruction. Cedar is among the injured. She is uncharacteristically quiet.

It is clear that I killed the orphans, and that humans alone could not have done it. They mourn their losses and they thank me. The female Glassmakers thank me.

Plants rejoice, too, and not just the irises.

"Smart work," says the locustwood. "You bamboozled the pest animals to death."

"Good riddance," pineapples say. "There's no need for bad animals."

The oranges are silent.

The orphans made themselves expendable, but this is not at all what I wanted. Most of the Glassmakers are dead. Far too many humans are dead, each one with a name, each one a treasure, and I will miss Lucille the most. She said moderators can do terrible things whether acting rightly or wrongly, and I now understand.

I am the ultimate cause of the situation. I acted out of selfishness. I wanted Glassmakers to join us Pacifists and help us, and I ignored my doubts. I wanted more service animals so that the city would prosper, so that someday we could go to the stars. Instead, I could not control the situation. I failed my animals and myself.

Rainbow bamboo is made to create slaughter. When the time came, I could kill as efficiently as my ancestors. Like all plants, I am naturally aggressive. But unlike a tulip or a snow vine, I am intelligent. I am the biggest and most powerful creature on Pax, and the most dangerous, and I have made mistakes I cannot rectify.

But I meant well. I meant greater happiness for all. I meant to create a new and different and better life. I thought I would not repeat the past.

I failed.

BARTHOLOMEW
YEAR 107–GENERATION 5

A moderator may resign at any time by giving written notice to the Committee. A moderator may be removed by a two-thirds vote of the entire Committee at a meeting at which not less than three-fourths of the entire Committee is present.

—from the Constitution of the Commonwealth of Pax

"Water and sunshine," I said, and made myself comfortable, physically, at least, in the chair in the greenhouse. Would Stevland answer? He'd hardly spoken since the attack three days earlier, and if he didn't answer, then I'd have to do what I could by myself to solve his situation, and we all had enough to do already. He ought to be more considerate. And yet we who were functional had to protect the shattered.

I arranged my books and papers. Sunlight sparkled on the broken edges of the glass block dome overhead—not a big hole, but enough to change the greenhouse into a new and discomforting place. Outside, broken glass and crockery still lay in corners of the streets and gardens, and several houses were burned-out shells reeking of smoke. The clinic's beds were full.

I closed my eyes and listened to the somber voices in the street, including the chortles and whistles of Glassmade. Only three days ago, destruction had filled the city. We'd since buried the dead and resumed our lives as best we could, but we still wore old clothes for mourning. Blood stained the paving stones. It would take years to get back to normal.

Outside, a Glassmaker screeched. For a moment I was back in that night, with Bellona shouting orders, majors rushing toward me, and Lucille pleading. . . . Not again. I snapped my eyes open. I had work to do.

I hadn't wanted to take the job as Stevland's advocate, but someone needed to defend him in the coming legal procedure and I was most suited to do it. I wanted to defeat Cedar more than anyone. And he needed to collaborate, to talk to me.

I took a deep breath to tell him so, then remembered Tatiana's habit—may she sleep soundly—of never speaking quickly. Stevland knew why I was there. But he hadn't even given a eulogy at Lucille's funeral, a dereliction of duty, pure and simple. Most people had forgiven him, since he had saved the city, after all—although not by himself. He still did his job at the clinic and provided minimal reports at the nightly Committee meetings, and perhaps he was too exhausted or sorrowful to do more. Grief had brought down a number of people, but he was the moderator, and we needed him.

I rehearsed a few words to scold him. As the counselors said, talking helped, and so did getting on with life. Busy and duty-filled days, that's what I strove for, and as a woodworker I had plenty to repair. Other people could dissolve their evenings in truffle or lotus root, lie in bed unable to move, or wander at night unable to sleep, weeping and jumping at nothing. No sense scolding, though. We were all suffering.

I looked at the Constitution again. It was a flawed document, yet I was going to have to make it work. I imagined myself at the Committee meeting that night: "Speaking for Stevland . . ." What would I say? Enough waiting.

"Obviously," I began, willing to talk to myself if I had to, "we have no real precedents for removing a moderator. The details involving Vera are inapplicable—"

He interrupted: "Vera was not voted out."

What did he know about that? For the past year, I had been thinking of writing a history of Pax as my best so we would understand where we had been and where we were going. But if anyone else had read the old record books, they never talked about it, and neither did I. Sylvia's revolt had been quite different from a vote, and the accepted history much more than a lie. But I could question Stevland about that another day. "That's not an issue now. Our concern—"

"I will resign. I will plead guilty and resign."

"No, you won't." Grief had unhinged everyone, and I was getting tired of it. Envious of it. But I wasn't about to hand Cedar a victory.

"You cannot tell me what to do," he said.

"I can tell you what you ought to do. First, we don't know what the exact charges are. Second, I believe you are incompetent to enter a plea."

After a moment, he wrote, "Then I am incompetent to be moderator also."

"An interesting paradox. But irrelevant, at least for me. Cedar wants you voted out. My job is to be your advocate throughout the process. Period. I believe you saved us from disaster. I believe Cedar used the attack to—"

"I caused the disaster, and many humans and Glassmakers and plants and animals died because of me. My error killed your son because I was unable to provide a warning."

"Orphans killed my son. You saved my life and the lives of many people." Words began to appear on his stem. "I am not going to debate your resignation." And I wasn't going to relive that night through yet another pointless debate.

"Then there is nothing to discuss."

"Still, I have things to advise you on, and you have choices to make. At this point, we must agree to procedure, which the Constitution doesn't give us, unfortunately. We owe it to Pax to set the best precedent we can."

No response.

"So, on your behalf, I will call for a step-by-step process. We'll want a specific written complaint from Cedar that will be reviewed by the Committee. We may wish to ask for a hearing or a trial. Anything you say to me will be held in strictest confidence. I will give you the best advice I can."

"However, you will not follow my instructions."

"I'm your advocate, not your servant. Do you agree to insisting on a thorough process?"

"If it is good for Pax."

"Good. I'll speak on your behalf at the Committee meeting tonight." I began to gather up my papers, since I had repair work to get to and then a visit with my grandchildren.

"The orange trees must be cut down," he said. "The entire grove."

"Yes. We've been busy, but we haven't forgotten. We ought to use the wood to make a memorial, but we can't decide how. Do you have any suggestions?"

No response.

I stood up. "Until the Committee meeting tonight. Water and sunshine."

He didn't answer with, "Warmth and food." Should I have felt miffed or worried?

As a little boy, one day I was stamping on rainbow bamboo shoots— for no good reason, just a little-boy antic, destroying things because it was possible. Because at that age almost anything was a novelty. Because at that age, stamping on a plant seemed like an appropriate way for me to assert mastery over my environment.

Sylvia saw me and picked me up. Her face, the same age then as mine now, at the time impressed me as unimaginably old, and it was unimaginably sad.

"The rainbow bamboo is our friend," she said. "Many plants are our friends, but this is our special friend. Did you know it can talk to us?"

I had noticed a fuss about it. I nodded, too intimidated to talk.

"What do you suppose it might say?" She set me down and pretended to stamp on my foot. "*Oh, no, you're stamping on me!* You have to think about what you do. You can hurt your friends and not mean to. We all have to help each other. If we hurt each other, we hurt ourselves, too."

"I'm sorry," I blubbered.

"We should tell the bamboo that," she said, and led me to the front gate, where the leaves on the tall stalks were still a rainbow of colors, stalks that loomed over me like giants, and I knew that the bamboo filled the city and much of the land around it. I blubbered again that I was sorry, wondering how something so small—me—could be important to something so big. It was as if I took a personal interest in every caterpillar in the fields.

And yet Sylvia seemed certain the bamboo was personally interested in me, thus I believed that must somehow be true, and I also stopped stepping on caterpillars intentionally because they were good for the dirt, so they were our friends, too. Now Stevland and I were equal citizens under the Constitution. The little boy, now a man, was defending him the way Sylvia had.

But now I knew why Sylvia's face had been so sad, and it had nothing to do with Stevland.

As for me, how could I understand Cedar's refusal to rescue Lucille and Marie? Combative, smug, unreasonable—that was Cedar, and it wasn't the Pax way. I needed to defeat her the Pax way: peaceful, proper, reasonable—and soon.

Cedar hadn't arrived at the Meeting House when the Committee meeting began, but we had a lot to handle before her part of the agenda, anyway.

The human co-moderator presided at meetings even in normal times. Violet, the head of the Philosopher's Club, had volunteered for the job—a capricious, youngish Green, a farmer with a too-delicate jaw overwhelmed by heavy dyed-green eyebrows, and her best was raising uncommon cacti. She kept a garden of them tethered around the main plaza, sometimes arranged by color, shape, size, age, or species, according to whim, which changed often. Most of the cacti had survived the attack.

If it weren't for defending Stevland, I would have volunteered to preside. I had coached Violet on what to expect from me so she could handle that part of the meeting adequately. At least she couldn't blame me if things went wrong.

I sat at the Committee table near Stevland, ready to speak for him. See-You sat on a bench at the side of the room, with Nye explaining the proceedings. Some people thought she should already have a seat on the Committee, sidestepping everything involved in citizenship, but the Constitution didn't matter to everyone. She would deserve the seat eventually, if Glassmakers indeed shared the Commonwealth's goals, and likely they did, but matters had to be handled correctly. Stevland had proven himself over generations.

Violet opened the meeting. "Things are getting back to normal, aren't they? That's what we need." But she fidgeted with her collar, which wasn't normal.

And no one chatted during the opening, they sat grimly silent. Usually, a few citizens always came with concerns or complaints about their work group assignment or procedure or size, but I knew the Beadies had come to see Cedar lodge her complaint. Yet the Meeting House had room to spare because most people had too much work to do or didn't have the emotional energy to sit through a contentious meeting, and some Green generation members had encouraged abstention to protest Cedar's complaint. That was normal, the split between Greens and Beadies, and as a Green myself, I would have just as soon been elsewhere.

Lumberjack report: Firewood split and ready for the next three days. "Cutting down those orange trees tomorrow," the old senior lumberjack said. "The team is taking volunteers."

"Who has time?" someone whispered.

"It's too bad Harry died," Violet said, ignoring the whisper. "He could make a fitting memorial. Although, I don't know, do you think it ought to be with orange wood? It seems kind of spiteful."

"Spite is just fine," a Beadie said.

"It's not the Pax way," a Green answered.

"Now, let's be nice," Violet scolded.

"I thought you wanted normal," Hathor said, and someone chuckled.

People muttered. Cedar had supporters, and they were as detestable as she was.

The fippmaster reported: Two kat teams available tomorrow. One team could help with the orange trees—if there was a kat task, and there was, holes to be dug.

The cooks reported: Glassmaker and human dietary requirements overlapped enough to cause minimal problems. "Stewed trilobites tomorrow because the flood has made it easy to gather a lot, so come with an appetite."

"That would be normal," Hathor joked, since who really liked trilobites?

More mutters, and then people shushed the mutterers because at least there would be plenty, and someone said, "I'm still too upset to eat anything."

More reports: Injuries mending, some crops replanted, urgent repairs under way, Glassmakers joining work teams, an uneven march toward recovery, but Stevland remained abnormally mute, which Violet ignored.

Still no Cedar.

"And how are the Glassmakers getting along?" Violet asked with a strange smile. See-You apparently knew the question was coming, for without waiting for Nye to translate, she whistled and kakked a report, and something she said reminded me of queens arguing that long night in the Meeting House, but their voices couldn't drown out the screams from outside, and my eyes had filled with tears. From fear? Or from a horrible smell the Glassmakers were giving off, the smell of fear, and we were all terrified, but I had to pretend I was not. I had to . . .

I had to pay attention. I was in the Meeting House, but it was a different night now, and I wasn't terrified anymore. But I was tired, very tired.

"We would like to resume language classes," Nye was repeating for See-You. "We wish to become part of the city as quickly as possible." A few people nodded. Soon, their voices might become a normal sound, and I wished for that perhaps more than Violet did.

And then Cedar limped in and took a seat toward the front, clutching a piece of paper. She whispered to Hathor and Forrest, the Generation 4 twins. I probably could have overheard if everyone else wasn't whispering—about her. "What right does she have?" "It's about time." "Be brave!" And: "She doesn't look well." That was true. And: "But what about Stevland?"

Cedar had an odd look on her face, maybe anger, maybe sadness, maybe even fear. Or pain. Orphans had attacked her with shredders for rayon working, making tatters of her skin. As mourning clothes she wore a loose, threadbare dress instead of her usual slacks and sleeveless shirts, a ragged scarf around her head that covered bandages, and lots of strings of beads—battered, broken, discolored, some singed by fire.

Violet tapped her fingernails on the table and frowned. Amazingly, the whispering died down. "Any other reports?"

A few: hunters, bakers, children's activities, assessments of the damage from the spring floods, and the weather forecast. Finally, it was time for new business. Violet recognized Cedar, who stood.

"I propose that Stevland should be voted out as co-moderator," she nearly whispered. She was not the same Cedar of three days ago, when she had said that there were no good Glassmakers, that she ought to be head of our defense, that we needed to control Stevland. We knew how to fight and we ought to fight! . . .

I shook my head to clear it.

"I have a formal complaint. Violet said to bring one." She began reading stiffly:

"Stevland should be removed from office immediately. He is not in sympathy with the spirit of our Commonwealth. He has different goals for Pax. He does not understand human culture. He is a parasite on us, and mutualism is a lie. He can control us with drugs, and he does, because he believes he is superior to us, and he does not trust us. He lies, and he keeps secrets." She paused, teeth clenched. "He is timid and patient because he is rooted in one spot. His mistakes cost us lives and livelihood. He is too powerful to be controlled. He should be removed from office and have his citizenship revoked."

She looked around, eyes narrowed. Stevland's stem showed nothing.

No one said anything, but the looks being exchanged between people debated the issue in depth. For some, she was a true fighter. For others, a nuisance or worse.

I stood, wanting to say that the Constitution did not allow for the revocation of citizenship, that her complaints were self-contradictory and a waste of time when we had important things to do, and most of all she was blaming Stevland for her own misconduct. When he was burning, she had said that there was lots of Stevland, as if hurting him didn't matter, and as for Lucille and Marie . . .

With forced calm, I said, "I can speak for Stevland. He would like the opportunity to make a formal rebuttal and would like both the complaint and his response to be evaluated by the Committee and by the people of Pax. This complaint deserves the utmost deliberation. This won't be quick or easy, and we urge the Committee to act without haste."

I noticed that See-You had left the room. When? Why?

"He wants to waste time," Cedar said. "We need Stevland out now. He's not fit to be moderator. He should resign and save us a lot of trouble."

"But he's not doing anything," the old hunter Orion said, waving at the blank talking stem. "There's no reason to worry about something that's nothing."

"How do you know what he's doing?" she said. "And the Glass-makers, they don't belong here. They tried to kill us and they'll try again, and they're eating our best food. We should throw them out." A few Beadies applauded. It was shameful.

Daisy, thank goodness, exploded. "Throw them out?" She stood, arms outstretched, pleading. "That would be tragic, and after so much tragedy, how could we bear more? Stevland is so exhausted by what happened he can hardly endure to speak." She started crying, as usual, to add dramatic effect. "The Glassmakers mustn't be sent away. We've worked so hard for peace and now we have it."

"Cedar was right about the Glassmakers," a Beadie said.

"Just about the orphans," a Green answered, "and they're all dead now."

Violet should have called for order, but she just sat there looking expectant. A wind had begun blowing outside, then developed into a faint chant, filled with whistles and buzzes. The sounds of Glassmade. What were they doing? Out in the streets again, scurrying through them like orphans preparing to attack? But the queens wanted peace, and they were smart enough to know they couldn't survive without us. We could trust the queens. But what were they doing?

Daisy didn't seem to have noticed the noise. "Oh, how can Cedar even think of such a thing? These are our friends!"

"They're not citizens," Cedar answered, "so we can do what we want."

Orion tilted his head, then tapped Carl on the shoulder and made some hand gestures that hunters used to communicate. Nye and Violet exchanged little smiles. Others began to listen to the chant.

Cedar wasn't listening. She said: "Peace! Talk! People like you are going to drag this whole process out until something awful happens again. 'Let's domesticate them!' And look what happened."

The sound outside grew louder, became a tune, and split into harmony.

"Glassmakers," Orion announced.

They were singing, but nothing like the horrible songs they had used to harass us. This was a sweet lullaby by old Uncle Higgins. It surrounded the Meeting House, one part of the harmony on the west side, another at the north addition, constantly moving and changing.

Cedar looked wild-eyed from one side of the room to the other. Violet had closed her eyes with eyebrows raised like they were riding a dream. Nye frowned, concentrating.

The melody split again into more harmonies and grew louder, the lullaby about a gentle snowfall that had soothed us all as children, but it reminded me of drums and singing at night, of trying to sleep during the siege and, because the Glassmaker noise was keeping me awake, worrying hour after hour about how much worse things could get. . . .

But I was awake, in the Meeting House. I had clutched my pen so hard that the reed tip was broken.

The song ended the reverse of the way it had begun, with harmonies coalescing and regrouping, and then the melody faded away into the wind.

"That was beautiful," Violet said. Cedar stared at the floor. Hathor and Forrest nudged each other, lips pursed. Orion sat still and smiled. I inspected a scratch on my finger from a reed splinter.

The Glassmakers walked in, the queens leading their families up the center aisle. "That was beautiful," Violet repeated.

Everyone applauded—except Cedar and her followers, of course. Stevland remained blank. The queens knelt on all four legs and lowered their heads, and their families repeated the gesture. The air smelled like roses.

Cedar asked, "What was that about?"

"Now, Cedar," Daisy said. She was well past her crying spell.

"The Glassmakers sing to honor our dead," Nye announced. "The harmony divides and moves apart to indicate lives leaving us, and then they join to show that the lives become treasured memories. They offer their condolences and their thanks for—for everything, for their chance to live in the city again."

"That was beautiful," Violet repeated again. "On behalf of all of us, thank you. And thank you, Nye." She looked around. "So, is there anything else? I don't think so."

"My complaint," Cedar said. "But you won't consider it. We have to treat Stevland nicely, we have to humor him, we have to defer to him because—"

"Because without him we have about as much chance to survive as the Glassmakers did," Daisy snapped. "Oh, why can't you see that?"

Violet looked around the table. "The Committee will accept the complaint, right?" No objections. Technically—unfortunately—none were possible. She looked at Stevland's stem, still blank, and she said something else, but I couldn't hear her over the din of voices, everyone with something to say about the meeting, the music, or Stevland. The Glassmaker song hadn't changed many minds.

I visited Stevland the next morning, bringing reddog tea, bread, and a piece of his fruit, feeling achy although I had slept well, or at least I thought I had slept well. He was speaking before I had time to sit down.

"I have spent significant time over the past few days meditating, which was why I have been quiet. I have tried to imitate human existence by isolating groves to experience your viewpoint, although isolating my viewpoint in my humor root offered insights of doubtful utility."

"I'm glad that you're feeling better." It was about time he started talking.

"The world offers many surprises when one is a small individual, because concentrated awareness is highly sensual. The Glassmakers' music last night caused emotional changes for my isolated grove. How did you react?"

"I . . . remembered other music." Counselors had told us that grief caused unstable emotions.

"Beauty is a link among Glassmakers, humans, and myself. The beauty of their architecture and music shows that we regard the world more alike than unalike. These similarities make our mutualism a joy and a satisfaction."

I looked for a pen and paper. "Let me make a note of that for our reply."

"We must participate in each other's beauty. I will make a request of the Committee. During the orphan attack, I identified a need to make sounds of warning. I would like a voice, perhaps even the ability to sing."

A singing plant.

"My humor root suggests that I am becoming more like an animal."

And if he were burning again, he could scream. I tried not to imagine it.

"You were right not to allow me to resign. The complaint says that I am patient and timid because I am rooted to one spot, but I can act aggressively. Moreover, I am a dominant species, and it is my nature to dominate. Each of us needs to be what we are, perhaps even be more of what we are. If we are true to ourselves, we will help our best natures flourish."

The bakers had boasted that the morning bread had been made by the Glassmaker apprentice start to finish. I bit into it, and it could not

have been more tender. "Does this mean you won't resign?" That was
a relief. A big change. Troubling, actually, because he had changed so
fast.

"I was wrong to wish to resign, as Cedar's complaint has helped me
see clearly. I owe the citizens of Pax my best. She has physical and psy-
chological injuries, but not scarlet fever brain disease. I checked while
she was being treated in the clinic. Cedar can be befriended if I apply
mutualism with sufficient rigor."

"I don't think she wants to be your friend. And I think that she's a
serious problem. She has followers."

"Befriending her does not mean emotional compatibility, it means
removing her necessity to fight. She is a valuable member of Pax, and
we must redirect her aggression to a suitable target, such as an ecological threat. She has provided leadership at decisive moments, despite
her recent failures."

"You know, your mood has changed a lot since yesterday."

"I have isolated my emotional imbalances in particular groves, so
each grove can work toward balance, leaving my major operational roots
more able to deal with immediate problems. One imbalance wishes the
orphan attack had not happened at all, so I have centered it in the roots
of the grove that the orphans burned, where the reality is most undeniable. Does that seem reasonable?"

"I suppose," I said, but I couldn't parcel out feelings here and there.
I had learned that long ago.

"However, I am still sorrowful. Higgins sang a song about grief
ever-green. It is a rich metaphor. When your wife was killed by coral,
was it like losing an arm or an eye?"

I didn't want to talk about that. But he needed help, and that was
my job. "Yes. More than an arm or eye. I lost decades of time, our future
together."

"Have you not grown another, correction, healed, since as an animal
you cannot grow a lost body part?"

I had been at the top of the bluff when the boat came back from the
coral plains, the boat Bess had taken in a trip upriver. Her traveling
team lifted her out of the boat, her stiff corpse like a log wrapped in

her blanket, and at a glance I knew what had happened, and I turned and ran back into the city, everything void. "No, I merely adapted. I can't replace her."

"Please elaborate about replacement."

I thought I had made myself clear. "Some people change partners like . . . like bats changing roosts, one is as good as another, but Bess—I can't replace her. I don't want to replace her. No one could be like her. What I did was continue to love her even though she isn't here."

After several moments, he said:

"We plants keep the venatoris coral out of our forest to protect you, but we cannot control the plains. I am sorry that Bess died. Others had esteemed her for her kindness, and observing her I learned much about the idea. It may be that Cedar wants to keep an enemy the way you want to keep Bess. But by my balance, it is better to maintain love than hate. Is it easier?"

"Yes." Bess had kissed me and left, and the next time I saw her face, she was in a funeral basket, and for a time I had thought I had lived a day too long, not realizing how much more I would love her after losing her. During Lucille's funeral, for the first time I felt glad I had not traveled upriver with Bess and seen her die. "Yes, she was kind. Thank you."

But he was wrong about Cedar. An enemy kept the blame off her, and that was why she wanted one.

I looked at the angle of the sunshine on the roof. "I should go to help with the orange trees. Water and sunshine."

"They are enemy trees. I am sorry for more killing, but I hope this will be the end of slaughter. The locustwood will help. Warmth and food."

Erasmus, the senior lumberjack, sized up the volunteer work team, about twenty of us plus a dozen kats playing leapfrog while they waited, a large team considering how much else needed to be done, but a small one considering how much people hated the orange trees. Erasmus was

Generation 4, tough and square as a brick, although a wispy beard and white fringe of hair somehow made him look frail.

He nodded in approval and turned to size up the orange trees: tangles of slim, supple trunks, each unable to hold much weight, so every branch sent down a dangling root that eventually became another trunk. Big green leaves veined in black made the trees look dark and hulking, and thorns like arrowheads studded the trunks and branches.

Ugly trees. Guilty trees. Another chance to fight the orphans and win, using a normal, everyday Pax work team. An emotionally charged work team. A team ready to finish the destruction that the orphans had started. One woman already sniffled tears.

"It's like this," Erasmus said. "Suppose we start cutting at one side and work our way through. The tree'll tip and fall on the logger. We have to chop branches as well as trunks, easier to say than do because of the thorns. We'll need ladders. That's the reason we don't harvest them often. Locustwood, now there's a tree that's a pleasure to cut down. Cooperative, too."

"Why don't we set fire to them?" said Fabio's father, a man deep in his suffering, axe in hand, fondling it, dreaming of worse things to do. He turned to me. "They got your son, too. How about it?"

"I'm only here for justice," I said. Fire . . . I was trying not to remember fire.

"Fire," Erasmus said. "Not a bad idea, and I like the sentiment. The thing is, the fire would hurt other trees, like that ponytail over there next to the oranges, those pines, even these friendly little palms. No, wouldn't be right. Good thinking, though."

People nodded. It wouldn't be the Pax way.

Piotr stood next to me. The downy hairs on his upper lip had darkened in the last year. He had loved Lucille and he would have been blind not to, the only grown woman in Generation 7. She had been his future, and she had died before his eyes. Could he heal, or could he replace her? If I talked about Bess, would he understand?

"Did you paint your face green to be like Lucille's?" I asked.

He looked away, fumbling with something in his pockets. "No." Then, "Yes," in a louder but not stronger voice on the edge of a squeak.

"That's a nice gesture," I said. He nodded and tried to smile and failed utterly.

Maybe we could have saved Lucille. Did he need to know that? Cedar had refused to act, but then Pacifists arrived, fought, and almost won. Almost. If the fighting had started a minute earlier, maybe . . . No. The orphans already had the acetone, they already had a plan to burn the women to distract us.

But Cedar hadn't known that. Could I forgive her? Would that be good for Pax? Would that be just?

Piotr was suddenly hugging me. "Take care of yourself," he said, as if I were the one needing care. He turned and left down a path, whistling in something like Glassmade, and two Glassmaker majors followed him. They'd bring back locustwood saplings to plant in place of the oranges, and the locustwoods would hunt and kill any remaining orange tree roots.

We fetched ladders and got to work, one tree at a time. I held a ladder for Fabio's father and tried to hold it steady, but he chopped wildly, long swings with more force than precision, almost knocking himself off the ladder, though he didn't seem to notice. He couldn't notice. He was attacking in his own private battle, and how could I not sympathize with the loss of a son? Tears or sweat filled the fine lines around his eyes. I kept my feet planted firmly, my eyes on his swinging arm to know when to tense, listening to the rhythm of other axes and the crunch and crackle of live wood yielding to steady assault, and to sniffs and sobs and relentless progress making way for good trees.

Fabio's father swung the axe at another branch. A Glassmaker would have hacked like that, axes and clubs swinging at the end of long, sinuous arms. All around me, axes opened up bright orange raw wood, too much like blood-red flesh. The morning after the battle, they had found Osbert's body, his head smashed open, thrown into the thistles, on a day with so many dead that we didn't have enough funeral baskets and buried them in bare soil.

"Are you okay? Bartholomew, are you okay?" Fabio's father was talking to me.

"Fine. I'm fine."

"Do you want to chop for a while?"

"No. Thanks. I'm good down here."

But was I where I ought to be?

The fight was over. We had won, the orphans were gone, and the surviving Glassmakers wouldn't turn on us. But Cedar could turn on them, and they could lose their last chance to survive. I had more important things to do than kill trees.

I checked the kitchen and several workshops, and found Cedar in the Meeting House. All the doors were propped open.

"I am pleased to have a chance to speak with you," Stevland's stem already said when I ducked in, probably addressing Cedar. She looked up from a law text.

"Keep the doors open," she told me. "Stevland isn't going to put anything in the air to control me. Only the Committee can vote out a moderator, right? But we vote for moderators. Everyone votes for them. Why can't everyone vote a moderator out? That's what they did with Vera, right?"

I sat down across the table from her. Take away her need to fight, that was what Stevland had said. No, take away her ability, that was it. I didn't know how to begin, but now would be the time, and no time to be tired or let my mind wander.

"We can all count," I said. "The Committee supports Stevland and the Glassmakers. Most citizens support them, too. You'd lose in a vote."

"Not by much," she said, then turned to Stevland. "That's what you want, isn't it? You win, we all lose. You get to stay in control."

"I do not wish to fight you," he said. "I forgive you for letting Lucille die."

She turned red and opened her mouth, teeth bared, ready to explode with denial.

I didn't give her the chance. The first rule of argumentation is to appropriate the argument. "No, Stevland, you won't forgive her."

"You cannot tell me what to do."

"I can tell you what you ought to do. First, forgiveness isn't that easy. Second, she doesn't want it."

"I don't need it!" she said.

A few people, attracted by our arguing voices, peeked into the Meeting House, unsure if they should listen. I gave them a nod to encourage them to stay. I would need witnesses—if I could figure out what to do.

"I can forgive," Stevland said, "because I understand killing. I did not wish to make Sylvia kill Vera, but I did."

"Sylvia did that back in the old village," I said. "You weren't involved."

Two people already sat on benches halfway toward the front. A few more lingered near the back, while another leaned out, gesturing at others to come.

"What actually happened is a secret passed on by moderators," Stevland said. "You are not a moderator, thus you do not know."

I pointed to the document bureau. "The facts are in the old record book, there for anyone to read." The book had been written by a record keeper named Nicoletta.

"I have the knife Sylvia killed Vera with," Stevland responded. "Lucille told me that Sylvia had killed her, and Lucille forgave me because I had not wished to make her kill, thus I can forgive others."

"What are you talking about?" Cedar demanded. The people on the benches—a lot more now—looked perplexed.

I tried to unravel his logic or his emotions, but I couldn't. "I'll get the book. Where's the knife, Stevland?"

"It is beneath the paving tile next to Harry's waltz box. It is steel, and it is from Earth. It has been passed down from moderator to moderator, but as a secret."

Cedar rose as fast as she could, limped over, and knelt to pry up the stone. I climbed on a chair and pulled down volume two, bound in worked leather and dusty. I hadn't looked at it for months. Cedar stood up, holding the knife vertically like a bouquet of flowers: a shiny, silver-gray metal blade.

Two dozen people sat on the benches now, with more arriving fast.

I turned to Stevland. "Let's see if this account agrees with the story passed down to you. There's a paragraph here among the notations about births and deaths and such, written about five years after the events. It says, *The Parents knew about Rainbow City but thought that the rainbow bamboo would be worse than snow vines. Sylvia and Julian*—Julian was a young man, Sylvia's first husband, I think—*discovered the city and wanted to move the colony here.*"

A few Glassmakers arrived. Cedar stood near the upturned tile, knife in hand, looking every minute more like her old self. I continued, trying to think and talk at the same time.

"The record says that to suppress the idea of moving the colony, Vera, who was the moderator, had Julian and Octavo the Rulemaker killed, she had Sylvia attacked and hurt, and she had several people beaten. It concludes, *Sylvia killed Vera during Octavo's funeral and declared herself the moderator. She was actually underage, only a teenager. That was the revolt. There was a vote, but only the votes in favor of Sylvia were taken.*"

The room was quieter than it would have been if it were empty.

"Stevland," I said, "is this the story as you know it?"

"I did not know that Vera had killed other Pacifists. This changes Sylvia's culpability."

"Indeed. Sylvia had to protect herself. However, Cedar had a chance to try to save Lucille and Marie during the orphan attack, but she did not."

"That's not true," Cedar said, waving the knife, perhaps unconsciously. "We were outnumbered."

"Bartholomew's account is again correct," Stevland said. "You were hiding beneath one of my groves, so I was able to observe. As Bartholomew suggested at the time, you only needed to create a diversion, and you said you would get killed doing so. At the time, I believed you were afraid."

"I was not!"

"Now," I said, facing the audience, "to forgive, first we need to understand what happened. Sylvia was in danger and she protected herself. During the orphan attack, Lucille and Marie needed help, and Cedar failed to act. If she wasn't afraid, then what motivated her?"

"I—" She stared at the knife in her hand.

People began to do more than murmur. Violet had arrived, and I
looked at her across the room, hoping she would realize she ought to
keep order. She marched to the front, faced everyone, and said, "We're
eavesdropping here. Let's be quiet and listen." It was a counterfactual
order, since I was addressing the audience directly, but it seemed to
work.

"If you weren't afraid," I said, "then what? We have two models for
behavior. Sylvia acted for the good of Pax. Vera acted to retain power.
Allowing Lucille and Marie to die did not help Pax, but you have long
felt you should be moderator. Allowing Lucille to die would be a step
toward acquiring the moderator position for yourself, rather like Sylvia, but—"

"No! I didn't want her to die! I . . . I was afraid. I was. I was afraid
of the Glassmakers. And I was right. Look what they did. Lucille didn't
know how to defend the city. They caught her and killed her. Marie
made mistakes from the start of the mission. Stevland—he didn't know
what to do."

"I have made many mistakes," Stevland said.

I didn't wait for him to list them. "You were afraid, then. Would we
all have done the same? We can forgive acts we could have committed.
Many of us were afraid that night, many of us hesitated, and we all
made mistakes, some big, some small. Some made no difference. Could
we have saved Lucille and Marie? The orphans already had the acetone and planned to use it. Cedar could have tried to rescue them, but
she would have failed."

Her eyes snapped up to meet mine. "Lucille would have died anyway?" There was relief in her voice—maybe. That would change everything. That needed to be confirmed.

"You thought that she died because you had failed to act."

"There were so many orphans! I didn't know what weapons they had.
I . . ." She paused again, looked down at the knife, at the floor. "I didn't
know what to do. I pretended I was brave, that it didn't matter. I . . .
But you said I couldn't have saved them. I didn't like Lucille, but she
was the moderator! I wanted to save her, I did, I . . ." She had run out
of words.

"I understand," I said. "You hesitated out of fear. An error we all could have made."

She nodded, still looking down. My own emotions were slowly shifting, but I hadn't undertaken this effort for my emotional benefit. People had begun to talk among themselves again, which was a good sign.

"You were afraid, and you hesitated," I summarized one more time to make sure everyone understood. "Had the situation been different, Lucille and Marie would have died because of what you failed to do, but in this case, their death was certain regardless." I turned to Violet, sitting up front. "What shall we do?"

She blinked a few times. "This isn't a proper meeting, so we can't do anything. We'll need to think about all this."

"Let's get back to work," Hathor said, disgusted. Could she forgive Cedar? No, she and Forrest never forgave anyone. People stood up to leave.

Cedar threw the knife down on a table and began to limp out, but she looked back at me, less smug than usual, maybe even ashamed. Not murderous. Not more likable, but that wouldn't matter anymore. I could forgive fear. She left.

I sat down at the table and pondered Stevland's talking stem, now blank. He had said he wanted a voice. He had wanted to remove Cedar's ability to fight. He had wanted to understand grief. He had wanted to become balanced again.

A few fellow Greens came up to the table.

"Thank you," one of them said.

"This is going to help a lot," another said. They did not seem triumphant. Good.

"It had to be done," I said.

"And you didn't hurt anyone," yet another added. "That's the way to do it."

I looked at them, old friends, companions in joys and sorrows and whatever the current moment was—hollow satisfaction, perhaps.

"We'll be at dinner when Lux sets. See you?"

I nodded, and one of them patted my shoulder as they left. By then only Violet remained. She walked over to the upturned paving tile and began to set it back in place.

"Stevland," I said, "what should we do with this knife?"

He didn't answer right away, and for a moment I worried that I had sent him back into silence, but then he said, "I believe it belongs in the museum. You were right not to allow me to forgive. It is more complex than I had believed. I attempted to balance emotions with facts, yet the weight of emotions seems hard for me to estimate."

"For us, too," I said, "even our own emotions. Sometimes they gain or lose weight over time."

I suddenly remembered the smell of truffle in the Meeting House, a long night keeping the Glassmakers calm, and no sight of my son, Osbert, none at all, but we all knew without saying what had happened to the guards on the wall and what might happen to us.

"You ought to get some rest." Violet had sat down and taken my hand. "You know, you could be moderator."

I tried to imagine Sylvia as a girl. As a new, underage moderator. Someone who wanted to do more than survive, but so did the Parents, obviously, by the expectations written into the Constitution: aspirations to joy, love, beauty, and community. They had thought they had to leave Earth to achieve them. Were they right?

"Stevland wants to sing," I said. Violet raised her grand eyebrows.

I tried to imagine Earth, and I couldn't. I tried to imagine writing a history of Pax, and there was much that I would never know. Too much.

Yet it needed to be done. I could start with what I knew and what I could learn so our story could survive, so we could discover our true selves. Our future would be another discovery—or, if we understood how we had arrived at where we were, it could be a choice.

I stood up. It was time to get back to work. Back to the business of living. Back to a life that would slowly seem normal even if it was never the same again.

Violet stood, too.

"Look what I found." She held out a little mesh basket, and a cactus the size of a thumbnail floated inside, sky-blue underneath, brownish-green on top, bristling with long white thorns.

"It's an *Astrophytum echinocactus caeruleus*." She pronounced the words carefully. "These are common and they get big, a meter across, but they're camouflaged and high flyers, so we don't see them much. This seedling sprang a leak, and that's why it fell. Leaks can be fatal, you know."

"The danger from leaks is susceptibility to predation," Stevland said. "With your protection, it will recover."

"Oh, I'll take good care of it. Like all my cacti." She took my hand. "Let's go. Water and sunshine, Stevland!"

"Warmth and food."

Under a Sun close to noon, the city seemed different. Or I was different. Less damaged. The house closest to the Meeting House had remained untouched during the attack and its roof sparkled. I paused to admire it, and Violet stayed with me, her warm hand in mine.

Glassmakers had built that house, one of the few that had survived entirely intact over the centuries and disasters. They had made those glass bricks with internal air pockets that acted like facets, a technique we had never quite mastered. Thus, deliberately, the roof flashed color. I had seen it every day of my life and enjoyed it often. Had marveled at it from inside and from up on the walls. And now from down on the ground again.

"Stevland told me beauty is a link among all of us," I said, "a love of beauty, for us, him, and the Glassmakers. Will that be enough?"

"It's one link, but I suppose we'll need more. What do we have?" She tugged on my hand. "What keeps us?" She led me past a garden that had also escaped untouched, studded with flowers that would become fruit and seeds in time. "We came from somewhere else and we came here. Both of us. We both wanted to be here."

She had taken me in the opposite direction from the front gate, where fire still scarred the stones and Stevland. Her path avoided other destruction as well. I soon realized she could do so with ease. We had hurt each other more than our surroundings.

"Glassmakers farmed, too," she added.

"Yes. When Sylvia and Julian came here, they found the remains of fields."

"They've already been very useful in the fields now, the Glassmakers. They'll help us a lot. And technology, they had technology. It's in the museum, isn't it? They can help with that, too."

"They don't seem to remember much," I said, "but they have a history, too."

They did, and it shouldn't be forgotten. I could see to that. I had another project. Or rather, I had a single, bigger project that would unite us a bit more.

We turned a corner and paused as people filed past on their way to or from work, still in old clothing but with the occasional new head scarf or string of beads. A man said something beyond our hearing, and everyone around him laughed.

Violet held up her caged cactus. "I should take this to put it with the rest of them."

"I need to make some tools," I said—and suddenly realized something. "We'll need some tools made specially for Glassmaker workers. Shorter handles, and maybe smaller overall. I'll need to talk to them about it."

I released her hand to go to the workshop outside the city, where there was room to stack logs and lumber. I'd need to pass through the main gate. I stopped. No. I didn't want to do that. A lot of us still hadn't yet. We'd been leaving through the west gate.

"I'll go with you to the plaza," I said. Then I'd head through the west gate and take a long circular walk outside the city walls. But at the end of the day I'd walk back in through the main gate. I would see destruction, but from a different angle and already somewhat repaired. A new view and a new memory.

Stevland had said that in the roots below the gate, his wish that it had never happened was fighting with reality. I didn't have that problem.

Around me rose his bright stalks and graceful leaves, the curves of their boughs echoing the curves of the roofs. I had water and sunshine, and warmth and food. Some shards of broken crockery lay at my feet.

I'd have a long chapter to write about the meeting of Pacifists and Glass-makers. Yet it wouldn't be the last chapter. Or the longest.

"Do you really think I could be moderator?" I asked Violet. Someone had to do it, and I knew what it would involve. I had seen it done well. And I would leave the knife in the museum, no longer a secret.

ABOUT THE AUTHOR

SUE BURKE spent many years working as a reporter and editor for a variety of newspapers and magazines. A Clarion workshop alumnus, Burke has published more than thirty short stories in addition to working extensively as a literary translator. She now lives in Chicago.